Little Pink Slips

Sally Koslow

BERKLEY BOOKS, NEW YORK

THE BERKLEY PUBLISHING GROUP
Published by the Penguin Group
Penguin Group (USA) Inc.
375 Hudson Street, New York, New York 10014, USA
Penguin Group (Canada), 90 Eglinton Avenue East, Suite 700, Toronto, Ontario M4P 2Y3, Canada
(a division of Pearson Penguin Canada Inc.)
Penguin Books Ltd., 80 Strand, London WC2R 0RL, England
Penguin Group Ireland, 25 St. Stephen's Green, Dublin 2, Ireland (a division of Penguin Books Ltd.)
Penguin Group (Australia), 250 Camberwell Road, Camberwell, Victoria 3124, Australia
(a division of Pearson Australia Group Pty. Ltd.)
Penguin Books India Pvt. Ltd., 11 Community Centre, Panchsheel Park, New Delhi—110 017, India
Penguin Group (NZ), 67 Apollo Drive, Rosedale, North Shore, 0632, New Zealand
(a division of Pearson New Zealand Ltd.)
Penguin Books (South Africa) (Pty.) Ltd., 24 Sturdee Avenue, Rosebank, Johannesburg 2196, South Africa

Penguin Books Ltd., Registered Offices: 80 Strand, London WC2R 0RL, England

This is a work of fiction. Names, characters, places, and incidents either are the product of the author's imagination or are used fictitiously, and any resemblance to actual persons, living or dead, business establishments, events, or locales is entirely coincidental. The publisher does not have any control over and does not assume any responsibility for author or third-party websites or their content.

PRINTING HISTORY
G. P. Putnam's Sons hardcover edition / April 2007
Berkley trade paperback edition / May 2008

Berkley trade paperback ISBN: 978-0-425-22131-0

The Library of Congress has catalogued the G. P. Putnam's Sons hardcover edition as follows:

Koslow, Sally.
    Little pink slips/Sally Koslow
        p.   cm.
    ISBN 978-0-399-15415-7
    1. Women periodical editors—Fiction.   2. Women's periodicals—Fiction.   I. Title.
PS3611.074919L58   2007   2006037339
813'.6—dc22

To Robby

Acknowledgments

I am in debt to many people who gave generously to me throughout the writing of this, my first novel.

I could not have asked for a more delightful editor than Jackie Cantor, whose enthusiasm and insights have made the process a dream. I am honored to have worked with her and others at Putnam, especially Ivan Held, Catharine Lynch, Marilyn Ducksworth, and—too briefly—the legendary Leona Nevler. To Annette Fiore, thanks for imagining a *Little Pink Slips* cover that is as elegant and eye-catching as her name.

I am fortunate that fate brought me to Christy Fletcher, who believed in *Little Pink Slips* from the start. I appreciate her unerring judgment and continuing guidance, and that of Elizabeth Ziemska in Los Angeles and Araminta Whitley in London, as well as the attention of Kate Scherler.

Charles Salzburg deserves huge thanks for allowing a rogue fiction writer to invade his nonfiction writing circle. I value his friendship, strategic suggestions, and deadlines, without which I'd still be tweaking page one. Vivian Conan is a fine writer whom I am happy to count as a friend. I am grateful for her common sense and questions—the more nitpicky, the better—and those of other good-luck charms in our workshops, especially Kimberlee Auerbach, Patricia Crevits, Sarah Doudna, Judy Gorfain, Sharon Gurwitz, Erica Keirstaad, Stephanie Klein, Patty Nasey, Naama Potok, Marian Sabat, Ellen Schecter, Sharon Samuel, Betty Wald, and Richard Willis.

To Amy Stewart and Thomas Gallitano at Conn Kavanaugh Rosenthal Peisch & Ford, LLP, many thanks for developing Magnolia Gold's legal argument as if she were a living, breathing client.

My friends in the wonderful, wacky world of magazines have a collective wit and energy equaled in few other industries. There are a lot of Magnolia Golds out there, but I owe a special debt to the incomparable Ellen Levine, who mentored me and so many others, as well as to Catherine Cavender, Emily Listfield, and Diane Salvatore, whose friendships supply a reality check and a bottomless well of wry observations. I also wish to acknowledge my remarkably talented former staffs at *McCall's* and *Lifetime.* I hope I was a better boss than some; if not, let's all just move on.

I definitely have the world's most giving friends, who offered hugs, hospitality, and editorial advice during the long writing process. My friendship with Barbara Fisher flowered during the adventure of writing *Little Pink Slips;* she deserves loving thanks for her gentle encouragement and remarkable resiliency. Very special shout-outs also go to Anita Bakal, Sherry Suib Cohen, Margie Rosen, and Ina Saltz—who all critiqued early drafts and said *yes!* with warm enthusiasm—as well as to Michele Willens. Dale Singer asked probing questions and buoyed my spirits as I started a fresh chapter. Thanks to her as well.

The women in my family are extraordinary—every one strong and inspiring. I owe a great deal to my sisters, Betsy Teutsch, Dale Berger, and Vicki Kriser, and to my gorgeous mother-in-law, Helen Koslow Sweig.

My love of fiction comes from my mom, Fritzie Platkin, the Fargo

Public Library's most regular customer. I wish that she and my father, Samuel Platkin, could have seen their daughter publish a novel and know how much I thank them both for a lifetime of quiet gifts.

My extraordinary sons make me proud in about a thousand ways. Thanks to Jed and Rory for cheering me on, as I do them, as we chase new dreams. It is a wonderful thing to be able to receive excellent advice from one's children.

Most of all, my husband, Robert, has always seen the potential in a girl from Fargo and was most of the reason I moved to Manhattan. I thank him for his humor, love, and support, which I return.

Chapter 1

From Fargo to Fabulous

The Chanel sample sale, holy of holies for the aspiring fashionista. Magnolia Gold, editor in chief of *Lady* magazine, could imagine few other reasons to get out of bed before dawn. She hurled herself into a sleeveless black dress that showed off her biceps, and slipped on the stilettos she'd found in Milan, the ones you could almost mistake for Manolos.

When she usually left for her office, three hours later, you'd sooner find a five-carat diamond in the garlic bin at Fairway than an empty taxi on the Upper West Side. At this hour, though, she all but collided with a cab. In minutes, she zipped down West End Avenue, headed around Columbus Circle, and turned on to Central Park South, arriving early enough at the Park Lane Hotel to snag a good place in line.

Lady's beauty director, Phoebe Feinberg-Fitzpatrick, had given her the drill. "People get there at six, though the doors don't open till eight," she lectured, an echo of Long Island left in her voice. "Dress comfy—it can get intense." They both knew *comfy* wasn't code for Eddie Bauer jumpers and sneakers.

Magnolia figured she scored a solid 7.5 on the cosmic scale of attractiveness. She had mahogany brown hair—shoulder length, thick, cut with bangs that framed big green eyes; a God-given nose which, to her horror, called to mind the word *perky*; and, despite a nuclear metabolism, a butt no one could miss. Thanks to Phoebe, who dispensed discounts and freebies wherever she landed, Magnolia had her frizz regularly deleted by the latest Japanese process ($800 for just anyone, zero for her) and benefited from gratis cosmetics that allowed her to make the most of high cheekbones and wrinkle-free skin, the continuing payoff of the teenage oilies. She hoped the last gift would keep on giving well past next fall's thirty-eighth birthday.

Today's invitation came via Phoebe's best friend, the PR girl for Chanel. Normally, editors in chief of old-time women's magazines never made the cut. In the Manhattan court of publishing, they were ladies-in-waiting. Fashion royalty came first—*Vogue, Elle, Bazaar, Elegance, W,* and even *InStyle.* Next were the shopping glossies, led by *Lucky,* tied with *Marie Claire, Cosmo,* and *Glamour,* magazines for women who'd murder for a date. The celebrity rags, *Dazzle, Us, InTouch,* and *The Star,* had street cred, too, because all the showroom girls read them. But even though hausfrau magazines like *Lady* were far more popular—with millions of readers—their clout in the world of fashion fascists was down there with tapered, pleated jeans.

Magnolia entered the hotel, all five feet five inches of her, and scurried past sleepy doormen and tall stands of calla lilies. She shot up the thickly carpeted crimson steps. At least thirty women were strung out along one wall, sitting on the floor. She recognized . . . no one. Parking herself, she idly opened her *New York Post.* What was their freakishly accurate horoscope witch warning today?

Stop playing second fiddle. As Mars moves into your birth sign, you need to convince people you are special, that you were born for bigger and better things. First of all, convince yourself.

Indeed. Magnolia knew it seemed as if she was on the top of the heap—the great job, the enviable dividends that came with it. The inner Magnolia was, however, less than 100 percent sure she deserved what she'd scored. Just as she began to ponder how, exactly, she might jump-start a confidence transplant—she'd had the name of a shrink on her nightstand for months—she was saved from the burden of precaffeinated self-analysis by Phoebe, who was cheerfully shrieking her name.

"You made it. Can you believe this dedication?"

Magnolia could. She'd be perfectly happy still buying her clothes at H&M. But she happened to want to keep working. Along with dancing at office parties, the unwritten job description of being an editor in chief at Scarborough Magazines—or Scary, as insiders christened the company years ago, when, in a putsch remembered as Bloody Monday, five editors in chief were canned in one day—included managing her image. This was at least as important as keeping tabs on an $18 million budget. No one at Scary had a Condé Nast–level clothing allowance, but every editor and publisher was expected to look as if she did.

At a luncheon a few years ago, Magnolia overheard the president of a major publishing company snort, "That woman will never work for *us*," while critiquing an editor in a ruffled peach suit more suited to the Scottsdale Country Club than the podium of the Waldorf. In a flash, Magnolia got it, just as she understood that the editor-in-chief position she was appointed to the next year came with migraines, fourteen-hour days, and densely numbered Excel sheets.

"When the Chanel ladies open the doors, race to the handbags," Phoebe instructed, placing her hands on her hips, which, despite the eighth month of a pregnancy, were so slim they appeared to have been modified by Adobe Photoshop. "They'll be on the far wall and they let you buy two. Grab them right away. Go to the opposite wall next and hit the shoes, but don't get sucked in by the short boots. They're so over. Then the clothes. Save the jewelry and sunglasses till the end. They have plenty."

Okay, Magnolia thought. She might be a piece of wood at yoga, but if she could migrate from Fargo to Manhattan, she could manage these moves.

Truthfully, once you got over the accents, Fargo had been less frozen wasteland and more an agreeably Type B place to be a kid, good for cruising the mall and dating cute boys named Anderson or Olson. On vacations from the University of Michigan, she'd return home every summer, with internships at *The Forum*. But when the newspaper offered her a job after graduation—she was one fine obit writer, that Maggie—her mother and father couldn't hustle her to the airport fast enough.

"Fargo—no place for a Jewish girl" could have been the family bumper sticker. For Maggie Goldfarb, there'd be little postbaccalaureate mooching. Recognizing she'd hit her sell-by date in the state the country forgot ("You're the first person I've ever met from North Dakota"), she'd need to get out, ready or not.

Maggie headed for Manhattan and morphed into Magnolia Gold. Later, when people asked her what connections she'd exercised to snag her job at *Glamour*, she fessed up to ignorance as her sole advantage. If she'd grown up in New York, she'd have been too intimidated to have cold-called Human Resources.

"Mags! Magnolia! Hey, Gold!"

Magnolia's head was in Fargo, but Darlene Knudson, publisher of *Lady*, was definitely here, dripping a tall latte on Magnolia's bare leg. She and Darlene were equals at *Lady*, each ruling her own dominion: Magnolia headed up the editorial staff, and Darlene managed sales and marketing. Both reported to Jock Flanagan, the company's president and CEO, and a former publisher himself. Most heads of magazine companies climbed the corporate ladder by starting as publishers, and though they feigned fascination for creative types, in a standoff, it was publishers who garnered their sympathy. When ad sales faltered, invariably an editor got the boot.

Big-boned and braying, Darlene plopped down next to Magnolia, ignoring scowls from the women—more than 150 by now—behind her in line. Darlene had never met a mirror she didn't like and, at forty, was still bragging about her SAT scores. She was a Midwestern transplant, too, but while Mr. and Mrs. Goldfarb failed to receive the memo that self-esteem had been invented, Darlene drank it in her mother's milk. The child of Iowa über-WASPs, Darlene was now an Upper East Side mother of three, with a nanny for each daughter. Everyone on her staff knew Darlene took mental health days every Friday to make up for rarely seeing Priscilla, Camilla, and Annabel the rest of the week.

She always tried to stick it to Magnolia, who considered Darlene her frenemy—more enemy than friend.

"First-timer?" Darlene asked, throwing down her bulging black satchel. "I hate this stuff myself, but Mother loves it."

"Yes, I'm a virgin," Magnolia responded in a tone she hoped was airy and ironic. But Darlene was already thumb-dancing with her BlackBerry. Conversation over.

By now the sisterhood of shoppers snaked down one long wall and back around the other. The latest arrivals were nearer to the door than sleep-deprived zealots who'd blown in at dawn. The crowd ranged from fashion victims—whose unfortunate garments represented every trend from the past four seasons—to dozens of adorable answers to the question "Who could ever wear *that*?"

As the clock neared eight, a Chanel representative emerged, arms brimming with papers. "No one will be admitted without proper ID," she shouted above the din. "Complete these waivers before we let you in."

"Forms?" countered a member of the *Lucky* pep squad. "What's up?"

"We need to make sure no one will resell on eBay," announced the gatekeeper.

"Last year one woman made over $60,000," the girl next to Magnolia whispered. Just as she was considering the brilliance of that energetic consumer, a tussle broke out. A new arrival (she must be past sixty—her face was Botoxed and Restylaned to perfection, but the neck told all) had tried to maneuver herself to a spot near the door. Two women half her age blocked her entrance.

"Where do you think you're headed?" one demanded.

"To shop like everyone else," the interloper responded as she plucked a speck of lint off her yoga pants.

"Like hell you are," said early bird number one.

"Don't be crass," answered Miss Sixty. "We have equal rights here."

"Not if you don't wait your turn," the friend said as she raised an arm to bar her elder.

"No one's going in till you all calm down, every one of you," yelled the Chanel rep, her camellia trembling. "No one."

Calm prevailed. For thirty seconds. Then the doors parted. The room, bright as a casino, swallowed Magnolia. Neatly boxed shoes and boots, carefully arranged by sizes, and every sort of brooch and more were piled high on tables, which ringed row after row of tightly packed clothing racks. Where to begin? The handbags, the handbags. Totes the size of labradoodles, clutches too small for a Tampax, purses worthy of a Jackie O impersonator. Not a style in sight a workhorse could live out of from morning till night.

Then she spotted it, the black kid classic. Interlocking C's stood chastely back-to-back in a quilted V. She'd seen this number advertised for $2,100 in the *Times*. Here, $150.

Magnolia grabbed the bag and a furry carryall that she could wear with—well, she'd figure that out later. She scat to the shoes, and furiously began trying on every pair of size sevens. Powder blue ballerina flats with huge C's. Even in her delirium she realized they were more appalling than appealing. The ankle boots? Phoebe's orange alert sang in her ears. Pumps with thick ankle straps? They'd make her legs look like stumps. Maybe the kitten heels. *Elle* insists—again—that pink was spring's newest neutral. They would do.

Under a chair she spied an unopened box, the crisp white logo an island of dignity in the middle of funereal ebony. Inside, the slingbacks' toes narrowed to a sexy point. The lizard soles, which no one but the wearer would even see, glistened like sexy snakes. *"You need to convince people you are special,"* her horoscope had warned. These shoes had her name all over them.

Now, the clothes. Magnolia cursed herself for not having researched her size at Saks. Six, she guessed, eyeing her behind. For princely occasions every woman was supposed to trot out a Chanel jacket, but there were few here without buckles and pockets run amok. Only one jacket looked acceptable—dove gray tweed with silver threads, a few discreet buttons rimmed with rhinestones, C's linked in the silk lining. Like intrepid pom-pom girls, they were everywhere, those C's. She grabbed the jacket and sprinted to evening gowns. Magnolia considered the red chiffon, but it was too bare for a bra. While ogling her nipples, the testosterone club that ran Scary would declare such a dress in poor taste. She settled on a demure black cocktail dress. Maybe she'd be invited to a Catholic charity dinner.

Arms filled, Magnolia headed to the ad hoc try-on area. Women in all manner of undress were madly pulling clothes on and off, quickly discarding selections that retailed for thousands. They seemed grateful for the males in the room—gay guys shopping for their sisters had opinions you could respect. As she was trying to decide if the dress actually looked like something from the Ann Taylor Loft 60 percent-off rack, she saw them. The publishers.

Four of Scary's hotshots were stripped to their bras and thongs, zipping one another up and lobbing compliments. Darlene Knudson, *Lady*'s publisher, towered above the publisher of *Elegance*, Charlotte Stone, a perfect lady trying valiantly to outsell *Vogue*. Charlotte waved over Magnolia. Like every editor, Magnolia deeply distrusted most publishers, believing they would sell you down the river for a Depends ad. Charlotte, however, was reputed to be decent.

"Magnolia! Honey! Did you see the trenches they just brought out? They're only $75!"

On size-zero Charlotte, the belted green coat looked soigné. "Check out the lining," she urged. The name Coco was knit into the fabric. They really did have the branding thing going on. Magnolia guessed that the lumpy coat might give her all the grace of a gorilla, but grabbed the last one without a try-on. She dragged her purchases to the cash register. It took another fifteen minutes to check out.

"Thirty-nine hundred," said the Chanel girl, without looking up.

Magnolia took another look at the handbag. If you added a chain, it could double for her lunch box from fourth grade. Was she really going to spend almost four thousand dollars on purchases she wasn't even sure she liked? If she'd ever wear these clothes, she wished she could accessorize with a disclaimer that read, "Do not judge the wearer, who may look deeply shallow, but is truly a person you'd want to know."

"Are you paying or not?" a woman behind her shouted. Magnolia whipped out her credit card. She lugged her bags to the street, hoping the hotel doorman could flag a taxi. It was 8:45. Magnolia was famished, thirsty, and needed to get to the office for a nine o'clock meeting.

Finally, she slid into a cab. As it turned right past the old Plaza Hotel, Darlene, Charlotte, and the other Scary publishers—each on her cell phone—passed her in a company limo. The light changed. Magnolia looked at her watch, a Cartier tank she'd indulged herself with in honor of getting her job. She realized now she'd certainly be late for her meeting.

She might have the title. She might be the youngest woman to ever edit a magazine as huge as *Lady*. But Magnolia Gold felt, not for the first time, as if she were a big, fat fake. Any minute now, she'd be exposed as the cubic zirconia she truly believed she was.

Chapter 2

The Grunt Work and the Glory

"Ah, the couture shopper," Sasha Dobbs greeted Magnolia as she entered her office on lower Fifth Avenue. "The sale—all it's cracked up to be?"

"Bought a lot, sweat a lot," Magnolia replied to her assistant. She glanced at her watch. Five after nine.

"Not to worry. The meeting's pushed to four because Little Jock broke his arm in an equestrian event yesterday. Or so they say."

Jock didn't strike Magnolia as a Mr. Mom who'd hang out at a child's bedside, even if it was his first son after five tries in three marriages. More likely than not, he was enjoying the happy ending of a very late night, probably with someone cute and young and not his wife. But it was a gift to Magnolia just the same. She'd have the better part of the day to rehearse for the meeting.

Sasha handed her the morning's messages. Three were from publicists, one from her friend Abbey, and another from Natalie Simon, the town's current alpha dog editor, who headed up *Dazzle*. She'd hired Magnolia for her first job, as her secretary, a title you were still allowed to use twelve years ago at *Glamour*.

"Okay if Cam pops in?" Sasha asked.

"Two secs, Sash." As Magnolia scanned her e-mail, Sasha arranged a fresh bouquet of peonies. Twice a week, Sasha stopped at the corner grocer and managed to discover flowers that looked as if they came from Takashimaya. Nonetheless, Magnolia made a mental note, when salary renegotiations came up, to ask for a weekly stipend to order fresh flowers every week from a real florist—ideally, that guru of design known for supersimple, superexpensive monochromatic bouquets.

She'd be useless without Sasha. When Magnolia's previous assistant, the plummy-voiced Fiona, had failed to return from a vacation, Magnolia seriously considered hiring the Oberlin grad who was temping for her. Then she got a peek at her pierced tongue. The next day Sasha showed up, dressed in a slim black suit by Theory. Sasha had limited experience beyond Teach for America, but she clinched the deal with her thank-you.

Magnolia never hired anyone who didn't send a follow-up note; to not thank a potential boss for her time, and make a case for how perfect you were for the job, was just plain dumb. Sasha's note was literate and hand-delivered on creamy, engraved Smythson of Bond Street stationery.

Sasha had begun six months ago at $41,000 and had earned every penny twice over. Speak to the folks in New Delhi about fixing Magnolia's BlackBerry. Check. Book tickets to L.A. and make sure Magnolia gets a window seat. Check. Order from Cupcake Café for office party. Check. For the tenth time explain to Darlene's assistant that she can't put an appointment on Magnolia's calendar to call on a client without clearing it. Check. None of these chores required the double major in film studies and philosophy Sasha had earned at Wesleyan, but she was so efficient she always had plenty of time left over for writing the magazine movie column.

"Okay. Ready for Cam," Magnolia said, leaving the rest of her e-mail for later.

"No problem," Sasha said. Magnolia despised that expression. Yet if she complained about it to Sasha, she knew she risked getting as steely a warning from Human Resources as if she'd asked her assistant if she'd tattooed her private parts.

Cameron Dane, the magazine's managing editor, excelled at the extreme sport of keeping *Lady* on time and on budget. When Cam told her to hurry, because a page needed to ship, Magnolia did. When they were at risk of overspending—last month, it was obscene sums on messengers—Cameron blew the whistle. Just as important, if *Lady* hadn't eaten up as much money as Scary allowed, he'd figure out where to use it or lose it, rule number one of corporate budgets.

Straight, six foot two, and in his early thirties, Cameron was one of the industry's less typical managing editors. If he hadn't been an aspiring novelist in need of health insurance, he'd never have been in the job. As usual, he was wearing Levis, and his shaggy blond hair hung over his collar. He placed his large mug of coffee on her desk.

Forty minutes later, after the two of them worked through his list of emergencies—including hiring a coach for the new lifestyle editor, who had impeccable taste but whose organizational instincts were a weapon of mass destruction—Cam was ready to leave. But not before he reminded her: "Time to write your editor's letter."

"It's written in my head," Magnolia said as Cam walked out the door. Her eyes followed him. If I weren't his boss, if he didn't have a girlfriend, if he weren't five years younger, and if he showed the *least* glimmer of interest—Magnolia thought—there's a guy I'd like be with naked. And so on. But she couldn't allow herself the luxury of a fly-by fantasy. She had to wrap her head around her work, not her sex life, which was currently on pause.

She'd get to the editor's letter. First she needed to look at the three baskets on the antique pine table she called her desk. Magnolia swore by her supremely low-tech system. The basket on the left was the outbox—currently empty, a glaring reminder of all she had yet to do. The middle basket she considered a black hole for items she could postpone, hopefully for eternity. The overflowing basket on the right contained whatever she needed to read.

Each upcoming issue's priorities were in a different-colored folder. September, which they were working on now, was purple. Title options were in a brown folder, waiting for Magnolia to choose or rewrite. All the financial stuff was in green, naturally. A blue folder labeled READ swelled with manuscripts and story pitches that hadn't been bought or assigned and maybe never would be. It stayed on the bottom of the basket. If Magnolia waited until the weekend to get to READ, it wouldn't stop up the plumbing—providing Sasha hadn't deposited any time-sensitive material there ("The White House requests the honor of your presence. . . ."). Magnolia's most important folder was red, signifying a rush.

The folder she inevitably dove into first, however, was pink: invitations. Today's offerings were meager. Another osteoporosis luncheon—worthy, but Magnolia had hosted one herself two months ago. A screening for a movie geared to adolescent males—even Sasha wouldn't want it, although she might go to the club opening, a category of event Magnolia stopped attending when the cocktails became undrinkable. Red Bull, OJ, and rum?

Magnolia turned to her computer screen to begin "But I Digress . . . ," her editor's letter. What in God's name would she write about this month? To plug something in the issue, she only had space for a few paragraphs, but she needed to lead with deep thoughts. It was worse than composing haiku.

This month, Lady *introduces two new columns,* she started to write. Bor-ing. Maybe she should focus on the section about child care? *Can there be a bigger guilt machine for working mothers than the job of finding quality child care?* Better. *But this is real life. Mary Poppins isn't landing on your roof. . . ."*

Sasha buzzed again. "Ruthie's ready to show film." Magnolia hated the interruption, but if she didn't pick photos for the September issue, the art department couldn't design. She walked down the hall to the large room filled with cutting-edge computers and girls in clothes from Club Monaco. The only designer who felt compelled to dress up was

Fredericka von Trapp, the art director—today in head-to-toe Jil Sander. She was huddled over a light box with Ruthie Kim, the fashion director.

"You can't see her dress." Fredericka complained, tucking a lock of platinum blond hair behind one ear. "Vy did you have the photographer come in so close? She's got pores like craters." Fredericka hadn't lived in Germany for twenty years, but her accent was as strong as Marlene Dietrich's.

"Because she's breathtaking," Ruthie said.

"Try bulimic. Remind me vy ve booked this model?"

"Amber bailed. Look right here. She's gorgeous. Gorgeous."

Ruthie adored every photo from every shoot she'd ever supervised. Thirty minutes flew as the three of them picked nine photos.

Back to her office. Another three sentences on the letter. The phone, this time Scary's attorney.

"You can't say that." He was ranting about a celebrity profile. "Does the word 'libel' mean nothing to you?"

"We have the quote on tape from a writer for *The Wall Street Journal.*" Magnolia loved sparring with the lawyers, who tried to suck the blood out of any story.

Truth was, Magnolia Gold loved everything about being a magazine editor. Publishing disease-of-the-week articles that saved people's lives. Rooting out gifted writers from small-town newspapers. Turning flaccid manuscripts into vigorous prose. Giving people jobs, tickets to Broadway shows, and invitations to press junkets, which whisked them off to resorts in Bali that their salaries would never allow. Knowing which button to push, thus motivating an employee to produce her best effort and shimmer with pride.

Okay, to be fair, Magnolia also liked her perks, and not just the free flu shot. Company retreats at Canyon Ranch, where the surprise speaker might easily be a randy former president. The vacation, five weeks of it—although she got hot and cold running FedEx's and faxes wherever she traveled, even to Cambodia. Knowing that her friends from Fargo watched her on TV.

Magnolia liked it all. Being an editor in chief was the ultimate job for the editor of the high school newspaper, especially one with questionable grammar. There was never a morning when she didn't want to go to work. Her staff, she suspected, prayed she'd take the occasional sick day, but Magnolia had the constitution of a mule, and feared that if she took off, just to play, she'd be struck with a legitimate, lingering illness. Her open secret was that she relished the grunt work as much as the glory. When the digits on her computer suggested, "Go home, kid," she had to force herself to leave.

Magnolia Gold felt born to be a magazine editor. When she was growing up in Fargo, magazines had given her a window into a world where people watched indie movies, wore clothes paraded on red carpets, and referred to Donatella Versace as if she were their college roommate. Now, working on a magazine required every talent God granted her, and overlooked those He forgot, like the ability to pass trigonometry. At the end of it all, a product existed that she could see and women liked. It didn't even bother her that most of *Lady*'s loyalists read it on the toilet. Hey, they were busy.

So was Magnolia. Every morning, there was more to do than she could ever complete in a day. That was fine, because inside her lurked a procrastinator hanging around in flannel pajamas, and she had to suppress her at all costs. Magnolia was no good at knitting or parallel parking, but she almost always knew what women wanted to read before they themselves did. Editors who grew up anywhere cooler than Fargo—which is to say, everywhere—had probably never even been in the same room with your average coupon-clipping, Wal-Mart shopping American woman. Magnolia grew up with her, respected her, and was her—if you could overlook the cosmic good fortune of a sprawling Manhattan co-op and a plus-size expense account.

Her favorite moment was knowing she'd written just the right line to impel hundreds of thousands of shoppers to stampede through the supermarket because they *had* to find out what the twelve steps were in this month's hair rehab story. Early in her career, when she'd dashed off "How Not to Be Fat After 30," it had garnered a "Dear Pussycat, That was absolutely fabulous" note from Helen Gurley Brown. Magnolia kept the treasure—typed on fading pink paper—in a folder marked OPEN WHEN FEELING SUICIDAL.

Plain and simple, Magnolia had always adored magazines. They'd taught her to relieve flatulence, give a hand job, and handicap the marriage prospects of Prince William. Now her fun wasn't so much from reading magazines, as from working on them, and the juicy center was being surrounded by smart, talented people. Each editor, proofreader, and production associate on *Lady* was a jewel, handpicked. While Magnolia didn't feel these gems belonged in a tiara she expected to wear forever, she appreciated that her top colleagues had followed her to *Lady* from her last job.

She swiveled her tall leather chair toward her Mac, banging out the editor's letter. At half past one, Sasha brought her the usual from the deli downstairs—grilled chicken, chickpeas, beets, cherry tomatoes, and romaine tossed with low-fat honey mustard dressing—which Magnolia gobbled along with *USA Today*.

A few manuscripts later, she looked at the clock. Could she call California yet? Two o'clock. Excellent.

"How are we coming with December?" she asked. *Lady* still needed a cover.

"Reese Witherspoon—definite maybe," replied the overpriced, L.A. celebrity wrangler. This was good, very good. Booking the dead-on perfect star guaranteed that *Lady* would sell 70 percent of its copies, which was roughly double that of most magazines.

When Magnolia looked up again, it was 3:45. Already? So much for rehearsing her presentation for the meeting. She brushed her teeth and combed her hair, glad she'd worked in an appointment over the weekend to have her amber highlights refreshed.

It was time.

Chapter 3

Oprah Envy

The boardroom was filled, every seat readied with a fresh yellow legal pad and an extrafine felt-tip pen, Jock Flanagan's preferred writing instrument. Darlene Knudson, in black Prada from plunging neck to rounded toe, positioned herself—as always—at one end, opposite Jock, as if she were his equal. Like synchronized swimmers, numerous high priests from circulation, marketing, publicity, production, and research—several outranking Darlene—flanked each side of the twenty-foot rosewood table. Everyone was waiting for the master and commander. As usual.

At 4:25, he entered. As company presidents went, Jock was prime time ready, from his monogrammed cuffs to his recently barbered head of wavy hair, whose blackness he owed as much to chemistry as genes. If it weren't for an unfortunate overbite, he'd be truly handsome, and he looked a decade younger than his fifty-five years. Taking his seat at the head of the table and offering no apologies for detaining twelve executives who, collectively, earned close to five million dollars, Jock let several minutes pass before he beckoned for Darlene Knudson and whispered something in her ear. Finally, he spoke.

"Ready, kids?" he asked the group. "I'm going to turn this meeting over to Magnolia, because I know you can't wait to see how she's going to reinvent *Lady*, everyone's favorite dowager."

What's with the snarky tone, Magnolia wondered? Whose fault was it, anyway, that *Lady* needed a facelift? It's not as if during her interviews for the job Jock happened to mention that the magazine was two million dollars in the red. The magazine looked like a frump when she signed on, and she'd vastly improved it, even without the redesign she was proposing today. Anyway, she could certainly hold up her head in public. As of a year ago, *Lady* had turned a profit. Plus, Magnolia had brought down the average reader's age to forty-two, practically prepubescent among traditional women's magazines. Jock should consider her a sorceress. Still, there were limits to how much she could accomplish with her current resources. After presenting to the group today, Magnolia hoped-hoped-hoped they'd finally approve the investment for which she'd been pleading. The magazine needed everything— glossier paper, a larger format, more room for jaw-dropping art, and the budget to pay for top-notch photographers and writers. What any editor would require to drag an aging diva into this century. If Magnolia's great-grandmother had lived in the United States, and not a shtetl near Minsk—or was it Pinsk?—she'd have been a *Lady* subscriber: the magazine was more than one hundred years old.

"Magnolia? Drumroll."

She realized she hadn't listened to a thing her boss had said in the last ten minutes.

"Thanks, Jock," Magnolia rose from her seat and walked to the wall. "You're all going to love what you see."

Magnolia had been shocked but pleased when Jock had agreed to Step One of her master plan, and had allowed her to hire the city's premier design consultant to help her make over *Lady*. The vote of confidence had propelled her through the last two months of work. Until at least ten on most evenings, she'd been working with Harry James, a well-mannered Englishman. Medium height, with ramrod-straight posture, he had longish hair which was receding ever so slightly, combed straight back from his forehead. His chin had a pronounced cleft.

As they pored over logos and layouts in his downtown design studio at the end of Magnolia's regular workday, it surprised her that Harry wore a suit, always in a dark color with skinny lapels and a narrow tie. He dressed impeccably. From this, Magnolia didn't want to jump to the conclusion that he was gay, though a fair number of designers certainly were. Harry never mentioned a boyfriend, but he didn't flirt with her, either. They kept to the business at hand, which was tricky.

It was hard to change a beloved magazine, no matter how dowdy it may have grown. If *Lady* did a one-eighty, its identity would vanish—and so might its readers. Improvements had to be subtle. Yet the design needed a distinctive point of view; when the magazine flopped open, any woman in Random U.S.A. needed to know instantly she was looking at *Lady*, not another clone of *Real Simple* or a neon replica of *Us*.

Today, each sample page of the magazine was mounted on heavy black boards, turned back side out on ledges that lined the long wall of the conference room. Magnolia inhaled deeply. "This is how we'd treat the cover," she said as she flipped back the first board. "We'd clean it up—fewer coverlines. Refined logo. Richer colors."

Jock and her colleagues got up from their seats and scrutinized the design, gathering behind Magnolia. They all waited for Jock's appraisal.

"Impressive," he finally said with a nod.

One by one, she turned around the remaining forty boards, showing how *Lady*'s columns, special sections, and the splashy pages in the middle—where no ads were allowed—would appear redesigned for a woman who didn't want to buy a magazine that looked like what her mom threw in her shopping cart with the mayonnaise.

As she took her seat, no one spoke. Magnolia thought she could hear the head of marketing sucking an Altoid.

"You've nailed it, Magnolia," Jock said. "This magazine is fresh, friendly, and modern—everything *Lady* should be."

"Congratulations." "Great job." "I love it." The compliments popped like champagne corks.

Magnolia felt like dancing on the table. She hadn't admitted to her top editors how nervous she'd been—only Abbey, her best friend, knew. Most editors in chief were years more experienced, and Magnolia always worried about making beginners' mistakes. Maybe now, finally, she could let herself relax. She smiled and thanked Jock and the group.

"This magazine has Estée Lauder written all over it," Jock added. Omigod, sweet. That was truly high praise. The beauty advertisers were the most coveted—and cosseted—because they tended to have the biggest budgets, and their ads looked so good they gave a magazine an upgrade. Half the time, readers couldn't tell the beauty ads from the magazine's editorials anyway. Among the dozens of big-name beauty advertisers, Lauder may as well have been named Leader. Every other company waited to see where they put their ads, and followed their direction.

"I appreciate the hard work you've done on this, Magnolia," Jock continued. He cleared his throat and fidgeted with the lapels on his Brioni jacket. "And now let's consider Darlene's idea."

Darlene's idea? Whoa. This was her meeting, Magnolia's. Her head was suddenly full of noise. Her publisher's name wasn't on yesterday's e-mail that had confirmed the agenda. Why hadn't she known about this? This was reminding her of last summer, when Darlene scheduled a critical six-month review with Jock for eight A.M. on the Monday morning when Magnolia would be returning, jet-lagged, from a two-week vacation in the Yucatán.

Magnolia scanned the faces up and down the table. None of the others looked surprised.

Darlene stood up, smoothing the wrinkles on her snug black pencil skirt. She walked to the door of the conference room and let in her assistant, who distributed a shiny red folder to each person at the table. Darlene turned to Magnolia and smiled. "Great design, really great. But what I'm going to show everyone today is a license to mint money. We have an extraordinary opportunity at hand, and I know you're all going to want to get on board." She grinned at the group, revealing her large, frighteningly white teeth. "You all know Bebe Blake," Darlene, a former Big Ten football cheerleader, said in her stadium-worthy voice.

Who didn't? Bebe's name was in the tabloids every other day. She was always suing someone. After a career as a singer, then as an actress, she had a syndicated talk show, which Magnolia knew had been in steady decline. Somewhere in there had been one or two five-minute marriages. Bebe had been on *Lady*'s cover twice since Magnolia had taken over. Not only did neither issue sell especially well, both experiences were odious. The last time, Bebe's publicist, the profession's head harpy, had ordered *Lady*'s art director Fredericka off the set because Bebe couldn't abide the woman's Düsseldorf diction.

"Bebe wants her own magazine, and she'd be willing to take over *Lady* and turn it into *Bebe*."

She'd be *willing*? Take *Lady*, where Eleanor Roosevelt used to write a column, and turn it into a magazine for show business's leading flake? Is Darlene smoking crack?

"Trust me, *Bebe*—that's what she wants to call the magazine—could be like minting money," Darlene concluded.

"Like Darlene says, this could be just the ticket for *Lady*," Jock chimed in. "Bebe is a marketing genius. When she plugs the South Beach Diet peanut butter cookies on her show, the next day cookies fly off the shelves. And she'd be willing to promote the magazine on air. Take a look."

"Minting money," Darlene repeated. And again. And again, as if a computer chip had malfunctioned. Magnolia wanted to knock Darlene on the head to get her to stop.

The group opened their folders. Inside were four pages of article ideas, most of which Magnolia recognized as recycled from other magazines. But what stood out was the red type. Now that she was reading on, she saw that the color red, Bebe's signature hue—which extended to her hair—would be featured prominently throughout the magazine. Every cover would have a red background. The magazine would end with "Seeing Red," an essay Bebe planned to write herself, where she promised to "vent, no holds barred." Oh, yes, the world was waiting for a download of Bebe Blake's opinions, of that Bebe seemed to be sure.

"The magazine that's *well-red*, that's the kicker Bebe wants," Darlene said. "Genius, no?"

Okay, joke's over, Magnolia thought. Everyone is going to groan now, then toast my idea. She pictured confetti raining on her head.

Apparently not.

"Well, done, Darlene," Jock said. "But this isn't a dictatorship. I value the opinion of everyone in this room. Tell me what you think. We know where Darlene stands, so we'll start with Milt."

Milt Herman, one of the grand poobahs, was the son of Scary's former president and was the same guy who advised Magnolia, based on an obscure study from 1987, never to use a celebrity's photo if her teeth were parted. When she'd ignored that dictum with a laughing shot of Jennifer Aniston, she'd put out *Lady*'s best seller of the year. Milt had never forgiven her the success.

"I go with Bebe. I see it as a huge win-win, just like Oprah's magazine," he proclaimed.

That's it. Oprah-envy, Magnolia thought. From its premiere issue—which needed to be printed twice because her fans snapped up all the copies in two days—Oprah Winfrey's magazine was the biggest triumph the magazine industry had seen in the last twenty-five years. Every other company—and apparently Bebe, too—was jealous of Oprah's slam dunk.

One by one, all the good soldiers fell in line praising the Bebe idea. Magnolia spoke last. "I beg you to reconsider," she said, trying to stay calm. "First, Bebe's not Oprah. Nobody is. Oprah's the closest thing this country has to a saint. You can trip any woman anywhere and she can explain what she stands for. If Oprah ran for president with Tom Hanks as VP, she'd win by a landslide."

No one in the room said a word, so Magnolia went on.

"Bebe doesn't stand for anything bigger than herself—she's just a collection of interests. Doughnuts, kittens, country music. Interests change."

She was definitely on a roll. She thought about the photo shoot when Bebe wouldn't wear the designer clothes they'd had specially made in her size and relived the incident with Fredericka. Should she mention that Bebe was notoriously difficult to work with? Nah, her colleagues wouldn't care—that would be her problem. Besides, whenever you complained that someone else was a pain, people always assumed *you* were the difficult one.

She flip-flopped about whether to go on, fearing that the head of Human Resources would crash through the door and haul her to P.C. court. But Magnolia had to say it.

"Third, it's pretty much an open secret that Bebe is . . ." She searched for a delicate word. ". . . a player." Who was she kidding? She's a slut. "This doesn't bother any of us, but remember how our clients refused to place their ads next to that story we ran about the call girl who became a pediatric oncologist? They aren't going to like it if Bebe and her latest boy toy get splashed on *The National Enquirer,* and many of *Lady*'s more conservative readers—you know we're mostly read by red-state Republicans—may be upset by it, too."

Magnolia took a deep breath. "Seriously, guys—you'll rue the day you sign a contract with Bebe Blake."

She looked the table up and down, waiting for one of her colleagues to see the wisdom of her impassioned homily. Silence.

"Okay, then," Jock announced, grinning his beaver smile. "Meeting adjourned."

Was there a clue she'd missed? Would a shrewder editor have seen it all coming? Maybe. Somebody who slept with Jock, perhaps? Definitely. Was the idea hatched by Darlene to make her suffer? Magnolia, even in a spasm of paranoia, doubted it. Darlene was more treacherously ambitious than pointlessly cruel; she cared about making money, the primary credential—along with the ability to avoid getting bogged down in pesky introspection—for succeeding as a publisher. If *Bebe* could guarantee Scary the direct route to a bigger pile of cash than *Lady* did, the company might get behind it. *If.*

Magnolia collected her thoughts, along with her boards, and headed back to her office.

Chapter 4

The Two Women Who Still Eat Carbs

When it came to running with Abbey Kennedy, Magnolia was what the United States Postal Service used to be. Neither snow nor rain nor gloom of night—hangovers, insomnia, upstairs party people—kept her from the appointed rounds. If the two made a date, she'd show on the dot of 6:45 A.M. Running wasn't all about protecting her butt from gravity or a sincere interest in heart health—no matter how much *Lady* preached on the subject. A couple of spins around the reservoir was her Prozac.

Magnolia had returned home late last night; walked Biggie and Lola, her Tibetan terriers; poured a glass of Shiraz, and promptly crashed after three sips. She'd had every intention of returning Abbey's call, greased with apologies, but exhaustion triumphed. Guilt trailed her as she ran a few blocks east and turned on to Central Park West to pick up Abbey.

To run, Magnolia wore the usual—whatever was clean and a base-ball cap from a trip to the Golden Door, where for two days Julia Roberts had been her best friend. "Mea culpa," she said to Abbey as she entered the oak-paneled lobby of her apartment building. Abbey quickly popped on her big, black Audrey Hepburn sunglasses, but not before Magnolia noticed she'd been crying.

Next to Abbey, Magnolia was Babe, Paul Bunyan's ox. Abbey could shop in the teen department and barely looked twenty-four, though she was ten years older. Crying jag or not, this morning she was adorable in tiny black running shorts, an orange racer-back running bra, and shoes that gleamed brand-new. Her dark brown ponytail looked as sleek as always.

"Okay, tell me," Magnolia pleaded gently. "Sorry I couldn't return your calls yesterday. Work tsunami. First, talk."

Abbey started to run and stared ahead, her smile zipped into a tight line. "It's Tommy."

"And?"

"Gone."

As they entered the park, Seymour, a neighborhood golden retriever who'd become Abbey's surrogate canine child, bounded up to them, Frisbee in tow. Normally Abbey would have given Seymour a hug, and the Frisbee a long toss. But today she ran past him, pushing uphill on her twiggy but powerful legs, leaving Seymour looking as confused as Magnolia felt.

"When I got back from San Francisco Sunday night, I noticed Tommy had made brownies. They were arranged on that stainless-steel platter he'd got for me at Moss on Valentine's Day." Magnolia remembered how annoyed Abbey had been—she was romantic to her last cabbage rose print—when she'd received a serving dish as a gift from her husband of three years. And from SoHo's bastion of ultramodern design, when she was the countess of the flea market.

"I went to cut a brownie in half and the knives were gone."

"Huh?"

"It took me a few minutes until I saw the note taped to the fridge. 'Abbey, I will always love you, but it wasn't meant to be.' It took a few minutes to sink in. I kept looking for a P.S.: 'I'm outta here and you're outta eggs.' What kind of bullshit way is that to leave your wife?"

Tommy bullshit. "I was out all night working on a story" bullshit. "I've stopped seeing Stephanie" bullshit. "The trip to Turks and Caicos is for work" bullshit. The kind of bullshit Abbey chose to believe.

Magnolia disliked Tommy O'Toole, deeply. She guessed the feeling was mutual, as it is when someone knows you've got their number, although she could understand why Abbey fell for him. Two years younger than Abbey, a model turned anchorman for the local news, broad shoulders, no waist, that faint shrimp-on-the-barbie accent, curly brown hair, terrific piano player. Also quite the baker boy and, according to Abbey, extraordinary in bed. But ever since Tommy came on to her, a month before his wedding, Magnolia wanted to snarl at him whenever he entered the room.

"I've been hysterical," Abbey said. "Blindsided. Haven't been to my workshop once. Or eaten a thing except for a whole pint of Chunky Monkey last night between three-thirty and four."

What were Ben and Jerry putting in ice cream? Abbey picked up the pace and kept talking. "I feel like such a fool. I want to claw his eyes out. I miss him. I'm embarrassed. I feel pathetic. I'm in disbelief. I hate him. I love him. I'm exhausted from all this emotion. How can he really be gone?"

What do you say to a friend who hurts everywhere? "Tommy is an asshole." Why state the obvious? "He tried to kiss me once, but I said, 'Fuck off.'" Instead Magnolia said, "Abbey, he'll be back." As soon as she heard her voice, she realized any devotee of Dr. Phil could have done better. Plus, she doubted it was true.

"Magnolia, you're wrong. This time I know he's never coming back. He took his cell phone charger, that navy Asprey blazer we had the fight about. Nineteen hundred dollars for a jacket that looks like Brooks Brothers? I'm still pissed. And the good knives. What kind of a man takes knives? Oh, and his passport. At least I never have to look at that Vuitton case again."

Abbey and Magnolia had bonded long ago over how much they loathed Louis Vuitton anything, and now that Magnolia thought about it, she was suddenly convinced that Tommy's passport case was probably a gift from a woman with whom he'd had an adventure, probably in a humid place in a faraway time zone.

"Do you have any idea where he went?"

"No clue."

They ran in silence, completing their laps. This was the first time Magnolia remembered a lull in their conversation. She and Abbey were perfectly matched as two of the slower runners around the reservoir—although today's shock appeared to be propelling Abbey to a speed that Magnolia had to work hard to match—and their chatter always made the runs seem more like a phone call than exercise. Whether they were discussing if Abbey should use citrines or garnets in one of her designs—her jewelry line, Abbey K, had just been shown in a recent *W* ("worn by Hilary Swank to the Oscars")—or analyzing last night's dream, talk carried them through.

After finishing their run, they headed to a nearby coffee shop for the fifteen minutes of breakfast Magnolia allotted herself on a workday. Not only were she and Abbey the only two women on the Upper West Side who still ate carbs—they shared a scone whenever they ran—she guessed they might also be the neighborhood's sole adult females who got through the day without antidepressants, although Magnolia was thinking that it would be handy right now for Abbey to have some pharmaceutical voodoo.

"Tommy will be back," Magnolia insisted. "He adores you. You're his life." Where was this drivel coming from? Abbey burst into tears. Magnolia grabbed a stack of napkins, handed them to her friend, and hugged her hard.

"Forget me," Abbey said through her heaving, Italian widow moans. "What's going on with you?"

"If I start venting, I will never stop," Magnolia said. "I'll give you two words. Bebe Blake."

"She walked off another photo shoot? What do you care? She sold, what, eleven copies for you last time."

"Oh, that it were so simple. I'll call you tonight and give you the whole deal." Magnolia got up to leave, remorse pulsing. She wished she could take off the morning, tuck Abbey under a downy duvet in a cool, air-conditioned room, and hold her hand while they listened to Harry Connick Jr. But there was rarely a day to be late for work, and this was definitely not it. Scary was the court of Henry VIII—make a mistake and you could be beheaded.

They said their good-byes. Magnolia raced home and rushed into the shower for a quickie shampoo. She went over her clothing options. Today called for skyscraper heels, definitely, and the confidence-building Stella McCartney dress she'd been saving for a very important occasion. With water dripping across her pale gray carpeting, she checked her schedule. Did she have a lunch? Yes, Natalie Simon for their monthly sushi pig-out.

Magnolia could use a dose of Natalie just now. A sit-down with Natalie could be better than finding money in your pocket: her advice was that astute. The vox populi was that Natalie was the cagiest editor in town, having earned her chops over the course of thirty years. The only problem was that Natalie seemed to have a selective memory and so many industry friends sucking up that you couldn't always count on her to recall promises she'd make to you, even if your discussion was yesterday.

Thirty-five minutes later, Magnolia was out the door. As she left the elevator downstairs, she collided with a delivery boy. "For you," shouted the day doorman. A magnificent white orchid—pale, perfect, a botanical Uma Thurman—was on its way up.

Magnolia accepted the present with curiosity. Flowers at *Lady* were routine, although it was usually the beauty and fashion departments that cleaned up; you could barely walk to the bathroom without seeing a glorious floral tribute. The untrained observer might think someone on the staff got engaged every day, but, no, the deliveries were almost always attached to press releases for, say, a new ultra-hydrating, pro-vitamin hair complex a publicist wanted mentioned in the magazine.

Could the orchid be a guilt gift from Darlene? Unlikely. She'd never given Magnolia a present, not even at Christmas. She opened the card. "Can't wait to see how yesterday went."

Uma was from Harry James, the designer who'd worked so hard on *Lady*'s potential facelift. Their months of late nights had been all business but not unpleasant. Harry. What a lovely thought.

Magnolia checked her watch. She realized that for a full five minutes she'd forgotten about Bebe Blake hovering on the horizon, ready to turn *Lady* into a caricature of a magazine and her job into something worse.

That is, if she still had a job.

Chapter 5

The Corner of Grapevine and Yenta

"Make yourself at home," Natalie Simon mouthed to Magnolia, a phone to her ear.

That wasn't hard. Except for a computer Natalie used as little as possible, her enormous space—twice that of Magnolia's, although both of them were editors in chief at Scary—was more a salon than the hub of a working journalist. As Mozart hummed in the background, a sea of azure prints, chosen by Natalie's decorator to set off her blue eyes, enhanced an effect of unhurried calm. Flanking the sole fireplace in the building were twin love seats. One featured a needlepoint pillow begging the question, *"What part of meow don't you understand?"* while the other observed that *"Many complain of their looks, few of their brains."* The pillows were gifts to Natalie from her mentor, the famously silver-haired Hearst editorial director Ellen Levine.

Natalie loved to dress as if she were still the 100-pound sylph she was in 1975. Today she wore an olive military coat and periwinkle blue polka-dot shirt over a knee-length yellow satin bubble skirt, a mix of vintage and, as Natalie—an Anglophile from Scarsdale—liked to put it, the high street. Her tangled, blond hair balanced like a cumulus atop her head, and stacks of turquoise and silver Navajo bracelets jangled at her wrists. One finger sported a substantial sapphire ring, another bands of lapis lazuli and gold.

She looked like a homeless woman who'd robbed a jewelry store.

One of Natalie's many talents was to attract people, and Magnolia thought of her office as being located on the corner of Grapevine and Yenta. Like a cat presents mice to her mistress, New Yorkers on their way up and/or on their way down liked to reward Natalie with juicy tidbits, and her phone fairly vibrated with this-just-in innuendo, deep background, and the occasional fact. This not only benefited *Dazzle*, Scary's cash cow, but made Natalie very good company when she was in the mood to share, which was often. To show her appreciation for information that sustained her place as the magazine world's reigning queen bee, Natalie liked nothing better than to find people jobs, doctors, and dates.

More than once, Magnolia had benefited from Natalie's aid. She had given Magnolia her first job, as her assistant at *Glamour*. She'd recommended the dermatologist Dr. Winnie Wong, who never let a little thing like FDA approval deter her; because of Dr. Winnie's signature glycolic acid potions, Magnolia hoped to forestall cosmetic surgery for decades. Natalie had also introduced Magnolia to her cousin Wally Fleigelman, who except for his name turned out to be a perfect first husband.

Magnolia didn't hold it against Natalie that she and Wally stayed married for only one year. For all of their hasty courtship, Magnolia was crazy in love, but unfortunately, after the wedding, she and Wally realized they were from different solar systems. He was an unabridged New Yorker, from his accent to his out-there sarcasm, and ten years earlier, she had yet to understand what was funny about a Woody Allen movie and buttered a roast beef sandwich. And how was Magnolia to know that her bridegroom's idea of foreplay would become watching the Golf Channel side by side? Recognizing a youthful folly—they were both only twenty-four at the time—the newlyweds parted amicably, not so difficult when the bride gets the real estate.

"Magnolia, sit." Natalie pointed to one of the love seats. Their sushi waited on delicate bamboo trays. They might be eating takeout from Yamahama Mama, but Stella, Natalie's number-two geisha—the one in charge of food, travel, and expense accounts—made sure the presentation was up to Natalie's specs.

"A shame about yesterday," Natalie offered, as she popped a piece of unagi into her mouth, careful not to smear her plum lip gloss.

Magnolia avoided Natalie's eyes. She'd pretend the possibility didn't exist that Natalie and others might be feeling sorry for her. Magnolia knew pity was the first symptom of a swift but fatal corporate disease.

"The thing is, the design Harry James and I created was wonderful," Magnolia said, pitching her voice low to make sure she wasn't whining. "We'd finally found an approach that's not the same old, more-white-space-than-words clone of every other magazine. What's up with Jock that he can't see what a bonehead move it would be to scuttle all this good work?"

"Since when, Cookie, does the smartest decision ever get made?" Natalie offered, parking her polished ebony chopsticks at the side of a red lacquer plate. "Everyone's got his own agenda. For now, forget the redesign. Although from what I hear, it's spectacular."

Was Natalie gunning for Magnolia to show it to her? That wasn't going to happen. Magnolia had learned the hard way that Natalie was like every other editor, who believed what was yours was yours—writers, headlines, ideas—until she decided it was "in the public domain," a time which could arrive with surprising alacrity.

"So, I shouldn't appeal to Jock's higher plane of reason?" Magnolia asked, getting up from her chair and walking to the window. If Magnolia wasn't mistaken, that was Darlene getting into a car with a rotund redhead poured into black leather pants, a fitted jacket, and spiky boots.

"There's no such place," Natalie said with a laugh. "Right now Jock's thinking Bebe Blake will lead him to Oscar parties, weekends in Malibu, and his own pilot and plane." They both knew how it got to Jock that his kid brother, who headed a media company deep in the corn of Nebraska, had a GV at his disposal, when Jock didn't even have a share in a NetJet.

"But, Natalie, it doesn't make sense," Magnolia said. "*The Bebe Show* is sliding in the Nielsen's. Will she even get an option to renew?"

"Magnolia, have I taught you nothing? Use a little *sechel* for a change." Only with Magnolia did Natalie throw around Yiddish, this time invoking the term for shrewd judgment. They were often the only Jews at Scary meetings and on those occasions Natalie used less Yiddish than your average Leno-watching Southern Baptist.

"Get all orgasmic about Bebe?" Magnolia asked.

"Precisely. What's to lose?"

Integrity? Face? Time? Still, she tried to focus on the bigger picture. "I get your drift."

"Besides, Bebe's not that bad," Natalie said as she twisted a stray tendril into her unruly topknot.

"And you would know this how?"

"We had lunch recently and she's hilarious. Curses a blue streak. I was peeing in my pants."

This was the first time Natalie had ever mentioned lunching with Bebe. In fact, after her last *Dazzle* cover, which featured a paparazzi photo which made the entertainer look like the blue-ribbon sow at the Texas state fair, there was talk of lawsuits. Magnolia weighed the options. Should she ask Natalie if she was aware of Bebe's proposal before her meeting with Jock and the gang—or let it go? Better not. If she knew nothing, Natalie would do a slow burn at the implication that she was sitting on dynamite.

"How's that friend of yours with the jewelry?" Natalie said as she poured green tea from a fragile celadon teapot.

Magnolia sometimes felt that before a conversation with Natalie she should pop a Ritalin, but frankly she was relieved that they'd moved to a new topic.

"Abbey?" Magnolia asked.

"I can never remember her name," Natalie said. "Was that one of her necklaces I saw Charlotte wearing the other day?"

"Could be," Magnolia said. She knew where this was going and decided to get there fast. "Want me to see if she'd give you a friends-and-family discount?"

Natalie feigned surprise. "Magnolia," she said. "You are the sweetest. But now that you mention it, maybe something from the new line I hear she has coming out. The one at Bergdorf's"

In the next ten minutes they discussed whether or not Magnolia would go out with Natalie's husband's partner (Magnolia waffled—he was a troll), why the editor of *Elegance* ran Penélope Cruz on the cover every six months (desperate), and who'd become the next editor of the *Star* (each of them offered a short list). When Natalie's assistant buzzed her, Magnolia was glad. It was almost two, and their lunch had failed to have its desired effect of making her feel fabulous merely from being in Natalie's wake.

"Oh, I know it's last minute, but I'd love it if you'd join us for cocktails in the country a week from Saturday," Natalie said as Magnolia got up to leave. "Throwing a book party for Dr. Winnie. A small group. Very casual."

Magnolia couldn't remember when she'd ever actually had fun at one of Natalie's parties, but if she declined, Natalie might be angry. Magnolia couldn't risk it. Natalie shifted from friend to foe like other women changed underwear.

"Love to," Magnolia said.

"Bring a guy—that is, if you're dating someone."

Her little imaginary boyfriend? They could drive in her pretend Porsche.

"Bebe promised to come," Natalie added.

"Your new best friend?"

"Grow up, Magele. You're way too paranoid."

The minute she said it, Magnolia knew that she wasn't. On the way back to her office, Magnolia decided to make a pit stop at the lobby newsstand. She paid for her lottery ticket and dashed into a closing elevator.

"There she is," Jock said to a short, rumpled man next to him. "Our own steel Magnolia."

Magnolia cursed the day the movie had ever been released. "Jock!" she said, and forced what she hoped was a smile.

"Magnolia, meet Arthur Montgomery."

Arthur Montgomery. The name sounded familiar but the face— long and hawkish—wasn't. "Mr. Montgomery, hello."

"Miss Magnolia, what a lovely name," he drawled. If they ever had a real conversation, this gentleman was going to be disappointed to find out she was from North Dakota, not Carolina. Could she help it if her mother chose the name "Magnolia" on her honeymoon to New Orleans?

"Magnolia, call me," Jock said as the elevator opened to her floor. His tone was neutral, but an order nonetheless.

She stopped in the art department on the way to her office. "Can we work on the cover together in about an hour?" she asked Fredericka. For the 80 percent of *Lady*'s readers who were subscribers, you could put a can of pork and beans on the cover and they'd barely notice, but to attract elusive newsstand buyers, the image and words were life-and-death; developing covers stretched for weeks. As she hovered over Fredericka at her computer, her art director was endlessly patient while Magnolia suggested colors and type and tweaked coverlines. At the end of each session, Magnolia walked away with numerous versions, which she'd stare at for days, trying to choose the most arresting one. She'd stare so long the words—*Free! Hidden! Sex!*—began to look like a Slavic language. Her last step was to take the covers home, so her doorman could weigh in.

"Ready when you are," Fredericka answered. "The film's scanned."

"An hour then," Magnolia said. As she walked into her own office, Sasha gave her a new batch of messages. Harry had returned her thank-you call about the orchid and Cam had stopped by. Magnolia was sorry she missed him, since she'd decided to tell him about the Bebe situation—not that it was a talk she looked forward to having.

"Almost forgot," Sasha said. "Darlene's assistant set up a breakfast for this Friday. You're supposed be at Michael's at eight-fifteen to meet you-know-who."

Sasha looked at Magnolia, waiting for more, but Magnolia walked into her office and slammed the door. Seven manuscripts and one editor's letter later, she went to work with Fredericka. At 5:55 she called Jock. It was a brief conversation. Jock didn't think it would be necessary for him to join Magnolia, Darlene, and Bebe when they met for breakfast. He and Arthur Montgomery, her attorney, were seeing eye to eye on everything and he was sure she and Bebe would, too.

Chapter 6

A Legend in Her Own Mind

"Good morning, Miss Gold," the perennially cheery young greeter announced. "Mrs. Knudson's already seated."

In the evening, any visitor from Nome to nowhere could snag a prime spot at Michael's Restaurant, but at breakfast or lunch the room was unofficially reserved for *le tout* media, who came to check out one another. Only after Michael's crack team verified your name, rank, and serial number to make sure you were—or still were—who you claimed to be. The unspoken rule was that if the maître d' and his fembots didn't know who you were, they weren't interested in taking your $27 for eggs and toast. The seating chart was planned with the precision of a $500,000 wedding. Executives from advertising, fashion, and beauty favored the back room, which won for appeal, given its peek at what passed for a garden. The front space, with its Hockney lithos, drew this minute's superheroes from Scary, Condé Nast, Hearst, Time, and big-ticket literary agencies. Television folk swung both ways.

It was up front that Magnolia headed. She spotted Darlene bouncing from table to table, floating photos of her sturdy Nordic daughters and bestowing kisses as if she were campaigning for the New Hampshire primary. Magnolia waved to several buddies from other companies as she walked across the room, stopping only to acknowledge the mayor's press secretary, who had just been featured in a *Lady* "40 under 40" roundup. Today Darlene's bag wasn't parked at her regular pied-à-terre, #12, but at a table that seated four. Magnolia positioned herself across from Darlene, who'd claimed the chair against the wall, the one with the good view.

"She should be here any minute," Darlene said to Magnolia. "They're on their way."

"They?"

"Bebe never goes anywhere without Felicity Dingle. She's her producer, memsahib, groomer, whatever." Magnolia remembered that at the last *Lady* photo shoot it was Felicity who'd barked to the publicist about Fredericka and had her banished from the studio. Darlene did a few hits on her BlackBerry, then locked eyes with Magnolia. "Bebe's a force of nature," she said. "You'll see."

Darlene turned to the Marketplace section of *The Wall Street Journal*. Other than the local business pages—especially on Monday, when they traditionally decimated the magazine industry—it was all she read. No one would accuse her of being a seeker of wisdom and truth, nor would Darlene apologize for that—or much. She parsed her time to reach her goals, and since she'd entered magazines ten years ago, had been on a fast upward trajectory. Darlene left investment banking to begin as an ad salesperson at a small magazine about decorating (or "shelter," as Darlene always reminded people, even if they weren't in the industry, and mistook her for speaking Finnish). She got hired as publisher of *Lady* last year. At forty, the statute of limitations had run out on her classification as a wunderkind. She needed a grand slam, and she needed it now. But so far, *Lady* had only been number three in its category, with number four nipping at her heels, and her ad sales had slipped an eyebrow-raising 9 percent.

As Darlene perused her newspaper, Magnolia looked at the menu, a waste of time. She'd be having oatmeal, as usual. Make a call? Not here, where the guy at the next table might be a tabloid spook.

Suddenly, the room grew silent. Magnolia turned. Bebe Blake was heading toward them, a long-haired animal—a ferret? No, it was a cat—peeking out of her burnt orange Birken bag. Bebe was wearing tight jeans—Juicy Couture, Magnolia guessed, although she wasn't sure they were made in Bebe's size—a V-neck Grateful Dead T-shirt that showed deep décolletage, and boots that looked compromised trying to support her. She had a heart-shaped face; a small, pointy nose; and when she removed her Gucci sunglasses, close-set dark eyes not unlike those of her pet. Bebe's hair was the color of ketchup.

Carrying an ostrich-leather-trimmed canvas tote loaded with papers and liter-sized bottles of Evian, another sturdy woman arrived. Her inky hair, which matched the feline's, hung close to her head in an asymmetrical cut that recalled Austin Powers's shagadelic London. In her aqua pants and zippered top, she looked ready for a power breakfast in any Atlanta suburb.

"Darlene!"

"Bebe!"

"You adorable thing, you. And you must be the editor, Gardenia."

In fact, this was not their first meeting. Every time Bebe had been on *Lady*'s cover, Magnolia had stopped by the photo studio to personally thank her and drop off a gift. Last time, to nibble during takes, she'd given Bebe chocolates in a specially ordered box the size of a laptop.

"It's Magnolia. Magnolia Gold. Thank you for coming."

"You're so much younger-looking than your photo." Bebe squawked, and both Darlene and the other woman joined her in noisy laughter.

"And you're so much . . ." Magnolia began.

"Fatter?" Bebe offered. It was just this kind of self-deprecating remark that won her fans, who were considerable in number. "I read minds," Bebe continued. "Meet Felicity." Magnolia shook hands with Bebe's cashmere-clad sidekick. "And this is Hell, the current man in my life, who's going to need some cream. Got some tongue on him, doesn't he?" She lifted the cat into her lap and let him lick her face.

"Shall we order?" Darlene said.

"I'll have raspberries with soy milk," Bebe announced. When she smiled, her small eyes got smaller. "Felicity? Will it be soy yogurt? We just returned from that new ashram in Santa Fe. We're vegans now."

Magnolia wished she'd gone for the eggs Benedict. But her oatmeal had arrived with efficiency.

Bebe yawned. "What's this I hear about your wanting me to take over a magazine?"

Magnolia almost spit out her cereal.

"Jock and I have been scouting for a new take on *Lady* for months now," Darlene began.

Total con, Magnolia thought. Unless it's true.

"We adore your show," Darlene continued. "I TiVo it and watch it every night on my Stairmaster. Gotta work on the old tush." She patted her rear.

"Your tush is a work of art, honey," Bebe said. "But let's cut to the chase. Flattered as I am by your attention, magazines are over. They're bor-ing. Never read 'em. Can't tell 'em apart. Beige, beige, blah. Dull, dull, dead."

Magnolia shot a glance at Felicity's bag, which was knocking against her leg. At least one of them bought magazines. *W* stuck out. And *O*. Plus obviously they were all going to pretend that Bebe's bright red memo for her own magazine, which they'd seen just days before, didn't exist. Magnolia realized she had officially entered an alternate universe.

"We think that your stamp on any product would make it stand out, and a magazine isn't any different from, say, designing clothes," Darlene countered. Bebe's brand of plus-size studded denim routinely sold out at Target.

Hell lapped up his dish of cream, at which point Felicity emptied the table's milk pitcher into his saucer.

"If I would even consider this little venture, I'd insist on a few deal points," Bebe announced.

"Shoot," Darlene responded.

"For starters, I require one hundred percent creative control," Bebe began. "Can't be second-guessed. That's a given. Ground rule two, I work when I work. Never sleep, so it's not a problem. I spend July and August in Hawaii, December in Aspen, and I'm thinking of buying in Tuscany. Anyway, Felicity can make any decision for me. She's my go-to bitch."

The two of them high-fived. Since "Good morning," Go-to Bitch had said not one word. Magnolia saw mouths moving, heard laughter coming from a faraway place. Drops of perspiration trickled down inside her new linen jacket. She would rather be enduring a Brazilian wax after a long, bushy winter than be here.

". . . and I don't intend to renew my show. Fuckin' noose," Bebe said with enough conviction to turn heads at other tables.

Magnolia came to. No show, no endorsements, no visibility for the magazine, if it should sink to that. No! No! No!

"Bebe, I'm surprised to hear you'd think of leaving *The Bebe Show*. It's such an audience-pleaser. Your fans would be outraged." Magnolia hated the sound of her own voice, although she wasn't surprised Bebe would be taking this step, with her ratings slip-sliding away. She hadn't made the list of *Fortune*'s wealthiest women in the universe for the last four years by being a pea brain.

"We'll see," Bebe said, popping the last raspberry in her mouth. "I'm looking at a lot of opportunities. Maybe open my own ashram. Or a chain of foot reflexology salons."

"If we're lucky enough to get you on board, is there anything you like and would want to keep from the current *Lady*?" Magnolia ventured, hearing her voice squeak, but feeling incapable of lowering it.

"Well, it's clever the way you do the product endorsement thing, your seal of approval."

"That's *Good Housekeeping*."

"And I like that column, 'Can This Marriage Be Saved?' Read it all the time at the podiatrist's.

"That would be *Ladies' Home Journal.*"

"You ladies, you're all alike." Bebe snapped, although Magnolia had to admit that she'd heard the exact remark many times in focus groups. Which was why she'd planned a redesign of *Lady* with Harry James. She could feel her temples throb at the epic injustice of the whole situation.

"I'm sure we can work out any little details later," Darlene broke in. "This is just get-acquainted time. Felicity, do you have anything you want to ask?"

Felicity's voice was low, her manner confident, and her accent, decidedly northern English.

"Only if Magnolia thought there would be anything unusually difficult about doing a magazine this way?"

Magnolia wasn't entirely sure what answer she could cough up, other than that handing over the magazine to Bebe and/or Felicity was the worst idea since bald guys with ponytails. "Typically, a magazine's editor in chief is a benign dictator," she responded. "What she says, goes. For better or worse, it's her vision, her success if the magazine's a hit, her disaster if it bombs. In this case, the vision would be Bebe's. It's an unorthodox arrangement, but I'm sure there's a way to work it out."

"Dictator?" Bebe said. "Sweet."

Chapter 7

Marshmallow and Mademoiselle

Manhattan offered far posher nail salons than Think Pink, where the only frills were a bowl of miniature Snickers and two jade plants in the jaws of death. What the establishment lacked in luxury it made up for in location, which was equidistant from Magnolia on West End and Abbey on Central Park West. The real draw, though, was its owner, Lily Kim, the mother of Ruthie Kim, Magnolia's fashion director.

In Korea, Lily had been a midwife. Here, she labored seven days a week in her shop, her real mission being to make sure that her daughter Ruthie achieved profound success. The tutors who helped Ruthie get into Stuyvesant High School—the Ferrari of New York City public education—paid off when Wellesley gave her a full scholarship. While picking clothes and arranging fashion shoots wasn't quite what Lily had projected for her daughter—her ambition ran along the superhighway of concert cellist–Olympic skater–McKinsey consultant—Lily had accepted Ruthie's choice. Now she made it her business to know Nina Ricci from Narciso Rodriguez, and she never hesitated to offer fashion advice or to comment on the appearance of Ruthie—or any-one else.

"Maggie, you look tired," Lily announced, as she arranged Magnolia's polish shades: Marshmallow and Mademoiselle, one coat of each, to create the subtle pink of a blushing bride.

"Week from hell," Magnolia responded. She had to be careful what she said, since every detail would bounce back to Ruthie. "But it's been worse for Abbey." She turned to her friend. "What's the late-breaking news?" she asked. This much Magnolia knew: as of 11:30 last night, Tommy was still MIA.

Magnolia thought it a testament to the donation of her precious Ambien stash that Abbey had even shown up today for their weekly manicure. She'd bombarded her with calls to make sure she wasn't still home in her nightgown on a sunny afternoon watching *You've Got Mail*, which every single woman in Manhattan could lip-synch.

"Got a message last night," Abbey said. "The prick's alive."

Anger, Magnolia thought. Excellent. Abbey's still alive, too. "Where is he?" she asked.

"Hiding in cyberspace," Abbey reported. "That's all I know." She blinked away a tear. Clearly, wrath was only a topcoat on a fragile base of fear, hurt, and anxiety.

"What did he say?" Magnolia pressed on, while Lily quietly began filing her nails, not too long, square with rounded edges. The Saturday afternoon opera played quietly on a boom box.

"Needs time to think," Abbey reported.

"Code for 'I will take my own sweet time to fuck around while you squirm and writhe,'" Magnolia said. She couldn't remember the last time any woman benefited when a man got to thinking. "What are you going to do?"

"Throw myself into work," Abbey said. "Become the world's most prolific jewelry designer. I was up all night sketching. I'm seeing lizards, lizards everywhere. Lizards with slinky diamond bodies.

Lizards with cowardly topaz stripes. And strangely, these lizards have no balls."

While Abbey and Lily debated the anatomy of scaly reptiles, Magnolia tried to ignore the fleeting thought that Abbey might actually produce one of these critters for her birthday—preferably in a size big enough to make a statement around her wrist. "Did you read your husband the riot act?" Magnolia asked.

"My *estranged* husband?" Abbey asked. "Not in so many words. I'm such an ass. I was actually relieved to hear from him."

"Did you e-mail back?"

"Told Tommy to get his butt home," Abbey admitted.

Magnolia thought Abbey might have asked a few more questions. Like where was he? Who was he with? What were his intentions? Why did he think he could treat her this way? She knew it would be up to her to play rottweiler. "If he writes back—correction: *when* he writes back—give him a deadline."

"I hope you never put his name on the lease," added Lily, ever the pragmatist, as she warmed Magnolia's hands with a steamy towel.

When they married, Tommy had moved into Abbey's rent-stabilized apartment. For the cost of a Queens studio, the couple luxuriated in six rooms and nine-foot ceilings capped by dentil moldings, a butler's pantry, enough closets to hide a family of fugitives, and a view of the park. The desire to keep a real-estate jewel of this caliber had kept many a faltering New York marriage together forever. Lily had clearly hit a nerve, and Abbey gave both of them her look that telegraphed: "Back off. This isn't a drug intervention. I am not the idiot wimp you think I am." Directed toward Magnolia, the look seemed to also say, "I'm married, even if my husband's not exactly around. You, on the other hand, are single. Perhaps terminally."

"Enough," Abbey said.

"Natalie loves your jewelry—especially the pieces she heard Bergdorf's commissioned" was all Magnolia could think to say.

"But of course Mrs. Simon would know this," Abbey said. "Is there anything she doesn't know?" She could not forgive Natalie for never remembering her name.

"She doesn't know who I am bringing to her party next week," Magnolia said. "Because I don't know myself." Magnolia's social life had gone into remission five months before when she broke up with Alec the architect, who had long black hair and an inability to hit an ATM. When he asked for her to pay his car leasing bill, Magnolia ended it, finally accepting the fact that he'd been as stingy with emotion as he had been with cash. "If I don't come up with someone—and you know she'll harass me about it all week until I do—Natalie will remedy the situation herself." As a matchmaker, Natalie believed in the classic combination of beautiful women and rich, ugly men, although for her, another rule applied: Natalie's husband happened to look like Jeremy Irons's baby brother.

"In that case, we need to be creative," Abbey said. "What about Cameron in your office? I've always loved him."

Everyone did. "Next," Magnolia said.

"J-Date," Lily insisted. "You need Jewish man." She gave the same advice to her own daughter.

"Find a guy online?" Magnolia responded. "What kind of loser do you think I am?"

"The kind who got no man," Lily said with a laugh. Lily and her manicurists were always cracking up. Either they found the world infinitely amusing or their customers imbeciles.

"You shrews take it down a notch," Magnolia said. "What you don't know is that this week a gentleman sent me flowers."

Abbey and Lily swiveled their creaky vinyl chairs to face Magnolia. "The designer I worked with on the *Lady* redo sent me a magnificent orchid in a tasteful white china pot."

"He's looking for more work," Lily said. "Doesn't count."

Magnolia hated that Lily might be right.

"Is he interested in Magnolia the delightful divorcée, or Magnolia the on-the-rise editor?" Abbey asked.

"I'm trying to decide whether I should find out. When we finally spoke last night, he suggested meeting for a drink."

"You accepted?" Abbey asked.

"Gave him the 'I'm on deadline.'"

"Technically, he's not your employee," she pointed out. "You should have said yes."

"Okay, I'll ask him to join me at Natalie's party. It's a business thing, so I can't embarrass myself that badly." In fact, bringing along Harry, who'd only recently moved here from London, might even elevate her stock. He was a hot design consultant, and Americans always thought anyone who sounded like Ralph Fiennes was profoundly intelligent.

Lily gave Magnolia's fingertips a final coat. Abbey's nails were now a shiny crimson, as they sat at the dryers at the far end of the shop. Magnolia noticed the latest *Lady*, along with any number of tattered *People*s. "Good, we've escaped Lily," Magnolia whispered, as she began thumbing through her own magazine. As soon as *Lady* was printed, she always found at least two dozen things she wished she'd done differently. "I've hit a little, ah, speed bump at work." She filled her in on the Michael's breakfast.

"She brought a cat to a midtown restaurant?" Abbey asked.

"That was the highlight. This whole Bebe thing is spiraling out of control. Very soon it's going to be the cheese stands alone, and I will be a piece of very stinky Limburger." Magnolia tried for breezy, but she knew Abbey would see straight through to the hollow spot inside of her that exposed her worst-case scenario. Humiliation! Loneliness! Financial ruin! That's what she saw for herself if Jock pulled the plug on her magazine. Working didn't just pay the bills—it made her whole.

"You've got to talk to Jock," Abbey insisted. "Get him to see reason."

"Natalie thinks that's a vile idea."

"Natalie? The only good advice she ever gave you was never to incriminate yourself in e-mail. If your magazine turns into Bebe Blake's Christmas letter, Natalie has nothing to lose. Fight!"

"Jock's totally dollar-happy," Magnolia said. "I'm afraid his mind is made up. He thinks going with Bebe is a blue-chip deal."

"How can you be sure?" Abbey asked.

Magnolia didn't know whom to believe. Her friend's love was never in dispute, but she thought like an artist, not a corporate strategist, while Natalie had stayed at the top of her game for close to twenty-five years, when some colleagues as young as forty were already roadkill.

"I say, 'Feed me,'" Magnolia said. "Omelets at Nice Matin?"

"Bye, Lily," they shouted. "See you next Saturday."

"Don't forget your newspaper," Lily called out.

Magnolia had almost left her *Post* behind. "Hold up, guys. Let's see what Miss Universe has in store for me today."

Can you trust other people's advice? Today's stars warn that not even close colleagues and confidants can be relied upon to share good information. They may not be trying to deceive you, but how do you know that they themselves have not been deceived?

Always with the questions, that witch. This mess, she could see, she'd have to figure out on her own.

Chapter 8

Cleavage Never Hurts

Magnolia had forgotten how much effort a woman needed to look good, really good.

The week had been too busy for a fake-and-bake at Brazilian Bronze, so the night before Natalie's party on Saturday, starting at midnight, she anointed herself with self-tanner, which dried while she fell asleep right before Ingrid Bergman discovers Cary Grant was actually single in *Indiscreet.* Fortunately, the next morning she awoke even and bronzed, not like the mutant tiger she'd feared.

Magnolia ran at eight, the earliest hour Abbey deemed civilized for weekends. Her shiatsu massage guy, Eli Birdsong, showed up at 9:30 for an hour of bliss-by-kneading. After a quick shower, she had just enough time to cab it to Frédéric Fekkai for an eyebrow shaping and blowout. Satisfied that her stylist didn't completely obliterate the body in her hair—the ramrod-straight look made her nose look the size of a muffin—she tipped handsomely and walked up Madison Avenue, scoping out shops to see if she could improve on the clothes she'd laid out. So, of course, she was late for this week's manicure.

It was 4:30 by the time Magnolia got home. Biggie and Lola

assaulted her, hyper and indignant—they'd been deprived of Saturday afternoon's usual rampage at the dog run. One short whip around the block was all the time Magnolia could spare if she was going to detox even a little, look over a bit of work, and do her makeup right. She'd drawn the line at a professional job, even if Natalie's guest list would feature a column's worth of bold-faced names. In fact, now that she thought about it, she'd have to scratch the work. Harry was picking her up at 6:45.

As she poured the last of her precious and now extinct Ralph Lauren Safari bath beads into the tub, the phone rang.

"Running a tad late," Harry said. "I'll bring round the car and have the doorman ring up. Will you forgive me for being the kind of cad who expects a lady to meet him on the street?"

I am such a sucker for a proper Brit accent, Magnolia thought. Give him a Hugh Grant stutter and I'd marry him even if he were a television evangelist. "Take your time, Harry," Magnolia said. "We'll make an entrance."

She poured herself a glass of Pinot Grigio, switched on a Norah Jones CD, and let the glorious bubbles wash off the week, which she gave a B plus. On the upside, she, Cam, Fredericka, and the gang had—as of 10:59 the previous night—shipped the September issue. They'd needed to work late every night. September was always a monster—three-minute makeup, fall fashion must-haves, a sixteen-page parenting section underwritten by Toys "R" Us, and one article she knew each *Lady* reader would memorize: the five secrets to getting a good night's sleep. That last coverline alone would sell the issue. The women in America may as well have a big pajama party between three and five in the morning—the adult female half of the country was all up, ruminating.

But the best part of the September issue was Magnolia's off-the-charts cover girl: a sweeter-than-Krispy-Kreme portrait of Kate Hudson and her adorable, hipster toddler. Home run. Eighty percent newsstand sell-through, at least, maybe 85, plus she'd be the envy of every other editor.

Magnolia had had to wait almost two years for that photo shoot, performing due diligence with Kate's celebrity flack by featuring several of her less fabulous stars—actresses way past their sell-by dates or no-name wannabes. It was a form of blackmail the industry shrugged off and accepted. The cabal of publicists who controlled celebrity coverage put all the magazines in a rotation. This meant that it would be at least nine months—when Kate's next movie premiered—until one of *Lady*'s competitors would be allowed to feature her on a cover. That's if the publicists were true to their word. Sometimes a promise was a promise, and sometimes just a suggestion. An editor could think her cover was locked, only to be told there were "extenuating circumstances" . . . which turned out to be that the celebrity preferred to be on *Vanity Fair*.

It took at least two years to get to the front of the line and by then, anything could happen. A young mom celebrity could, for example, decide once her baby became older, "for security reasons," never to allow her child's face on a magazine again. Editors had it easier at *People* or *Dazzle*, Magnolia thought. They used paparazzi photographs, although the fights for the best ones got ugly and monstrously expensive. Still, it didn't matter if the star had lettuce in her teeth, as long as readers recognized her. Magnolia and all the editors of more traditional publications needed a perfect studio shot, where the celebrity locked eyes with the reader, Mona Lisa–style. And forget about recycling a photograph from a few years ago. Any of the stars you'd want bought the rights to all the photos that had ever been taken. Every single one. It was an arcane system. You needed the approval of a celebrity's publicist to reprint a photo and if you tried to sneak around and approach the photographer or his rep directly, they would alert the publicist who, by midday, would be on the phone, taking your name in vain as she drove to work in L.A.

So the Kate Hudson cover was good news, very good. On the downside, though, Magnolia hadn't been able to meet with Jock. It took her all of Sunday to convince herself that confronting him—make that, gently reasoning with him—was her best move. His assistant had rescheduled an appointment three times over the course of Monday, Tuesday, and Wednesday. Then Jock flew off with Darlene, Charlotte Stone, the publisher of *Elegance,* and two other publishers to weasel the Detroit car lords into doing a lucrative joint buy of Scary ads.

Magnolia tried not to think about the whole nasty business. It was time for the evening's first big decision. What to wear? She didn't know whether tonight was the equivalent of a budget meeting washed down with a few martinis or a potentially life-altering first date. Magnolia tried on the new Tuleh floral. It showed tasteful "I'm a woman, not just a working girl" cleavage, and Abbey had lent her a pair of dangly tourmaline earrings that made her eyes look as green as Granny Smith apples. Her orange mini and halter? Did it say "festive dress," as Natalie had requested, or "tranny hooker"? Should she go for understated chic with the Chloe cream eyelet pants and semisheer shirt? The outfit was her seasonal splurge—she could have gone to Paris for a week on what she'd spent—and now she wondered if it looked like she'd grabbed it from Forever 21. Maybe she should default to her five-year-old black Gucci pants (thank you, Abbey, for insisting that Loehmann's wasn't a waste of time) and compliment-generating $69 Pearl River chinoiserie jacket. With that getup at least no one would be staring at her chest.

Dressing for Natalie's little party was harder than writing a résumé. In terms of self-promotion, more depended on it.

Tuleh won. Cleavage never hurt. As Magnolia slipped on the frilly frock, the doorman rang to announce Harry. She gave herself a spritz of scent, slicked her lips with gloss, and looked in the tall mirror that leaned against the foyer wall. Good to go.

She'd never seen Harry in anything but one of his dark business suits, button-up shirt, and narrow ties. But there he was in a pale pink shirt, linen trousers, and a three-button black jacket. And damn he had blue eyes, blue as a '57 Chevy. His wavy brown hair, combed straight back, looked as if he'd just stepped out of the shower, an image she'd never considered until this very moment.

Harry walked around to give her a peck on one cheek and then the other—he smelled good, too. He opened the door of his car. Magnolia hated to be behind the wheel of a car—she didn't know a clutch from a carburetor—but she was reasonably sure this was a vintage Jaguar. Sinking into its nicely broken-in tobacco brown leather upholstery as they headed toward Westchester, Magnolia once again thanked Harry for Uma, who was still in full bloom on her coffee table, and told him for at least the fifth time how much she liked his *Lady* redesign.

"Now tell me what you're not telling me," Harry said, laughing and turning his eyes from the Henry Hudson Parkway to Magnolia's face—and if she wasn't mistaken, her legs. The self-tanning had been worth the effort.

"Just that I'm not sure the design's going to go forward," Magnolia said, hating that corporate-speak was the best she could do, wearing a girlie dress on a balmy June night with Diana Krall in the air and a handsome man to her left.

"This toiling artist demands a reason," Harry said.

"My publisher has an idiot big idea, high concept, never gonna happen, but I have to make nice."

"Big how?"

"Bebe Blake."

"She's big all right." Harry roared. "We're talking wide-angle lens. But I'm not connecting the dots. What does she have to do with *Lady?*"

"Bebe wants to do an Oprah. Start an empire, mold nubile minds, preach to the little people. The Scary folks are thinking of giving her *Lady* on a silver platter."

"Which makes you the turkey?"

"Stuffed, trussed, eaten alive."

"Magnolia, luv. Dial back. They can't just give away a magazine. Utter rubbish. Wouldn't get all worked up if I were you. The folks at Scary have got to be smarter than this."

"Have you met Jock Flanagan?"

"Only in Liz Smith."

Magnolia raised her eyebrows and gave him a long, skeptical look.

"I take your point," he said.

As Harry smiled at her, she noticed a dimple. That and what a fast driver he was. They were already beyond Scarsdale, sailing through that slice of good-school-district burbs to which most of Magnolia's college friends had migrated with their reliable husbands and fast-track toddlers. By the time Exit 4 on 684 came into view, an hour had melted away. They'd covered all the safe subjects: their first jobs (his was at *Rolling Stone*), their last vacations (Barcelona for her, Reykjavik for him), and their dogs (could she warm up to a hyperactive Jack Russell?).

Magnolia guided Harry through the twists and turns of what New Yorkers loved to refer to as "the country." Then they entered the grounds. It was 8:30. Showtime.

Beyond stands of evergreens and birch, elegant gray gates parted on a winding road. At the top of a hill stood not a condo development but the house Natalie had christened Simply Simon. Every lamp and chandelier was ablaze, rivaling dozens of Chinese lanterns strung along an open front porch and swinging from old oaks in the soft breeze. The only thing missing was Bambi. That and the paparazzi—though for all she knew, Natalie might have hidden a crew in the bushes. They got out of the car, handed the key to the valet parking attendant, and walked to the front door.

The first time Magnolia laid eyes on Natalie's house, her envy was like a rash. Natalie and her husband had bought their mini-estate only three years before. After a contractor had gone belly up, he'd unloaded his family dream house and its nine hilly acres to Natalie and Stan ("all cash") Simon. Within a year, Natalie had nestled a swimming pool and Jacuzzi into rocks that looked cloned from the set of *The Flintstones*—if Wilma and Fred had lived beside a man-made waterfall and hot tub. She and her decorator had tag-teamed at every antique show on the Eastern seaboard for insta collections of McCoy pottery, folk art tchotchkes, and flower-sprigged English china, which crowded into imposing cupboards with their requisite peeling paint. Outside, weathered European garden furniture dotted the lush, rolling grounds. An herb garden sat next to two tennis courts surrounded by a tasteful log fence. A cutting garden wasn't far from the basketball court and campfire circle, should anyone have a Kumbaya moment.

"Cookie, you made it," Natalie shouted as she encircled Magnolia with a warm hug. Natalie wore a heavily embroidered purple kimono over silky black cigarette pants. Her hair was secured by chopsticks. Magnolia was glad she'd ixnayed her Chinatown jacket.

"And you must be . . . ?" Natalie asked.

"Harry. Harry James," he said as he extended his hand.

Natalie clasped Harry's hand with both of her own. "Harry, I'm so glad you could join us." But when Harry began to thank her, she had already turned to receive the next couple, whom Magnolia recognized from the Sunday *Times* Evening Hours photos as a Park Avenue plastic surgeon and his bony wife. Natalie didn't bother to introduce Harry and her, and motioned them toward the door to the back veranda. Waiters circulated with delicate walnut-stuffed artichokes, gooey Brie tartlets, and spears of asparagus to dip in a lemony sauce. Magnolia and Harry maneuvered past a throng to the bar, trying to avoid eye contact with the head of Scary circulation, who looked like the missing Marx brother but who, sadly, lacked the family's wit. Drink in hand, Magnolia noticed an old-fashioned glider at the end of the porch. She weighed whether she might park herself with Harry for a respectable length of time, dodge the small talk with other guests, and get to know this man just a little better. She didn't know if it was due to the magical combination of dusk and high-voltage electricity—or the fact that she hadn't eaten so much as a six-ounce yogurt all day—but during the ride, he seemed to have grown more attractive.

No such luck. "Magnolia, speaking of the devil . . ." It was Darlene, coming at her like a tornado and speaking with that natural disaster's force. "Charlotte and I were wondering if you'd be here. I knew you were a Wong girl."

Magnolia had almost forgotten that the party was in tribute to

Dr. Winnie Wong, the dermatologist, and Darlene and Charlotte were patients, too. Not that Natalie would have left them out even if tonight's celebration honored the assistant to the head of sanitation in Queens. Charlotte and Natalie were the best of friends and Darlene was, well, Darlene, who got herself invited everywhere.

Charlotte, she suspected, had done a bit better at the Chanel sample sale than she had. As Magnolia was complimenting her on her satin pants and tiny beaded halter, both of which exactly matched her Gwyneth-blond hair, Darlene was leaning dangerously close to Harry, snorting at something he'd said. Magnolia tried to eavesdrop while nodding attentively as Charlotte described in footnoted detail the house she was building in Sagaponack.

"After a lot of thought, we decided to go with bidets in three out of five bathrooms," she said. "You know, from Waterworks. The white, not the bone. Definitely not the ivory." As Magnolia tried to concentrate on the stress of picking high-quality porcelain fixtures, she realized Darlene had commandeered even more of Harry's personal space and was now whispering—she hoped only that—into his ear. Magnolia waited until Charlotte drew a breath, then turned to Darlene.

"What are the girls doing this summer?" she asked. Magnolia knew Darlene always shipped the three of them and the two senior nannies to her parents, the ranking royalty of Des Moines's country club set. Then in August she and her husband spent two weeks *en famille* on Martha's Vineyard. But Magnolia suspected that Darlene wouldn't want to out herself to Harry as a young matron with a large family.

"The Vineyard. The usual," Darlene responded, with less than complete enthusiasm. But Darlene was not to be bested easily. "Harry, have you met Jock, our president?" she asked.

There he was, strolling toward them, arm in arm with Bebe and Felicity, each of whom was dressed as if for the Grammys. In her red sequined pants and flowing top, Bebe appeared ready to accept her trophy with thanks to Jesus and her band, the Mother Fuckas. Felicity took it down a notch, in a black-and-gold-striped caftan. A vaguely familiar-looking man trailed them. Oh, yes, the Southerner, Arthur Montgomery, Jock's elevator friend and Bebe's lawyer.

"Can you imagine anything more ideal than all of us meeting up here?" Jock boomed, pecking Magnolia's cheek.

Magnolia could, actually. She and Jock exchanged introductions. "Magnolia, I believe you've met Arthur," he said.

"Mag-knoll-ya, the magazine girl," Bebe asked. "Who's the hottie?"

Bebe zeroed in on Harry. Arthur disappeared to refresh both Magnolia's drink and his own. Darlene, Charlotte, and Felicity attached themselves to Dr. Winnie, who was being led around like a show dog by book publishing's glamour girl, Rachel Wright. Wright had made the doc's book, *The 30-Day No-Wrinkle Diet*, the top of her summer list, along with political screeds from both the right and the left. That left Jock holding a double-malt Scotch, waiting for Magnolia to speak.

"I'd hoped to get to you this week," she began.

"Right."

"About Bebe."

"Change of heart?" Jock asked. He wasn't making it easy.

"Not exactly," she began.

"But you'll trust me to make the right decision?" he said.

Magnolia began to answer, but there was Arthur, back with the drinks. "My lovely Magnolia," Arthur said, "you've done up one pretty little magazine. Good girl."

"We made a big change when we brought Magnolia Gold in as editor in chief of *Lady*," Jock said. "Our job right now is to support her, to give her both the time and the room to perform."

Magnolia thanked him, although nothing he'd said or done in the last two weeks suggested that his statements were anything but hooey.

"You are a generous man," Arthur said, "given the numbers you showed me."

Score one for Bebe: her attorney had seen *Lady*'s books, although not necessarily the ones with the figures Magnolia had been shown. Magnolia downed her second martini.

"Magnolia, care to join us tomorrow at Winged Foot?" Jock asked. "Arthur, Darlene, and I are in hot pursuit of a fourth."

During her marriage, whenever conversation drifted to putters and the back nine, Magnolia's boredom began to simmer. She'd explained to her ex, Wally—who'd always wanted her to join him at his parents' country club—that if he'd read the editor bylaws, he'd know that it was expressly forbidden for her to even learn to play golf. Maybe there were some female editors somewhere who loved golf—she just didn't know any.

"I'm going to have to beg off. All I know about golf I can summarize in three words: bad Bermuda shorts."

"Golf. Did I hear my second-favorite four-letter word?" The question was coming from Bebe, still glommed onto Harry.

"You play?" Jock asked.

"My favorite outdoor sport," Bebe said. "I am thinking of planning the Bebe Blake Invitational Pro-Am. Already in conversation with ESPN. Ford's on board as sponsor."

"Stupendous marketing opportunity for *Lady*," Arthur added. "But we'd have to talk soon. Deal's almost done. I'm sure your readers would be interested."

Felicity wandered over, locking arms with Bebe and Jock. "I am having the best time," she said. "Dr. Wong promised me an appointment for Monday. It's not at all like what people say. You magazine people *do* know how to party. Bebe, have to steal you away. Here, kitty, kitty, kitty."

The two of them wandered back into the crowd. Harry pulled Magnolia into a corner. "May I rescue you?" he asked.

Magnolia was already way past her usual two drinks. Even Jock was beginning to look attractive, and forty-five years old was her cutoff. "You may," she said. "We are so finished here."

Chapter 9

Good, Clean Manhattan Fun

Magnolia was not hallucinating. That really was Harry James—he of the excellent pecs and other lovely body parts—snoring softly in her bed. She threw on a silk kimono and tiptoed into the kitchen, careful not to wake him.

As she began to brew a pot of coffee, extra strong, she attempted to reconstruct last night. She remembered trying to get out of Bedford while the getting was good. Then her publisher, Darlene—no, it was Bebe—stormed in her direction, offering an invitation she felt she could not refuse: meeting up at Bebe's suite at the Ritz-Carlton back in Manhattan. There were curt words with Natalie, who was probably peeved that she, too, couldn't go to Bebe's after-party, not with a hundred guests attacking pecan tartlets, colossal strawberries, and chocolate-covered fortune cookies that the caterer wasn't presenting until eleven.

When she and Harry arrived at the hotel, Bebe's cat, Hell, rubbed against her leg. That Magnolia recalled. Jock—whose third wife, Pippi, always seemed to be visiting her family in Houston—was canoodling with *Dazzle*'s entertainment editor, a corkscrewed, brunette poptart in a dress slit past the boundaries of corporate propriety. Jock's hand seemed glued to her left hip, all 34 inches of it. Bebe's lawyer, Arthur, played the piano while Felicity, in a booming alto, belted out Billy Joel. Did Bebe and Darlene start a game of strip poker? That was too awful to try to remember.

Everything about the evening melded—everything except the kiss. During the drive back into the city, she and Harry bantered away, hitting every broad target from Bebe's behind to the number of plastic surgery procedures per guest. Good, clean Manhattan fun. At Bebe's, as the Veuve Clicquot flowed, Magnolia and Harry began to feed each other oysters. One for Harry, one for Magnolia, and on and on. They'd staked out the balcony, its Manhattan vista as timeless as a torch song. As if he'd done it hundreds of times, Harry put his arm tightly around her waist, and pulled her close. It was just one kiss, one long, slow, warm, champagne-y kiss.

He'd been together enough to call the front desk and have his car brought around. With two crisp twenties, Harry thanked the doorman, Felix—he seemed to know his name. As they turned onto West End Avenue, a parking spot opened in front of Magnolia's building, which she took as a portent. It would have been rude, then, not to invite him up. Magnolia liked to think of herself as a well-mannered Midwesterner. Who was she kidding? Manners had nothing to do with it. It was two A.M., Harry was clearly available and she hadn't had sex in seven months.

The phone rang, jarring Magnolia back to Sunday morning. Who'd be phoning at this hour? She looked at the clock. Anyone—it was almost eleven. What was indecent was that she'd just got up after sleeping with a man with whom before last night she'd never discussed anything more intimate than a font.

"How was the party?" It was Abbey, sounding bizarrely chirpy for a wife who knew her husband was floating in cyberspace, and not much more. God bless her antidepressant, which she'd decided to start two weeks ago. It must have begin to kick in.

"Either amazing or a catastrophe," Magnolia answered. "Too blitzed to decide."

"Details, sweetie. Cough 'em up."

"Better-than-average food and much swanning around in off-the-charts clothes."

"Yeah, yeah, another dull night for Magnolia Gold. More, please. Anyone fabulous there?"

"An impressive showing of the New York narcissists' delegation," she said. "Plus Bebe, Felicity, Jock, and Darlene. Oh, and Bebe's lawyer."

"I see, all the cool kids from high school."

"Starting to feel that way," Magnolia said, as she walked to the coffeemaker to fill her mug.

"Did you hold your ground?"

"It's become a slippery slope," she said. "But, to be honest, work is not the first thing on my mind this very minute."

"And what is?" Abbey asked.

"Not a what. A who," Magnolia whispered, stirring milk into her coffee. "Harry."

"Magnolia Gold, you harlot," Abbey screamed. "You do me proud. I think I'm gonna cry. Was he worth it, or are you already suffering dater's remorse?"

"Box number one."

"Do we think he's interested?"

"Can't talk. I hear him rustling around and I may be experiencing post-traumatic stress disorder—the kind where you want to rip the guy's clothes off all over again."

"As your mental health adviser, I feel obligated to speak up. Miss Gold," Abbey said. "You may be in the first stage of an all-too-common condition we refer to as first-degree lust, which is often brought on by an extended drought."

She suddenly felt Harry massaging her neck and beginning to work his way down the back of her thigh-high robe. "Dr. Abbey, you are a brilliant diagnostician but don't hate me. Gotta go."

Magnolia stood up and turned to him, to say . . . what? . . . some party last night, huh? How about those martinis? Fortunately, there was no need for conversation, cheesy or otherwise, because while his hands slipped inside her lacy panties, he was kissing her in the most determined way. Harry was neither tall nor short, and for a guy in his late thirties who mostly sat around making computer magic, he was in commendable shape—an attribute equal to his ability, just then, to multitask.

Harry pressed her against the refrigerator. Twenty-five minutes later, Magnolia realized that Sub-Zero would no longer be an appropriate name for that particular kitchen appliance.

Drying off after their shower, Magnolia decided this would be an opportune moment to locate her inner Frenchwoman. She pictured them washing down flaky pastries with steaming café au lait while they lingered over the *Times*. The best she could offer, however, was stale granola topped with acidophilus yogurt and some rather mature strawberries. Magnolia sensed that her standard breakfast would squelch the mood faster than a dog pooping on the rug—which would be happening any second.

"After I walk Biggie and Lola, how do popovers sound?" she asked.

"Popover Café?"

"It's just a short walk." Magnolia gave Harry her most fetching smile. Famous for popovers as big as cantaloupes, the restaurant—four blocks away on Amsterdam Avenue—was one of Magnolia's favorites, despite the fact that it appeared to have been decorated by an eight-year-old girl—there were more teddy bears than you could count, and calico curtains snatched from Snow White's cottage.

"I'm not sure I could handle the double-stroller gridlock, luv," he answered. Much as she appreciated her nine-closet co-op, vigilant doormen, and proximity to parks and the Dakota—which Magnolia considered her ultimate destiny (she'd be a very considerate neighbor to Yoko)—on the coolness scale, her neighborhood scored, maybe, a five. It was family land, filled not just with strollers, which must have been made by Hummer, but with unshaved foodies, both male and female, loading up as if Hurricane Shlomo would hit the Hudson any minute. She thought it best not to suggest Barney Greengrass, the sturgeon king, as a brunch alternative.

An awkward pause later, they both started talking. "I've got so much work to do," Harry and Magnolia said in unison. For Magnolia, at least, it was true—even if she'd happily prepare performance evaluation reports all night long just to have Harry close to her for a few more hours.

"It's been———"

"Magnificent," he interrupted. "The most delightful night. And not unexpected."

Harry put on his jacket. After one lengthy embrace, where she memorized the scent of his freshly showered neck, she closed the door behind him. I-will-call-you-later, he recited, five words that lobotomize even the most self-assured single woman. She walked the dogs, collapsed on her unmade bed, pulling the rumpled Frette sheets up to her chin, and fell into a dreamless sleep.

At five o'clock Magnolia awoke, ordered chicken with cashews from Imperial Dragon, and worked straight through *60 Minutes*, an *Entourage* rerun, and a Lifetime movie where a washed-up actress plays a psycho who buries alive a tycoon's wife. She had a mountain of manuscripts, potential book excerpts, and layouts to review, which she turned to during commercials. Usually she was a patient editor, writing clear, detailed comments in the margins. But today, more than once, she scrawled "Huh?" or "Is English this writer's first language?" in barely legible handwriting.

Just as Magnolia was going to find out if the movie's victim would rise from the grave, the phone rang. It was Abbey, filling her in on Tommy's latest and waiting for Magnolia's social weather report. At 10:45 she got another call, from Sasha, to give her the heads-up that she was stranded in the Pittsburgh airport and would be late in the morning.

Magnolia let her mind wander. She could picture Harry across the room at the desk, her laptop replaced by a sleek designer's computer. He'd be calling her over, saying they had to stop what they were doing, that he had other ideas in mind.

She should be focusing on work. On tomorrow. On deconstructing what to do about Bebe. But she didn't want to think about her—she was too busy deconstructing Harry's "not unexpected." Did that mean that she, Magnolia Gold, was as luscious a morsel as he'd imagined— or that she, Magnolia Gold, was as easy to bed as a porn star?

Why couldn't men come with instruction manuals?

Chapter 10

Manhattan Is High School in Heels

At home, Magnolia's taste led her to Paris, circa 1965. She'd painted the living room a pale yellow to mitigate Manhattan's gray light and loved curling up with a pile of manuscripts on the curvy, panther-print chaise, which she'd positioned next to the baroque, white marble fireplace that had drawn Wally and her to the place eleven years ago. Framing the windows were gossamer draperies. They reminded Magnolia of her prom dress at Fargo South—and the night she and Tyler Peterson celebrated their true love in the backseat of his father's Pontiac. The latest addition to the apartment was a chandelier, tastefully dripping with crystal teardrops, which she indulged herself with last year when her bonus came through.

Just looking at the chandelier made her feel like Simone de Beauvoir—or Gigi—depending on her degree of literary pretension: some days she saw herself as a serious person taking charge of her own future, others as a ditz with charm around the margins. She could imagine stepping out for an espresso and a Gauloise at Café de Flore—or was it Les Deux Magots?—on the Boulevard Saint-Germain, even though she'd never smoked a cigarette in her life. Marijuana didn't count.

This morning, however, as she opened the door to her office at Scary, she landed in a world where Little Bo Peep met Ralph Lauren. Scary hadn't wanted to spring for redecorating, so she'd inherited the furniture of the previous editor, who was in love with American country. Magnolia worked amid coffee-stained sisal carpeting, black wing-back chairs, and white walls due for a paint job. At one end of the room sat her big, pine desk; at the other, a cozy couch with baggy, cream-colored slipcovers. Enormous bulletin boards covered two walls. On a four-week cycle—*Lady* was a monthly—one filled up with miniature versions of layouts and full-sized cover options for the next issue. The other had developed into a Smithsonian of postcards, pages ripped from other magazines, and Roz Chast cartoons.

Magnolia loved an early morning at work. She could quickly dispense with her e-mail and savor *The New York Times, The Washington Post,* and *The Wall Street Journal.* Unfortunately, it was too soon to phone her parents, who'd traded Fargo for Palm Springs, feeling they'd earned the right to sun 365 days a year.

Soon Cameron would arrive and find a warm body to fill in for the missing Sasha. This would require Magnolia to explain her nitpicky systems to the terrified temp. She briefly considered whether she might tell Cam that, thanks anyway, she could manage on her own today, then recognized that he—being all but clairvoyant in the Magnolia department—would attribute such an action to her being worried.

On that point, he would be correct. She counted on laser-beam focus. Just now, though, Magnolia found it hard not to dwell on how quickly she'd slid from the exhilaration of buffing *Lady* to a gloss not seen in thirty-five years, to wondering whether the poor old dear would soon be transmogrified into a magazine carnival act. Between Bebe's harangues on subjects only she cared about and all that bloody red, Magnolia couldn't imagine readers buying *Bebe* more than once.

There was a knock at her door, which she'd left slightly ajar.

"Mags, good morning." She liked that Cam called her Mags. He was the only member of the staff who claimed this familiarity and he spoke her name in a deep, commercial-worthy voice—one of his several earlier careers was acting.

"Hey," she said. "How was the weekend?" Cam owned a house upstate, where he retreated every Friday. Magnolia had never seen it.

"Major bike ride. Other than that, just cooking and weeding. Wrote. Reread *Middlemarch*."

"I'm becoming illiterate," she said. Lately she'd definitely been more Gigi than Simone de Beauvoir.

"That can be our little secret, you with the fancy New York life."

From anyone else, Magnolia would have been allergic to the sting. But Cam actually knew how hard she worked, how many evenings she surrendered to Scary.

"If you're referring to Natalie's party, I came, I drank. I listened to people pontificate. I did not lose my cool or any brain cells that I'm aware of." Magnolia decided not to share the Harry part. She presumed that Cam still had the same girlfriend, a Belgian photographer who was always flying all over the planet for *National Geographic,* and Cam was polite enough not to ask her if she'd starting dating anyone after Alec the architect.

"What's going to happen next?" Cam asked.

"That question may have been answered by the eighteenth hole at Winged Foot Country Club. I can hold my breath."

"Good. That means you and I can do performance evaluations all morning long." He said the last three words very, very slowly.

"As soon as you nab a victim to be Sasha for the day."

Cam returned forty-five minutes later, temp in tow. He and Magnolia then began to hash out who would get a raise. Scary, not known for generosity at the lower levels, had declared 2.5 percent as the norm. That meant that if Magnolia wanted to reward a star employee with an increase she'd actually notice, another staff member would get stiffed. As far as Magnolia was concerned, every employee deserved more than the paltry standard. She'd rather have root canal than look a talented, underpaid editor in the eye, slather praise like Crème de la Mer, then announce that at the end of the next year she'd be richer by $759.31. "You're brilliant, you've slaved for twelve months, now after taxes you can blow yourself to a weekend at Motel Six and a Happy Meal."

They chewed through the evaluations for as long as they both could stand. Only when Cam left her office did the temp remind Magnolia that in ten minutes she needed to be at the 21 Club to hear Candace Bushnell speak at a luncheon. In magazine mythology, Candace held a vaulted place. Not many assistants started by sharpening pencils at *Ladies' Home Journal* and ended with *Sex and the City*, hot novels, and the studliest dancer ever to perform with the New York City Ballet.

Sasha would have known to order a car to take Magnolia thirty-seven blocks uptown, but the temp didn't, and it was too late to book one. Magnolia dashed out to hail a taxi. She got lucky, and only eighteen minutes later a cab dropped her off in front of 21, whose welcoming lineup of puny lawn jockeys always made her think of every jerk she'd dated since tenth grade. The interior of the old-time speakeasy-turned-club continued the equestrian theme, with horse paintings grazing on the walls. You could almost smell the dung.

The minute Candace started her speech, Magnolia realized that Sarah Jessica Parker had modeled Carrie's delivery after Candace's excitable speech—or vice versa. Candace sounded exactly like Carrie did whenever she was drunk, especially when she described a party she'd attended in the eighties where the men wore only diapers and the women dressed as nannies. "Some sort of English thing," Candace recalled, then started taking questions.

What are you writing? A book that sounded overdue to her editor. When did you marry? Not until forty-three, which made the crowd exhale with relief. What kind of shoes are you wearing? Candace took off a sparkly blue stiletto and placed it on the podium for everyone to admire. Candace made Magnolia feel good about being a single woman in her thirties, trying to earn a good salary.

The luncheon over, Magnolia flew upstairs to a tiny powder room she knew would be emptier than the one the horde would hit on the ground floor. As she emerged from the stall, she found herself face-to-face with Candace, who was even tinier than she'd appeared from the podium—a size 2, tops. In the split second during which Magnolia pondered if she should introduce herself and ask Candace if she'd write for *Lady*—and then decided that, no, she was way too big a deal for that—Candace greeted her by name.

"Magnolia Gold?"

"Yes, oh, that's me." Magnolia felt like an idiot for not responding in a more articulate fashion, but was flattered—and shocked—to be recognized.

"Is it true what I'm hearing?"

What *was* Candace hearing? Did Candace want to be her friend? Before she could concoct a witty retort, Candace continued.

"Bebe Blake taking over your magazine? That's rich! Man, am I glad I've left women's magazines. And I thought television was low." With a toss of her long, blond hair, Candace was off, leaving behind only a whiff of delicious perfume and her empty champagne flute, which she'd parked on the marble countertop.

As Magnolia settled back at her desk at 2:45, the temp buzzed her on the intercom. "Jack wanted to see you fifteen minutes ago," she said.

Jack the IT guy? Every time he touched her computer, it developed tics in new places. "Please tell him that now isn't a good time." Magnolia had a December planning meeting and it would take hours. It might be almost the Fourth of July, but at *Lady* they needed to be thinking eggnog, *bûches de noël*, and, every year, a new spin on Hanukkah latkes. December was their biggest seller. By mid-November, you could count on American women to instinctively scour their supermarkets for a comforting magazine full of artery-clogging cookie recipes.

"Jack's secretary said it was important."

Jack from IT had a beeper, not a secretary. "Could that have been Jock Flanagan's office?" Magnolia may as well have asked her to recite the periodic table. The temp stared at her, blankly. "Did the secretary have a name?"

"Vera? Viola?" This temp had just graduated from Penn and, four hours ago, told Magnolia she'd kill for a magazine job.

Magnolia called Jock's office herself. "Magnolia, we were expecting you fifteen minutes ago," Elvira said. "Jock's waiting, and he's got a three o'clock."

He could keep you waiting, but the behavior wasn't tolerated in reverse. "Be right up," Magnolia said. "Minor administrative snafu. Sorry. You don't need to hear explanations."

As the elevator opened on the tenth floor, Magnolia collided with Darlene.

"Cute skirt!" Darlene bellowed as she rushed by at her I'm-more-important-than-you pace.

Jock's door was closed. Twenty minutes later Elvira allowed her in. His office looked like a movie set—it rarely showed any evidence of an executive who did actual work. Jock motioned Magnolia to a black leather chair.

"Water?"

"No, thanks," she answered, her heart thumping like Biggie's tail when he sniffed a pig ear hiding behind her back.

"Magnolia, you've been courageous in defending your position on *Lady*."

Whenever someone called you *courageous* you knew they really meant nuts.

"I'm sure you've recognized that going with Bebe is, however, too good a deal not to do," Jock said. "It's plain and simple."

Plain, simple, shatteringly mediocre—take your pick, Magnolia thought. She held her breath, waiting to get voted off the island, determined not to be embarrassed by a meltdown. She'd never been fired, not even from the babysitting job in high school when the Gustafsons arrived home early and discovered her making out with Tyler Peterson in their bedroom.

"I'm going to count on you to teach our girl Bebe the ropes," he continued.

"Excuse me?" The words stuck in her throat. Magnolia coughed, lowered her voice, and started over. "Excuse me, Jock. Could you, uh, clarify?"

"Bebe Blake will be big picture. I'll expect you to work with Felicity Dingle to turn Bebe's vision into a magazine."

"Her vision?"

Jock walked back to his massive mahogany desk, raised one brow, and eyeballed Magnolia.

"Of course, you don't have to stick around. Your choice. If you wish to break your contract, HR has been alerted. Which will it be?"

This could be her moment to impersonate Katharine Hepburn and tell Jock where he could put his big idea.

Magnolia thought of how much she loved her work, the only thing she'd ever wanted to do—perhaps the only thing she could do. Was she an idiot savant? She didn't care. She pondered the pleasure of writing a clever headline, teaming the right idea with the right writer, finding the one photo image among hundreds with the best smile on the best star, which yielded a stupendous sale. She considered the high she got seeing *Lady* lining the airports' racks—and the kick of observing a real reader take a crisp copy to the register.

Magnolia thought of her $3,500 mortgage payments; her $1,900-a-month in co-op maintenance, the $1,000 she donated every year to the University of Michigan, and Biggie and Lola's vet bills. She thought of how she had no man to share her financial load, or parents who were still giving handouts, and pictured herself home at 12:30, in need of a shower, her dark roots three inches long, trying to concentrate on the

Tom Friedman column when everyone she knew was at Michael's. Perhaps someone there would be saying, "Whatever became of Magnolia Gold?"

The plebiscite approach to editing a magazine—she couldn't begin to imagine it, but she didn't feel she had a Plan B. "Sure, Jock, I'll give it a go," Magnolia said, in a jaunty voice she didn't recognize.

"I thought you'd see it that way. And I think you'll be able to manage just fine in the office we'll move you to."

"Bebe's getting my office?" she asked. Her voice quivered with just the faintest tremor, but in her stomach she felt sucker-punched.

"Not right away. The decorator will be in first thing in the morning, though, so you'll need to move out. Don't worry—you'll get plenty of help with that."

Chapter 11

Avalanche of Reality

Bebe Blake Beheads Lady. That's how the *Post* summed it up, accompanied by a photo of Magnolia, mid-bite, at a cocktail party four years earlier. Magnolia could carbon-date the shot from her unfortunate short hair. She had a lamb chop in her hand, as if it were a weapon.

BOLD GOLD FOLDS was the New York *Daily News* spin. Usually Magnolia didn't give the Snooze a glance, but today she made a run to the closest newsstand to gather all the papers, even the ones that would be delivered to her office later.

The New York Times treated the Bebe takeover in a subdued Business Day item alluding to *Lady* as one of many beleaguered women's service magazines. The *Times* reporter suggested that the whole category, with its fifty million readers—enough to sway a presidential election—might, by the end of the decade, vanish, like the VCR.

The Wall Street Journal ignored the story. They generally hung back and, months later, came out swinging. Magnolia could imagine their suggesting—on page one of a slow news day—that both readers and advertisers were shying away from magazines in favor of digital media. Young people don't read anything but blogs, they'd lecture.

USA Today focused only on Bebe, with the headline OPRAH, WATCH YOUR BACK. As if she were sweating one drop.

Magnolia dumped the newspapers in the recycling bin near her back door. By the end of the week, the weeklies—not just celebrity-studded periodicals but newsmagazines as well—would also feature the Bebe takeover. Then there would be the online newsletters, and e-mail blasts that each editor received, and they all received plenty—*Mediaweek, Iwantmedia, Media Life, Media Industry Newsletter, Media This,* and *Media That.* Since the media loves no subject more than itself, it would be a festival of narcissism.

The worst part was that thanks to Google, her misfortune would live on for years. According to Magnolia's unofficial tally, *venerable* had already been used nineteen times to describe *Lady,* causing Magnolia to refresh her understanding of the term. "Commanding respect by virtue of age, dignity, character, or position" was the dictionary definition. Magnolia suspected no one associated venerability with dignity, character, or position—the common understanding linked venerability simply to old age. The word smelled decrepit. Industry insiders who'd never bothered to study *Lady* (it was an open secret that most decision-makers were "too busy to read") would believe the news and assume that *Lady* was a dentured, bunioned, whiskered old hag. This pained Magnolia almost more than the fact that she'd effectively be reporting to Bebe Blake, a fact she hadn't got her head around yet.

Hurt didn't begin to describe how she felt. Sick was more like it, too sick to eat or talk or even call her parents. But she couldn't waste time now being hurt or sick or humiliated. She needed to focus.

The most frustrating aspect of this avalanche of reality was that it was out of the question for Magnolia to tell her side of the story to anyone but her nearest and dearest—who, over the last day, failed to include Harry, who hadn't even e-mailed. One thing Scary did exceedingly well was to control its press coverage. Elizabeth Lester Duvall, their storm trooper of corporate communications, monitored every sound bite an employee might want to shout out. She delivered her gag order in person the previous day the moment Magnolia left Jock's office.

Elizabeth pulled Magnolia into the executive-floor conference room and shut the door.

"Don't worry, honey," Elizabeth said in the rat-a-tat-tat speech that almost belied her Mississippi Delta roots. "We'll handle this. Bebe will give a press conference tomorrow afternoon. We've booked the Pierre. Be sure to get your hair blown out, because we're giving *Entertainment Tonight* an exclusive."

"We'll have makeup at the ready," Elizabeth continued, breathlessly. "Back to the press conference. You won't speak. Darlene and Bebe will handle the particulars. Just go home. Have a cocktail!"

She gave Magnolia a big grin and patted her hand. "You're taking this so well!" With that, Elizabeth was off. A kiwi green cashmere cardigan knotted around her shoulders billowed in her wake and her silver hair sparkled under the hallway's fluorescent lights.

It wasn't until after Elizabeth had left that Magnolia realized, when she talked to Jock, her title had never come up. Perhaps Bebe would get the "chief" and Magnolia would be downshifted to "editor," "deputy editor," "executive editor," or the truly opaque "editorial consultant." Or maybe she'd remain "editor in chief," and Bebe would become, what, "editorial director"?

Did it matter, really?

It did. An editor in chief was far more glorious than a plain-Jane editor, and usually got better pay. When a company wanted to be cheap, they'd promote an executive editor into the top job, and name her "editor" with a token raise. But it was all very confusing. An "editor" at one company might be paid four times the salary of an "editor in chief" at another, and even at the same company, people with seemingly identical positions had widely variable power, perks, access to upper management, and compensation. Magnolia suspected that at Scary, Natalie Simon, for example, was first among equals and earned at least $200,000 more than she did.

What a lot of bunk, Magnolia thought. Even if her title became Your Royal Highness, everyone in her world would read the invisible ink and know that Bebe was running the show. Still, she would like to stay a chief, and if her title hadn't been decided yet, perhaps she could bargain for it later. If Jock had a pixel of guilt, she might get him to agree.

She took the elevator down to her floor. Magnolia had wanted to announce the change to her staff personally, but when she walked into her office, she could tell from the hush that everyone already knew. A flock of assistants was already helping Sasha arrange her belongings in neat brown boxes for the move down the hall.

Sasha pulled her aside and whispered a report. While Elizabeth had been delivering her orders to Magnolia, Jock had addressed the troops, using words like "eye candy" to describe Bebe, assuring editors that Bebe had a "dynamite idea" she'd explain herself. Later. When "later" he didn't say.

"Did Jock mention me?" Magnolia asked Sasha when her helpers had left the office to replenish supplies. It humiliated Magnolia to be seeking information from her assistant, but she had to know. Sasha stopped unpinning Magnolia's elaborate bulletin board collage, which she was carefully dismantling and putting into folders.

"He said you were totally behind the Bebe change, that you'd be working with her." Sasha paused and bit her lip.

"Spit it out," Magnolia said.

"I'll still work for you, right? I'm not going to have to work for *her*, am I?"

Magnolia hated to admit she didn't know the answer to the question almost as much as she hated the thought of losing Sasha. "We're working that out, Sash," she said, hoping Sasha would buy it. "Don't worry. Change is good."

Magnolia walked to her new office and slumped at the desk. The space was cramped. The office's most unfortunate aspect, though, was that—inspired by newsrooms—one wall was transparent glass. The architect's fantasy might have been to motivate editors to feel like

Lois Lane chasing the page one story, but for the staff who inhabited these quarters the primary activity seemed to be carping about lack of privacy. Magnolia knew her new office would make her feel like a monkey at the zoo.

Cam knocked softly on her door. "There's no use talking about this," he said. "For now, I have the solution."

"A brick wall?"

"Getting hammered." Cameron enclosed Magnolia in a quick bear hug.

In ten minutes, Cam and Magnolia were sitting at the bar at the Mesa Grill, and by six o'clock Magnolia had lost count of how many margaritas she'd downed. One by one, the wake expanded to include all of the top *Lady* edit staff—a very pregnant Phoebe Feinberg-Fitzpatrick, Fredericka von Trapp, Ruthie Kim, and several others.

As the afternoon turned into evening, the digs about Bebe got deeper, and the jokes, increasingly lame. "Do you think she'll do a cat cover?" Phoebe Feinberg-Fitzpatrick asked while she absentmindedly pattered her pregnant tummy. "*Catwoman*, the prequel? Halle Barry, get out of town."

"My fashion department can supply a red leotard," Ruthie suggested.

"That would put the scary back in Scary," Cameron said.

"*Nein*," Fredericka said. "She'll vant boys on the cover. Young boys."

"There could be a tagline: *Where IQ doesn't count.*"

Magnolia realized she had to shut down the conversation. "We're going to make this work," she said, hoping she didn't sound as drunk as she was. "Celebrities are the future." At that, she whipped out her corporate AmEx card, paid the $350 tab, and escaped into a taxi. A half hour later, when she arrived home, her phone indicated fourteen phone messages. All were from editor pals, and except for Natalie Simon, she didn't return any of them. Nor did she reply to the dozens of "Oh, shit" e-mails.

"Of course, you know I had nothing to do with it," Natalie said the minute she heard Magnolia's voice. "Obviously, it's dreadful. But, Cookie, just deal. Rise above."

Natalie completely understood about Magnolia's not wanting to give up Sasha, however. Natalie's two assistants kept her life humming with gracious precision. The First Lady could take lessons. "Power's for the taking," she advised. "Proceed as if you assume Sasha will continue to work for you. Believe me, nobody's thinking about her right now."

"Do you think I can pull this off?" Magnolia asked.

"My God, of course!" Natalie all but screamed into the phone. "You're so talented, so everything, but sometimes I absolutely want to bitch slap you. Or at least send you to my mother for a self-confidence tune-up."

Magnolia had met Estelle, Natalie's mother, numerous times. The woman could have run General Motors if she hadn't been too busy negotiating delicate country club politics, taking on issues as onerous and portentous and divisive as whether kids in diapers should be allowed in the pool. Certainly, Estelle had done a number on Natalie. No flagging confidence there.

"The press conference is what you should be concentrating on," Natalie said. "Look sharp. Wear your Michael Kors suit."

Later in the evening, while walking Biggie and Lola, she thought again that in the avalanche of attention, all unwanted, there was still one person she hadn't heard from who might have made her hellish day easier. Why hadn't Harry sent flowers or at least called? But her head reverted to work. Change is good, she repeated to herself. Change is good.

What a lot of crap, she decided. Whoever thought up that proverb clearly had always been in charge of her changes.

Chapter 12

Bushwhacking at the Pierre

Magnolia knew she had talent. That, and the pluck common to those who hail from the middle of nowhere, who realize that if they want to succeed in a more stylish time zone, they must learn early the value of hard work. Her ability to toil like an indentured servant was, Magnolia thought, one quality that might set her apart from editors who came from more privileged backgrounds. But was it true that she never doubted herself? Every editor Magnolia knew possessed some measure of self-doubt, even the prep-school princesses and Ivy grads.

At thirty-seven, had she already redeemed her quota of hit-the-jackpot coupons? Her cynical side understood that she and all the other top names on an editorial masthead owed their job security to serendipity. Only deluded egomaniacs—and Magnolia had a few of them on speed dial—convinced themselves that talent alone truly engineered big breaks and continued success.

The hiring gods giveth, but they also taketh away. Today was one of those away days. When you might least expect it, you're heading off to the Pierre to watch a celebrity begin the public tango of let's-pretend-I'm-an-editor, while you try on the unfamiliar role of wallflower.

Magnolia dressed in the suit Natalie had suggested. She unearthed her Chanel sample-sale handbag, and hoped no one thought she'd scored it at the Chinatown spider hole that her assistant Sasha swore by for dead-on knockoffs. She sat silently through her blowout. Afterward, she stopped at Tiffany's and sent out an Elsa Peretti baby spoon to her college roommate's infant daughter. It was only June, and the sixth baby present she'd given this year, three to little girls named Isabelle. She arrived at work around 11:30, knowing her presence, just now, made everyone around her twitch with discomfort.

At 1:30, Elizabeth Lester Duvall, sunlight bouncing off her silver head, peered through the glass wall of Magnolia's new office, mouthing, "Time to go." The limo ride to the Pierre gave Elizabeth ample opportunity to bark a few more orders.

"If you're asked about *Lady*, defer to me," she said.

"Got it," Magnolia answered.

"When Bebe enters the stage, stand up, so everyone will do the same."

"I hear you."

"Make sure your hair isn't in your eyes," she said. That wouldn't be a problem for Elizabeth, since her hair literally stood on end. "And smile!" Elizabeth continued, grinning at Magnolia just in case she'd forgotten what that facial expression looked like. "It's going to be great."

Why the president hadn't put Elizabeth in charge of FEMA, Magnolia didn't know. No man-made crisis or natural disaster was beyond her range. In the time it took Elizabeth to call Jock and review a few more strategic details, she and Magnolia arrived at the Pierre.

The very fifth-arrondissment Pierre had always been Magnolia's favorite Manhattan hotel. Whenever she walked through its hushed lobby, a study in almost faded elegance, she looked forward to making a turn into the blue oval salon with its cloud-covered ceiling. She pictured herself in a simple satin wedding dress, climbing the marble stairs to meet her bridegroom in the ballroom a short flight up.

Unfortunately, the anteroom to the ballroom was the very space that Elizabeth had commandeered for today's press conference. Magnolia stepped into the room. Apparently oblivious to the charms of its gray stone trompe l'oeil walls, which created the effect of a classical piazza, reporters were stuffing their faces with the pastry, cheese, and fruit the covey felt was their due. Magnolia realized that, from now on, the Pierre would be forever linked with Bebe. She'd need to manufacture a new dream.

"What's the deal, Maggie?" shouted Justin Fink from *Business-Week*. "Are we sitting shiva for *Lady*?"

She walked over to Justin. Despite his downtown affectation—geeky black glasses, thrift shop shirts, and Puma sneakers—she knew him as one of the sharper press journalists. At least he had a memory extending back further than a year. Magnolia swallowed hard, and greeted him with a friendly peck on the cheek.

"*Lady*'s moving over for the next big thing, Justin. You'll see."

"But why?" Justin asked with a wide smile. "It doesn't compute, unless Scary's been putting out bogus circulation numbers. You guys selling half of what you claim? Any comment?"

"Justin, are you delusional?"

"A little off-the-record, Magnolia, just for me, your favorite reporter?"

Already, he'd bushwhacked into feral territory. From across the room, Elizabeth spotted them chatting, causing Magnolia to wonder whether she hadn't secretly been fitted with a house-arrest ankle bracelet. "Justin!" Elizabeth said, separating them with her skinny shoulder blades. "Patience, honey. You know better than to give our Magnolia the third degree. Bebe Blake will explain it all."

"That Justin—he's a dog." Now Mike McCourt, the genial reporter from the *Post*, had joined their circle. Everybody liked Mike, but you didn't need a Sergeant Elizabeth to tell you to close down when he accosted you at an event or surprised you with a call. You could count on Mike for being relaxed with the facts. Then again, he could be useful. At least one editor had incorporated him into her long-term strategy. She was widely known for leaving him messages indicating that she was rumored to be up for absolutely every job—generally, when she wasn't—hoping Mike would print the tip. Mike, with a daily column to fill, happily obliged. As a result, the untrained reader assessed her as a hot magazine stock.

"When will we be getting the pleasure of your star's company?" Mike asked. "Her helicopter still circling?" The speeches were supposed to start ten minutes earlier.

"Patience, y'all," Elizabeth drawled, her Mississippi accent conveniently restored. "Talk amongst yourselves." She pushed Magnolia toward the dais, positioning her to the right of the podium.

Fifteen minutes passed. No sign of Bebe. Ten more minutes. Above the rumble in the room, Magnolia heard a stir. Darlene, looking like a Girl Scout leader, led the pack in a sleeveless safari-style sheath, not afraid to expose her meaty arms. Felicity followed in a mumsy pantsuit and clunky, gold-trimmed shoes. The two of them placed themselves to the left of the podium and began whispering.

And then she entered, on Jock's arm. In a bow to her vision of a working editor, Bebe wore red Harlequin glasses trimmed with rhinestones. On her right, middle finger she flashed an emerald-cut diamond the size of a sugar cube.

"First, there was Martha." Jock began, in his deep, sonorous tones. "Then there was Oprah. Now Scarborough Magazines proudly presents Bebe Blake, the country's most multitalented celebrity and a passionate devotee to causes that interest women everywhere."

Magnolia adjusted her face to a few notches above blasé but comfortably below bootlicking.

"And here she is, Bebe Blake," Jock said with a flourish. The room, filled with at least eighty reporters and photographers, thundered with applause. Bebe exploded onto the podium.

"Can't you give these guys some booze?" she yelled. "Jock, you cheapskate, this is an occasion, for God's sake."

Jock, standing behind Bebe, looked paralyzed, then switched on a big guffaw and matching grin. Magnolia checked out Elizabeth hovering near the wall. Anyone who worked at Scary knew she became homicidal if an employee strayed off script. Elizabeth looked as if she might shoot a howitzer at Bebe any second now.

"Okay, okay," Bebe continued, beaming a wide, engaging smile. "I get it. We have to sell some magazines and then we get to drink. Well, gang, that's what we're going to do. Sell mags. More women are going to buy *Bebe* than buy maxipads. Why? Because *Bebe*'s going to be fun. Fart-out-loud fun."

The crowd roared.

"It's going to be pee-in-your-pants fun. It's going to be fun, fun, fun till Daddy-takes-the-T-Bird-away fun. It's going to be all the things I stand for. Darlene Knudson—she's my publisher—can attest to that. I'm told that woman could sell a page of advertising to the pope."

Bebe blew a kiss to Darlene, who shouted "thank you" in her no-amplification-required voice, and then to the audience, and they all blew kisses back.

Darlene joined Bebe and blathered on about what a great opportunity *Bebe* would be for every product in America to reach its target audience, although she didn't declare who, exactly, that would be. Magnolia looked out to the crowd. She expected one of the reporters to start asking hard questions. "What do you stand for, Bebe?" "Why do we need your magazine?" And even if she'd wince at the answer, Magnolia wanted someone to press Bebe, or Jock, or at least Darlene, on why *Lady* was being abandoned, just so she could hear the creativity of the answer. But the usually brutal crowd demurred. To Magnolia's horror, she realized they adored Bebe, and were awestruck to be close enough to an authentic celebrity to feel her spit on their faces.

"Ever since I was a kid, I've been into magazines," Bebe was saying, and—dammit, Magnolia thought—it sounded genuine. "My dad's

Playboy, my mother's *National Enquirer*—I've loved 'em all. But regular, old women's magazines—"

As Bebe continued, Magnolia heard a cell phone ring. Once, twice, three times. The noise sounded as loud as a car alarm. Elizabeth glared.

Bebe stopped talking. Magnolia couldn't understand why everyone was looking at her. It took until the fifth ring for Magnolia to realize the phone was in her bag, which she'd plunked behind her.

"Mag-knowl-ya, answer the damn phone," Bebe demanded, with a big grin. "You all know Mags, right? I love that gal and she's quite the looker. She's going to be my deputy. Which I guess makes me the sheriff."

"Magnolia, who is it?" shouted Justin from *BusinessWeek*.

Magnolia grabbed her bag—happy that she'd switched to the Chanel—and quickly turned off the cell. But not before she saw the number.

"Condé Nast on the line?" Mike McCourt asked. "Your lawyer maybe?"

"Justin, Mike, you'll be happy to know it's my boyfriend," Magnolia shouted with what she hoped was an adorable smile. "Excuse me, everyone."

"Who's the cutie?" Bebe asked? "The guy I met Saturday night?"

Elizabeth walked to the podium, shooting Jock a look that implored him to take charge *now*. Jock grabbed the mike. It took another minute for the bedlam in the room to subside.

"Time for all of you to see *Bebe*, our new baby." He yanked the cord on a silky curtain and revealed the cover of an eight-foot magazine featuring a life-size photo of Bebe, her arms stretched forward as if she were going to perform a kung fu move. She was wearing a halter top and a rose in her hair. The background color was red, the logo gold.

"How ya like it, guys?" Bebe said. "I want you to know that's one hundred percent God-given cleavage. I am not an implant gal." She stood back and mimicked the cover.

"Or do you like it better this way?" She struck a different pose. "Or like this?" Bebe began to dance, first alone, then with Felicity, Jock, and Darlene, and finally with Magnolia. The podium became a hoedown.

Bulbs began to flash as Elizabeth supervised various constellations for photo ops—Bebe and Jock, Bebe and Darlene, a large group shot that included Magnolia, then Bebe posing one by one with many of the reporters. The members of the feared Manhattan press corps were probably going to each ask for Bebe's autograph, Magnolia thought.

No one paid attention to Magnolia as she peeled away to play back her voice message and return Sub-Zero's call.

"Harry, it's about time you called," she said. She failed to sound angry.

"Sorry, sorry, sorry, Magnolia, luv. I am a bad boy, but I was trying to think of the right words, and I'm never very good with that. But enough about me," he said. "You poor chickadee."

"What's this about you missing me?" Magnolia asked.

"What can I say? We English like a woman who appreciates a good, juicy chop," he said. "Oh, and I like your bum."

"I like yours more."

"I need to rescue you from this hell you seem to have fallen into, don't I?"

"I'm not saying no."

"Can I talk you into dinner Saturday? Please tell me you're not one of those women with a tattered copy of *The Rules* next to her bed, who needs weeks of notice."

"I hardly have any rules at all," she admitted.

"Lovely. A woman with no scruples is the one for me. So, eight. Pick you up. I have just the place."

"Where?"

"Surprise."

"Date."

Date. Magnolia liked the retro ring of it. She popped her cell back in her bag and returned to the reception. Jock was giving sound bites to Mike. Darlene had snagged the *WWD* guy. Elizabeth was steering Felicity away from the *New York Times* reporter.

As Magnolia scanned the room, she felt a tap on her shoulder and turned.

"Nice touch, Gold," Bebe said, embracing her. "Loved the cell phone bit. Priceless. Got to admit, I never thought you had it in you, upstaging me and all. God knows, I respect a worthy adversary." She shook her head in admiration and held on to Magnolia's arm, in a best-girlfriends way. Then she gave Magnolia's arm an affectionate squeeze. "Are you ready to rock and roll?"

"I'm ready if you're ready," Magnolia said, wishing she actually had been crafty enough to have planned the mishap.

Chapter 13

Extra Virgin

Waiting for their manicurists, Abbey and Magnolia huddled on a black leather love seat, heads down, hooting at movie star photographs in *Dazzle*'s "What Were They Thinking?" section.

"Will you promise to stage an intervention if I ever buy anything this short?" Magnolia asked. "The statute of limitations for wearing skirts like this is just about over for me."

"The thing about age-appropriate dressing is that the rules keep changing," Abbey said.

Magnolia hoped she'd evolve into a wiser version of herself and that woman would want a wardrobe she couldn't even imagine right now. She closed the magazine, and focused on Abbey, who had the look she got when she wanted to spill a secret.

"What is it?" Magnolia asked.

"Tommy and I had ex-sex last night," Abbey announced, as seriously as if she'd disclosed that she'd fornicated with a beagle.

"It's not technically sex-with-an-ex," Magnolia pointed out. "But give me the goods."

"We've been e-mailing and text messaging," Abbey said, moving over to her manicurist who, today, was Lily Kim.

"Stay away from that man." Lily had joined the conversation. "Bad, very bad." With her normal efficiency, Lily began to file Abbey's nails square and short, which made her hardworking jeweler's hands look even more like tiny paws.

"I couldn't turn him away. He wanted to stop by and talk."

"Run that conversation by us," Magnolia said, sliding into the chair next to her. She immersed her fingers in the china bowl her manicurist presented before her. As Abbey continued to speak, Magnolia closed her eyes and let the warm, jasmine-scented water wash away the last few days.

"First we went to dinner at Balthazar, and you know how much I love it," Abbey started. "We'd gone there for our last anniversary."

When you fought about the gift you received, Magnolia recalled.

"Dinner turned into coffee back at the apartment," Abbey said.

"Did he seem mildly contrite?" Magnolia asked. "Deeply apologetic? Fraught with anguish?"

"No, no, and yes." Abbey said. "'Disabled' was how he put it."

"Well, we all want to embrace diversity," Magnolia said, striving for funny and realizing she'd failed. "How did the conversation go?"

"Quickly, with a trail of clothes to our bedroom," Abbey reported. "Sex was never the problem. It was almost like the first time."

Magnolia thought back to her own first time, which had been fast but worth the wait. Reverend Peterson's Pontiac after the prom. She and Tyler Peterson, the preacher's son, had dated for two years. Soon she'd leave for Michigan and he to St. Olaf, where bright Lutheran boys with good baritones go. During the summer he'd be in Montana, working cattle or whatever you did with cows. The end was closing in on them—graduation, college, another life. The nightly phone calls and Saturday movie dates would be fading to black. They both knew it and never discussed it. Tyler couldn't imagine he'd ever again meet a girl as full of dreams as Maggie Goldfarb and she, a sweeter guy—or better-looking. The Norse gods had kicked in, and Tyler had shot up to well over six feet.

"Magnolia, are you with me?" Abbey asked.

"I'm listening to every word," she said. "Does this mean you guys are back on track?"

"Hardly. Even when we were kissing, I knew it was a mistake. Not the kissing—he can still speak in tongues—but change is not in Tommy's vocabulary. Talk about fraught, though. I was definitely fraught. With lust fraught. Incredible night."

"And the morning?" Magnolia asked. She believed in the revealing powers of mornings after.

"There was no morning," Abbey answered, shrugging. "I asked him to leave at around four A.M." She drew her hands away from Lily and turned toward Magnolia. "Tommy's always going to be a baby. Who can wait for him to grow up?"

"How do you feel?" Like backup singers in a Motown group, Lily and Magnolia begged the question in unison, giving the last word emphasis.

"Sad. Resigned. Pretty sure it's the end."

Magnolia wished Abbey could be happier—she deserved to be happier—but her assessment of Tommy was dead-on accurate. "You're tough," Magnolia said. "You'll get through this. I'll help you. Do something today that will make you smile."

"Such as?"

"Hmm . . ." Magnolia said. "Make dessert lunch?"

"Pecan pie and cheesecake," Abbey said. "And buy slutty underwear."

"That's a start," Magnolia said.

"Pick different polish," Lily insisted. "Your nails have been Dead Red since 1999."

The three of them deliberated over Lily's newest choices. Abbey chose Kinki in Helsinki. Magnolia considered Chocolate Moose, but decided it would make her fingers look as if she'd been digging for worms. Pink Slip? Definitely bad karma. She settled for Jewel of India, a shade the red of Shiraz. Magnolia guessed she could live with it for a week, and if things didn't work out at *Bebe*, perhaps she'd get a job naming cosmetics. Or erectile dysfunction drugs.

Kinki in Helsinki and Jewel of India progressed to the nail dryers. "Give me your world news of the week," Abbey said. Magnolia hit the high notes, compressing Bebe, the new office, and her cosmic panic to a chunk of conversation that she felt came across with minimal self-pity and admirable cheer. Magnolia wasn't up to analysis. She wanted only to coax herself into the right mood for tonight.

"All I'm thinking about now is Sub-Zero," she said, knowing Abbey would see through her fiction but wouldn't press.

After lunch, Magnolia took a nap and didn't dream of Bebe, Jock, or Darlene, just a long riff involving Jude Law and chocolate. She awoke refreshed, and dressed quickly. Magnolia had insisted to Harry—who lived in the Village, as did most ex-pat media Brits—that he didn't have to pick her up just to drive her back downtown for dinner. Women who played the high maintenance game infuriated her.

On the cab ride downtown, she ruminated on how second dates were loaded, especially when Date One lasted for eighteen hours and ended with a tasting menu of I'd-forgotten-how-this-feels sex. Would the two of them fumble for conversation—the bioethics of lobster boiling, perhaps? Magnolia often wondered why couples in long relationships didn't run out of chat but then considered her own parents. After thirty-eight years of marriage, Fran and Eliot Goldfarb never failed to find something about which they didn't agree; conversation thus wasn't a problem.

Just this morning, when they called her—as they did every Saturday morning on the dot of ten—Magnolia's father thought he had the sure cure for her work-related problems. "Quit and move out here to Southern California," he said. "I don't know why anyone in their right mind would put up with New York."

"But, Eliot," her mother interrupted, "Magnolia is a magazine editor and New York is where all the magazines are. That's why she moved there. Am I right, Maggie, honey?"

"Right, Mom," she said.

"Now tell me about Bebe," she said. "I've read that her last husband was ten years younger and she had to pay him a fortune after they divorced? Is that true?"

"Mom, she's not exactly confiding in me," Magnolia said.

"Fran, you're wrong," her father said. "She's gay."

"Eliot, you're crazy," she said. "That's Rosie."

The bickering raged on, until Magnolia told them she needed to get off the phone because she had a date and wanted to get a manicure.

"A date, honey?" her mom said. "That's fabulous. Is he Jewish?"

"No, Mom," she said. She had no idea what Harry's religion was, but she was fairly sure he wasn't Jewish.

"It's the most important thing, doll," her father said. "Never forget that."

"Because it's been the charm for you two?" Magnolia said, and instantly regretted it.

"Do you ever hear from Wally?" her mother asked.

"Not in years, Mom," she said. "And, anyway, he remarried."

"You blew it, kiddo," her father said.

"Eliot, shame on you," her mother said. "What's wrong with you?" And on and on.

Magnolia relived the conversation until she arrived on West Fourth, the kind of tranquil, leafy street where she could easily picture living. She opened the door to Extra Virgin and found Harry waiting at a corner table. He stood as she entered. Tonight he wore faded jeans, a white shirt with the sleeves rolled up—a jacket hung on the back of the chair—and a faint scent which, when they hugged, recalled long walks in Nantucket.

"Magnolia, duckie, the week you've had," he said, holding her face in his hands and giving her a short, tender kiss. "Has that big bully, Bebe, stomped all over you?"

"I have a little bruise right around here," she said as she pointed to her heart. "But don't underestimate me."

"You?" he said. "Never. Here, have a look at the menu. The chef here is a genius."

Magnolia's appetite usually left men asking "Where do you put all that?" For this biological blessing, she thanked her mother, who still fit into a Pucci dress from her honeymoon. Magnolia started with Chardonnay-steamed mussels, but nibbled one of Harry's roasted artichokes. He continued with the branzino. She wavered between crabmeat ravioli and lamb tangine. Ravioli won. Having eaten dessert for lunch—her own flan and half of Abbey's tiramisu—she slowed, but couldn't resist a taste of Harry's tarte tatin, sipped with strong espresso. Tonight she hoped she'd be up for hours.

"Caught a moment of that press conference on the telly," Harry said. "You looked ravishing, if a little frightened. Or was it bored?"

"Maybe I should be frightened, but for the moment I'm wearing the red badge of courage."

"Bebe—she's got eyes like a nasty little hedgehog," Harry said, sliding his hand on top of Magnolia's. "I knew her stunt double at university. Or maybe I'm confusing her with the mean nanny of my nightmares. Is she the type who hangs around with a lot of poofs?"

"I'm told she likes real men," Magnolia said, "and lots of them, the younger the better. Her last husband was twenty-eight."

As the candles burned low, dripping on the roughly hewn wooden tables, Harry's hand slid under the full skirt of her gauzy white sundress and skillfully climbed her bare thigh. While they discussed work—tactics to handle Bebe, how he could land an account with Banana Republic—Magnolia's mind settled between her legs. She knew Harry lived only blocks away, but he wasn't rushing to end their dinner. He was setting the pace, slowly and confidently.

"Amaretto?" he asked. At this point, the only thing she wanted to put in her mouth was an appetizing part of his anatomy, but he nodded to the waitress. A brunette with long, silky hair and a personal trainer's body sprinted across the room.

"Heather, luv, two Amarettos, please," Harry said, letting his hand graze the waitress's slim waist.

"Mr. James, of course," she responded, holding his gaze and never glancing in Magnolia's direction.

Harry brushed her hand, but turned back to Magnolia and stroked her arm. Twenty minutes later, she and Harry were the last diners to leave Extra Virgin. Magnolia tossed a tiny bottle of olive oil—compliments of the chef—into her bag, in which she'd stashed a toothbrush and an extra thong. Without discussing it, Harry steered them toward his brownstone. They entered through a foyer containing a small table with an antique brass bowl for keys and a slim Steuben vase filled with several deep purple dahlias. The foyer opened into a large room dominated by an enormous kitchen, as full of equipment as a small restaurant.

She noticed several black-and-white paintings on the far end of the room, which held low, oversized, red leather couches and a grand piano. The canvases were well over ten feet tall. Just as Magnolia realized the sensual form in the largest painting was female, Harry wrapped his arms around her from behind, caressing her face and sliding down over her breasts to her hips.

"She reminds me of you," he said. "Curves in the right places, but understated. Not too showy."

Perhaps it was his regular line. Maybe he was silver plate. But at that point, "Miss Gold, please remove your clothes and put on this paper gown" would have worked. They walked upstairs and entered Harry's spartan bedroom—a simple black iron bed, a dark walnut Empire armoire, a table, a chair loaded with art books, and a painting featuring another fertility goddess. Harry gathered Magnolia's clothes and carefully hung them on a heavy wooden hanger on the back of the door.

For a split second, an image of Harry and Extra Virgin's waitress, together in this very room, crossed Magnolia's mind. She imagined them naked, clinking Amaretto glasses, sharing a postcoital joke at her expense. "Did you catch the business-class-sized butt on her, Harry?" the girl would say. But then Harry pressed Magnolia to him, drew her down to the cool, cotton sheets, and pinned her body under his.

"Magnolia Gold, my darling, surrender your red badge of courage," he ordered, in a low growl. "I am the big bad wolf."

Chapter 14

Whatever Turns You On

"Magnolia Bakery?" Magnolia said.

In every relationship, the man came up with the same idea. Harry just thought of it sooner than most. On Sunday, a few weeks after they'd started seeing each other, Magnolia met Harry at the front of the bakery's line. Hipsters and tourists alike trailed out the door, waiting for sugar transfusions. Magnolia Bakery might be in the Village, but inside, under the swirl of a lazy ceiling fan, you could easily imagine Scarlett waving a confederate flag. Magnolia found Harry's gesture as endearing as the bakery's signature cupcakes iced in the hues of little girls' party dresses.

"Four, please," he said to the guy behind the counter.

"Four?" Magnolia said. "I'll be as big as Bebe."

"On you it would look good," he said, putting a piece of cupcake in her mouth. She wondered what life might have been like if she'd been named, say, Hermès: smaller butt, better bags.

It was definitely the gold rush. She and Harry had been seeing each other two or three times a week and last night, at bedtime, he signed off his phone call with "You're growing on me."

"Sweet dreams," she replied. And that's what her dreams were. She was gaga over Harry, and his attentions arrived with superb timing. Which made it all the harder to be sitting in her crowded new office on Monday morning, watching a leftover cupcake disappear into Sasha's mouth as she sought Magnolia's opinion on her new blog.

"What do you think of me calling it Almost 24/7?" Sasha asked. "I'm almost twenty-four, and I'd yak about everything in my life—oral sex, work, my 32AA boobs. Other women should know what it's like to go through life built like a playing card. I'll call that entry 'No Boobies, No Rubies.'"

"Almost 24/7? What will you do when you turn twenty-four?" Magnolia asked.

"Not going to work," Sasha realized. "I'll give it another think." She licked cupcake crumbs off her fingers. "Nutritious breakfast. Should we go over your agenda?"

They both knew the daily ritual was pointless. Without discussing it, Sasha had canceled the meetings she'd engineered weeks in advance, her normal drill in order to accommodate editors' frantic travel and shoot schedules. Except for an 11:45 dental appointment, Magnolia's calendar stood empty.

Downtime at work had never existed before, and Magnolia didn't like it one bit. Yet at the magazine it would be impolitic to charge ahead—assigning features, approving photographs, interviewing applicants for unfilled positions—as if Bebe weren't down the hall, at least theoretically. The painters were still at it in Magnolia's old office, and Bebe was nowhere in sight. Magnolia freshened her lipstick and wandered over to the office next door. She stood for a full minute before Cameron became aware of her, took out his iPod earphones, and smiled.

"And so it begins," he said.

"Have you done magazine 101 with our Queen B, explaining that we actually have deadlines?"

"Planning a sneak attack for noon," Cameron said. "If she shows." With Bebe apparently not realizing she needed to be the orchestra leader, *Lady*'s symphony had ceased. The staff hadn't reached complete cacophony—all her colleagues were still at their desks, nervously awaiting orders, whispering into phones, and dashing off e-mails they tried to conceal should anyone approach their computer screens. But it was already July. In weeks the October issue, compressed to a few computer disks, would be due at the printer. The deadline could be stretched only a little—and at great expense.

October wasn't the only problem. November needed to get well under way, along with the issues after that. To save money, smart editors always photographed in season. This very minute they should be planning next summer's food stories to be shot now, at a nearby beach, instead of spending $17,000 to fly a crew to the Caribbean in the high season next February.

Editors were dodging calls from photographers' reps eager to confirm dates. Writers, needing reassurance from motherly assigning editors, whimpered for contracts. Freelancers were threatening to defect to other jobs.

"I hate that you have to be the badass, Cam," Magnolia said. "But with it coming from you, maybe Bebe will listen."

Felicity's voice rang out down the hall. "Yoo-hoo, Magnolia. Cameron. Is this beyond exciting?"

Both Magnolia and Cam would have chosen a different word.

Felicity had a cat carrier in her hands. In it was Hell, wearing the smirk of a serial killer. Magnolia backed away as the feline stuck out a clawed paw.

"We're moving in!" Felicity trilled. "Jock told us to camp out in the conference room until the paint dries. Don't you just love that perfect *rouge*?"

"Felicity, just the woman I was hoping to see," Cameron said, a little too heartily, Magnolia thought. "If you wouldn't mind putting the tomcat down for a minute, I was wondering if I could steal you to go over some dates?"

"I'll leave you two," Magnolia said, backing out of the office and pondering where she could, with a modicum of dignity, pounce next. She entered the art department, walked beyond the three designers, past the photo editor's desk and her assistant's cubicle, and into Fredericka's elegantly spare taupe office. Fredericka, her tanned arms loaded with silver bracelets, hovered over her light box.

"Magnolia!" she moaned. "Vat am I going to tell Fabrizio about his October cover?" Fredericka had shots of Sarah Jessica Parker spread out, tenderly looking at each one as if it were an in utero image of her unborn child. Just a few weeks earlier, Fabrizio daVinci had finally agreed to work for *Lady*—the result of Fredericka's considerable persuasive abilities and magnums of Cristal sent to his cavernous downtown studio.

"Fredericka, his rep probably has ten offers for those pictures," Magnolia said. "First, remind him that Scary still holds a six-month embargo on the images." Maybe this whole *Bebe* nonsense will disappear and we can restore *Lady*, Magnolia thought fleetingly and—she realized—stupidly. But Scary did own the pictures, and she'd be damned if another magazine would benefit from her misery. "Then promise him the premiere *Bebe* cover."

Fredericka blanched, her skin almost matching her platinum hair. Apparently she hadn't yet fully absorbed that she and her photo editor would be responsible—issue after issue—for turning Bebe Blake into a cover temptress. She looked at Magnolia like a raccoon in a trap.

"But Fabrizio vould never, never agree to shoot Bebe," she said. "You know he only likes gorgeous vomen."

Fredericka was right. And Magnolia realized no good could come from hanging around her office. Even if the dentist told her he'd need to pull a front tooth, she'd rather be in his chair than here. She returned to her office, packed her Tod's tote with the latest *Vogue*, and left for his office, arriving forty minutes early.

Two hours later, her face looking like a stroke victim's, Magnolia heard her cell phone ring. Sub-Zero, she hoped. While sitting in the dentist's chair, she'd happily relived every stroke and thrust of both Saturday and Sunday nights. At one point, in her dental stupor, she worried that she might be doing a pretty fair "yes! yes! yes!" from *When Harry Met Sally*. But it wasn't Harry.

"I've been calling and calling," Sasha said. "How quickly can you get back here?"

"Fifteen minutes," Magnolia answered, overly optimistic. She'd already been standing for ten minutes on 57th Street, searching for a taxi.

"They're gathering," Sasha said. "Drop quiz. Cameron's looking for you. Surprise staff meeting."

A half hour later Magnolia bolted off the elevator onto her floor. She listened for the raucous laughter that usually erupted during a meeting, the rising voices of editors interrupting one another with ideas that trumped the next person's. An amped-up, competitive staff meeting was better than a basketball game at Madison Square Garden, and sometimes just as sweaty.

She heard nothing.

When she entered the conference room, however, the gang was there, stony and mute. Bebe presided at the end of the table in Magnolia's usual spot. For her first day of work she wore a silvery satin bomber jacket embroidered with dragons, and coordinating pants. With the ceiling spotlight shining on her you, had to squint.

"Sam here told me it was high time that we, uh, convened," Bebe said, looking at Cam. "I was just telling the girls—oh, 'scuse me, Sam—about my idea for the first cover: posing in a tub full of bubbles."

Bebe's gaze caught Magnolia's lopsided mouth. "What the hell happened to you, Mags? Wild nooner?"

The staff turned to Magnolia, who ignored Bebe's comment.

"Bubbles. What, exactly, would you be trying to convey in that image?" Magnolia asked Bebe in a level tone.

"That I'm all about fun," she answered, staring at Magnolia as if that weren't as obvious as the fact that they both had boobs. "Life's a hoot. Join in. Party on."

"I'm not sure most women want to hop in a tub with another woman, Bebe," Magnolia said.

"Holy Jesus and Mary, my women aren't that literal," Bebe answered. "Felicity, what do you think?"

"Your crowd would follow you anywhere, Beebsy," she said.

"Who are 'your women'?" Magnolia asked. "We need to establish that."

"Every woman. That's who watches my show. Nuns, truck drivers, inmates, old biddies, teenagers. Here, the cover would look like this." She sketched herself next to words marching down the right, instead of the left. Bebe's rendering looked reversed. Perhaps it would sell well to the dyslexic—or in Tel Aviv.

"Bebe, maybe we should brainstorm about the cover later in a separate meeting," Magnolia said. "Fredericka has some drop-dead ideas—Ruthie, too." She turned to her lieutenants. Fredericka flashed her whiter-than-white teeth, but Magnolia noted she had chewed her fingernails to the quick. Ruthie, not usually a poster girl for perfect posture, appeared starched.

"How about turning our attention to what's going to be inside the October issue," Magnolia said. "When you think of fall, what comes to mind?" She hadn't a clue how to tease great ideas out of Bebe, assuming she had some.

Bebe leaned back in her chair and put her boots on the table. "The fall makes me think of . . . Harleys," Bebe said, finally. "Tearing up a quiet country lane on a big road hog."

"I see models posing with bikers," Ruthie ventured. "It could be a great way to show denim."

"But not those skinny bitches," Bebe said, opening her jacket and pulling at a roll around her middle. "Every woman hates 'em."

Bebe had a point. "So are you seeing a plus-size fashion story?"

Magnolia asked. She noticed her anesthetic was wearing away. Had she wanted to, she could now smile.

"Plus, minus . . ." Bebe answered. "You all can figure that out. Just find me a bunch of biker babes."

"Ah, real people—that makes it much harder, Bebe. We have to find the women, be sure there's geographic and racial diversity, see when they can be flown to New York, be fitted for clothes—it takes planning, and real women don't usually fit into sample sizes."

Magnolia answered in a tone even she identified as prissy, but the fact was that organizing real people stories was like planning the invasion of a small country. They were ten times the trouble of regular fashion stories, where you phoned an agency, cast a few models, and called it a day. Real people stories required massive effort and yet often looked amateurish.

"They can wear their own clothes," Bebe said.

"But women want to be able to buy the clothes they see," Magnolia said, thinking that the bigger problem would be with Darlene. Periodically, Darlene gave Magnolia a list of the fashion advertisers she was wooing, and she expected the magazine to flog their clothes in the editorial pages, even if they came with price tags way out of reach for the readers.

"You work out those details," Bebe said, frowning. Her eyes looked even closer together than usual. "You and Sam must be gangbusters at that. Now in the fall, I also like to eat. Well, I always like to eat. Felicity here bakes bread, believe it or not."

"Mother taught me," Felicity explained with pride. "I'd be happy to be photographed teaching the readers. I bake a mean pumpernickel."

"Sounds delicious, Felicity," Magnolia answered. Now that her painkiller was gone, she remembered that she hadn't eaten a bite of anything today. "But most American women try to stay away from bread."

"Bullshit, Mags," Bebe said. "Show me one."

"Ladies?" Magnolia looked to her staff. A few timid hands shot up, but several editors refused to yield, even though Magnolia knew they'd rather give their Jimmy Choos to the homeless than eat the crust of a pizza.

"Okay, bread, done." Bebe switched on to a higher voltage. "And then I'll write a sex column. Answer readers' questions. Nothing off-limits." She nodded her head in enthusiasm. "We'll need a great name. I'm thinking 'Pussy Talk'?"

According to polls, if you believed them, *Lady*'s readers—and Scary would send *Bebe* to all of those subscribers; that's how it worked—had husbands and children, but no one ever admitted to having, liking, or being the least bit curious about sex.

"You think it might be a smidge too graphic, Bebe?" Magnolia asked.

"How about 'Getting Naked,'" she suggested.

"Love it," Magnolia said, "but some other magazine uses it."

"'Sex Ed,'" an editor shouted.

"'Your Pleasure Starts Here.'"

"'A Course on Intercourse.'"

"Not just intercourse," Bebe said. "Get real, girls."

"'The B Spot! The B Spot!'" a very pregnant Phoebe, who usually never came up with an idea beyond her annual "Metallic Makeup for the Holidays," screamed the suggestion.

"'The B Spot,'" Bebe hollered it back. "I get it. I like it. 'The B Spot.'"

"Whatever turns you on," Magnolia snickered softly.

"What's that? 'Whatever Turns You On!'" Bebe repeated. "'Whatever Turns You On.' Yup, that's it. Magnolia, you little genius. 'Whatever Turns You On.'"

Magnolia realized she could transform the meeting into a Roman holiday, with every editor feasting on the gore and barbarism of watching her tear out Bebe's squinty little eyes. Or she could encourage Bebe to create a magazine in her own image and have it die a natural death.

That is, if the magazine would fail. With the American public, who knew? Bebe could be right. Women might adore these ideas. Maybe every woman was secretly dying to hop on a big old Harley, stuff her face with a loaf of pumpernickel, and have mind-blowing sex on a quiet country lane with a three-hundred-pound biker named Runt.

"So Mag-knowl-ya, what do you think?"

"Whatever Turns You On . . ." Magnolia said. "Let's make it happen."

Chapter 15

In This Life, One Thing Counts

During the two years Magnolia had reported to Jock Flanagan, he had not once popped into her office for a schmooze. So it was curious that today, Friday, the end of her first full week as Bebe's deputy, Jock arrived like a missile. He landed on her new guest seating—an armless, royal blue swivel job, pilfered from the conference room—as if it were time for their weekly therapy session.

"So how's it going with Bebe?" he asked, trying to smooth his thick, wavy hair. Jock required regular mowing, and if he missed a trim, he looked as if he'd been coifed by a Cuisinart.

Magnolia flashed on the last few days. She and Bebe had settled into a no-routine routine. A few times Bebe had buzzed her to demand a drive-by meeting, but either she hadn't learned to turn on her Mac or didn't care to use it, so no e-mail volleys existed. Felicity kept regular hours to supervise the fluffing of Bebe's office, and could be heard squealing with glee as each mirror, poster of Bebe, or carnivorous-looking plant found its home in the red lair. Bebe fit the magazine around rehearsals and tapings for *The Bebe Show*.

Magnolia wished that Jock were, in fact, an actual therapist. Then she could have told him how she felt. Ridiculous, pissed off, and stuck—she couldn't afford to walk out since no guardian angel had dangled another opportunity in her face. This didn't surprise her; she'd counted on the redesign of *Lady* to project her into the orbit of hotshots who circled from big job to bigger job. But she also felt guilty—she knew she should be grateful for the well-paying, well-percolated position she still had, even if it was at a lower rank than at the first of the month.

"Magnolia, I asked you a question," Jock said.

"Everything's fine," she answered. "Really. We're developing a terrific sex column, we're stalking biker chicks for fashion, and we've got a story in the works where we're all over leopard—clothes, shoes, dishes, furniture, everything except the big cat itself."

Jock seemed to cringe a little, but offered no response, so Magnolia continued.

"There's a special section called 'Don't Get Screwed—Get Everything,' where matrimonial attorneys advise divorcing women. Bebe came up with the idea, based on her last settlement. She's been married several times, you know? Husband number three demanded a fortune in alimony—I'm sure you read about it. He was her agent, ten years younger. It's sad the way he ripped her off."

"Hmm," Jock said.

She thought, given Jock's marital history, that at least the divorce story would have piqued his interest, but now it was Magnolia's turn to wait. It hadn't sounded like a good *hmm*. The staff *was* busy, she thought defensively. Whether it added up to a unique magazine was not for her to say. Not that anyone was asking.

"Magnolia, from what I hear you haven't been, well, the most cooperative."

"What?" she snapped, wondering who might have slimed her. She thought she'd been as neutral as Switzerland. Well, maybe not sweet, stern little Switzerland, but definitely more Western European than

Middle Eastern. If someone—most likely Darlene, that sociopath masquerading as a publisher—had portrayed her as a suicide bomber of Bebe's plans, it was outrageous. "You heard this where?"

"Where doesn't matter," Jock said, staring at his manicured nails as if he'd just noticed they were attached to his hand. "You get how serious this is, don't you? How much money Scarborough has on this horse?"

Magnolia took Jock's measure. She wasn't convinced he was angry: she'd seen him in this state enough times to recognize his version of rage. Once, when he'd swooped down on an editor whose newsstand sales had plummeted 62 percent, you'd have thought she'd shot his bulldog, Grover Cleveland. Magnolia decided Jock probably just needed reassurance. No doubt, he was getting heat from the Scary brothers who owned the company. They rarely left Santa Barbara, but tortured him by phone, fax, and summons to California.

Magnolia calculated that she'd best kick it up a notch. She'd need this job until something better came along. "You have my word that I will get and keep things in line," she said, in honor student mode. "Bebe's first cover shoot's today, and I'll be there to run interference. Elizabeth's people have arranged for an *Access Hollywood* crew to film the shoot. Build buzz. They'll air the film the week of the launch."

Would she be insane to spit out what she was thinking of saying next? "Would you like to come to the shoot?" Magnolia held her breath, thinking how the photographer they'd booked—Francesco Bellucci, a fading star known for grand opera tantrums—would very likely walk out if the president of the company showed up to cramp his style.

Jock appeared to consider the invitation. But then he said, "Oh, please, that won't be necessary," and waved away the thought. "In fact, I'm catching a plane. I know I can count on you, Magnolia."

He looked at his vintage Patek Philippe and stood to leave. Should she spring her next question, the one that kept her up every night and had, as a result, cost her four hundred dollars for a QVC chinchilla wrap too faux for even a ho? Magnolia went for the red meat. "I'm glad you stopped by, because I was hoping we could discuss my . . . title." She delivered the request with bluster she thought would be mistaken for male confidence. No one ever damned a man for a bold gesture.

"What is your title," he asked. "Remind me?"

"Bebe seems to think it's deputy."

"Makes sense," he said. "Although I don't recall if we ever discussed titles, Bebe and I."

"Three years ago I'd have been thrilled with that title, Jock. But it doesn't reflect the job I'm doing. I'm managing this magazine down to the last semicolon." Surely, that was how Jock saw her role, a copy editor who'd mated with a lion tamer. "You know that."

"Do I?"

"If I have to sleep in the ladies' room, I'll make this magazine the best it can be."

"Why, for God's sake, do editors carry on about titles? It's about bucks. Don't you people get that?"

In this life, one thing counts. In the bank, large amounts. . . . For publishers and other business-side folk, it was a philosophy they may as well have had on their business cards, but editors always wanted their monetary entrée rounded up with tasty side dishes, including a respectable title.

"Editor then?" Magnolia said. It was a big step down from editor in chief, but at least it wasn't deputy.

"Editor. Magnolia the editor."

"You'll tell Bebe?"

Jock had already stepped halfway out the door, but turned to give Magnolia an appraisal that, if she wasn't mistaken, lingered rather long on her chest. "I'll try to remember," he said.

Chapter 16

Bebepalooza

Traffic was light at this hour of the morning, and it didn't take long to arrive at Washington Street, not far from the Hudson River. Most local photo shoots took place in vast studios—Manhattan's stand-ins for back lots—tucked into downtown loft buildings, and Magnolia's favorite was Industria Superstudio, where she was heading. Fredericka had pulled in every chit to book Studio 6. It was small enough to be intimate, yet large enough to drive in a tank and photograph a minor jihad—which is what Magnolia feared might take place today.

"Good morning!" Fredericka spotted her and left her *Woman's Wear* on a leather armchair as she sprinted across the shiny wooden floor in Magnolia's direction, her platinum bob flying.

"*Guten tag*, Fredericka," Magnolia said. "*Was ist das?*" She pointed to a tall structure swathed in white drop cloths.

"The backdrop," Fredericka explained. "Vhen ve decided to go vith leopard, Francesco suggested a leopard vall, so ve had a muralist paint one."

"How much did this set us back?"

"Three thousand? Six thousand?" Fredericka answered and shrugged. "Francesco has in mind to pose Bebe draped over one of those leopard chaises in front of the background." She pointed toward a cluster of furniture being unpacked by several beefy deliverymen. "Like an odalisque."

Magnolia knew not to be surprised. Photographers saw themselves as *artistes* and cared far more about whether a day's work would enhance their portfolio than if it fit a magazine's image or budget. It mattered little that *Bebe* would be paying Francesco's fee—half of today's $50,000-plus bill. Photographers ruled their photo shoots, and if they chose to treat an art director like a summer intern or take only half the shots the editor in chief expected, they stamped their feet and got their way.

"Check out the clothes," Fredericka said, taking Magnolia's hand and pulling her toward the other end of the room, where Ruthie and several assistants were setting up what looked like a good-sized boutique, removing garments from bags, steaming away creases, hanging everything on aluminum racks, and salivating over choices.

"Some Bebepalooza." Magnolia whistled.

"The shoes!" Ruthie said. "You've got to see them."

Magnolia inhaled the smell of expensive leather and listened to the promising rustle of tissue paper as a double for the Bergdorf's shoe department came into focus. The troops carefully removed at least twenty pairs of leopard-print size tens: Manolo Blahnik stilettos; Lambertson Truex skimmers with toes so pointed they could open letters; Stuart Weitzman calf-hair pumps you'd feel the need to pet; girly, bow-bedecked Christian Louboutin peep toes. The only footwear missing were actual leopard paws.

Ruthie slipped her size six-and-a-half feet into the bowed pumps. "Don't you love these?"

"Not for $700 I don't," Magnolia answered, knowing she sounded like a social worker. "The reader could feed her family for months on what these shoes cost."

"We're not telling people to buy the shoes," Ruthie said. "Anyway, they're what Felicity said Bebe liked."

Luca Luca, Moschino, Marni, and Roberto Cavalli were all here, along with lesser labels. Since Bebe didn't wear a sample size—not by several digits—Ruthie and her junior varsity had called in dresses, pants, and blouses from every chic store in Beverly Hills and all points east. Magnolia and Fredericka combed through the garments, grouping first choices together. As Magnolia held up a ruffled Alexander McQueen cocktail dress, she heard the voice.

"Sheena, Queen of the Jungle, reporting for duty," Bebe boomed. "You don't actually expect me to wear that?" she said as she got close enough to see the dress in Magnolia's hands. "Christ, I'd look like a heifer."

"Not at all, Bebe," Magnolia said. "You're going to look like you." Just not exactly like the Bebe who'd arrived in bike shorts, a long sweatshirt, bare, lady wrestler legs, and running shoes. In one hand, she carried a half-eaten doughnut and under her arm, Hell.

"I loathe photo shoots," Bebe said. There was an edge to her voice that Magnolia couldn't quite identify. It took a second for her to realize that what she was hearing was honesty. Bebe was just as freaked about being photographed as any woman who wasn't a 100-pound, fourteen-year-old model from Eastern Europe.

"That makes two of us," Magnolia said. Every time she had her editor's letter photo taken, she'd found the experience so ego-shredding she practically needed rehab to recover. "Most of my pictures wouldn't even make the cut for the Westminster Kennel Dog Show. But don't worry. We've got the very best for hair and makeup."

Fredericka broke in. "Before ve get going, you need to meet Francesco." She nodded toward a short man in wireless glasses, loose white pants, and a long shirt billowing over a sizable tummy. A do-rag was tied around his head. "Ciao," Fredericka shouted, as he ambled in their direction.

"Ciao, *bellissima*," Francesco said to Fredericka. "And this beautiful lady must be today's star," he sang out, bestowing kisses on Magnolia's reddening cheeks. "I will make you so magnificent, like the most desired concubine in a sultan's harem. But it will not be hard."

Fredericka interrupted. "Francesco, darling. You know Magnolia Gold. Remember the *Lady* shoot with Nicole Kidman? *This* is our cover girl." She swiveled toward Bebe. Francesco turned in Bebe's direction. "Please meet Bebe Blake."

"You were expecting someone gorgeous perhaps?" Bebe said with a grin. "Frank, better have a drink. Catwoman ain't coming. You got your work cut out for you."

Francesco blinked twice and kissed Bebe's hand. "Apologies, my lovely lady. You will see. I will make you divine."

"Bovine? I can do bo-vine standing on my head." Bebe laughed. Alone.

Francesco looked confused and motioned toward the breakfast buffet. "*Mangia,* everyone," he said, waving. Pineapple spears, three kinds of berries, yogurt, brioches, and bagels covered a long table set with heavy taupe pottery and a linen cloth. "We're still prepping the first shot," he said. "It all must be perfect." Two male assistants in tight blue jeans and black T-shirts were unfurling an enormous white background. Several others were setting up a galaxy of lights. "You must excuse me."

Magnolia looked at her watch. Nearing eleven. The breakfast hour would drag on another twenty minutes. Then makeup, which takes a good hour, followed by hair, an hour there, too. By then it would be 1:30, and the whole crew—close to thirty people, counting Francesco's aides-de-camp plus Elizabeth Lester Duvall and the *Access Hollywood* crew who'd be arriving at noon—would announce that, no, they're not hungry, but, sure, they could use a snack. The caterer would present another, far more sumptuous, meal and the gang would chow down as if they were gearing up for a Yom Kippur fast.

They'd be lucky to start shooting by two.

Magnolia wished life would allow her to age in photo-shoot time. It wasn't just the slo-mo pace that got to her. It was the talk, endless hours of it, during prep and between takes. "Did you hear about Dogbone, the new club?" "My boyfriend and I got totally trashed there last night." "We got cut off at the pass. Had to go to Schiller's Liquor Bar." "Did you want to kill?" "Totally." "I so need to lose ten pounds." "You're insane. I want your hips." "Then be ready for lipo." And on and on. Magnolia knew that even at *Lady* she wasn't exactly brokering peace in the Middle East, but at photo shoots she could feel IQ points literally melting away. Plus, she thought crankily as she took a deep breath, this was a smoking crowd. Then there was the music, which as the day wore on, would throb at migraine-inducing decibels, all in the name of trying to "create energy."

Why, she wondered, did anyone think shoots were glamorous?

Magnolia wandered off to a corner, and began to read *Men's Health*, the only magazine she could find. She got almost to the end of "Put the Tiger in Your Wood—9 Hard-and-Fast Rules for Awe-Inspiring Erections." Just as she was thinking how her ex, Wally, could have benefited from the information, Bebe gave a shout-out.

"Magnolia!" she yelled. "Whattya think?"

Bebe looked ready for a revival of *Cats*. Her face was spackled to a Formica smoothness, and smoky gray eyeliner extended almost to her temples. At least Akiko, the makeup artist, hadn't added whiskers.

"Honestly, Bebe?"

"No, lie big. Of course, honestly."

"Too, too, too . . . Akiko, could you make it more . . . natural?" Magnolia asked. Akiko smiled sweetly and continued to sculpt faux cheekbones into Bebe's well-fed face.

"Hey, I like it," Bebe said. "The eyes stay. And Jean-Luc here"— she pointed to the town's premier makeup man, who was cursing his boyfriend in French on a cell phone—"we've already decided on spiky hair. A whole new me."

A Bebe who readers might not recognize, Magnolia thought. A Bebe who could frighten small children. But time was marching on. Elizabeth and *Access Hollywood* had shown up with a truckload of equipment. As Elizabeth bossed them around like the secretary of defense, their presence added an element of chaos, which only slowed the tempo as they directed Bebe in their filming and interviewed Francesco.

Magnolia bivouacked with Fredericka. "If we can finish Bebe's hair and get her into the first outfit, will Francesco be ready in thirty minutes?"

"I'll ask," Fredericka said. She returned in five minutes. "Francesco thinks ve should break to eat."

The lunch, which Francesco had ordered from Tabla, his favorite Indian restaurant, was worthy of New Delhi in high summer. Normally, chicken tikka with mango chutney and mint, coconut rice, and orange glazed carrots would have appealed to Magnolia. But today she could only look at the clock. Their star hadn't even tried on clothes. Toward the end of the break, Magnolia approached Bebe. "We've got to keep moving," she said, and motioned Bebe toward the clothing while she held up a Marni dress with a forgiving cut.

"Hate it," Bebe said, as she polished off a big bite of a pink sweet everyone else had left on the buffet.

"How about this?" Magnolia pulled out a simple gown by Calvin Klein.

"Nope." Bebe chewed loudly.

Magnolia offered Bebe a jacket by Michael Kors, followed by a Moschino Cheap & Chic skirt and sweater. Reject. Reject.

"You're kidding, right?" Bebe said, yanking off her sweatshirt and exposing her black lace bra. From the back of the last rack she withdrew a flimsy leopard T, and stretched it over her head, smearing her eyeliner. "Love it," she said as she stripped to her panties, which, to Magnolia's relief, were grannies. "Help me find a bottom."

Ruthie and Magnolia searched and returned with eight pairs of pants. Nothing fit. If the pants were made with back or side zippers, Ruthie would be able to cunningly split a seam and no one would be the wiser, but every style zipped up the front.

"Houston, we have a problem," Magnolia said. "Ruthie, have your assistants run out and look for plain black pants."

"No-no-no-no-no," Bebe said. "I'll wear my bike shorts." Bebe began to squeeze back into her spandex.

"Bebe," Magnolia said. "You can't."

"Watch me," Bebe responded, grinning.

"Seriously. It's all wrong for the cover."

"It'll be fun," Bebe said, gathering Hell into her arms. "What do you think, you big, bad boy?" She tickled the cat's neck until he purred. "Doesn't Mommy look fucktabulous?"

"Do you think we could let Francesco decide?" Magnolia asked, peeking out from behind the curtained dressing area and motioning him over.

"Like I care what that fat old fart thinks? Magnolia, are you forgetting whose magazine this is? This is me. I live in bike pants. End of story."

Francesco stepped behind the curtain. Bebe danced to the sound of Prince. "So, Frank, can you make me bo-vine?" she asked, striking a hands-on-hip pose.

The photographer glared.

"Francesco, let's just try a few shots in these clothes," Magnolia said, softly and evenly.

"They will not do." He folded his arms over his belly. "I do not see it."

"See it," Bebe said, mirroring his stance.

"Excuse me?" he asked.

"See it, Frank," Bebe repeated, shimmying to the music.

"*Basta, basta*," Francesco answered, walking away. "I will not be insulted. I am Francesco Bellucci."

Magnolia closed her eyes and hung her head. When she took a look around, Fredericka was grinding her teeth and cursing in German. Bebe was laughing, and Francesco had escaped. Magnolia looked at the large clock on the wall. Four o'clock.

"Serious scumbag, that Frank," Bebe said. "Remind me why you booked him." Because as soon as they heard you were the celebrity, six photographers we asked first said no, Magnolia recalled. And one of them was polite about it.

"Bebe, I'll talk to him," Magnolia said, looking for Francesco, who'd walked out the door. She found him murdering a cigarette butt with his Gucci loafer.

"Francesco, I know she's—how can I say this?—unconventional, but could you see your way to finishing the shoot?" Magnolia said. "Please."

"I have my reputation," he answered. "Sweet Jesus, who does that woman think she is?"

"She's an investor," Magnolia said, slowly and loudly. "The magazine has her name on it, for God's sake. It might be huge."

"I am very sorry, Magnolia. But this shoot is a category five hurricane. I must withdraw."

Magnolia considered her options. It didn't take long. She had no options. Well, maybe one. "What if we up your rate by ten percent," Magnolia said. "Combat pay."

"Twenty-five," he countered.

"Ten," Magnolia said. "Think of how you'd like to continue working for *Elegance* and *Dazzle* and all the other Scarborough magazines. Ten firm."

Francesco lit up a second cigarette, sighed deeply, and wiped his brow with a monogrammed handkerchief. "I shall proceed," he said gravely.

Four hours later, Bebe's hair and makeup had been redone several times. Magnolia and Fredericka had cajoled her into several wardrobe changes. Francesco had finished off eight roles of film, including one round in front of the white backdrop—without Hell—as an alternative to the leopard. This was a good move: Magnolia had no idea how Fredericka would get coverlines to read over those spots. *Access Hollywood* was packing to leave. Francesco was just about to shoot a final roll of film, when Magnolia heard a familiar bellow, growing louder and louder, like the horn of an approaching ocean liner.

"Gold!" it said. "Gold! Mags! How's it going? Bebe! Oh, Bebe, you look fabulous." It was her publisher, Darlene, hurrying toward the camera, her Prada suit a mess of wrinkles. "I was in the neighborhood on the way home, and asked my driver to swing by," she said. It was a curious detour. She lived on Park and 80th and that wasn't all. Publishers were never invited to photo shoots. An art director and photographer would sooner extend an invitation to their archrival than to their magazine's publisher.

"How's it going?" Darlene asked.

"Dandy," Magnolia hissed, turning away from Darlene.

"Can I see the Polaroids?" Darlene asked in her pushiest tone.

"Please, Darlene," Magnolia said. "Not now."

"Frank here is one helluva photographer," Bebe said. "I did a Janet Jackson with my tit, and he didn't even blink. But I guess you don't like girls, huh, Frank?"

Darlene plunged in Francesco's direction. "I'm *Bebe*'s publisher," she said to the startled photographer, picking up a Polaroid from the table where his assistant had left them. "Mind if I look through your lens?"

"Mind if I read your tax return?" Francesco responded.

It was close to nine o'clock. Magnolia had canceled a date with Harry. She was starving, exhausted, and wanted to kick Darlene with the pointiest stiletto in Ruthie's collection. She regretted that Ruthie hadn't called in steel-toed work boots.

"Darlene, don't even think about it," Magnolia said. "This shoot is over."

Chapter 17

Too Much Information

Several workdays later, at 6:45, Magnolia was relieved to see that Ruthie was still working with her assistant to account for the clothing from the Bebe shoot which needed to be returned "Ready for an intervention?" she said.

"Big date?" Ruthie asked with a smile, looking unwilted, even at the end of the day, in a vanilla skirt and shirt and pale stilettos. Her straight, shiny black hair framed her dark almond eyes. She looked like a fashion editor doll.

"I wish," Magnolia replied. "No, it's a black tie, last minute, Waldorf hell."

Every year Scary bought tables at the Bowel Bash, a favorite charity of the older Scary brother, the skinny one with irritable bowel syndrome. Bebe and Darlene were tapped to represent *Bebe*. At 6:30, however, Felicity sent word that Bebe was "indisposed"—taping her TV show, Magnolia was to believe. She would be pressed into action to replace her.

Usually, dressy events were excuses for Magnolia to wear real jewelry. Maybe her sapphire chandelier earrings, her parents' gift for her thirtieth birthday. Or she might borrow one of Abbey's pieces, like the coral and black jet Maltese cross from her short-lived Frida Kahlo period. But today there would be no time for a trip home to root around her jewelry box, hidden underneath the heating pad. There would barely be time to see if Ruthie could lend her more appropriate clothes and shoes than today's plaid jacket; stretchy, butt-forgiving Capris, and flats. Magnolia blinked away an image of her Chanel sample sale dress sadly awaiting bright lights in the big city. The dress would have to wait a little longer.

By standards of a legitimate fashion magazine, the *Bebe* fashion closet—an uncarpeted space roughly twenty-by-twenty, lit by fluorescent lights—was touching. To an innocent female bystander, though, it was paradise. Shoes and boots filled shelves along every wall. Belts, hats, and scarves dangled from pegs. Hosiery and socks were arranged in drawers along with jewelry, sorted like fishing tackle.

In the middle of the room stood racks of clothing. Here was the coat that had to be purchased because a model's cigarette burned a hole in the sleeve. There was the baby blue halter the talk show host demanded because it matched her eyes, then refused to wear because it exposed her ham-shaped arms. In a corner was the complete Target line Isaac Mizrahi had sent one Friday afternoon with a challah and a note that began, "Good Shabbas, Magnolia bubbe."

A fashion closet was one of those giddy ties to glamour taken advantage of by even the lowest of the low on the editorial masthead. If an editor needed to replace rain-soaked shoes or swap her turtleneck with a clingy Hoorywood top for a last-minute date, Ruthie and her team always obliged. Like now.

Right now, however, Ruthie was fixated on Magnolia's hair. "Let's not talk about it, okay?" Magnolia said. This morning she'd forgone a shampoo, and tied her hair into a ponytail, which now hung like a small dead rodent waiting for the taxidermist.

Ruthie shrugged and ducked behind a rack. She quickly emerged and offered Magnolia a clingy black panther of an Armani dress.

Magnolia scowled and stuck out her rear end. "I'm not nearly skinny enough for that."

Ruthie nodded and returned with a black printed chiffon gown encrusted with beads. Magnolia stripped to her underwear and pulled the dress over her head. The bell sleeves hung below her hands. She was Morticia in a muumuu.

"Off, off," Ruthie shrieked and disappeared again, mumbling something about Valentino. The name warmed Magnolia's heart, until she saw a ruffled purple leopard gown in silk georgette. Obviously, even Valentino had an off day.

"Please, anything but leopard," Magnolia said, politely ignoring the gown's other faults.

"Even with this to cover it up?" Ruthie held out a gray fox stole.

"Ruthie, I'm not accepting an Academy Award."

"Got it," Ruthie said. "Glitz-lite."

"And forget about décolleté," Magnolia called out as Ruthie foraged further. "Tonight's about gastroenterology, not tits."

Time dribbled away as Ruthie pulled out clothes and shook her head. Finally, she emerged, bearing a pale pink sweater. Were it not for a diamanté-jeweled neckline of the softest cashmere, it could have been sold at Old Navy. Magnolia loved it. She pulled on the sweater, which made her waist look tiny and her breasts ample but not obscene.

"With this skirt," Ruthie insisted. The sequined scalloped skirt, in a darker pink, hit her legs right below the knee. The woman who stared back in the mirror reeked chic.

"Stick this on," Ruthie commanded. She handed Magnolia a white gold ring showcasing a hunk of lemon quartz the size of a cherry tomato. "And these for your ears."

Magnolia fingered the dangly spirals that Ruthie was now proffering. "Garnets?" Magnolia asked.

"Rubies," Ruthie answered.

"Not too much with the sweater? Don't want to look like a petit four."

"Trust me, you need to distract from the hair," Ruthie said as she handed Magnolia a small beige satin envelope bag.

"You're right. They're fabulous. But shoes, Ruthie?" They both looked at the red flats she'd kicked off.

Ruthie eyeballed the fashion closet's size nines and tens. Models might be skinny, but they were tall girls with enormous feet. Magnolia was a seven. "Here," she said, taking off her own bone Manolo pumps.

"You have saved my life, Ruthie Kim, and I will be forever grateful," Magnolia said, slipping on the shoes, which were only a little snug. She gathered her work clothes and flats; dumped them back in her office; stuck her cell phone, twenty dollars, and a lipstick in the bag, and pinned her hair in a chignon with the help of an unidentifiable hair product she found lurking in her desk.

Five minutes later she was in the elevator. As was Natalie Simon. "What's with the pink?" Natalie asked. "We're doing bowels, not breast cancer, right?"

"Cut me some slack here, Natalie," Magnolia said, wondering why a woman wearing the twin of the purple Valentino leopard dress she'd rejected fifteen minutes ago had the temerity to be critical.

"You know I'm kidding, Cookie," Natalie said. "You look adorable. I'd like to rip that sweater off your back. Whose is it?"

"Honestly, haven't a clue," Magnolia answered, eager to change the subject. "What's going on?"

"Meaning to call you," Natalie said. "I just shipped our cover and I have you to thank."

"Why is that?"

"Sarah Jessica Parker," Natalie said. "Those pictures were knockouts. As soon as I saw them, I postponed Angelina Jolie. She scares the bejesus out of people anyway."

Corporately, of course, it made sense. In the boilerplate of the standard Scary contract, the company had paid for the shoot, not *Lady*, and the embargo extended for months, so it was too soon for the photographer to resell them. Why not let *Dazzle* run the pictures shot for *Lady*? Still, it stung. Just as a courtesy, Magnolia wished Natalie would have at least asked her if she took advantage of the photos—not that Magnolia owned them in any way beyond emotional.

"They've been lucky already," Natalie grinned. "Online tests predict that cover's going to blow out of the newsstand."

Natalie Simon luck, Magnolia thought.

Natalie offered Magnolia a ride to the Waldorf, and the two chatted about other things—whether it was true that Jock was doing it with Mitzi, Pippi's sister, and the pissy e-mail they'd all got demanding that each magazine cut back 20 percent on color Xeroxes.

By the time the two of them arrived at the hotel, most of the cocktail hour had passed. As they entered the room, Natalie got plucked off by a Brooks Brothers type who Magnolia suspected belonged to one of the three corporate boards on which Natalie sat. Magnolia scanned the sea of overdressed humanity but, since it wasn't an event exclusively for the magazine industry, she didn't recognize a soul. One short man on the arm of a tall, willowy woman looked familiar, but she couldn't place the face. Was he a friend's father? She started to walk in his direction, but when she got close, several people cut in front of her.

"Mr. Mayor, we're honored you could be here," they said.

Magnolia quickly reversed directions and grabbed a glass of champagne from the nearest waiter. And then she saw her publisher, who was eyeing her as if she'd come to the event dressed in sweats.

"Magnolia, only you could wear that!" Darlene said. "Interesting hair." Even in the din of the crowded reception room, Darlene's voice could be plainly heard. "Great that you're here—there's someone I want you to meet," she added, pulling Magnolia into a three-minute sales call to a pharmaceutical advertiser. "*Of course*, our readers would be interested in a new drug for premature ejaculation," Darlene insisted. But before the startled client had a chance to respond, the lights blinked. Time to take their seats in the grand ballroom.

Magnolia looked for her place card, a touch Elizabeth Lester Duvall always engineered; if she could help it—nothing in the Scary domain was ever left to chance. When Magnolia arrived at her table, however, she had the distinct feeling that the seating arrangement had been reshuffled. Surely Bebe's seat, which she was filling, would have been next to Jock, or at least one of the Scarys. But, no, she was at the second table. To her right was the chatty wife of the production director. To her left was the number two guy in circulation, a pudgy, bow-tied fellow who she knew would be only too happy to offer a letter-by-letter reprisal of his winning game at the regional Scrabble tournament.

Magnolia looked to the other table. There was Charlotte Stone, the publisher of *Elegance*, Natalie, Jock, Darlene, Elizabeth, the brothers, their matching blond wives, and the pharmaceutical executive. "Two bottles of champagne to start," she heard Jock say, snapping his fingers at the waiter.

Throughout the evening, Magnolia seethed about the *Lady* photos gone to *Dazzle*. This was just as well, because her rage kept her awake, which the evening's speakers might have failed to do. The waiters removed her tuna tartare before she'd finished it, and quickly replaced it with a leathery hunk of filet mignon.

"May I please have fish instead?" she asked.

"See what I can do," the waiter snarled. By the time he returned with a dry slab of salmon, the lights had gone dim for a fifteen-minute film. She fidgeted in her seat. There could be no discreet escape hatch, not with Scary's table front and center in the ballroom.

Six speakers followed, as did the skinny Scary brother, who began handing out the annual Bowel Booster awards. Even an enormous serving of chocolate mousse in a bittersweet chocolate shell—an unfortunate choice, given the evening's theme—couldn't tempt Magnolia to stick around. As soon as the third of five awards had been bestowed, she found her evening bag, stood up, and said to no one in particular at the table, "You've got to excuse me," she said. No one even looked up.

As she listened to Comedy Central an hour later, Magnolia carefully folded her borrowed clothes, removed her makeup, and laid out running clothes for the following day. She checked her office e-mail and answered the phone twice—a short call from Harry, who suggested she not get her knickers in a twist over the Natalie picture heist, then offered a long monologue on knickers in general, and Abbey, who patiently listened to an accounting of Magnolia's day.

Just as she was starting to set her alarm for 6:15 A.M., Magnolia heard the intercom. She thought her doorman might be saying, "Gentleman wants to see you." The building's system made the subway's loudspeaker sound elegantly clear.

"What's his name?"

"Harry," the doorman said. At least she hoped that's what he'd said. Harry might have been in a cab on the way uptown when they spoke and had called on his cell, not his landline.

Was there time to switch into the new black camisole set nestled in her drawer? The thong had two tiny bows at the V above her butt cheeks, which the top's matching bows marched down to meet. She tossed off her SpongeBob T-shirt and pulled on her new underwear just as she heard the knock.

"Be right there," she said, hoping the outfit would cause Harry to overlook her hair, which was not improved by the gel she'd used to cement it into a chignon.

"Can't wait to see you, gorgeous," Harry said. Only it wasn't Harry. As the knocking got louder, Magnolia looked through the peephole. "Magnolia, gorgeous, it's me. Open up."

There he was, catapulted from cyberspace. "Tommy O'Toole, where the hell have you been?" Magnolia screeched through the door. "You've been AWOL for months, and Abbey's a twitching mess. And what in God's name are you doing *here*?"

Since their postbreakup tryst, Tommy had been communicating with Abbey, but only through e-mail. He'd last claimed to be in New Zealand, though for all Abbey knew, he'd been holed up at the Hotel Gansevoort in the Meatpacking District.

"Gotta see you, Magnolia," he answered. "Give a guy a break. Open up."

"One minute," Magnolia said. She put on her robe—her ratty one—and let him in. Tommy immediately pressed her to his chest and covered her mouth with his. Magnolia pulled away quickly but not before she smelled Scotch.

"Hey, Magnolia, you've never been such a tease," Tommy said. "Come to Tommy boy. You know I've always thought you were hot." He circled his arms around her again, then grabbed her wrists and planted her arms around his back, holding her tight. Magnolia couldn't escape his grip. His tongue probed her mouth.

"I want to see you naked, Magnolia," he whispered.

"Too much information, Tommy," Magnolia said, as he momentarily relaxed and she was able to push him away.

"You smell good," he said, his blue eyes half-shut "You've got a beautiful shape. I've always thought of you as a fine wine."

A wine, she thought. I'm a wine? Did he think she was *old*? Magnolia realized she didn't have time to analyze Tommy's train of thought. She just needed to get him to stop this horseshit.

"I think about you all the time," he said. "At work, at the gym, when I'm with other women."

"You don't, Tommy," she yelled. "You're just drunk. My God, you're vile. And what are you doing with other women anyway? You're married!" The loudness of Magnolia's voice appeared to penetrate his psyche. He sat down on the bench in her foyer, cradling his head in his hands. Biggie and Lola, awakened by the ruckus, circled around, barking.

"You've hijacked my heart, Magnolia."

"The hijacked organ is your brain, Tommy," Magnolia said from the other end of the foyer. "No, you have no brain. It's your prick talking. And to think Abbey's been carrying on about you. She's down to ninety-eight pounds."

"My sweet Abbey," he said, as he started to whimper. "I love my little wife."

"Of course, you do, Tommy," Magnolia said. Maybe Tommy wasn't vile. Maybe he was just an idiot drunk. Abbey deserved better, of course, but he wasn't a total villain. Definitely not. Magnolia walked over to him and began to stroke his arm as if he were a child. "Now I'm going to make you some coffee, and then you're going to get out of here, go see Abbey, and figure out your life."

He looked up with tears in his eyes. "Magnolia, I love Abbey, but I love you, too. You're a wise, sexy woman."

Magnolia pretended she didn't hear him. She walked into her kitchen, thinking how it would be at least ten minutes until the coffee would brew, and she would force Tommy to drink a cup and start to sober up. Then he'd leave, and she could fall into her bed.

Magnolia made the coffee, superstrong. "You're going home," she said, handing him a mug. "I'm going to take you down in the elevator myself." Just to make sure he didn't hang around the lobby like a lost shoe. She let him almost finish the coffee, then yanked his arm. Tommy put down the mug, spilling coffee on her rug, and followed her out to the hallway. They stepped in the elevator, Tommy first.

The doors closed. Magnolia faced forward, pressed the button, and started to tell Tommy they were both going to forget this ever happened. But when Magnolia turned, Tommy was at it again. He embraced her from behind, pressing his frame tightly against hers. She tried to ignore the sensation of his well-muscled body close to her own. He *had* been going to the gym! Struggling to free herself from his embrace, she started to groan.

"Oh, Tommy," she said. "This is just too much."

She heard the elevator open, and sensed that someone was in the doorway. Let it be Manuel, the night doorman, she prayed, worried about her because a neighbor had reported a ruckus. Thank God she'd overtipped him last Christmas—and thrown in a Burberry scarf.

It was not, however, Manuel. When she twisted around and looked up, she could see the doorman at the far end of the lobby, and hear him laughing uproariously at a Spanish television program playing on the small set he hid behind the concierge's desk. But she knew the man waiting to get into the elevator, the man who'd taken in everything and was now observing Tommy wrapped around her like a tortilla.

It was Harry. "Well, Magnolia, aren't we the lady of the evening?" he said.

"It's not how it looks, Harry," she said.

"It never is, luv," he snickered.

"Yeah, man," Tommy added, as he swayed to keep his balance.

Harry shook his head. On his forehead she noticed small beads of sweat. "Magnolia," he said, "you have really disappointed me. Did the last few weeks mean nothing to you?"

"Harry, this is Abbey's husband—" she started to say.

"How does that make it better?" he said. "Whoring around with your friend's man?"

"You scumbag," Tommy said. "Don't insult Magnolia,"

Harry straightened his shoulders and turned. "Sod off, the both of you," he said as he stomped out of the building.

Chapter 18

Mistress Tortured

It was past midnight. Magnolia returned to her apartment and tried Harry's cell phone five times, hoping he'd turn it on. He did not. She tried sleeping, unsuccessfully, and couldn't even take a sleeping pill, since she'd given her stash to Abbey. So she attempted to organize her closet, a task so tedious that whenever she started it, she fell into a coma.

Magnolia began with the suits, wondering if she should hang on to a gray pinstripe Max Mara, just right for the job she would never want or get at a Fortune 500 company.

"The suit stays—it cost over two thousand dollars," argued one voice in her head—her mother's, to be exact.

"You haven't worn it in three years," the other voice answered. "Dump it."

"It's a classic," retorted Mom. "You can keep it forever!"

"What a crock" came the answer. "Classics are cauliflower."

"Hang on to that suit—you might need it for a funeral."

She dropped Max Mara onto her chaise and walked into the bathroom to draw a hot, sudsy bath. Just as she slid into the tub, the phone rang. She bolted upright, ran across her tile floor to the bedroom, and grabbed the receiver.

"Hello," she said, trying to disguise the fact that she was out of breath. She could hear loud, labored breathing on the other end. The phone display indicated a restricted number. "Who *is* this?"

The creep clicked off. Magnolia gave up on her bath. She wrapped herself in a towel, lay down on her bed, and pulled the duvet to her chin. "This is not happening," she repeated.

The next thing she knew, she'd overslept for the day of *Bebe*'s launch party. Magnolia checked her phone log. She'd managed to snooze through a second call, but again the number wasn't identified. Tommy or Harry—which was worse?

Magnolia grabbed the garment bag of clothes she'd laid out the previous day for this evening and—lucky break—found a taxi to take her to work. Luck's a commodity I could use a little more of, she muttered as she settled herself in the cab. Her cell phone rang. Let me not get hang-ups on this phone, too, she prayed. But the caller offered a cheery hello.

"Ready for the big freak show?" Abbey asked.

"Not my night," Magnolia answered. "I just need to show up and hope for a cataclysm. Any locusts coming our way? You'll be there tonight, right?"

"Well, the thing is, Mags, I'd love to—give you moral support and all—but something's come up, and, well, will you hate me if I miss the Bebelicious party of the year?"

"You won't be missing much. But what's up?" she asked, working to sound casual.

"Tommy," Abbey said.

"Oh, really? Tommy?"

"Magnolia, don't jive me. I know."

What did she know, and when did she know it?

"Yeah, I know," Abbey said. "And thanks, you're the most wonderful friend."

Magnolia didn't know how to respond.

"You there?" Abbey said. "I know that you convinced Tommy to try and reconcile—he told me all about how you insisted he stop by my—make that our—apartment. He was here till two A.M., a perfect gentleman, full of unexpected insights. God, I forgot that's one of the things I love about that man." If Abbey were angry, she was disguising it with enormous bravado.

"Abbey, you have nothing to thank me for," Magnolia said, relief breaking through like sweat. "I hope you guys work things out—if that's what you want."

"I don't know what I want," she admitted, "but we're having dinner tonight. He was sweet yesterday but seemed kind of strung out. I think he's got a lot on his mind."

Could she ask Abbey if Tommy had made calls during his visit? Magnolia could not.

As Magnolia entered the lobby of her office building, she stopped at the newsstand to pick up some magazines. That's when she saw him, pretending to read *The Wall Street Journal.* Magnolia wondered what story he'd fed the security guards to skulk past the front desk, but then a handsome Englishman in a long, black cashmere coat isn't ripe for profiling. To get to her office, Magnolia would need to pass him, and she was too late to duck out and return later. May as well swallow the big pill, she thought, even if I gag.

She walked over to Harry. "I can explain," she said.

"Fine," he said. "Go ahead."

She looked around the crowded lobby. "Magnolia, I'm back!" she heard someone say. "I'll stop by your office later." It was Phoebe, returned from a brief maternity leave and already fitting into her jeans, as if she'd produced a Barbie, not a nine-pound baby. Magnolia noticed that motherhood hadn't prevented her beauty editor from finding time to color her hair the perfect caramel, or that Harry wasn't too upset to give Phoebe an approving glance.

"Obviously, this isn't a good place to talk," Magnolia said to Harry. "You want to come up to my office?"

The scowl on his face said no.

"There's a Starbucks across the street." She had no business arriving late to the 9:30 production meeting. Cameron wouldn't be happy having to deal with Felicity solo. But she followed Harry across the street.

They stared at each other over their coffees.

"Let's cut to the chase," Harry said. "You've really disappointed me. I couldn't sleep all night and I doubt I can work today until you explain yourself. The last thing I need in my life is a woman I can't trust—I've had a string of those."

Magnolia's mind flashed to their last long, luxurious day together over the weekend. It began at MoMA, the Barney's of museums, where she always found the art lovers—with their fine fabrics and well-cobbled shoes—as inspirational as the paintings. After a late afternoon stroll through a few galleries in Chelsea, they walked in the soft rain to Harry's, where he cooked a perfect dinner—grilled tuna, risotto cakes, and snap peas. For dessert, he made crème brûlée. Not only did he own the cute ceramic dishes, he burned the sugar with his own blowtorch.

"You're going to be Torch from now on," Magnolia had said. "Sub-Zero no more."

"Then you're Mistress Torch," he had said. But she wasn't feeling like Mistress Torch right now. More like Mistress Tortured.

"You've got to believe me when I tell you the man you saw was my friend's husband, Tommy O'Toole." Magnolia said, fatigue draining her voice. "He dropped in, shitfaced. There's never been anything between us and never will be."

"The thing is, I wasn't seeing a whole lot of resistance going on there," Harry said. "Close friends? And the look on your face . . ." Harry gulped the last of his coffee. His face was red and his knuckles, white.

"The look on my face?" Magnolia asked. "What do you think my face is saying now?"

"You're angry," he said.

"You got that right," she said, "but I'm feeling disappointed, too. Didn't these past two months teach you to trust me? Can't you just cool off and realize that what you thought you saw wasn't what you thought you saw?" She put her hand on his. He didn't pull away.

Harry gave her an inscrutable look. But at least he said, "I'll try." He got up from the table, leaned over, and gave her a kiss, more of politeness than passion, but a kiss. "I'll think about it," he said as he got up to leave.

Magnolia watched him walk away. Should she ask whether he still planned to come to the *Bebe* launch party? She decided she could live in suspense.

Chapter 19

Not Great, Not Grateful

The Mandarin Oriental was in a glitzy tower that in any other city would rightly be called a vertical mall. Bebe stood in one of its ladies' rooms and twirled, showing off her new dress, which Magnolia recognized from *Harper's Bazaar*. "Magnolia, opinion!" she said. Magnolia remembered the "price available upon request" caption, magazinespeak for "Don't even think about it." In the photo, the ruffled pouf skirt and balloon sleeves made the model's waist even waspier. But Bebe had no waist. She looked like a bundt cake.

"Magnolia?" Bebe repeated, and struggled to undo the tiny buttons the designer had clearly intended to stay fastened up to the wearer's neck. Apparently satisfied with her deep cleavage now on display, Bebe smiled in a way Magnolia had never seen before. My God, she thought. That smile isn't the least demonic. She's not slicing and dicing a soul in sight. If I'm reading her right—Bebe was now shifting from side to side—Bebe Blake is anxious about her launch party and she's insecure about the way she looks. The woman is human!

But she stayed that way only for a second.

"I look fabulous," Bebe declared. "Felicity, have I ever looked better?" She turned to Felicity, who was perched on the ledge of a marble sink. She was trying to attach a brooch to her suit, whose skirt and jacket had rhinestones the size of thumbtacks circling the cuffs and hem like neon bulbs announcing a Times Square attraction.

"Beebsy, you are ravishing, and Magnolia—" Felicity said, talking to Magnolia's reflection in the mirror while she applied coral lipstick, "—you look sweet."

Weeks before, Magnolia entrusted herself to Ruthie and Elizabeth for tonight's styling. "Not too showy," Elizabeth insisted. 'Cause it wasn't Magnolia's show. For the occasion, Elizabeth was wearing a simple gray suit that matched her hair. For Magnolia, Ruthie had come up with an homage to Twiggy—a short, black mink pullover; tight, cropped pants; and black kitten heels. A shame the getup had to be returned the following day, because Magnolia thought she looked quite the minx. A perspiring minx, however. There didn't seem to be air-conditioning on at the hotel. It was October but unusually hot.

"Thanks, Felicity," Magnolia said. She was saved from returning the compliment by Elizabeth's charging into the bathroom with Darlene, whose look for the party recalled Pocahontas. She wore a rust-colored, shearling-lined coat. On her feet were snakeskin sandals whose heavy soles made Darlene appear to be walking with snowshoes.

"Darlene's finished with hair and makeup and they're ready for you two, Bebe and Felicity," Elizabeth barked. "Magnolia, come back in forty-five minutes."

Magnolia walked to the lobby outside the ballroom. On an ebony grand piano, red roses spelled out the *Bebe* logo in an arrangement that might well have been sent by Staten Island's leading crime family. She peeked inside the ballroom. A caterer's assistant was constructing a tower of glazed doughnuts. "One, two three, testing," blasted through the empty room, as the sound crew checked the mikes, while in the back of the room a DJ who called himself Slow Mo—he ruled Williamsburg—was setting up equipment.

"Smile, Foxy," Slow Mo shouted, taking off his earphones. "Life can't be that bad."

Magnolia shot him a grin.

"What's this party for?" Slow Mo asked. He was in his late twenties, had wavy auburn hair, a closely trimmed beard, and a high-voltage smile.

"Just a bunch of magazine people pigging out on free food," Magnolia shouted back.

"No dancing?" Mo said. "You're breaking my heart, Foxy."

Magnolia considered continuing the volley. She'd dated younger, a run of T-shirt designers, aspiring filmmakers, and so many law students she could pass Contracts. But now? She was in a mature relationship. Or was she? Her life was messy enough, she decided, with no Mo. She waved him good-bye, exited the ballroom, and walked down the winding stairway to the blissfully cool lounge on the thirty-fifth floor.

Magnolia settled herself in a buttery leather armchair and took in the Central Park view. Location, location—that was the point of this hotel. Autumn leaves clung to the trees in a medley more opulent than anything the Mandarin Oriental's decorators had imagined. I should be happy to be here, she thought, as she began to sip her martini. Grateful. I could still be writing obits for the Fargo *Forum*, spending my days on the phone to funeral directors.

She was feeling her drink's first tingle of relaxation when she overheard familiar voices. Magnolia turned. Across the room, Jock and Darlene had their heads close and appeared to be making a toast.

"Magnolia" was all she could pick up of their conversation. There was no way to leave without passing them. She paid her tab, and walked toward the lounge's entrance, hoping Jock and Darlene were too involved to notice her.

"Ms. Gold," Jock called out. "Magnolia. We were just saying how this night would never be happening without you."

Right, Magnolia thought. And I am Jackie Onassis's love child.

"You look fabulous, Mags," Darlene said. "Love the fur."

More fabulous than I looked twenty-five minutes ago when you saw me and didn't say a word, Magnolia wondered? "You flatterers," Magnolia said. "Thanks, guys, but you'll have to excuse me."

"No time for a cocktail?" Jock asked.

"Hair," Magnolia tugged a few locks. "And makeup. Elizabeth will kill me if I blow it off." She bolted to the elevator and rode to the ground floor. Breathing heavily, Magnolia walked outside and ducked into Pink, the shirt shop, simply because it was nearly empty.

"May I help you?" said a salesgirl.

If only you could, Magnolia thought. If she were being honest—which in regard to her mental health Magnolia often viewed as an overrated policy—she had to admit that until tonight she hadn't realized how depleted she'd become by the last few weeks. Bebe! Let her jump out a window. With Jock. And forget grateful. In her heart, Magnolia knew what she really wanted was to be great. All-on-her-own, sweat-equity, toast-of-the-town, Englishman-optional great.

She walked out of the store. Dusk was falling. Soon klieg lights would be shooting a loop of comets into the Manhattan sky, and a thousand of Bebe's nearest and dearest would descend from limos and walk the red carpet past flashing cameras into the hotel.

Magnolia rode back up to thirty-six. Elizabeth was pacing.

"Magnolia," Elizabeth said briskly, her face flushed and her silver crew cut as motionless as ever, "Alessandro and Akiko are waiting. You don't want to grace that stage all mousy and shiny."

Elizabeth directed Magnolia to the hair and makeup station, where Akiko was powdering Bebe's face with a big, pink poof. Alessandro looked on, horrified, while Felicity bombed her hair with spray. Bebe and Felicity left the room, and twenty minutes later, Magnolia had been buffed to a gloss.

She walked into the ballroom, which was filling rapidly each time the elevators opened. Waiters circulated with dark red drinks, heavy on the pomegranate juice, which they were forced to call Bebepolitans. There hadn't been a major magazine launch party for at least two years, and tonight's invitation, which arrived in a red leather, leopard-lined box, turned out to be as coveted as a ticket to next week's Yankee–Red Sox series. Bebe, Felicity, and Elizabeth had spent weeks planning the party, including a forty-eight-hour standoff until Bebe abandoned the idea of a stripper pole. Only when Magnolia saw the list of the final invitees two weeks before, did she get a chance to open her mouth.

"You forgot to invite the staff," Magnolia pointed out.

"The whole staff?" Bebe hooted. "I don't even know most of them."

"Bebe, they made the magazine," Magnolia pointed out. "And it's just forty people."

"Forty people! What do they all do, forty people?"

"Now that I think of it, closer to seventy-five with sales and marketing," Magnolia added. "It's only fair." She heard herself whine ever so slightly. "You're inviting your whole staff for *The Bebe Show*." She decided not to bring up the fact that Bebe's maid, driver, herbalist, veterinarian, cook, tarot card reader, and broker also made the cut.

"Okay, no squabbles." Elizabeth said. "We'll squeeze in the staff. But no dates."

"Fair enough," Magnolia agreed.

"Except Magnolia's hottie," Bebe said. "We need guy candy."

Tonight, as she began to roam the room, Magnolia realized that on that count Bebe had been correct—available heterosexual males were in seriously short supply. It was a sad day when Mike McCourt from the *Post* was one of the hotties. He was walking toward her now.

"What do you think of the new issue?" As Mike took a gulp of his drink, a drizzle of red slid down the lapel of his tan corduroy jacket. "Is *Bebe* going to march toward world domination?"

"What do you think?" Magnolia responded, kissing him on the cheek. "Oh, that's right. You won't see the magazine until you leave." *Bebe*'s premiere issue would be handed out with tonight's goody bags.

"You're not sounding over the moon," Mike said. "Shall I take your tone as a critique?"

"Critique-wise . . ." Magnolia cleared her throat. Elizabeth had rehearsed her, knowing she'd be questioned again and again at the party. "I think we've done a superb job of defining *Bebe*'s unique perspective."

"Magnolia, you're talking to me," Mike said. "*En inglés.*"

"It's . . . interesting." Magnolia gave Mike a little smile.

"What does Miss Understatement think is 'interesting' about it?"

"You'll see," Magnolia said. "I'd love to schmooze, Mike, but I think I see Darlene," she added as the crowd thickened. Darlene would be one of the last people she'd want to hang out with tonight, but she didn't trust herself to play at pro level this evening, and she'd be damned if Mike would corner her into a quote she'd regret. She found Fredericka instead.

"I rode up vith Paris Hilton!" Fredericka said. "And isn't that Rosie O'Donnell? Are she and Bebe bosom buddies?"

"Maybe Rosie's her hair and wardrobe consultant."

"This is the oddest crowd," Fredericka said. "That's Bruce Villis, talking to Samuel L. Jackson, no? And that little person? Danny DeVito in drag?"

"Dr. Ruth."

"I think I'll introduce myself to Lindsay Lohan," Fredericka said, and walked off.

Magnolia took stock of her conversational options. The *WWD* reporter circled Bebe, who was draped over Jock. Two major players from Lancôme had caught up with Felicity. Some car magnates flown in from Detroit eyeballed the girls from the art department. Natalie Simon was chatting with Charlotte Stone. Magnolia made the round with each group. An hour later, hoarse from shrieking over Slow Mo's earsplitting sound, she gravitated toward a group from her staff as if it were running a halfway house.

"To our queen in exile," said Cameron, lifting a glass. "Long may she reign."

"Here, here," the others said, clinking. "To Magnolia!" Cam got grabbed by one of the publicists. This left Magnolia with the women.

"There's a serious dearth of straight men here," Ruthie observed. "Except that one over there talking to Phoebe. It's not fair. Why does our staff's only wife and mommy attract the best-looking guy?"

Magnolia swiveled to see Phoebe. In tonight's four-inch heels the beauty director, who was almost six feet tall barefoot, loomed not just above most of the other women but a good number of the men. This included the object of Ruthie's praise, who Magnolia couldn't see in the crowd. She extricated herself and walked toward Phoebe, who smiled and waved.

"You look super!" Phoebe shouted over heads as Magnolia approached. "Terrific party. I just saw Kelly Ripa. And isn't that Barbara Walters? She's my nana's age, but she looks amazing. Don't you think?" She directed her question to the person who was hovering near her, whose back was still toward Magnolia.

Magnolia got to within eight feet of Phoebe and froze.

"I'd love for you to meet my boss, Magnolia Gold," she said to her admirer, motioning Magnolia to move closer.

"Actually, Magnolia and I are acquainted," the man said, leaning closer to Phoebe than was necessary. "Rather intimately."

"Ah, okay," Phoebe mumbled, and looked from the man to Magnolia. "I'm going to grab another Bebepolitan. Lovely to meet you, Harry." Phoebe glided away on her elegant stork legs.

"See you later, luv," he said. "Saucy girl, your Phoebe," he said to Magnolia.

"Glad you could make it," Magnolia asked. She suddenly felt so hot she wanted to rip off her mink top and stomp on it.

"Did you really think I'd miss this little drinks party?" Harry said. "Seasonal highlight and all."

"So you're still not over last night?" she said.

"I don't know that I am," he said. The face that looked so handsome just days before was twisted in a snarl, and Magnolia could swear that his hairline had receded by another half inch.

"I can't deal with this right now," Magnolia said. "I want to talk, but our conversation is going to have to wait, Harry. This isn't an easy night for me. I'm sure you get that."

"But what could be more important than us?" he said.

From a distant place in the densely packed ballroom, Magnolia could hear a heavily amped country western artist—LeAnn Rimes? Faith Hill?—singing an upbeat ballad over the room's noise. Out of the corner of her eye, she spotted Jock and Darlene, who were now standing only four feet away, and if she wasn't being paranoid, she could swear they were listening to her with Harry.

"Magnolia, you're not answering me," Harry was almost shouting. "We still need to talk about you and that asshole ripping each other's clothes off."

Just as she had the impulse to throw her Bebepolitan in his face, Magnolia saw someone loping in her direction. Elizabeth all but tackled her and simultaneously gave Harry a chilly look. She had that gift.

"Magnolia, stage!" she snapped. "We're starting the presentation." Leaving Harry standing with his mouth half open, Elizabeth corralled Jock and Darlene and steered them, along with Magnolia, toward the front of the room, where Felicity was already waiting. "Don't move a muscle, any of you, while I find Bebe," Elizabeth said, signaling for the Nashville singer to continue.

Jock and Darlene stood aside while Magnolia tried to calm herself with breath after deep breath. "That asshole Harry, that asshole Harry," she repeated silently as she followed Elizabeth.

Ten minutes later Elizabeth returned, frowning. "Has Bebe swung by here?" she said. "Where could that woman be?" The party was called for seven to ten, although it hadn't got rolling until eight. It was now past nine, and Magnolia knew that Elizabeth was worried that guests would soon start to leave.

"Let me check around for her," Magnolia answered, just to be able to break away from Jock, Darlene, and Felicity. She'd passed Bebe more than twenty minutes before, holding court by a photograph of Frank Sinatra. Magnolia stopped there first. No Bebe. She walked down the stairs to look in the lounge. Bebe was sitting on the floor next to a glass sculpture that appeared to have been liberated from an ice carnival.

"What's up, Magnolia?" Bebe's head was in Slow Mo's lap, an empty champagne bottle next to the two of them.

"Foxy!" Mo said. "Bebe here knows how to party."

"Bebe here has a speech to give," Magnolia said. "Enough with the liquid courage, Bebe. *Achtung.*"

"Magnolia, Magnolia," Bebe said. "Calm down. Itsabeautifulnight." She drained the champagne like a bottle of Snapple.

"Mo, help me get her upstairs," Magnolia said. Mo stood up, and Bebe—still joined to him—did the same. As they began to walk, Bebe tripped. Magnolia got on her other side, and the three of them staggered to the elevator, Bebe hiccuping loudly.

"Gotta tinkle," Bebe said when the door opened on thirty-six.

Magnolia walked her to the ladies' room. As Bebe left the stall, she pulled up her skirt, took off her thong, and dropped it on the floor.

"Can't stand this damn string up my butt," she said.

Magnolia waited for Bebe to put her undies in the trash, which she did not do. Magnolia decided not to rise to that occasion. She took Bebe's arm, and together they walked into the ballroom and over to Jock, Darlene, and Felicity. Elizabeth motioned the singer to finish her number and lined up the five of them to go onstage. Jock welcomed the crowd and handed the mike to Bebe, who took center stage.

Elizabeth had written a seven-minute speech for Bebe, who was supposed to thank Jock, Felicity, and Magnolia, then hand the mike to Darlene, who'd cue the start of a $75,000 video that featured behind-the-scenes shots of Bebe "working" on the magazine. They'd rehearsed this drill six ways to Sunday. At the end, a velvet curtain would rise, revealing the premiere issue's cover.

"Hello, out there," Bebe said to the crowd. "We having fun yet? All I can say is you're going to love my magazine and . . ." She stopped. The crowd waited. "All I can say is . . ." She stopped again. The room became still. "All I can say is—" this time she found words to finish the sentence—"we have a great goody bag."

This wasn't the script.

"I'm not shitting you," Bebe continued. "Hey, I want to show you. Jock, where's a fucking bag?"

Jock looked confused. Elizabeth rushed to the stage with one of the red Coach *Bebe* totes. As the video started to roll, Bebe pulled out the gifts, one by one, and announced each. "Here we have a Bebe doll. Great knockers, huh?" She pointed toward her own. "Leopard cashmere slippers!" She threw her stilettos into the crowd and put the slippers on. "A stuffed kitten wearing a *Bebe* T-shirt! Looks like Hell! Bacardi raspberry rum? By the way, did everyone here have enough to drink? An itsy-bitsy red Canon camera! A sterling silver choker . . ."

To appreciative howls from the crowd, who were now chanting, "Be-be. Be-be. Be-be," she held up every piece of loot. Someone cued the video, but no one even noticed it or heard its worshipful voice-over, which was drowned out by the shouts.

Bebe was still unsteady on her feet. Magnolia considered the outcome if Bebe, now going commando under her dress, slipped. Magnolia tried to get her eye, to tell her to stop.

"'Scuse me, but Deputy Gold has something to say to all of you. Magnolia, you adorable thing, get your rear up here."

Magnolia walked forward and took the mike. "The magazine, Bebe. Don't forget to show everyone the issue! Hold it up!"

"Oh, the magazine," Bebe said, emitting an audible belch as she lifted a copy of *Bebe.* But by this point, the crowd—Harry included, arms linked with an assistant to one of the *Access Hollywood* reporters—was stampeding toward the door to receive goody bags.

"Stay, everyone," Magnolia implored, shouting as loud as she could. "We'd love to show you the magazine." But no one was paying attention to her. Not even Jock, Darlene, or Elizabeth. They were all glaring at Bebe.

As the ballroom emptied, Bebe linked arms with Magnolia. "I think that went rather well, Gold," she said. "Don't you?" Bebe's makeup was smudged and her dress, slightly ripped. At that moment, Magnolia wished she could dig deep and find some motherly instincts. What would *her* mother advise? If you can't say something nice, don't say anything at all. Maybe the advice was from Thumper in *Bambi* and not her mother. No matter.

She put her arm around Bebe's ample waist, and together they walked out the door, Bebe's leopard cashmere slippers padding softly on the empty ballroom floor.

Chapter 20

Cupcake?
I Don't Think So

"What's the latest from Planet Bebe?" Abbey asked. Given the trifecta of her and Tommy breaking up again, Harry's dwindling attentions—apparently holding a grudge, he hadn't called in a week—and Magnolia's thirty-eighth birthday, Abbey had decided to underwrite a beauty blitz in her honor. They were starting at the Exhale spa on a sunny November morning, waiting for massages in a dim Japanese-serene room.

"The technical term is, 'It sucks,'" Magnolia replied. "Bebe and Felicity flew to the West Coast, and Cam and I have been closing the issue through fax, phone, and e-mail. When it's just the two of us, for whole minutes it's bliss. Then I snap back to real life."

"Is Bebe still in the crosshairs of the columnists?" Abbey asked.

"Not at all," Magnolia said. "You'd think it would work against you to go full moon wacky at your launch party, but the magazine indus-try's collective memory has the depth of a pore. Bad behavior and bad results rarely correlate. Elizabeth had her send tickets for *The Bebe Show* to all the reporters—everyone's mother's a groupie. Since then it's been a big, wet kiss. She wound up on the cover of *Us,* and now the premiere *Bebe*'s almost sold out."

"She isn't haunted by the *Post* referring to her as Burpin' Bebe?"

"She'll probably brag about it in an editor's letter," Magnolia said.

Magnolia took out her *Times* and began to read aloud. "Get this. 'A report on November second about the wedding of Sarina Balfour-Smythe and Heath Farina included an erroneous account of the bride's education, which she supplied. Ms. Balfour-Smythe, the new publisher of Scarborough Magazines' *Dizzy,* did not graduate from Stanford University or receive a master's in business administration from Dartmouth University or a Ph.D. in anthropology from Yale University. Although she attended Stanford summer school, her degree is from the University of Wisconsin Oshkosh. The *Times* regrets that it did not corroborate the credentials before publishing the report.'"

"I'll bet they do," Abbey said.

"Why don't more people get outed for their whoppers," Magnolia said. "Darlene tells everyone she got a perfect SAT."

"What amazes me is a forty-year-old woman is still lying about her SATs," Abbey said.

"I take heart that as long as we both shall live, Darlene will always be older than I am," Magnolia said. Lately, no matter the situation, Magnolia defaulted to the subject of age, her brain trilling, "Thirty-eight! Thirty-eight!" like a taunting parrot. She'd started to ask new questions. Am I too old to show my navel? No, not as long as my abs stay flat, she decided. Is it time to start dressing like a lady senator? The world will reward me if I don't. Will I ever again be carded? Not likely. And the extra credit question: Should I harvest my eggs? Next!

Magnolia would be Googling a stray fact, and suddenly her fingers were researching the age of other editors. She was relieved to discover how many were older than she—a whole crop was born in 1964. But combing through the personals, she found herself wanting to throw a meatball at guys like "Genetically Swedish/Emotionally Italian SWM, 39," who only wants to hear from women thirty-five and younger.

Magnolia opened her *Post*. She stopped at a photograph of the *Vogue* soccer team, in fitted T-shirts emblazoned with their motto: We're secretly judging you. They trounced the Dazzlers. They could do with a better slogan than "*Dazzle* will beat you to a frazzle." Scary was rarely at the Condé Nast level, no matter the game.

Just as the New Age music began to give Magnolia a headache, her masseuse beckoned. Inside an immaculate massage room, Magnolia inhaled the lavender aroma, stripped, and slid between fine white cotton sheets.

"Any spots giving you trouble?" the masseuse asked, as she began to knead Magnolia's shoulder with a luscious lotion that smelled faintly of ginger and grapefruit. Magnolia could feel Bebe in her neck, Felicity in her left hip, and Harry in her lower back. For the past week she'd been hobbling around like Toulouse-Lautrec.

"Everywhere," she admitted.

"I want you to go to a place that makes you feel relaxed," the masseuse said in a gentle voice. Her old office, Magnolia wondered? Nope. There must be a law against thinking about work during a massage. Her living room with the dogs beside her? Better.

"Now take someone special with you to this place," the masseuse directed, as she began to banish the stiffness in Magnolia's neck.

You even need a date for a massage! She closed her eyes but could visualize no one with her. Definitely not Harry. She was still furious at him for making such a big deal of the Tommy incident and goading her into a spat observed by Jock and Darlene. He and Genetically Swedish could go to a singles bar together.

"Are you beginning to unwind?" the masseuse asked as Magnolia started to float into a zone near sleep, savoring every long, smooth stroke on each thirty-eight-year-old muscle group. Fifty minutes later she opened her eyes.

"Didn't want to wake you," the masseuse whispered, handing

Magnolia the thick terry robe she'd worn into the room. "You were totally out."

Was this sorceress a masseuse or an anesthesiologist? All Magnolia knew was she felt mercifully calm, as if her tension had been laid on the chair like a worn-out coat. She thanked her and dressed slowly, not wanting to abruptly reenter reality. In the outer lobby, Abbey looked similarly tranquil, but not too mellow to ask, "Ready for lunch?"

Crossing the street and walking along Central Park South and over to Madison, they entered the impeccably lit Barney's. They always stopped first at the jewelry displays—Abbey, for professional reasons, and Magnolia, because in a faraway bazaar, whenever she was tempted to purchase a bauble, she did the Barney's test, trying to imagine the treasure displayed under glass with just a few other choice pieces. If she could see it at Barney's, she rarely suffered buyer's remorse.

Ten minutes later, she and Abbey rode the elevator to Fred's, the store's crowded café, took a table amid the Black AmEx card crowd, and ordered their usual chopped salads. Today they were having them with champagne.

"To Magnolia!" Abbey said. "To the best year of your life. May it only get better."

"Amen," Magnolia said. "And to you, Abbey—to getting through this rotten Tommy stretch with unbelievable grace."

Abbey and Magnolia raced through their salads, and the waiter approached with a tiny fudge cake, which Magnolia was pleased to see arrived with only one sparkler and two forks. "Make a wish," Abbey insisted. "A secret wish."

A better man? A better job? Both, definitely, but not in that order. Bebe's hostile takeover was bothering her more than being disappointed by Harry.

Abbey handed her a tiny box wrapped in pale gray tissue and tied with yellow ribbon. Inside were earrings with yellow jade teardrops suspended from clusters of tiny gray pearls and turquoise stones.

"Abbey, gorgeous," Magnolia said, replacing her small diamond studs with the exquisite pair. "I adore them." The yellow jade reflected her amber highlights; the turquoise made her green eyes greener. "Thank you!" She gave Abbey a big hug.

"A Nolita boutique ordered them for Christmas, but you have the originals," Abbey said.

Ten minutes later, as they got in the taxi to go to Think Pink, Abbey's phone rang, which reminded Magnolia that hers had been strangely mute for hours, except for an early call from her parents. She removed it from her bag and saw why—Exhale required clients to silence their cells and Magnolia had forgotten to turn hers back on. When she did so, there were four messages. Three were from Bebe with variations on "Where the hell are you, Gold? We've got to talk. Very, very important. *Hasta pronto.* Divine weather in L.A. At the pool. New bikini."

The fifth was from Harry. "Cupcake, I really need to see you," he said. "I'm such an arse. Tail between my legs. Call me." Magnolia felt a twinge return in her back. Cupcake? I don't think so, she thought.

"Lots of birthday greetings?" Abbey asked as Magnolia clicked her phone shut.

"My parents," Magnolia said. "And Bebe."

"What about Dirty Harry?"

"Not a word," Magnolia lied. She didn't want to spoil a perfect day by discussing him. "Which is just as well. He might be somebody's Mr. Right—just not mine."

By five o'clock, afternoon darkness hung in the air. Magnolia walked home, careful not to smudge her newly red toes. She opened her cards. "Another year older?" Cam's read "*Crappe diem.*" She changed into white silk pajamas sent by her parents, settled in front of her fireplace, and started a novel. The only thing that can make this evening better is a big piece of leftover cake from my office party, she decided, and I'm not going to feel the least bit guilty about eating dessert twice in one day. Tomorrow, starvation. As she walked into her kitchen, however, the intercom sounded.

"Gentleman to see you," Manuel said.

Not Tommy! Magnolia gritted her teeth.

"Mr. James," Manuel continued. "Send him up?"

Magnolia hesitated. She'd managed to get through the day without any spikes in her emotional EKG. With Harry, who knew? Still, he'd arrived.

"Yes, send him up, please," Magnolia responded.

Standing in her doorway, he looked taller than she remembered. A man always looks taller when he carries a Tiffany bag.

"For you," he said, kissing her lightly on the lips.

"Take your coat?" Magnolia asked, aware that she sounded as formal as a fusty maiden aunt. At least she hadn't called him sir.

"Here's a better idea," Harry said. "I take off my own coat, you open this little gift, and then we play kiss and make up in your bedroom." He placed his coat on the bench and handed her the small blue bag. It felt light in her hand.

They sat down on the bench. His thigh touched hers. She pulled the box out of the bag and slowly unwrapped the white silk bow, carefully placing it on a table. She opened the box and fingered the blue felt bag.

Magnolia pulled out a shiny sterling silver cuff half covered with an ornate golden blossom. She gasped.

"Tiffany calls it their Magnolia bracelet," Harry said.

How many times had she noticed Tiffany's reliable upper-corner-of-page-three *Times* ads and admired this very bracelet advertised? Every time she saw the photograph—or wandered through the store and casually tried on the real thing, hoping the salespeople hadn't grown to recognize her—she coveted the bracelet, and, twice, she'd almost bought it. But where was that flutter of excitement tonight?

"Thank you, Harry," she said. "You have the most magnificent taste." That much was true.

"Isn't it gorgeous?" Harry said, taking the bracelet out of her hand. "Here, Cupcake, put it on. It looks so beautiful on your wrist."

She had to agree, as she twisted the silver and gold bracelet to catch the foyer's dim light. But the ad called "Magnolia" a cuff. If she accepted this gift, she'd be shackling herself to a relationship she knew in her gut would never be right. Maybe she was having a *Blink* moment she'd later regret, but she didn't want this gift, not from Harry. As he took her wrist, she pulled back and stood up.

"Really, thank you so much," she said, removing the cuff. "It's a hugely extravagant present. But I don't think so, Harry." Magnolia began to choke up.

He looked at her. A tear fell on the sleeve of her silk pajamas. "I know I've acted like a fool, Magnolia," he said. "But let's just forget about that." He stepped forward.

She raised one palm to block him.

"Let's talk about it," he said. "I'm willing to overlook all that business with Tommy."

"There's nothing to say, Harry. Except that it just doesn't feel right. Let's not make this more difficult than it needs to be. I've had my season's fill of scenes." Magnolia carefully placed the bracelet in the felt bag, the box, and then the bag. "We're finished."

"I'd like to know where I've gone so terribly wrong, Magnolia?"

"Let's see," she said. "Talk about blame the victim—you made me feel like a hooker when my friend's husband came on to me. You wouldn't see reason when I tried to explain. You started carrying on in front of my boss and publisher at *Bebe*'s party and I see how you look at other women. But a lot of it's me. With Bebe at the magazine, I'm stepping around land mines every day—I'm not going to make any man very happy right now."

As she said it, she knew she and Harry were just a miniseries, not a hit that would go into eternal syndication. "Harry, I like you." She decided not to admit that even a week ago, she thought "love" might be a more apt word. "But I'm getting too old to be in relationships that I know won't work."

"I see," he said. "I suppose this is some sort of womanly coming-of-age rite." He snickered and picked up his coat from the bench.

Magnolia handed him the bag.

"You know, I thought Englishwomen were batty. But you Americans are nuts."

For several minutes after Harry closed the door behind him, Magnolia was still standing in the same spot, feeling the special burn fueled by disappointment. She'd like to have a man in her life, preferably *the* man. But at least she was smart enough not to trick herself into staying with the wrong one.

Where was I, she thought. Ah, on the way to the kitchen. But nothing now seemed less appealing than leftover cake. She returned to her chair, threw another log on the fire, and stared at the flames. Lola brought over her squeaky mouse, which Magnolia threw across the room. The dog scampered off and settled down for a good long chew. Magnolia reopened her book and read the first page three times. She couldn't remember a word.

The phone rang. Magnolia welcomed the intrusion.

"Gold!" Bebe said. "Could you be any harder to get hold of? Why didn't you call me back? I said it was important."

"That you did, Bebe," Magnolia said, subdued. "I'm so sorry. Did you want to change a line on the cover again? Can you hang on a minute? My files are in the other room."

"Don't be an ass. It's not the magazine."

"Oh?"

"It's a delivery."

Magnolia was about to mention that it was her birthday and she'd just broken up with Harry—she wasn't in the mood to play messenger girl—but decided she'd let it pass. "A delivery? You want me to pick something *up*?"

"No, just stay put. Gotta go." Bebe clicked off without even thanking her for sticking around on a Saturday night. But what difference did it make? She was in for the evening anyway. Maybe a herd of goats would arrive for the weekend and camp out until Bebe moved them to the farm she was buying upstate. Perhaps they'd be good company.

Magnolia settled herself again in her chair and started channel surfing. She could at least manage a movie. As she tried to decide between *The Way We Were* and *Sleepless in Seattle*, however, the doorbell rang. Had Harry been standing in her hallway all this time, pleading for a second chance? He had more stamina than she.

Magnolia looked through the peephole. All she could see was an enormous bunch of yellow roses.

"Special delivery," said a familiar British accent. Only it wasn't Harry's.

"My good friend Bebe Blake asked me to deliver these to you," the voice said. "If you'll open up. Oh, and from both of us, a very happy birthday."

Was that a Hugh Grant impersonator standing in her hallway?

Chapter 21

Hugh Grant and the Glamazon Girls

"I looked through the peephole and there he was," Magnolia repeated before an expanding circle of editors and designers crowding her office and overflowing into the hall. She felt as if she were lip-synching a stump speech—she'd already told Abbey and her parents the whole story—but it wasn't half bad to revisit life at the red-hot center of the universe.

"'Care for a short drive?' he said." Magnolia tried to get the accent right.

"'Mind if I change?' I answered."

"'Well, shoes might be in order,' he said, 'but as far as the rest goes, you look quite swish. I'll be Tracy to your Hepburn.' So there I was, in my jammies—they were fancy, but I was wearing zilch underneath—and off I went. We got in a normal black town car, nothing slimy like a stretch. 'Spot of tea? Champagne? Gatorade?' he said. I fixated on his eye crinkles, the compact body, that voice. Bull's-eye look-alike. Then he handed me a red envelope."

Magnolia took a large gulp of her coffee as Fredericka, Ruthie,

Phoebe, Sasha, and the others listened attentively. Cameron, she noticed, walked away when she got to the part about no panties.

"It said, 'Yes, it's Hugh. You think I'd send a fake? P.S. You can have him—not my type. Bebe.'"

"Bebe!" Fredericka hooted. "Talk about a power present. Vat ever became of giving a nice scarf?"

"Now do we have to think she's adorable and kind?" Sasha asked, but Magnolia ignored her—the truth was, much of Bebe was adorable and kind—and continued to report on the drive, which lasted fifty-five minutes, exactly the length of a shrink session, but proved far more therapeutic than any she'd ever experienced.

"We chatted about how much he loved going on Bebe's telly hour," Magnolia said. "And he wanted to know if when American women told you what they want in the bedroom—down to the millimeter, in full sentences, practically with charts and graphs—they're being bossy or helpful. Both, I assured him."

Magnolia decided to edit out the portion when she gave Hugh the CliffsNotes of her most recent battered romance. "Did I do the right thing to break up?" she'd asked. "Did I blow it with Harry? He's such a hothead."

"Stay away from English public school blokes," Hugh cautioned. "Every one's a pack of twitchy nerves. Too much bad mommy/good nanny going on, yours truly included. Find yourself a red-blooded American and don't be fooled by those Ivy League almost-Brits. They're stunt doubles for the crew who went to Oxford with me."

"Oxford?" Magnolia asked. No wonder she'd always liked Hugh Grant. Without a brain, a penis didn't count for much. "What did you study there?"

"English," he said.

"Me, too," she said, although she left the Big Ten university out of it. For a moment on that birthday-that-trumped-all-others, Magnolia let herself wish that Hugh wasn't a mere cameo in her life, and that her charms might be sufficient to make him look at her like something beyond a Make-A-Wish recipient. But then he got out, giving her a quick embrace as he brushed both cheeks with his lips, leaving Magnolia clutching her arms around herself, as much to cover up her nipples as to keep herself warm. The frosty November evening drove her inside, and she immediately started regretting that she'd kvetched to Hugh Grant—Hugh-fucking-Grant—about her boyfriend problems. Idiot!

As she rode up in the elevator, she considered the possibility that she'd hallucinated the whole thing. When she opened the door, however, and saw three dozen long-stemmed yellow roses abandoned in her foyer, she smiled and laughed out loud. At least six times that evening and throughout Sunday, Magnolia left effusive messages of thanks for Bebe—but never got through.

Magnolia switched her head back to Monday and the colleagues waiting for her grand finale. "He gave me a kiss on both cheeks and saw me to my door. . . ." Magnolia told the group. "I floated until bedtime."

Magnolia could see her audience deflate. "Meeting adjourned," she said in a chipper tone. "I'm only sorry I didn't bring my digital camera to document the whole event."

After her colleagues scattered, Cam returned. "Big birthday, huh?" he said with a sly smile. Magnolia suddenly felt like a fool that Cam had witnessed any part of her soliloquy.

"Thanks for the card," she said.

"Sorry I didn't have it delivered by Brad Pitt," he said, pushing his wire-rimmed glasses up on his nose, a gesture which made him look about ten—and adorable, Magnolia couldn't help but notice. "Any emergencies in the last ten minutes I should know about?"

"Nope," Magnolia said, glad they were switching off her private life. "Have to read all these proofs—then I'm meeting Darlene and Bebe at Glamazon." Which, of course, Cam already knew.

"Why do you suppose Darlene wants you there?" he asked. Bebe and Darlene had been doing every ad call together—exactly what Magnolia expected. She'd never loved making sales calls, particularly when Darlene and her clients gossiped like college roommates. Still, not being invited was another reminder of her grand unimportance.

"Because then she can blame me when we don't get the account?" Magnolia suggested.

At the end of the calendar year, Glamazon—the new prestige cosmetic line—had found some extra funds in its budget and invited three magazines to a bake-off for the prize of a few choice ad pages. Darlene didn't know who the other contenders were, only that the command performance for *Bebe* was scheduled for two in the afternoon. The plan was for Bebe, Magnolia, and Darlene to converge at Glamazon's headquarters.

"No prep needed," Darlene had said. "Just look sharp and bring your big brain. Meet at one forty-five."

Magnolia rode uptown, and arrived by 1:35. Plopping down on a stiff suede chair in the austere reception room, and unable to bear the thought of pulling out the *Bebe* she'd stowed in her bag, she looked for something else to read. Five fresh copies of *InStyle*—and only *InStyle*—were fanned out on the low limestone table in front of her. The publisher of *InStyle* obviously had had an appointment this morning and, when the receptionist wasn't looking, chucked whatever magazines had been displayed and left her copies in their place. Magnolia opened the issue to the Editor's Note, always the first page she read in another magazine, and considered what it would be like to have a position where she'd be paid to go to the couture shows in Paris and Milan, as this editor clearly was.

As she was reading, her head facing down, the publisher of *Marie Claire* and Susannah Slutsky, her associate publisher, walked past her. Magnolia slunk an inch lower and pulled *InStyle* close to her face.

"Yes!" Susannah said, high-fiving her boss. "That went *well*. Who do you suppose our competition is besides the *InStyle* ladies we saw leaving?"

"I'd guess *Lucky* or *Bebe*."

"*Bebe*, what a sorry excuse for a magazine," Susannah said. "Did you catch the looks on the Glamazon women when we did our page-by-page *Marie Claire/Bebe* comparison?"

"Priceless," she said. "Hey, gotta pee. Leave behind the magazines and I'll meet you downstairs, okay?"

Susannah turned toward the table to swap *InStyle* for *Marie Claire*. "Magnolia Gold!" she said, startled. Far fewer than six degrees of separation connected most people in the industry—Magnolia and Susannah had worked together years before at *Glamour*. "I've been meaning to call you. How's it going?"

"Dandy, Susannah, and you?" Magnolia asked, deciding not to rise and greet her with the customary hug.

"So I gather *Bebe*'s up for this account?" Susannah said.

"Isn't that a copy of it in your hand?" Magnolia asked.

"Oh," Susannah said, as if she were surprised to discover she was holding it. "I was just telling my boss how super the magazine looks."

"Really, Susannah?" Magnolia asked. "Because 'sorry excuse' sounded like scant praise."

Susannah's jaw opened and shut like a mechanical dog's. She and Magnolia took each other's measure.

"You're too funny!" Susannah said. Without leaving her magazines behind, she racewalked to the elevator door, which opened to dislodge Darlene. The two gave each other big smooches as Susannah ducked inside.

"Susannah Slutsky, that two-faced bitch," Darlene said, lowering her booming voice. "Can't trust one thing she says. Bebe arrived yet?" Darlene smoothly traded the *InStyle*s for *Bebe*, and walked over to the Glamazon receptionist with an engaging smile. "We're here for our two o'clock," she said. "Darlene Knudson. Publisher of *Bebe*."

"We'll call you when we're ready, thanks," the receptionist said. "Water?"

"Sure, great," Darlene said. "You're a sweetie." Darlene accepted the Evian, parked herself, and shot Magnolia a cranky look. "Where's Bebe?" she half whispered.

Magnolia shrugged. "Haven't heard from her."

"Well, Consuelo is a stickler for punctuality," Darlene said, pulling out her BlackBerry and trying Bebe's number. "She doesn't even have her phone on!" Annoyed, she started making another call.

"Ms. Everett will see you now," the receptionist announced five minutes later.

Darlene and Magnolia walked into Consuelo Everett's office, which matched the reception room beige for beige, as did Consuelo herself, from her shorn, honeyed hair brushed away from her chiseled face, to her vertigo-inducing buff suede boots. Consuelo walked toward the door to embrace Darlene, as did her twenty-five-year-old twin daughters, Consuelo Jr., and Sophia, who trailed behind her like bridesmaids.

"Bebe will be here in ten minutes—she just phoned from her car to say she's on her way," Darlene lied. "You know Magnolia Gold, right?"

Consuelo and her daughters offered gummy smiles and nods of hello.

"Consuelo, you've never looked better!" Darlene said with the enthusiasm usually reserved for someone recovering from major cosmetic surgery. "Thank you not just for your support"—Glamazon had eight pages and a potent scent strip in the launch issue—"but for joining us last week at Canyon Ranch. I appreciate how difficult your schedule is, and how hard it is to get away."

"I have you to thank," Consuelo said. "Lost five pounds." She pulled out the waistband of her size 0 café au lait leather pants.

"Shall we start with a PowerPoint, then," Darlene said, as she turned on her laptop. "Welcome to Bebe-world," the presentation began, narrated in Bebe's nasal voice. "*Bebe* is like no other magazine. It's where American women learn to take charge of their lives." The images showed Bebe playing with Hell, driving her red Porsche along the Pacific Coast Highway, interviewing Russell Crowe. "One of the things I've learned in life is that bravado can take you a long way. In fact, it can take you all the way." The images continued. Bebe skydiving, Bebe swinging on a trapeze, Bebe flying a plane.

Magnolia had already seen the presentation, created by Darlene's marketing director. What connection it had to the lives of *Bebe*'s readers she'd yet to determine.

The PowerPoint concluded with a shot of the cover accompanied by Marvin Gaye singing, "What's Going On." "You can see that *Bebe* captures the spirit of a bold woman, the kind everyone wants to become," Darlene intoned. "The kind of buyer Glamazon has in mind for Consuelo, its new fragrance, and its skin-care line." Darlene looked pleased. As she began to unroll the heart of her sales pitch, however, there was a persistent knock.

"Enter," Consuelo said. The receptionist stuck in her head.

"Excuse me, Ms. Everett, but there's a woman here who insists on seeing you and she won't tell me—"

Bebe shouldered her way past the young receptionist and walked toward the round glass table where everyone was seated. "Damn gridlock," she said, as she threw off a sleeveless black coat that appeared to be made of monkey fur. She deposited the garment on the edge of Consuelo's pristine desk.

"Bebe, I'd like you to meet Consuelo Everett," Darlene said.

"Hey, Connie," Bebe said, offering the executive her hand and a grin. "So what do you think of my magazine?"

"Well, Bebe, we were just getting acquainted with it," Consuelo answered, leaning forward with her elbows on the table, her long, French-manicured fingers crossed over one another, which gave Magnolia a close-up of Consuelo's hunky, canary diamond solitaire. "You couldn't have arrived at a more auspicious time."

"Suspicious?" Bebe asked. "Of what?"

"Auspicious, Bebe," Consuelo said. "I was wondering why you believe Glamazon belongs in your magazine."

"Come again?" Bebe asked.

"Our products, Consuelo parfum, Glamazon exfoliators, and age-defying eye enhancers—how do we know the *Bebe* reader will embrace them?" Consuelo asked evenly.

Bebe stared at Consuelo as if she'd just noticed she had a large mole on her nose.

Darlene jumped in. "I can answer that. We know our reader's an upscale shopper—she buys more department store brands than drugstore, she's young, she's sophisticated, and she has a significant disposable income, $76,000. She's Glamazon all the way."

What rot, Magnolia thought. We know nothing. We don't even have final numbers on how well the first issue sold. The readers could all shop with food stamps.

"I appreciate that, Darlene," Consuelo said, "but—"

Bebe woke up. "When you buy *Bebe* you're buying me, the complete Bebe Blake experience," she asserted with conviction. "I stand for independence. And don't your cosmetics?" As she leaned toward Consuelo, the woman leaned back ever so slightly.

"Well, I wouldn't put it that way," said one of the matching daughters.

Bebe and Darlene began talking over each other in increasingly shrill tones. Magnolia tried to follow both conversations at once, but it was as if they'd switched to Zulu. All she could pick out were the occasional buzz words like "must buy" and, from Bebe, "dog doo." Then she heard her name spoken.

"Magnolia, would *Lady*'s reader have purchased Glamazon?" Consuelo asked. "From what I hear, those subscribers have been sent the magazine." All eyes turned to her.

"Glamazon's new," Magnolia answered, "so I can't quote you hard facts, but we know the *Lady* reader always regarded high-end cosmetics as an affordable indulgence she felt she deserved. I can compare to, say, Chanel. The *Lady* reader couldn't, frankly, afford the clothes or the bags, but she was a huge consumer of Chanel No. 5, the lipsticks, and the nail polish. I'm positive the analogy would extend to Glamazon."

Consuelo looked satisfied. Darlene, Magnolia thought, looked relieved. Bebe looked radioactive.

"Chanel No. 5 is for tight asses," Bebe said, scowling. "Wouldn't wear it to a pig roast."

Magnolia saw Darlene roll her eyes, although she was sure Consuelo and her daughters did not. They were fixated on Bebe. Darlene shot up.

"Isn't she hilarious, our Bebe?" Darlene said to Consuelo. "That's what we love about her, complete and unbridled candor. I'm going to be following up by phone this afternoon." Darlene looked at her watch. "Two forty-five? We've eaten up way too much of your time. *Muchos, muchos gracias.*" With that, Darlene herded Bebe out of the room, and Magnolia followed.

Riding to the office, Magnolia decided not to pierce the silence with in-person thanks to Bebe for her birthday gift. Darlene stared out one window, and Bebe, the other. Magnolia began to imagine the amusing recap of the meeting she'd be able to give Cam. Then it dawned on her—a bad meeting was not necessarily good news, especially not for her. No one talked for the rest of the ride.

"Damage control, damage control." Magnolia muttered as she rang Jock's office after she returned. If she got to him immediately, she could offer him her own carefully crafted summary—witty but damning—of how Bebe had blown the ad sales call and how she, Magnolia Gold, had tried to save the day. Score: Magnolia, 15; Bebe, love.

"Any chance of getting a little time with the man?" she asked Elvira, Jock's gatekeeper. "Fifteen minutes?"

"And the purpose of the meeting is?" Elvira asked, reflected power oozing through the phone line.

Manipulation? Retaliation? Garden-variety ass-saving? "Just a Bebe update," Magnolia answered.

"He's got a heavy schedule for the next week, and then there's a trip to Shanghai," Elvira replied. Magnolia could hear her making blowing sounds as if she were drying her nails. "How about a week from Friday at three forty? Oops—he'll be off to Key Largo." The season had arrived for the Sun God to go south on weekends.

"The following Monday?" Elvira suggested. "Ten-twenty?"

By then the Glamazon decision would have been announced—not to *Bebe*'s advantage, on that Magnolia would bet Biggie's best bone—and her vigorous self-defense would be moot. "Elvira, please call me if there's a cancellation," Magnolia said, knowing it would never happen. "Even better, ask him if he couldn't squeeze me in, okay?" So much for having showered Elvira with the cosmetics she'd asked Phoebe to assemble for her birthday last summer. She may as well have given the grab bag of Bobbi Brown and Lancôme products—Elvira's favorites—to the night maid.

Magnolia proceeded to Plan B and called in Sasha. "Do a drive-by outside Jock's office," she instructed.

"Got it," her assistant answered. "I'll be back in five minutes."

Glass walls throughout Scary extended to Jock's vast, leathery domain. While Magnolia knew better than to walk by his office herself, an innocent stroll from Sasha—an invisible assistant—would never be noticed.

"He's in there with Darlene and Bebe," Sasha reported back, calling Magnolia from her cubicle ten minutes later. "Bebe was smoking one of his cigars, and all three of them were whooping it up."

"Thanks, kiddo," Magnolia said, careful not to reveal an iota of emotion. "Just as I thought." Rats, rats, rats, Magnolia thought. Despite the frost in the taxi less than a half hour ago, apparently Bebe and Darlene had decided to mount a unified defense.

Magnolia began to pace. Given the diminutive proportion of her new office, three steps equaled one good pace, and she found herself racewalking straight to Sasha's desk across the hall. Upon seeing her, Sasha quickly closed her *Post*, which reminded Magnolia that in her Hugh Grant afterglow, she'd neglected to even open her morning paper. She could read it now. Anything for a distraction. As "Mind if I borrow your paper?" slipped out of her mouth, though, Sasha dumped the tabloid in her trash can and finished it off with the remains of a Diet Coke.

"Aren't we being a little hostile?" Magnolia asked. "What'd the *Post* do to you?"

"Nothing in it today," Sasha answered, and offered a high-pitched giggle.

"Sasha, there's always something in the *Post*—a body ID'd in a Brooklyn dumpster, a rat caught lounging in a Dunkin' Donuts—something." Magnolia watched Sasha turn to tidying papers on her already neat desk.

"Give me that paper, Sasha," Magnolia insisted.

"You don't want to see it."

"God will punish you, Sasha Dobbs," Magnolia said, walking toward the elevator. "You are going to get the worst acne."

Five minutes later Magnolia had returned from the newsstand downstairs. She opened the Hershey bar she'd bought along with the paper, settled herself at her desk, and flipped to the business pages that announced industry news. Nothing. Maybe it was an item about Harry. Had he catapulted into a photo-worthy relationship? She turned to Page Six, which today was on page fourteen. There was a tragic-looking Julia Roberts photographed with five Bergdorf's bags—being elected to the Worst Dressed list could inspire the most secure woman to shop—and an item declaring that a certain adorable Hollywood couple was still together, in case you were up nights stressing over whether their marriage could be saved.

Then she spotted it. "*Just asking,*" the three lines began, "*which glittering editor is no longer solid gold? A certain English-accented, top-of-another-masthead lovely may soon be replacing the tarnished blossom taking orders from Hollywood's lovable loudmouth.*"

Magnolia dropped her candy bar, leaving a skid mark on her white cashmere V-neck.

Her first impulse was to call Mike McCourt and let him know he'd obviously been bamboozled by "a certain English-accented" editor. But what if he hadn't been? Manhattan was littered with UK roadkill who snatched New York jobs when their Fleet Street careers stalled. In their

West Village tea shops, they privately laughed at American executives awed by inglorious northern England accents. Harry must be friendly with every one of those ex-pats, Magnolia realized. What if, together, he and an ambitious Keira Knightley clone had crafted the tale and passed it on to the *Post*? Magnolia picked up the phone to call Harry's office and sound off. She dialed his number. One ring. Two.

What *was* she doing? Thank God, he hadn't picked up. Harry might be a hothead, but even if he did have something to do with this, what exactly was she going to say to him? Magnolia slammed down the receiver just as she heard the recording of his painstakingly acquired, well-modulated BBC English announcing, "Good afternoon." Magnolia had no idea whether Harry's studio's landline—his cell seemed too intimate at this stage of their extinct relationship—had caller ID or whether he would hunt her down later with *69.

Talk about damage control. Someone's got to gag me before I commit both social and professional suicide, Magnolia thought. I can't be trusted. Her next impulse was to phone Abbey, until she remembered that she'd flown to Los Angeles, where a number of Third Street boutiques were salivating at the prospect of buying her jewelry.

Deep breaths, she told herself. Deep breaths. Big news usually blindsides people—nobody gets telegrams, she reminded herself. Maybe the item is a scare tactic or someone's idea of a joke.

For the remainder of the afternoon—and the rest of the short workweek, because Thursday was Thanksgiving—Magnolia forced herself to polish an issue's worth of sentences to a gloss, even ghostwrite Bebe's editor's letter on how to bond with a cat, to be run with a portrait of Bebe and Hell. Yet all the while she was looking over her shoulder, trying to pretend people weren't gossiping about her. Was the item planted by Darlene? Bebe? Elizabeth at Jock's behest? Possibilities ran through her mind like an Andrew Lloyd Webber ballad—graphic, tragic, ultimately so relentless it made her want to howl—but she proudly refrained from leaving drama-queen messages for Abbey. You can handle this, Magnolia chanted. You're thirty-eight!

On Wednesday, in honor of the holiday weekend, Scary closed at noon. At *Lady*, this wouldn't have stopped Magnolia from working until eight, when—every year—she and Abbey would pull out their fox trapper hats; pile on parkas, mittens, and tired Pashminas; and spend hours on Eighty-first Street and Central Park West, watching their favorite balloons come alive for Macy's Thanksgiving Day parade. But today she decided to go home early. After stopping to buy the olives, cheese, cornbread, and pie that Cameron had carefully specified for his Thanksgiving dinner—friends knew better than to ask Magnolia to cook or bake—Magnolia lit a fire and turned on her television.

As she channel-surfed, Bebe suddenly appeared. The show was live—she'd seen Bebe in the identical orange mohair tunic that morning, wondering if she'd intentionally tried to impersonate the Great Pumpkin. Her guest today was Sharon Stone. The two of them air-kissed, and Sharon slinked across the set and settled herself next to Bebe. Sharon looked flawlessly young, another celebrity who proclaimed that plastic surgery was great for other people, just not her.

"This seems like an odd choice for you, Sharon," Bebe began. "A Western. You being such a rabid antigunslinger."

You could all but hear the inner Sharon summon her agent with "Get this crazy bitch off me—this wasn't the talking point we agreed to."

"Not sure what you mean, Bebe," Sharon said, however, utterly poised. "*Shoot* isn't just 'a Western.' It's a Clint Eastwood movie."

"Clint might be the most popular guy in Hollywood, but that's not the point. What I want to chew over is that I understand you've turned in your guns to the L.A.P.D., Sharon," Bebe said. "What's that about? You one of those gun-hating nuts? I never knew."

Magnolia dropped the channel changer. Bebe was leaning forward in her chair, jumping on Sharon the way Biggie would a pork chop. Magnolia heard two phones ring—her cell and her phone next to the couch—but she couldn't tear away to answer.

"Guns, Bebe?" Sharon replied, still cool. "Why are we talking about guns?"

"Well, don't you believe that owning a gun can help prevent a murder, Sharon?" Now Bebe was practically out of her chair and in Sharon's face. Sharon fixed Bebe with her ice-pick stare and tossed off a laugh.

"You've got to be kidding, Bebe," she said. "Guns *preventing* murders? I suppose you think chocolate prevents weight gain and sex prevents pregnancy." A few members of the studio audience tittered.

"Sharon, honey," Bebe was saying. "Scotland and Ireland have tougher gun laws than we do, and higher murder rates."

Sharon rose to the bait. "I'm not tracking you," she said, her mike now unnecessary. "Bebe, are you saying we should all go out and buy guns?"

"Well, I just did," Bebe said, leaning back in her chair and putting one of her chunky legs up on her desk. "Relax—it's not an assault weapon." The audience laughed, a little more vociferously than before.

"That's a relief," Sharon said.

"Keep going, Bebe!" Magnolia shouted to the TV. "Make an utter ass of yourself."

And Bebe did.

"I bought the cutest little handgun," she declared. "Fits into my handbag like a banana. Gives me a whole lot of peace of mind whenever I'm walking alone at two A.M."

"So now she's armed," Magnolia screamed—loud enough to rouse the dogs.

"I suppose you think I'm a monster for owning a gun?" Bebe asked Sharon with a jack-o'-lantern grin.

"People who own guns scare the crap out of me, I'll admit it," Sharon answered. As she ground her perfect white teeth, delicate cords appeared on the actress's swanlike neck. "You people say you need guns to protect yourselves, and the next thing you know you're going postal and your creepy kids are mowing down their friends at school."

"*'We people'?*" Bebe asked, glaring. "So now you're blaming me for serial killers?"

Magnolia's cell phone went off.

"I can't believe it either," Magnolia said quickly to Cam. "Bebe's trying to turn Sharon Stone into chopped meat. Can't talk. Need to see who'll self-destruct first." She clicked off.

"No one's blaming you for anything, Bebe," Sharon said wearily, as Magnolia returned her attention to the screen. "Hey, I didn't come on this show to be ambushed. All I want is to talk about my movie."

"Fat chance!" Magnolia yelled. "Strike back, Sharon! Attack!"

"So talk about it," Bebe taunted. "Didn't I read you have a genius IQ? Change the subject."

Sharon stayed mute, but her fingers pulled nervously at her hair.

Bebe picked up Hell and put him in Sharon's lap. "Cat got your tongue?" Bebe swiveled and looked into the camera. "You saw it here first, folks—a friendly discussion about the merits of gun ownership. I hope all you morally superior liberals out there have paid special attention."

"Who are you calling a 'morally superior liberal'?" Sharon asked, indignant. "Try law-abiding citizen who still has a brain." Sharon tossed a startled Hell onto the floor and stomped off the set.

"Guess we pushed *her* buttons," Bebe said with a malevolent laugh as her bandleader keyed her theme song. It took a good twenty seconds for the credits to roll.

Magnolia looked at her AOL mailbox. Nine new e-mails ranged from "that woman will do anything for publicity" to "call in the National Guard." On her phones she had messages from her parents, along with Natalie, Ruthie, Phoebe, and Sasha.

Immediately after *The Bebe Show*, every major network ran news of Bebe sandbagging Sharon. The celebrity shows followed, which left plenty of time for cable's talking heads, with Larry King snagging Sharon Stone, whose agent had wisely advised her to turn this into an opportunity for continued exposure. Sharon was joined on the program by Robin Williams, who did a brilliant Bebe. From ten until eleven there was more news, capped off by Jon Stewart, Stephen Colbert, David Letterman, and Jay Leno. "Did you see the gun gals face off this afternoon?" Jay asked in his monologue. "Man, I wouldn't want to be between those two cowgirls in a dark parking garage." Magnolia watched it all, flipping channels while she multitasked on the computer and phone dissecting Bebe's performance.

"What did you think?" Natalie asked.

"You first," Magnolia said.

"No, *you*," Natalie urged.

There was no percentage in revealing to Natalie how over-the-top-thrilled she'd been by Bebe's performance. How great it felt to have the world see that Hollywood's lovable loudmouth could be this vile and off. How much she was identifying with Sharon Stone. She wondered if Bebe's behavior breached some don't-act-insane clause in her Scary contract and if Jock would ditch her. How maybe she, Magnolia, would now get her sweet old job back and could return to the office on Monday to strains of "Hail to the Chief."

But then it occurred to Magnolia that if Bebe would self-destruct, she would sink with the ship or be asked by Jock to salvage it.

"Well, this could be very bad for *Bebe*" was what Magnolia said to Natalie. "Our readers are divided on the gun issue, although the one thing they see eye to eye on is etiquette. They're going to hate seeing Bebe in attack mode."

"They're a well-mannered demo," Natalie agreed. "You're right. They might turn against her."

Would that be good or bad? Magnolia would have liked to know what, exactly, Natalie would suggest as a next step, but Natalie suddenly took another call, which left Magnolia alone with her alternating worry and glee. Bebe was important and well-connected. Even if the public responded to her behavior as a gaffe, she would survive it, Magnolia finally decided as she turned off Conan O'Brian in favor of sleep. But then the phone rang one more time. It was Scary's spin mistress, Elizabeth.

"Stay calm," Elizabeth said, although it was she who sounded frantic. "By the end of the long weekend, this Bebe fuss will all blow over. Do. Not. Worry."

"I wasn't worrying exactly," Magnolia said. "At least not about that."

There was a long pause. "Oh, are you ruminating about that *Post* silliness?" Elizabeth asked. "Jock shopping your job?"

For a second Magnolia couldn't follow Elizabeth. Then she remembered the *Post,* which Bebe's performance had pushed out of her psyche for eight full hours.

"Well?" Magnolia asked.

"Well, silly goose, don't," Elizabeth answered. "Nobody believes the *Post.*"

Elizabeth had promised that after the weekend the Bebe coverage would evaporate. She was partly right. The next bounce came in the weekly celebrity magazines, which featured the stars inside their issues. They invited readers to take online polls declaring their loyalty to either Sharon or Bebe, who did her best to keep the controversy alive, appearing on *Larry King* herself. In a slower news week—without a Midwestern ice storm of biblical proportions (Magnolia noted that Fargo was once again the coldest spot in the nation)—she might have made the cover of *Time* or *Newsweek.* But by Thursday the ruckus had almost been forgotten. Except by the NRA.

"Magnolia, we've gotten the most fantabulous opportunity," Felicity trilled as she walked into Magnolia's office. "Beebsy could have the cover of their magazine."

Magnolia looked up from her proof. "What does Elizabeth have to say about it?"

"What's this got to do with Elizabeth?" Felicity asked, looking genuinely confused.

"A lot," Magnolia answered. "Everyone at Scary runs requests like this past Elizabeth." Who will say no. Did you not hear me? No.

"Magnolia, dear," Felicity said, her voice dripping with condescension, "Bebe Blake is not 'everyone.'"

No argument there, Magnolia silently agreed.

"I'll call her at the photo shoot and see how she feels about it," Felicity said.

"The photo shoot?" Magnolia asked. "What shoot?"

"Oh, didn't Sasha tell you the cover shoot got moved up a day?" Felicity asked, all innocence.

"Sasha's at a press conference," Magnolia said. "Why didn't you mention anything to me about the schedule change?"

"The photographer Fredericka booked was called to Paris for a funeral, so I lined up the woman who did Bebe's publicity stills. She's entirely capable. Magnolia, don't you think that Bebe can handle a photo shoot by herself?" Felicity asked as she walked away. It was just as well that Magnolia didn't get a chance to answer.

She walked into the art department. "Fredericka, what do you know about a rescheduled photo shoot?" she asked.

"Vich one?" Fredericka asked, looking up from the screen of her giant Mac, on which she was designing a food story. The triple-decker burger looked like it had escaped from the Sci Fi Channel.

"Cover," Magnolia said.

"Vat cover?" Fredericka asked, looking perplexed.

"Something about Philippe being called to Paris for a funeral."

"But I just had lunch vit Philippe and ve nailed down all the details," she said. "I'll call him. There's some miscommunication here." Magnolia stood by while Fredericka got him on the line.

"*Bonjour*, Philippe," Fredericka said cheerfully, but her face quickly contorted. "Could you speak a little more slowly, please? Vat happened? Canceled? You just found out? Fuck. Pardon my French. Never mind, it's just an expression. Of course, I know nothing about it! *Mon Dieu.* I totally agree. Yes, of course ve'll pay. I am so, so sorry. Yes, I already told you ve'll pay. I agree about protecting your reputation, Philippe. Listen, Philippe, I have to go. I'll call ven I get to the bottom of this."

Fredericka took to a minute to absorb the news. "Felicity canceled him, just like that."

They both knew it was too late to book another photographer, and that after this incident, it would never be easy to book one. Word would get around. Magnolia explained to Fredericka about the renegade photo shoot. "Check into it," she said.

Fredericka did. There had been a photo shoot: Bebe did it without hair and makeup, in the studio of a photographer no one had heard of, who promised the photos in two days. Fredericka explained to the photographer that she was the art director and asked that the photos be sent to her directly.

"Someone named Felicity gave me instructions to send them to her," the photographer said, sounding more worried than arrogant. So Fredericka and Magnolia waited. And waited. Two days turned into a week. When the photos finally arrived, it was Bebe who presented them, calling Magnolia and Fredericka into her office, where she and Felicity had the shots—far fewer then usual—laid out on a light box behind her desk.

"It's time for Bebe to make a statement," Bebe said. "The December cover was just too sappy." Granted, Bebe in an apron making cookies was a stretch—on that point Magnolia and Bebe concurred. "I need to be true to myself. And this," she said, radiating satisfaction, "is me. Have a look."

In every shot Bebe's index finger cocked straight ahead at the reader as if it were a gun. Her small eyes, devoid of makeup, shone with menace. She looked like a woman who'd fled the double-wide to take out her whoring, no-good, check-bouncing slob of a husband, Billy Bob.

"This is what I call taking a stand," Bebe said.

Chapter 22

The Intimidation Card

"Nathaniel Fine, is it?" Magnolia looked across her cluttered desk at the young man sitting soldier-straight in front of her.

"Yes." He hesitated and cleared his throat.

Magnolia hoped he wasn't thinking of adding "ma'am." She was feeling old enough already, which, for someone whom *The New York Times* just five years ago called a wunderkind, was an unfamiliar sensation.

"So, you'll be interning with us?" Magnolia said. Natalie had asked Magnolia if *Bebe* would take him. His parents were her friends, and the *Dazzle* art department already had four interns.

"Yes, Miss Gold."

"Magnolia," she corrected him. "Call me Magnolia."

He didn't. In fact, he said nothing at all as he shifted in his chair, uncrossing a long pair of legs. Magnolia got a glimpse of his powerful arms and chest. He was almost a man, although from moment to moment you could still see the Bar Mitzvah boy, an effect enhanced by a navy blue blazer a quarter inch too short in the sleeves.

"Natalie tells me you play water polo," she said, stretching for a topic to put him at ease. Magnolia didn't typically mind exercising the intimidation card—which in her world was required as often as AmEx—but she didn't want to spook a child, even one who looked twenty-three. Or maybe he looked eighteen, which he actually was; one sign of getting older, she recognized, was no longer being able to reliably pinpoint the exact age of a younger person. Magnolia wondered whether Nathaniel knew yet that he was handsome; he looked like the secret son of George Clooney. "All I remember about the sport is that guys wear swim caps with earmuff gizmos."

Her remark harvested a small smile, which spread across Nathaniel's face as he offered Magnolia details of the sport's finer points. "It's one of the hardest games to play," he concluded proudly, "'cause you can't touch the bottom of the pool—you always have to swim or tread water."

"Treading water—that skill will come in handy with our little games here," Magnolia said, hoping he might laugh. He did not. "Okay, then." She stood. "Our art director, Fredericka von Trapp, has found all sorts of work for you to do. Scanning photos, making color Xeroxes, logging photos—if we lose one, $3,000 gone, *whoosh*. You might, if you're very lucky, even get the chance to design a page—if you're not busy bringing in pizza for the whole department."

"I know I'm the bottom of the food chain," he said, standing as well. Magnolia estimated his height at five foot eleven. "But someday I want to run an art department. I appreciate this opportunity, Miss Gold." He caught himself. "Magnolia."

As she ushered him out the door, she noticed assistants to both Phoebe and Ruthie idling by Sasha's desk.

"I'm Jordan," the brunette said, flashing a smile she'd bleached one shade too white.

"Zoe," added the zaftig blonde, extending a hand with a hefty silver mesh ring on the middle finger.

"I'm Sasha and if you need anything . . . " She pointed to herself. "Forget those two slackers exist."

Ready aides for Nathaniel Fine were always going to be in supply.

Elite private school; promising applications to Brown, Princeton, Duke, and—for backup—Wisconsin; intact Upper East Side family: dad a senior partner at a major law firm, mom an in-demand interior decorator—Natalie's, to be exact; designer summer camps; good looks; even good manners. If this kid had talent to match the rest of the package, by the time he was twenty-nine he'd be running the art department of *GQ* and earning in the high six figures.

"Ladies, meet Nathaniel," Magnolia said.

"Actually, only my mom calls me Nathaniel," he said.

Magnolia pretended to wince.

"Please call me Polo."

"For the cologne?" Magnolia asked.

He looked at her as if she were brain damaged. "For the sport you play in a pool."

Magnolia marched him into the art department. There were the usual three designers developing layouts, the photo editor and her associate examining images on a huge light box, and an assistant answering the phone. But everything did not sound as usual. All Magnolia could hear was a Chris Botti CD faintly playing in the background.

She looked into Fredericka's office and understood the hush. There was Bebe hulking over Fredericka as the two of them worked on the upcoming cover. "Make the words huge," Bebe said. "Put them here." Her hand touched a spot on the upper-left corner of the computer screen, leaving a visible fingerprint. Fredericka will be Vindexing the minute Bebe blinks, Magnolia thought. Yet the art director offered no reaction except to dutifully move the coverline—"Guns: Why Every Woman Needs One"—exactly where Bebe pointed.

While Magnolia stood outside Fredericka's open office and debated whether she should interrupt to introduce Polo, Bebe glanced in their direction.

"Who have we here?" Bebe asked. If Magnolia wasn't mistaken, Bebe was sucking in her gut. "I see you've brought me a treat." Her gaze nailed Polo's reddening face.

"Polo Fine, our art intern," Magnolia said. "Bebe Blake. Fredericka von Trapp."

Fredericka walked toward them and extended her hand to Polo—Fredericka was pleased, Magnolia guessed, to briefly escape Bebe's intimate scrutiny.

"How'd you get that name, Polo?" Bebe asked.

"For water polo," he answered.

"I hope you're going to model your uniform," she said. He blushed. "You two, look," ordered Bebe, still by the computer. "So? Opinions!" Magnolia and Polo walked to the screen, which displayed an image from Bebe's I'm-gonna-blow-your-brains-out series.

"Bebe, you know what I think," Magnolia said, shaking her head. "Ditch this idea."

"Ignore her," Bebe said, as she rested her hand on Polo's arm. "Magnolia's not a risk taker. You have fresh eyes. Tell Mamma what you think."

Bebe's hand fell to her side as Polo crossed his arms and stepped back, taking a minute to consider the design. Magnolia watched a surge of Park Avenue confidence kick in.

"It's provocative," he answered. "Grabs my attention. Sends a strong message. I like how your eyes in the photo lock with the reader's."

Magnolia couldn't disagree with his observations. It would be an excellent cover—for, say, *Guns & Ammo*. Polo couldn't be blamed if no one had taught him ground zero of cover design: know and entice your unique reader, who in this case was a violence-abhorring, middle-of-the-road American mother/wife/church lady who wouldn't want *Bebe*'s emerging cover within a block of her Ethan Allan coffee table.

"You get it, kid," Bebe said, one hand back on Polo's arm, the other fidgeting with her neckline to lower it ever so slightly. "We're going to be great friends. Fredericka, see what he can do with the cover."

Fredericka looked startled. Magnolia knew the art department's other designers always campaigned to get a crack at cover design, but

Fredericka trusted no one but herself for that responsibility. A small wrinkle emerged between the art director's eyes as she placed her hands squarely on her narrow hips.

"I mean it, Fredericka," Bebe said. "See what he's got."

Magnolia tried to process the situation. If Polo worked on the cover, Natalie's friends, Polo's parents, would be picturing the result attached to his college applications. *Hello, Ivy.* But if Polo reported back to them that Magnolia Gold had blocked that opportunity, Natalie's friends would be less than understanding and Natalie would be pissed. Then again, this version of a cover would never sell. And she might get blamed.

How could she protect herself? She couldn't.

What the hell. Bebe wanted it. Let her have it.

Magnolia decided now would be a good time to get as far away from the art department as possible. As she was leaving, Fredericka was settling Polo in front of his own giant Mac. "Veel scan in the cover images and check back vit you in two hours," Magnolia heard her say in a quiet monotone, followed by a whoop and a "Hot damn" from Bebe.

"Well, *he's* going to be a welcome diversion around here," Sasha said as Magnolia stopped by her desk to pick up messages.

"Pants on, Sasha," Magnolia said. "He's a baby. Who called?"

"Message from Darlene. 'Glamazon big fat fucking zero' were her exact words." Magnolia crumpled the message and dropped it in the trash.

"And some woman asking if you could speak to the"—Sasha checked her notes—"Prairie Press Club. All-expense-paid trip to nowhere. Needs an answer ASAP."

Magnolia half-heard Sasha as she watched Bebe saunter down the hall, arm in arm with Felicity.

"Said she knew you from high school," Sasha added.

Magnolia perked up. "Oh, really?"

"A Misty Knight," Sasha said. "And if she's a stripper, she never mentioned it."

Misty Sandstrum, it has to be. Magnolia pictured a red-and-white cheerleader sweater a size too small to showcase her Miss North Dakota chest and a graduation speech that made Magnolia want to gag. Misty beat her to that glory by one white-blond hair and then put everyone to sleep with thirty-two minutes about rainbows.

"Where's her number?" Magnolia asked, answering Sasha's you-can't-be-serious look with her don't-even-think-of-asking glare before she entered her office. She closed the door and dialed.

"Misty?" Magnolia said in her best-girlfriend tone. "Sure, it's me. . . . Of *course*, you can still call me Maggie. . . . You married Bucky Knight? He's running the Ford dealership? Four kids? All named with B? Precious . . . And you . . . ? You're a restaurant reviewer at the Fargo *Forum*?"

Ten minutes passed as Magnolia listened to Misty. Did I ever talk that slowly, she wondered?

"So what's this speaking thing?" Magnolia finally asked. Misty ran down the details. The annual meeting of journalists wanted Magnolia to be the keynote speaker a week from Saturday. The pride of the Dakotas, Tom Brokaw, had been the original choice, but he'd bailed.

"Very tempting—thanks," Magnolia said. "Someone from my office will let you know by tomorrow. Promise . . . It would be great to see *you*. I'll bet you haven't changed a bit either." Magnolia wondered whether Misty considered this a compliment.

Her first choice would have been a long weekend in Paris. But for Magnolia Gold, an escape to Fargo would do just fine. Why stay here? To take the heat when Jock saw Bebe's gun cover? She'd rather not.

Magnolia opened the door and returned to Sasha's desk. "Clear my calendar—I'll be gone next Friday," she said. "We're going to need to update my *Lady* PowerPoint to make it *Bebe*-specific," Magnolia said.

"Would that 'we' be me?" Sasha asked.

Magnolia smiled. "Book me on Northwest Airlines," she said. "And call Misty tomorrow at six our time to tell her I accept."

"What did you ever do to this woman that there's some return favor you can't refuse?" Sasha asked.

"Change of scenery will do me good," Magnolia said.

"What scenery? I saw *Fargo* twice."

"It's just a trip."

"But it's forty below. North Dakota is the home page of the wind-chill factor."

"Sasha," Magnolia said as she walked away, "that's why God invented fur."

Chapter 23

Aw, Heck, What Would Jesus Do?

Magnolia stood with her luggage at the designated meeting place: directly under the vintage airplane hanging from the ceiling of Fargo's industrial-chic airport, Great Plains–style. Flying to Minneapolis, Magnolia had begun to picture Misty as increasingly wide and soft. Between Minneapolis and Fargo, she had ballooned in her mind to at least size 18. By the time she deplaned, Magnolia sternly reminded herself to be the soul of graciousness and overlook her childhood friend's maternal transformation.

The woman striding confidently through the airport could, however, easily pass for Christy Brinkley's younger sister. Her tall body—buxom but trim—would be comfortably at home on a black diamond ski slope, although you'd have to go to Montana to find one. Misty had tucked her jeans into a pair of Uggs, and under an unzipped white parka Magnolia could see a pink turtleneck which matched her blush-free cheeks. Her hair hung as long as when she was crowned homecoming queen twenty years ago. Around her enormous blue eyes, fringed with dark lashes, were fans of delicate crow's-feet but—overall—Misty appeared as fresh as newly fallen Norwegian snow.

Magnolia despised her on sight. She instantly regretted wearing her sheared mink. I'm the one who looks matronly, she thought.

"Maggie?"

"Misty!" Magnolia didn't know whether she should greet her, as she would Abbey or even her top editors, with a kiss on the cheek. Too New York. She settled for a long hug.

"Gosh, look at you," Misty said, sizing her up, top to bottom. "I can't wait for Bucky to see you, city girl," She lingered on Magnolia's high-heeled suede footwear. "But, jeez, I hope those boots don't get ruined."

You can kiss these Manolos good-bye, Magnolia said to herself.

Misty effortlessly grabbed Magnolia's heavy duffel and pointed her toward the exit, where a white Eddie Bauer–logo'd vehicle the size of a small garbage truck spit swirls of vapor into the crackly air. Magnolia pulled her Russian hat low over her forehead. The temperature made her nose run, and as Misty tossed her suitcase in the car's rear end—already crowded with a toboggan, two sleds, a shovel, cross-country skis, and a golden retriever—Magnolia turned away to blot the dripping with her black kid glove.

"Hey, Goldfarb!" Bucky got out of the car and swept her toward his barrel chest. She'd forgotten how Bucky had always found her original last name endlessly amusing—or what bruisers the men were here. He made his SUV look like a Matchbox car. "Hop in," he said. Magnolia hoisted herself into the backseat, where a rosy Polartec-swaddled baby slept sweetly in a car seat.

"That's our youngest, Bjorn," Misty said. "We're picking up the big ones on the way to your hotel. Be there in a jiff."

"No rush, guys," Magnolia said. "And thanks for meeting me. I can't believe I'm here."

"Say what?" Bucky asked.

"Excuse me?" Magnolia said.

"Ya, you're right, Misty," he said. "She did get herself a New York accent."

"Don't be a dork, Bucky," Misty said. "She has not." Misty paused. "Well, maybe a little. Like that woman on *The Nanny* reruns."

Magnolia, used to being complimented on her all-American diction, faked a laugh and looked out the window. It was only 3:45 in the afternoon but the northern light was rapidly fading. As Bucky drove on the crunchy, snow-packed streets, Misty delivered a voice-over. "See that house"—she pointed to a tidy split level surrounded by a few, bare trees. "That's where Scott and Jen live now." Magnolia guessed she was supposed to remember who they were. "And that one over there"—a vinyl-sided ranch already heavily illuminated for Christmas—"was Tom and Deb's, but he hooked up with Cynthia. Deb's a lesbian now. Moved to the Twin Cities." Misty raised her eyebrows in mock shock.

Just as Magnolia began to try to imagine what life might have been like had she never left Fargo—would she be with Tom, assuming she could recall who he was? would she own a set of jumper cables and know what to do with them?—Bucky and Misty stopped in front of a school whose playground had been flooded with water that had frozen to create a skating rink. The jolt awoke the baby, who started to wail. In one fluid motion, Misty exited the SUV's front passenger door, popped around and opened the back door, unbuckled the car seat, and plopped the startled child in Magnolia's lap, saying "We'll be back in two shakes—mind the baby, okay?"

The chunky little boy took one look at Magnolia and cried at twice the volume. She tried to bounce him on her lap—that's what mommies did—but he felt heavier than Biggie, and her jerks succeeded only in making tears stream down his little chapped face. The child pulled off one red mitten, tossed it on the floor, and shrieked even louder. This roused the sleeping dog, who leaped over the seat and began to slobber on Magnolia's mink and pant hotly in her face. She could see the dog's breath in the chilly car.

"What's your name again?" Magnolia asked the unhappy infant. Lorne? Porn? "*Bjorn!*" Had Misty named her child for that Swedish tennis champ with the scraggly hair and headband? When they were both thirteen, she dimly remembered his face on a cover of *Time* plastered to her friend's bedroom wall. Or was Bjorn the cool ethnic name here, the Upper Midwest equivalent of Jaden or Aiden?

She stared out the window, which was getting fogged. Where were Bucky and Misty?

The doors opened. Three apple-cheeked cherubs carrying ice skates crowded into the seat behind Magnolia, a blur of primary-colored jackets, pom-pom hats, and boots.

"I'm Brittany," said a mini Misty. "These are the twins, Brett and Brendan."

"Meet Mrs. Goldfarb, kids," Bucky said.

"Hello Mrs. Goldfarb," Brittany said in a singsong that matched her parents.

"Actually, that's my mother—you can call me Magnolia."

"That's a dumb name."

"Company manners, Brittany," Misty said, not unkindly, to her daughter. "Maggie can call herself whatever she wants."

She turned around to face Magnolia as she continued their tour—the coffee bar where Siegel's Menswear used to be, the sewage treatment plant, the nonexistent landscaping. And in less than five minutes, they were pulling up to her hotel. "You're going to love it here at the Donaldson—just like South Beach," Misty said.

I'll be the judge of that, Magnolia thought.

"Pick you up for supper at seven," Misty shouted out the window as the SUV huffed around the corner.

The last time she'd been in Fargo—twelve years earlier, before her parents abandoned the state for tennis in nonstop 70-degree sunshine—this hotel had been a flophouse. Now, from what Magnolia could tell, the whole town was getting subversively trendy. Loft condos had sprouted up where pawnshops used to be. A patisserie stood next to a tractor factory rehabbed into a sleek, postmodern office building that appeared to be furnished by Design Within Reach. Where were the endless freight trains whose cars she'd counted as a child, trains that dissected Fargo four times a day and made traffic—such as it was—come to a standstill? Magnolia hadn't seen a one. And had all the lumpy, polyester people of her memory migrated, perhaps to South Dakota?

At the Donaldson, a bellman opened the door to a suite twice the size of Magnolia's first New York studio apartment. The walls were decorator white and the carpeting, sisal.

"Is that a hot tub?" Magnolia asked the bellman, pointing to what looked like a small lap pool.

"Ya, you betcha," he said. "Welcome to the HoDo."

She wondered whether its water would freeze like the skating rink. As soon as he had left, she jacked up the thermostat to eighty degrees and kept her coat on as she unpacked. Maybe she would cancel Misty. HBO on the gigantic, flat-screened TV; a run-through of tomorrow's speech; and room service sounded like a fine night. She studied the menu, which promised "artisanal twists on classic regional favorites." What might they be? In the Goldfarb home, artisanal food was kugel, brisket, pastrami, and rye bread—imported from Winnipeg or Minneapolis—and the occasional Sara Lee coffee cake. Here, who knew? Lutefisk? Jell-O martinis? Perhaps she'd drop in at the bar and check out the R&B band. Or the poetry reading. Really, her stay was going to be better than Disney World, and all for $144 a night.

The telephone rang. She hoped it was Misty, canceling.

"Maggie?" asked a nervous, high-pitched voice.

It couldn't be.

"I read about your speech tomorrow in the *Forun*," he said. "Welcome home."

"Tyler! Or do I have to call you Pastor Peterson now?"

"You heard I got ordained?"

"Did you have a choice?"

"Ya, it's kind of a family business." When they grew up, Tyler's dad herded the flock of Fargo's largest Lutheran church, of which there were as many as Forest Gump had shrimp dishes. All of his older brothers had become ministers. "So, anyway, I was wondering . . ."

"Yes, Tyler?"

"If you could meet me? I'm in the bar downstairs."

Would Tyler wear a minister's collar? Carry a bible? Say grace? Magnolia threaded her way through the dark, crowded hotel lounge, searching for the dirty-blond hair that used to hang over her high school boyfriend's eyes. Next to several men in orange, deer-hunting clothing, a group of shrill college girls dominated one end of the smoky bar, their male counterparts circling them like the chorus of a Bollywood movie. Magnolia turned in the opposite direction, where a few couples were sipping margaritas and chomping tortilla chips. No Tyler.

Maybe he wasn't going to show. Worse, maybe it had been a joke instigated by Bucky, who would roar through the door, slapping his beefy thigh and shouting, "Got ya, Goldfarb. Still got the hots for Tyler Peterson, huh?" She sat at a table and waited, crossing her arms against her breasts. Even with a layer of silk long johns under her jeans and a thick cashmere turtleneck, Magnolia wondered how she had ever survived here in Iglooville.

She felt a tap on her shoulder. In place of the Tyler she remembered stood a serious man with wire-rimmed glasses and a blue knit ski hat. She could easily picture him at a desk in a bank, granting a loan to a customer in a John Deere cap. He stared at her and didn't seem able to speak. Nor could she.

"Maggie," he said, after what felt like minutes. "I like your hair long." He brushed away her bangs, and as his hand grazed her cheek, she shivered—this time not from the cold—and pulled him close, breathing in the clean scent of skin she'd know anywhere.

"Aw, heck, I didn't mean to make you cry," he said, as they sat down together. He pulled off his hat; his hair had turned brown. Magnolia blinked away her tears.

"It's just so great to be home." She lied. The truth was, if she wanted to go to a Starbucks or a Gap, she could find dozens at home in Manhattan, with the same caramel macchiatos and boot-cut jeans. Nothing about Fargo felt remotely like the sweetly unadorned town of her memory. Nothing except Tyler Peterson. As he settled into his chair, she could picture him on the bench in his football uniform, turning shyly to look for her in the bleachers.

"I don't suppose you want the local specialty, a prairie fire—tequila and Tabasco?" Tyler said, as he smiled for the first time and ordered them a pitcher of beer. "Tell me about your life in New York."

"Magazine editor. Two wheaten terriers. Good friends. Not a lot to tell," she said. Not a lot she wanted to tell. She didn't know how to edit the caption for her life in a way that wouldn't give Tyler the opportunity to denounce her as an urban sinner. Divorcée, workaholic, childless woman, big spender. "You?"

"Church in a town where the tallest building is the grain elevator," he said, looking at his hands. "Wife, two kids, small house, big mortgage."

"Circle back to that wife part."

"Jody's the sunniest girl I ever met."

"Sounds perfect," Magnolia said, thinking no one was ever going to call her sunny. "Tell me everything."

"She's a preacher's kid, too; knows the drill; makes a mean hamburger hot dish, teaches bible camp, can sew a Halloween costume that fits over a parka," he said, looking Magnolia straight in the eye for the first time. "But nothing's perfect."

The hue and cry of married men on the make, she thought, then squashed the idea. Don't flatter yourself, Magnolia. Tyler is probably here to save your soul. "I guess it's the not-perfect part that keeps your business alive," she said.

"Secret of my success—people don't show up on Sunday for my sermons."

"Pictures?" Magnolia asked.

Tyler reached into the pocket of his corduroys, pulled out a canvas wallet, and opened it to a shot of two young teenagers—a pudgy, sunburned girl and a boy who looked remarkably like the Tyler who had sat next to her in geometry class twenty years earlier. They were standing in front of an RV. "We took this last summer at Yellowstone," he said proudly.

"They're so old," Magnolia stammered. She had prepared herself for babies.

"We sort of had to get married," he said and laughed again, this time nervously, absentmindedly rubbing his bare ring finger.

"Tyler Peterson, are you blushing? It's not like you were a virgin." As soon as Magnolia said it she wondered if she shouldn't take down the smart-ass tone a notch. When she last knew this man, he did not have an ironic bone in his damn good body.

"My wife reads your magazine," he said. "She's been following your career."

"My *brilliant* career?" Magnolia said, bristling at the "wife" word. "So I guess you know that Bebe Blake runs the show now."

"Jody figured that out. Watches Bebe every day," he said. "I don't get that woman. Can you explain her to me?"

"I doubt it," Magnolia said. But the look on Tyler's face showed he expected an answer.

"Hot-and-cold-running ego. But just when you really start hating her, she does something decent. Then, when you let yourself like her, she ignores you completely."

"Why do you submit yourself to that?" he asked.

"Well . . ." Magnolia said. It was an utterly reasonable question, but she wasn't quite ready for pastoral counseling. Because even a not-great job is better than men, who never fail to disappoint? Because she was afraid that living in a place as regular as Fargo would be an e-ticket to hell?

"Maggie Goldfarb, are you blushing?" Tyler asked. He filled their glasses for the second time, put his hand on top of hers and slowly moved his palm toward her wrist. She felt warm everywhere, as if they'd both stripped and were breathing heavily under the universe's most luxurious duvet. "Soft," he said, as he moved his fingers toward her arm.

Soft, she repeated to herself. She time-traveled to their first date, when they'd French-kissed for hours in the back of the Fargo Theatre and she confirmed firsthand the definition of the term "orgasm." Tyler continued to stroke her wrist until he reached her watch.

Magnolia jolted back to reality. "Jesus, Tyler," she said. "Oh, Christ, sorry I said 'Jesus.' What time is it?" She yanked her arm away and quickly stood. "Bucky is picking me up in five minutes."

"That fool who hawks cars on Channel Four?" he asked, not sounding one bit like the Reverend-anything.

"Don't act like you don't remember Bucky," she said. "You were on the same football team." Is he jealous, she wondered? And are they both insane? "It's not a date—it's supper. Misty Knight is the one who invited me to speak tomorrow." Why was she explaining this to Tyler?

"But when will I see you?" he said as he stood up to help her into her coat.

"Tyler, get a grip . . ." she said, but this time she didn't finish her sentence because he leaped forward and kissed her. His tongue tasted like slow dancing, like high-octane teenage hormones, like midnight skinny-dipping at Pelican Lake.

She pulled herself away, ran out the door and into the street.

Magnolia had expected Saturday's event to be the equivalent of a lunchtime facial. It turned into a heart-lung transplant. Starting at 8:30, seventy journalists from Montana, the Dakotas, and western Minnesota assembled to praise and dissect one another in a drone of panel discussions. Only at 2:30, after the last cup of weak black coffee following pale chicken and limp broccoli bathed in hollandaise, did Misty approach the podium for Magnolia's introduction.

"I remember her as Maggie Goldfarb, my coeditor on the South High newspaper, but to all of you she's the famous New York magazine editor, the former editor in chief of *Lady* and now an editor with Bebe Blake on *Bebe*. Let's give it up for Magnolia Gold, Fargo girl made good!" Magnolia wondered if Misty, the former cheerleading captain, would finish with the splits.

Applause carried Magnolia to the front of the auditorium. She looked out at the sea of faces attached to Lands' End work clothes. Embarrassed to think of her Manhattan colleagues seeing her feted like a rock star, she waved for the crowd to stop clapping and signaled a tech wonk to begin her how-a-magazine-gets-made lecture.

When Magnolia read that public speaking was many people's worst fear, she never got it. Put her in front of a microphone and a trained monkey took over. Where this creature came from—complete with stand-up comic timing—she never knew, and she could rarely summon her on command. Today the audience laughed and clapped at all the right places, and, in thirty minutes that felt to her like five, her presentation was already done.

"Questions?" she asked.

"What do you pay celebrities to be on the cover?" asked a Missoula court reporter.

"Absolutely nothing," Magnolia said. "No money changes hands." Just a lot of tsuris, she thought, plus hairsplitting negotiations over locations, photographers, writers, stylists, hair and makeup crew, and photo retouching.

"Your edit doesn't begin until page 102," complained a food editor from Bismarck. "Why are there this many ads?"

"Without advertising, cover prices for magazines would be so high no one would buy them," Magnolia said, although every reader bitched about the same thing. "Newsstand sales are only a small part of the picture and it's money from ads that keeps the cost of subscriptions so low, even with soaring postal rates."

"Who gives a hoot about all those celebrities?" asked the fishing editor of a small Minnesota magazine.

"Much as I might love to feature a big-mouth bass on our cover, sir, we could hardly call a magazine *Bebe* and not go with Bebe Blake," Magnolia responded.

"How did you get your start?" inquired a white-haired woman with a gravelly voice.

"Miss Pierce?" Magnolia said. Could it be? Rosemary Pierce had been her ninth-grade English teacher, the woman who introduced her to Dorothy Parker and was the first nonrelative to tell her she had talent? "Is that you?"

"Yes, dear. We're all so proud of you." There was a ripple of applause.

"I moved to Manhattan and worked myself up from fetching coffee," Magnolia began, and summarized the last twelve years of her life into two hundred and forty seconds. Magnolia let herself feel a tremor of pride. It would be good to end now, she thought, but unfortunately one more hand was waving.

"Isn't it hypocritical to advertise cigarettes in the same issue with a '5 New Ways to Stop Cancer' story?" Misty asked, her face arranged in angelic innocence as she held up the current *Bebe*.

Magnolia locked eyes with her hostess and adolescent nemesis—a girl who got into Brown, where Magnolia only made the wait list, and then blew off the acceptance to attend the University of North Dakota, so she could join her mother's sorority. Of course it's hypocritical, Misty, Magnolia thought. But magazine publishing isn't a social justice organization, honey. Live a day in my shoes, you with your four-car garage, 5,000-square-foot house, six-burner Viking stove, wine cellar, media room, and snowmobile fleet.

"Those decisions are ultimately made by the publisher, not the editor," Magnolia answered and shrugged. "Division of church and state." But just the same, she resented the gotcha.

Satisfied or not by the answer, Misty thanked Magnolia and announced that the afternoon seminars, which Magnolia this instant chose to boycott, would begin. In fact, Magnolia decided that she would call the airline and see if she could stand by for the next plane out of Fargo. Later, she would tell Misty that an emergency back home prevented her from attending the cocktail reception and evening dinner dance. Magnolia could live without the karaoke.

"Great presentation," a woman called to her as she made her way out the door. It was Miss Henderson, the head of the high-school physical ed department, who had accompanied Miss Pierce. So they really were a couple.

"Will you sign my copy of *Bebe*?" said the man from Missoula. Autographs! No one in the office was going to believe it, not that she would mention it. Magnolia finally reached the coat check.

"I had a feeling I'd find you here," he said. "Good speech. I'm impressed." Tyler smiled warmly.

She hadn't noticed him in the audience. "Tyler, thanks for coming," she said, genuinely surprised.

"You're my whole point for driving into Fargo," he said. "C'mon, I'll see you back to the hotel."

She could hardly refuse him, considering that her chances of hailing a cruising taxi were right up there with finding a buffalo roam. And she had to admit that throughout the morning, her mind had drifted to Tyler once, twice, twenty times. It was another Magnolia who had burned for him all through high school and well into freshman year of college, but seeing Tyler brought her back. Magnolia realized she missed not just him but the girl she once was, a girl who wrote poetry for friends' birthdays, who cared more about a boy's calling than whether she would get a raise. She wanted to spend a little more time with both of them, Tyler Peterson and Maggie Goldfarb.

Magnolia followed Tyler out to the street, where a layer of light snow was dusting the icy sidewalk. She climbed over a steep snowbank— rather nimbly, she thought, considering her heels—and he opened the passenger-side door to his minivan. During the ten-minute drive, neither of them spoke. Magnolia, at least, was busy crafting a tender but final good-bye speech—how she'd cherished their history, how she'd love to meet his family if they ever visited the Big Apple, how they could e-mail if he wanted. When they reached the hotel, she opened her mouth to launch her oratory, which Tyler interrupted.

"Not such a good idea to talk here," he said, unbuckling his seat belt. "Didn't you listen to the weather?"

She looked at him dubiously as he zipped past Christian rock on the radio until he found the local news.

"—you betcha, ten to twelve inches of the white stuff. Get yourselves off the roads. Ya, gonna stick this time. Be a big one. Listen to Ole here. Throw a log on the fire, open a bottle, snuggle up with someone special. Settle in for the night. It's baby-making time in the Red River Valley."

"You heard the man," Tyler said and winked. "You wouldn't send an old friend out on the Interstate now, would you?"

Magnolia drew her coat around her in the frosty car as he reached for her hand. She gently pushed him away. "Seriously, won't your wife be worried about you?" she asked.

"Jody's clear across the state for a 4-H event, staying at her parents' farm with the kids. Judging from the weather report, she's not going anywhere."

"Pastor Peterson," she said slowly, "did you order this snowstorm?"

Magnolia walked out of the bathroom in her red plaid flannel pajamas and called Misty with apologies about skipping out on the evening's dinner. By the time she hung up, Tyler had stripped out of his clothes and slipped into the steaming hot tub placed squarely in the sitting area of the suite. Without his glasses, in the dimmed light, she could take him for the Tyler in her yearbook who'd signed, "I'll love you forever." The last time she'd seen his bare chest, it had eleven pale, blond hairs, which her teenage fingers had memorized. Now, a discreet patch of fur covered his sharply defined pecs. Clearly, a minister's schedule allowed time to work out.

"You look about twelve in those pj's, Maggie."

"You were expecting, what, a little pink slip and high-heeled slippers trimmed in marabou?" Tyler didn't need to know she had both items back home.

"You're everything I was expecting and more," he said, moving aside their second empty champagne bottle to pat the side of the tub. "C'mon in."

"Tyler, you're ripped," Magnolia said. "And this is wrong."

"I'm not drunk—I'm happy. We've been together on that bed and now you're saying it's wrong?"

She was covered with goose bumps—or was it guilt?

"We were both dressed on that bed," she said. "Well, practically dressed." In her ten years of postdivorce dating, Magnolia had redefined *appropriate* on an annual basis. She'd been with a college roommate's father; both her gynecologist and her periodontist, although not at the same time; and a senator twenty-five years her senior. But she'd never done the husband of a subscriber, at least not that she knew of. By the technical definition of any blow-jobs-don't-count, friends-with-benefits teenager in America, they hadn't had sex yet. Yet Magnolia felt queasy and was fairly certain it wasn't from the drinking.

"I care for you, Tyler," she said. "I really do." And she really did, in a way that felt love-song pure—and appealingly naughty. "But this is wrong."

"It'll be my sin," he said.

Magnolia flashed to the perfume she'd discovered at a flea market the past fall. "My Sin," it was seductively labeled. She loved the pristine bottle, but when she opened it, the 1950s Parisian scent had turned. Mosquito repellent smelled better. "My sin." Not auspicious.

"I've been dreaming about you for years—you broke my heart

when you stopped writing me," he said. Magnolia didn't respond, in hopes that he would continue. "I have a good life," he said, "but I need for us to be together again, even if it's just for tonight. I have to know what it would feel like."

The last time she'd seen a man this emotionally exposed, she was watching a movie on Oxygen. His letters—short, dear, pleading— kept coming all through that first year at Michigan. She'd return to the dorm after a date and tuck them away in the bottom of her drawer, always meaning to respond the next day. But the girl who got A's in creative writing could never find the words.

Maybe she owed him. Magnolia took a what-the-hell breath, divested herself of her pajama trousers, and walked over to the tub. As she slipped in next to Tyler and eased her legs through the water, her gooseflesh disappeared. He pushed aside her pajama top and began to run his hands over her shoulders and breasts.

"Like silk," he said.

Thank you, La Prairie Caviar Luxe Body Cream. She responded to his familiar mouth as her hands slipped below the water. There was nothing boyish about him. *Buzz . . . Buzz.*

They proceeded to explore, above and below the water, but Magnolia kept hearing the buzz.

"That the doorbell?" he asked, dreamily.

"My BlackBerry," she said.

"Your *what*? You lewd New York girls."

"Just let me check it," she said, hopping out of the tub and walking to her bag as she dripped water on the carpeting. *Package to arrive by five . . . call ASAP,* the message from Cameron said. "Just a minute," she said to Tyler who waited in the water while she dialed the front desk. "Any deliveries for me?" she asked.

"Golly, I'll check," said the front-desk clerk, who put her on hold. Magnolia, with just a towel around her, stood freezing. "The FedEx guy was late on account of the storm," the girl at the front desk said, "but something just arrived and I'll send it up in a sec."

Magnolia went to the bathroom for a thick white robe and handed another to Tyler. "Get dressed, please," she said.

"But . . . ?"

"It won't take more than a moment," she said, answering the knock as he disappeared into the bathroom. The bellman handed her a box containing an early, unbound edition of *Bebe,* gun moll cover included. But it didn't take a moment to read the issue in full. It took a good forty minutes, followed by just as long a wait on the phone with Cameron to rectify mistakes.

"Can't this wait?" Tyler asked when she was halfway through the ritual. He'd sat down next to her on the bed and was playing with her as she continued to read.

"The thing is, no," she explained, with her hand over the receiver. "The magazine pays for delays."

"Aren't your values a little out of whack?" he asked.

"Yours aren't?" she said.

"I'm just a guy, a guy in love, and God understands, if that's what you're wondering."

"You're not in love, Tyler," she said, rolling her eyes. "Well, maybe you are—I hope you are, with Mrs. Peterson."

"Take me seriously," he said.

"What I have to take seriously right now is this little bit of work." She continued the task at hand, happy to opt out of a discussion that had taken a turn for the uncomfortable.

Tyler started to doze. By the time she had finished talking to New York, he was fast asleep. Magnolia gently outlined the muscles in his strong back, then moved down to between his legs, but he slept as if he were drugged, tossing and turning and mumbling.

What was he saying? The Lord's Prayer? Magnolia moved away from him, got under the covers, and tried to sleep, but she stayed awake most of the night, wondering if she hadn't got an e-ticket to hell after all. A one-night stand with a married minister wasn't what she'd expected room service to deliver. The chemistry might be there, but it wasn't just a case of his being from Mars and her from Venus; they were from different galaxies. She could no more imagine him discussing the Whitney Biennial at a Manhattan dinner party than she could see herself running a bake sale in Wild Rice, North Dakota.

Magnolia rose at six A.M., baptized herself in a scorching shower, and hurriedly packed. As she tiptoed around the room, she savored one last look at Tyler's sleeping frame now stretched comfortably under the goose-down comforter. It took all of her willpower to slide into her coat and turn to leave. Before she closed the door, she kissed him softly on the lips and left a note by his pillow, still not sure that the writer in her had the words. "Dear sweet Tyler," it began. "God works in mysterious ways. . . ."

Chapter 24

In the Bleak December

"Magnolia, you're here!" Elizabeth waved at Magnolia as if they'd bumped into each other in the Amazon rain forest. Was she not expecting to see her tonight?

When the invitation arrived for Jock and Pippi Flanagan's party—which kicked off the holiday season the first Monday of every December—Magnolia's reaction was relief even greater than usual. She'd made the cut. Jock had been known to include the head of human resources, but not her counterpart in production; the publisher of a magazine without its editor, and vice versa. The chosen ones didn't scan the room to view who else was there as much as to see who wasn't. Even though the gathering was called from six to eight, to max out their exposure, guests tended to arrive exactly at seven, after—with uncharacteristic cheer—they greeted Mike McCourt, who decamped to the corner of Park and Ninety-fourth for note-taking. Tomorrow, the merrymakers would devour Mike's recital of the guest list, second in popularity only to his column about the Condé Nast Christmas lunch, whose seating plan he analyzed like a purloined state department document.

Scary folk made up only a third of the group: the rest was a flesh-and-blood Q-rating of Manhattan's reigning air kissers. As Magnolia checked her coat—for tonight, mink was fine—she looked around. The first two luminaries she spotted were the former mayor and his second wife, who'd attached herself to Natalie Simon like a barnacle.

"Honey, she can suck up all she wants," Elizabeth whispered, her Southern accent switched on for the party, as if she'd pressed CHARM. "Natalie's never going to make her a columnist. Doesn't she realize the ex-mayor's ex-wife is one of Natalie's best friends?"

"Pippi, you remember Magnolia Gold?" Jock said as she worked her way to the front of the receiving line. Pippi Flanagan looked at Magnolia blankly, though this was the third year in a row that she'd attended their party. "Pleased to make your acquaintance," Pippi said, fingering her dainty pearls as her eyes shifted from knee-jerk politeness to unbridled delight. Magnolia turned to see who'd arrived. She saw the top of a silvery head. Was it her friend, Dan Brewster? She started to walk in his direction and then saw, no, it wasn't Dan. That handsome hair belonged to Bill Clinton, with Hillary.

As well-wishers swarmed around Bill and Hill, Magnolia was pushed from the foyer into the Flanagan's double-size parlor. She heard Bebe before she saw her.

"The magazine's doing fantastic," she was crowing to a small circle, including Darlene and the head of Glamazon. Magnolia wondered if Bebe even recognized the woman who'd decided not to buy ads in *Bebe*. "Just wait till you see our next cover—designed by my secret weapon back at the office," Bebe said.

Noticing Magnolia, Bebe charged toward her, her long sleeves flapping. Tonight she was Mrs. Claus with cleavage, dressed in red velvet trimmed in white fur.

"Happy holidays, Magnolia, What, no drink? Let's hit the bar." She corralled Magnolia into an alcove off the other end of the parlor. "I'm so glad you're here," she said, handing Magnolia a cup of bourbon-heavy eggnog and quickly downing a glass herself. "Let's show Jock the cover. It's in my bag."

"Bebe, this isn't the place," Magnolia said. She could hear the adoring crowd that had swelled around the Clintons, and expected that Jock was reveling at its epicenter. Bebe began to fumble for the cover just as Jock ushered the royal couple into the parlor.

"Let's keep that cover between us, okay?" Magnolia said, but Bebe's attention had moved on.

"Holy fuck, it's him, isn't it?" she said, fixated on the former president. "And her." She began to dart in the couple's direction.

Magnolia saw a flicker of terror in Jock's eye. As the former president was swarmed by wide-eyed females, Jock swiftly created a no-fly zone around Hillary, whom he adroitly steered toward a cluster of kingpin advertisers. His moves were as smooth as a swan dive.

For a split second Bebe stood paralyzed, then replaced her astonishment with cavalier amusement. She turned to Magnolia. "Gotta get to my next party—one with real food," she said. "Want to join me?"

"But there's a whole spread in the next room," where Magnolia could hear Darlene.

"Suit yourself. I've had it with this crowd. An eggnog for the road and I'm history." She padded off to the bar, leaving Magnolia to head for the buffet to make sure that Darlene and the other Scary disciples registered that she was here.

By the standards of a ten-room Fifth Avenue duplex, the Flanagans' dining room was small. Magnolia found herself bosom to bosom with Darlene, directly under a portrait of one of Pippi Flanagan's disapproving ancestors.

"Have you met Raven?" Darlene asked, smearing caviar on a blini, popping it in her mouth, and motioning toward an exceedingly tall woman with hair and clothing as dark as her name. "Raven Kensington-Woods, Magnolia Gold. Raven's visiting," Darlene said as she chewed. "From London."

As if that weren't obvious the minute the woman opened her mouth. "Grand party," the Brit said. "Are you another of Jock's lovelies?"

"Are you?" Magnolia asked.

Raven laughed like wind chimes. As if on cue, Jock appeared and linked arms with her and Magnolia.

"Everyone drinking up?" he said.

"I'm told you press people here in the States don't like to drink," Raven said. "Not like us, who end every bloody workday with cocktails."

"You're going to have to change that, Raven," Jock said, and moved on as happy host.

"Here for long?" Magnolia asked Raven.

"Not likely," Raven said. "I doubt you all could afford me." She let her wind chimes tinkle one more time, tossed her sable hair, and floated off with Darlene toward the bar.

"Who—or what—was that?" Natalie asked, sidling up to Magnolia as they watched heads turn toward Raven, who cut an inky wake in a crowd that had abandoned its customary black for hits of festive color. Natalie wore a thigh-high caftan in blue iridescent silk, gold bangles on each wrist, and slouchy, calfskin boots. Her hair was in its customary Wilma Flintstone do.

"'Tis some visitor tapping at my chamber door,'" Magnolia said.

Natalie took a second to get Magnolia's reference. But she was an English major, too. "'Ah, distinctly I remember it was in the bleak December,'" Natalie recited. "I take it that's the Raven Something-Something I've read about?"

"Only her and nevermore," Magnolia said. "Or at least I hope there's nothing more."

"Don't do one of your paranoid numbers—I hear she's in town about one of the cheesy tabloid jobs," Natalie said, always making a point of distinguishing *Dazzle* from the only slightly trashier celebrity magazines that had overtaken the newsstands. "Stop thinking about that pea-brained Page Six item. Everyone else has."

"Okay," Magnolia said. "I'll try." She decided now would be a good time to leave the party and collected her coat from the attendant in Jock's lobby. Despite Natalie's order, she couldn't stop obsessing over whether Raven might be the mysterious Englishwoman rumored to be after her job, and, to clear her head, she started to walk south rather furiously.

Soon enough, she was in midtown. She passed Barney's Christmas windows, loaded with insider innuendo, walked over to Bergdorf's, whose displays were dripping with more layered opulence than she'd ever recalled, and past Cartier, whose whole building was wrapped in a red bow. She ultimately stationed herself in front of the towering tree at Rockefeller Center, standing before it as if it were the great Oz ready to spit out answers. Why can't anything be simple, she wondered? Not a store window. Not a party. Not a guy. Not a job.

Out of the corner of her eye, a tall man in a blue knit ski hat put his arm around a woman's waist and pulled her close for a kiss in front of the tree. Magnolia did a double-take. Could that be Tyler?

Magnolia blinked and the man disappeared. Had she made him up? She walked toward the skating rink in an attempt to see him again, weaving in and out of the crowd until she spotted him. He turned.

Blue Hat had a cropped red beard. Not Tyler. But why could she not stop thinking about him? Since she'd left the hotel room yesterday, she'd been marinating in both guilt and a persistent emotion she couldn't name that was dangerously close to longing. Magnolia could see him, taste him, hear him, and smell him.

Was she so needy and vulnerable that she'd lost all common sense? If they'd spent a whole weekend together, they probably would have run out of conversation by Saturday afternoon.

Had she used Tyler? She'd discussed their time together with Abbey, who tried to convince her it had been the other way around. You can't think about him, Magnolia told herself. And she didn't for most of the walk home, because she was back to ruminating about Raven, a certain head-of-another-masthead who Magnolia, informed by her intuition, knew had made the trip with the hope of becoming her replacement.

At the very least, Magnolia had distractions. Just as magazines glorified Christmas, whipping female readers into a froth of insomnia-inducing, chemical-dependency-seeking stress as they compared their ragged efforts to the results of photo shoots engineered by teams of professionals, so, too, the industry romanticized the season for its own amusement. First, there were the parties.

It was true what Magnolia had told Raven: during the rest of the year, if there weren't a profit motive to get together at the end of the workday, staffs splintered off to Westchester, New Jersey, Connecticut, and four of the five boroughs. (Magnolia had yet to meet anyone who worked on a magazine and lived on Staten Island.) But in December, they made up for it, with day after day and night after night of bonhomie, both real and faux.

Scary, for instance, traditionally invited every employee to the once-glorious Tavern on the Green, which they rented out in its entirety. Mail-room attendants showed off MTV-worthy dance moves with rhythm-challenged editors as partners. Those who didn't dance feasted from a pile of shrimp the size of the national debt.

For Magnolia, there was also Darlene's tree-trimming party at her Upper East Side brownstone. The evening masqueraded as a family fete, her velvet-clad daughters—Priscilla, Camilla, and Annabel—circulating silver trays of canapés to the advertisers Darlene treated as her nearest and dearest. Magnolia knew that the magazine paid the bill. But who was she to complain? *Lady* used to do the same for the staff brunch she threw at her apartment, featuring an ecumenical spread of Zabar's finest Nova Scotia salmon, sweet potato latkes, and Christmas cookies she had baked herself from the magazine's recipes. But this year, she wouldn't be giving her party. In its place was Bebe's Nashville rib-and-brew bash at Blue Smoke.

But that wasn't all. Until the industry flew west for skiing three weeks later, every venue from Mulberry to Madison was filled with mistletoe madness. The Estée Lauder gang, for example, invited the town's top editors in chief and beauty editors to a discreet cocktail party at the 21 Club. Glamazon staged a disco night around the pool at Soho House. And Scary threw an official no-executive-left-behind lunch at Daniel, which was decked out with trimmings fit for *Dr. Zhivago*. Between courses, Daniel Boulud himself greeted the guests to make sure the food was perfect. It was. Lunch ended with gifts— enameled cuff links for the gentlemen, fur shrugs for the ladies.

Presents flowed through the season. Magnolia gave and Magnolia got. For the staff, she decided on long, kiwi green gloves which Ruthie Kim ordered at a discount, though Magnolia footed the bill. She debated whether or not to stretch for the splurge. She wasn't the editor in chief anymore, and maybe her colleagues wouldn't expect it. But history and ego convinced her to go the distance; she didn't want to appear stingy, considering what she raked in from PR firms, grateful contributors, and the more senior staff members. While this year she didn't accumulate as much swag as in previous seasons, she adored the satin evening bag with its Swarovski crystal clasp, the cashmere hoodie and sweatpants, and best of all, a mad bomber hat from Cameron.

The presents were exhilarating, but the fake fun wasn't. By today—an afternoon on the final week of work before Christmas— Magnolia was as limp as the last piece of tinsel in the package. Natalie had invited her to *Dazzle*'s ho-ho-hoedown. Magnolia sat at her desk and realized that she didn't have a thing to wear—anything party-worthy in her closet was, by now, at the cleaners or had been on view again and again, and she hadn't gone shopping in at least two months.

Briefly she considered if, for her, that could be as credible a sign of depression as a sudden change in appetite. No problem. The fashion department could surely help, at least with the clothing challenge. Remembering a plum velvet suit she knew had just been returned from a photo shoot, she walked into the fashion closet.

As Magnolia began foraging in the racks, she heard a husky male voice at the far end of the crammed room. "What the hell are you doing?" it said.

"C'mon, babe," Bebe answered him, loud and clear. "I'm talking fun. Have another glass of Pinot Noir. I took you for a grown-up."

"No, thanks," he said. Magnolia heard a tussle. "No," he shouted. "Get away . . . not my type."

"Sweetheart, you're too young for a type." Bebe laughed loudly. "I can teach you a few things. You'll thank me for this later. And haven't I been good to you?"

"Yes, but—"

"Agree, cute butt."

Magnolia stuck her head through the racks just as Bebe started to unbuckle his belt. With the grace of a Bond girl, she pushed Bebe and Polo apart, shrieking, "Bebe, do the terms 'statutory rape' and 'jailbait' mean nothing to you?"

Bebe looked up, startled. Her beady eyes barely blinked.

"Paws off, Bebe," Magnolia said, having no idea where her conviction was coming from. "And you, boy, out!" Polo bolted.

"Calm down, you little buzz kill," Bebe cackled at Magnolia. "I am educating this kid. Don't get your tit in a ringer. And what's with the *CSI Investigates* bit anyway? Why are you snooping?"

"I didn't think I had to put on a HazMat suit to walk into our fashion closet," Magnolia said, staying close to Bebe and talking in a hushed tone. "Why I'm here is irrelevant. What part of 'normal' don't you understand?"

"Yeah, yeah, yeah," Bebe said, walking away. "I've always found 'normal' was highly subjective and sadly overrated. Get out of my face, Mag-knowl-ya. You're trying to turn a PG13 short into an X-rated miniseries. Go party and forget this happened."

"Your secret is safe with me," Magnolia said to Bebe's back. *You sleazy child molester,* she said to herself.

"And me." Magnolia spun around. Wide-eyed, her assistant, Sasha, had watched the whole thing.

Chapter 25

Fattened Up for the Kill

"Suing?" Magnolia asked. "Did you say they're suing?" It was odd for the phone to ring at 6:15 A.M., and even odder for an early morning caller to be Natalie.

"Magnolia," Natalie said, "you stayed too long in the sticks. Stop sounding like you're calling a hog."

"Natalie, I'm usually hitting my snooze button about now," Magnolia pleaded. "Can you just give me the net-net?"

"Let me spell it out. A little spook told our friends at the *Post* a story about Bebe coming on to Nathaniel Fine in the fashion closet."

Magnolia woke up fast. This was huge. "Back up!" Magnolia said.

"Someone tipped off my friends the Fines, and Nathaniel's dad is a $1,000-an-hour litigator," Natalie said. "Put together the pieces. We're screwed. It's on page three, and God knows where else it will end up." Just when Magnolia was going to speak, Natalie started again, yelling so loud Magnolia had to hold the receiver away from her ear. "I see what you must have been thinking. Bebe's reputation gets trashed. The company pulls out of her magazine. *Lady* rises from the dead."

"Whoa," Magnolia yelled back. "Are you accusing me? Of the leak? That's absurd, Natalie. You are so off."

Twenty seconds passed before Natalie said "You'd swear you know nothing about this?"

"I didn't say that." Magnolia paused. "I saw it all." Magnolia wondered if she was a moron to have admitted this, but Nathaniel would most likely report it eventually. "But call a newspaper? What possible good could come of that? I *like* Nathaniel. And he's just a kid." Why was she squirmy and defensive? Damn Natalie for having that effect on her. "Listen, I said nothing. To anyone." Abbey, she decided, didn't count.

"Oops, hold on." Magnolia waited while Natalie took another call. "Can't talk, Cookie," Natalie said as she clicked back on. "Jock and Elizabeth conference call."

Natalie called her Cookie—she must be calming down, Magnolia hoped, as she began surfing the net and TV to see what play this was getting. So far, nothing on the morning shows, though the blogs were banging the item as if the United States had invaded St. Barth's. She threw a coat over her nightgown and ran to the newsstand.

BEBE PLAYS WITH FINE BOY TOY headlined a story accompanied by Nathaniel's water-polo team photo, and either the *Post* had digitally enhanced his crotch or their intern had a future on male greeting cards. Magnolia raced back to her apartment, threw twenty dollars at her neighbor's sixth-grader to walk the dogs, and dressed so fast that it was only when she was in a taxi that she realized her boots didn't match.

The corridors at Scary were strangely quiet as she walked to her office. Magnolia immediately called in Sasha and closed the door.

"How did this item get in the *Post* and every fucking blog?" she asked, throwing the paper on the desk. "Did you rat them out?" Magnolia knew Sasha had been an eyewitness in the fashion closet; what she didn't know was if there'd been other flies on the wall that she hadn't noticed.

"Not me exactly," Sasha answered, biting her lip and looking like a high school sophomore.

"Talk," Magnolia said.

"I was in a bar last night, drinking to the point where this I-banker was looking cute, and when he asked me where I worked, I found myself describing Bebe and Polo—the material was just too rich. He joked about calling it into the *Post*, that he knew someone who knew someone who knew someone."

"Sasha, do you realize what you've done? Polo's dad is a partner at a major law firm. Making noises about suing for child abuse, sexual harassment, God knows what. You didn't think, did you? This is breaking-the-sound-barrier bad—for the magazine, the company, all of us." Magnolia stared at the ceiling and drummed her fingers on the desk. Though she might have made the same mistake herself when she was twenty-three, she nonetheless felt like ripping off Sasha's face.

"I'm so sorry—I just wanted to impress this guy," Sasha sobbed, as she pulled a tissue from the box on Magnolia's desk. "And I wanted to screw Bebe."

"You hit it out of the park on that last one," Magnolia said.

"Plus, I thought it might help you."

"Help me? If you wanted to help me, why didn't you at least warn me about this item? *That* would have helped me."

"But I only found out when I read it on the train."

"Okay," Magnolia said, finding a quieter voice. "Well, you're going to help me now. Get me every clip, every inch of loop tape, every Web site. We've got to be all over this. Now blow your nose and get out of here before someone walks in on us." She motioned for Sasha to leave, but her assistant didn't move.

"Am I going to lose my job?" she asked, sniffling.

"Really, Sasha," Magnolia said. "No one's going to lose her job." Hopefully. "But if anything like this ever happens again, I want my cell phone ringing, my BlackBerry popping. I want a frigging blimp outside my window. *Capeesh?* What I don't want is to be woken up to hear about it from Natalie Simon."

"I get it," Sasha said, still trembling. "No problem."

"And while we're at it, Sasha, don't ever say that again, ever!"

Magnolia screamed. "Now go act normal and don't breathe a bloody word to anybody."

As Sasha walked out, Cameron walked in, holding the *Post*. He closed the door behind him.

"You know, Magnolia," he said, chuckling. "I'm only thirty-six, and up until now I have never felt old. But Bebe fondling Polo? I'm crushed. And here I thought Felicity was the weirdo."

"Felicity?" Magnolia said. "She's just toady."

"Where Bebe is a real predator?"

"In the Hollywood sense, yes," Magnolia said. "Thinks everyone and everything is available for her amusement."

"So it's true," Cameron said. "Just when I was starting to like her."

"If you must know, I was, too," Magnolia admitted. She'd been living off the fumes of her Hugh Grant evening.

"Well, is there's anything I can do?"

"You can," Magnolia said. "Try to make sure people do some work today."

All day long, that's exactly what Magnolia tried to do. There was a numbing dearth of new information. She didn't hear from Natalie, Jock, or even Elizabeth. She definitely didn't hear from Bebe. The only call came from Legal, and other than Cameron, the sole person on the staff to acknowledge the incident was Felicity.

"A lot of hooey over nothing," Bebe's designated hitter said when she paid a visit to Magnolia. "This country is too litigious. And when a celebrity gets in the mix, all anyone sees is a cash register. It's not as if that snot-nosed Polo needs the money. Poor Beebsy."

"Poor Beebsy?" Magnolia said. "She was taking advantage of that boy!"

"It was a setup," Felicity sniffed. "Nathaniel exploited Bebe's good nature—after she gave him the opportunity to design a cover of a national magazine! It's shameful. I'm urging Bebe to take her lawyer's advice to countersue."

"Countersue?" Magnolia wailed. "There were witnesses."

"*Witness*—only one—and she has an ax to grind," Felicity said icily, apparently unaware that Sasha had been in the closet. "Magnolia, dear, I hate to break it to you, but you're not the most credible observer."

"Felicity, out!" She pointed to the door. "You codependent leech. What kind of shit are you shoveling?"

"Well, if memory serves, young Nathaniel's here courtesy of you and your friend Natalie Simon," Felicity said with a final smirk, as she slammed the door so hard the papers on Magnolia's desk scattered.

At five, Magnolia attempted a drive-by visit to Natalie, who hadn't responded to the three messages she'd left. As Magnolia got out of the elevator, however, Jock was walking toward Natalie's office and she aborted her mission.

A half hour later, Jock's assistant called to inform her she had a command performance: lunch with him tomorrow.

The next morning the Bebe story was bouncing around the Internet, but the television shows, both news and celebrity—to the degree you could tell them apart—had stopped reporting the incident, probably on advice of lawyers. Magnolia didn't know if she was in the eye of the hurricane or if it had blown out to sea and, as a result, she deliberated for twenty minutes about what to wear. Everything in her closet looked too giddy, too grim, or too prim. She ultimately defaulted to an old black velvet jacket, narrow tweed pants, and black suede boots that gave her three and a half extra inches of courage. Whether she was preparing for her own memorial service or a tête-à-tête on the post-Polo spin cycle—which her inner optimist decided was more likely—she felt well-dressed.

At 12:15, she waited at the appointed spot downstairs, the late December wind whipping her face. Ten minutes passed. She called Jock's office to see if he was delayed. No answer. Then she heard him.

"Over here, Magnolia." He was calling to her from his town car. "C'mon in."

She'd assumed they'd walk to one of his neighborhood joints—the Gramercy Tavern, perhaps, or Union Square Café. But a car? In that case, she hoped for Michael's or the Four Seasons. "Where are we eating?" she asked, forcing a smile, as she settled herself on the seat next to him.

"It's a surprise," Jock said.

They traveled south, crawling along Broadway in the seasonal slog. Might they wind up at WD-40? Nobu? That hole in the wall with taxidermy at the end of Freeman Alley? No, they kept going, and suddenly they were on a bridge. Jock must be one of those Manhattanites who's just discovered Brooklyn, Magnolia decided, praying they weren't headed for a slab of cow at Peter Luger's.

During the drive, the conversation skirted Bebe and Polo, though Jock did bring up the gun cover. "Not only is it nuts, that cover, this morning I found out a bunch of the supermarket chains won't display it," Jock complained. "As goes Wal-Mart, so goes our newsstand—right down the toilet."

Magnolia felt her stomach turn over. *He's going to blame me. What was I thinking, that today's lunch would be about making the Polo mess go away? I'm over. Talk about deluded.*

She had a sudden urge to tell the driver to turn around, that she just remembered her apartment was on fire. But then Jock switched to harmless subjects, and she zoned out, trying to respond at appropriate moments. After twenty more minutes, they arrived at a Brooklyn restaurant that Michelin had proclaimed one of the city's best. As they stepped behind a velvet curtain, Jock pressed his hand on Magnolia's back to guide her to a corner table in the tiny, avocado green room.

Jock ordered a bottle of 1997 ZD Cabernet Sauvignon—the restaurant was known for its wine list—and quickly downed a glass, urging Magnolia to do the same. "A toast," he said. "To Magnolia, a woman of exceptional talent, courage, and valor." He clicked her glass.

"Thanks, Jock," Magnolia said, suspicious of the accolade.

"You've been a great sport, kid," he said. "I thought you deserved a good thanks. Let's start with the roasted beets with goat cheese ravioli and toasted pine nuts. Or would you rather have the ratatouille-stuffed squid?"

"Beets, definitely," she said. To match my face.

"And for an entrée, I insist on the duck."

Magnolia studied the menu. *Slow rendered duck breast, braised sprouts and Aligoté in a caramelized red vinegar sauce.* Aligoté? She'd definitely missed the press release on whatever that was. Throughout both courses, Jock kept their wineglasses filled as he nattered on about his vacation to Dubai, Little Jock's Thoroughbred, and paintings he hoped to acquire at auction.

Magnolia responded in a language she was fairly sure was English, but her head was on her job, which she now convinced herself would be terminated by the end of the lunch. As galling as it was to have to report to Bebe, and to be second-guessed by Felicity, to be tossed out of Scary would be far worse. If she were to get a new job, she wanted it to be on her terms, not Jock's.

Finally, Bebe came up.

"She's quite the girl, our Ms. Blake," Jock said. "We haven't seen the end of this mess with that Fine boy. But at least we've put pressure on the media to bury the story so we can try and settle out of court— though Bebe's going to have to pay big, bigger than we will, to make it go away."

He finished off his wineglass and refilled it. "The newsstand mess, though," Jock said, "that's not a small thing." He looked as if his best friend had just received an HIV-contaminated transfusion. "I've got it coming at me every which way."

He's fattened me up for the kill, Magnolia thought. Here it comes, the rubout.

"There's a lot of stress with being in charge," Jock groaned. Wait— was he showing sympathy? Wrong. He was talking about himself.

The server came over to offer dessert: "Gingerbread pudding or chocolate fig cake?"

"I couldn't possibly, thanks," Magnolia said.

"A double espresso," Jock said. "And chocolate fig cake."

"Sir, will that be with coconut ice cream or passion fruit sorbet?"

"Passion fruit." As the waiter walked away, Jock leaned in closer across the small table and filled both their glasses with the last of their second bottle of wine. "We're headed for some hairpin turns, Magnolia. But you can help." He raised his glass, as if for a toast. "Do you know you are a very beautiful woman?" he asked in a soft growl.

He moved his face so near hers, she could smell the Cabernet Sauvignon and she instinctively—though she hoped not noticeably—backed away. This lunch was definitely not passing the sniff test. "Why, thank you, Jock, you are very kind," she said stiffly.

"Relax," he laughed, and took her hand. "Have I been good to you?"

Yeah, Jock, you've been great. Murdering *Lady*. Demoting me. Importing my replacement. "Yes, Jock. I appreciate everything you've done for me."

"Good. I've always thought the two of us could be a team. There's something between us. I know you can feel it. And I like the way you've at least tried to stand up to that bitch, Bebe. You've got, what's the word you people like? Chutzpah." He took her hand and rubbed his fingers slowly between hers. "What do you say?"

Coming on to her now, while a sexual harassment suit was whizzing through the air? He must be totally disassembling. Magnolia shifted in her chair and backed away a little farther. I say, *Ewww* that's what I'd like to say. "I am so fucked" also comes to mind. She considered telling a lie like "I'm very flattered, but I like the way things are now, Jock—although if you were single and not my boss and ten years younger . . ."

"Jock, maybe we should regroup when we haven't had two bottles of wine" was the most authentic and politic response Magnolia could muster.

"I know exactly what I'm doing," he said, trying to penetrate her eyes with a look she was sure he imagined was seductive.

"I don't think you do. Do you really see this, of all times, as the moment for you to start up with me?" she said, removing her hand from his grasp. "Do you want more scandal, more items in the paper?"

"Magnolia, who's going to know?" he said, the words a threat.

"Everyone," she said. "Because I'll tell them."

Jock stared at her.

"I will," she said.

After an uncomfortable pause, he cleared his throat, adjusted his glasses, and called for the bill. "I see," he said, putting on his coat without helping her with hers. The two of them walked to the car.

The ride back to Manhattan felt as long as a flight to New Zealand and allowed plenty of time for second-guessing. What made her be so harsh? Why hadn't she just manufactured a hidden fiancé?

Neither one of them spoke until they were just a few blocks from Scary. "I'm considering a new position for you, Magnolia," Jock said, "given everything that's gone down in that war zone between you and Bebe. Yes, I'm definitely thinking about 'corporate editor.'" He was staring straight ahead, delivering his announcement as gravely as if he were informing the Vatican that the pope had died.

"Corporate editor?" Magnolia squeaked. In a few companies, corporate editor wielded heft. But more often, just like editor at large translated to editor who's small, it was a hollow position. Jock might give her projects—should this position come to pass—but unless they came with his clear imprimatur, no one at Scary would take the assignments seriously, despite her sweaty efforts to wield vigilante authority. "Corporate editor?" It was like being named weather girl for the three A.M. news telecast in Tulsa.

"Yes, everyone around here needs a change." Jock hopped out of the car without saying good-bye. "Corporate editor. Magnolia, think it over."

Chapter 26

Pluck Sucks

"Run it by me again," Abbey said as they looped around the Reservoir. "When Jock said, 'You think it over,' was he talking about that other job or the Hot Sheets Hotel?"

"I wasn't sure, but figured Hot Sheets was like an airline reservation—forty-eight hours and the offer would expire," Magnolia said. "Which I let it do, although I was dying to know what name he'd use for reservations."

"So you have another new job?" Abbey asked.

"Scary's corporate editor," Magnolia said. "Last stop before oblivion." And for someone like her, who loved slaying dragons, living death.

"Did you have a choice?" Abbey asked as they ended their run.

"I could have quit," Magnolia said. "Call me a coward. I chose paycheck over trying to prove sexual harassment."

"Jock's word against yours? I'm no lawyer, but it doesn't sound like an airtight case," Abbey said. "Now tell me, what do corporate editors do?"

"Look busy," Magnolia said. "The job doesn't come with a training manual, so I'll have to write it myself. Jock will probably ask me to interfere at the other magazines—critique them, submit ideas, sit in on meetings—and all the Scary editors in chief will despise and ignore me." Magnolia realized as she was talking about work, she was getting increasingly tense, even though she'd just finished a four-mile run that was designed to obliterate stress. She knew she had to change the subject.

"I want to hear about you and Tommy," she said. "Are you really and truly over?"

"Done-d'-done-done," Abbey said. "I've sprinted through the five stages of breakup—denial, anger, depression, reconciliation sex, and Match.com."

"How goes online dating?" she asked as they walked into Abbey's apartment building. Upstairs, Abbey began to brew coffee in her cluttered but utterly charming kitchen with its checkerboard floor and tall, glass-fronted cabinets filled with white china.

"Women lie about their age—for men, it's height," she said. "Every guy I've met could be technically classified a carnival midget. I definitely have to post my own ad." She handed Magnolia pen and paper. "So I'm giving you an assignment. Be creative. Help me write one."

"Ooh, fun. Give me a few essentials."

Abbey took out her notes. "'Good listener,' 'great friend,' 'and 'compassionate'?" She looked for Magnolia's approval.

Magnolia shook her head. "That's fine if you want to head up the Red Cross," she said. "Lead with your looks."

"'Pretty'?"

"'Pretty' is code for 'not exactly hideous in the right light,'" Magnolia said. "Pretty is flowered dresses, jars of jam, Snow White, granny quilts."

"Got it. 'Beautiful'?" Abbey said. "As in 'my friends say I'm beautiful'?"

Magnolia thought it over. "Beautiful scares the nuts off men," she said. "Let's go with 'adorable.' And it's true. 'Adorable, sexy, artistic, laser wit." Magnolia made a list. "Are you writing this for you or me?" Abbey asked.

"Mine would say, 'Temporarily closed for renovation.' Back to you.

'Great with hands'?" Magnolia wondered. "Why not? Truth in advertising. Now we need something like 'more Guggenheim than Frick,'
'More *Breakfast at Tiffany's* than *Two for the Road*'?" She drank half
her coffee. "Think, Abbey."

"'More Paris flea market than Bergdorf's'?"

"Perfect. Clever but not too. You don't want to come off too Maureen Dowd. Brilliantly cutting *and* movie star gorgeous. Talk about a
killer combo—poor thing, we should invite her to brunch—she must
never go out. Although it doesn't help to write a book called *Are Men
Necessary?*"

"Enough words, don't you think?" Abbey asked. "Guys really don't
read that much."

"Or that carefully," Magnolia said. "You could write 'Man-hungry
hussy from hell looking for warthog to eat flesh' and you'll get
responses if your picture's hot enough. Show me what you've got."

Abbey pulled out her album. Many of the photos were neatly cut in
half, Tommy having been burned at the stake of Abbey's fireplace the
first night of Stage Two. Much of what remained was Abbey snapped
at black tie functions, where, given her love of vintage clothing, it was
hard to tell if she was wearing bag lady rejects or Yves Saint Laurent.

Magnolia flipped through the album twice. "I think we have a winner," she said when she got to one of Abbey in her Audrey sunglasses
and bikini top. "Can't wait to see who comes panting. If you get a good
response, I may run an ad myself."

"So are you still getting e-mails from Tyler?"

"Daily," Magnolia admitted. "They're dear. It's the purpose-driven
romance."

"Could it ever be the real thing?" Abbey asked. "He sounds awfully
sweet."

"Are you kidding?" Magnolia said. "He's a Lutheran minister in
Wild Rice, North Dakota, with a wife and two kids. I'm an ambitious,
divorced, Jewish Manhattan magazine editor who spends too much on
clothes. Do the math." She hugged Abbey and ran home.

The truth was, Magnolia had been enjoying their e-mailing more than she cared to admit. When she dated Tyler in high school, her father tried to discourage the relationship by quoting *Fiddler on the Roof:* "A bird can love a fish," he'd say, in his best Tevye imitation, "but. where will they live?" Now, Magnolia could answer him. In cyberspace. Every morning Hotmail would deliver a missive from Preacherman8. She was getting as addicted to them as to cashews.

When she'd written him about her counterfeit promotion—conveniently skirting what had inspired Jock's spite—he'd responded with "If your boss doesn't know by now what you are capable of, he must be blind or stupid or both. Don't try too hard to make sense of something that is illogical." She wondered what Tyler would think of the latest, which she'd e-mail him about tonight. Raven Kensington-Woods was replacing her at *Bebe.*

And what would he think of her publisher Darlene's slobbery send-off? "Magnolia, I wanted to tell you how much I appreciate all your hard work," she'd said in an audition for insincerity. "I've really enjoyed working with you these past few years." So much that you pushed me under a bus, Magnolia thought, her teeth grinding at the other end of the phone. You probably flew to London and lured Raven here with a trail of Prada.

Natalie—who'd been dodging Magnolia's calls—phoned yesterday as well. "You've got to approach the new job with pluck," she advised from her lookout atop Mount Success. "I've always believed power is for the grabbing." This philosophy had sustained Natalie for decades, along with *you've got to be a little bitchy to be interesting.* "*Bebe*—let that be Raven's problem," Natalie added. "Has Bebe called you, by the way?"

"Not a peep, not a cuss."

"Felicity?"

"She's still smoking over Polo. And, hey, what's happening with that?"

"They're settling out of court," Natalie said. "Let's just say that it's likely Nathaniel will have his tuition and therapy paid for throughout the rest of his life, and still have plenty left over for beach-front property."

Magnolia felt awful that Polo had been traumatized, which shouldn't happen to anyone, but she still couldn't help feeling she'd pulled the short straw, especially on Monday, when she opened the door to her corporate editor office. The walls hadn't been painted in years, and she was greeted by two roaches, one dead, the other in vigorous health. The office was tucked into the side of the executive floor where people never wandered unless they were lost. Sasha helped unpack her. Raven, Sasha's new boss, would be starting tomorrow.

"I'm never going to forget that you've kept my secret about the *Post*, Magnolia," Sasha said. "Good luck in this new job." Sasha surveyed the bleak surroundings. She didn't press Magnolia on what she'd be doing, exactly, in her new job. The e-mail announcement had been vague, though perhaps by now Sasha had learned to read subliminal messages whispered in corporate-speak.

Her second visitor was Cameron, who arrived with three dozen pale pink roses. "It's going to be damn odd not working for you," he said as he handed her the flowers and enfolded her in an enormous, long hug.

"You, too, but you've got to be my lifeline to reality, promise? A woman needs gossip to live." Isolation scared Magnolia as much as Fargo. "Promise you will be my personal eyewitness and prognosticator?"

"Lunch, e-mail, hanging out whenever," he said, "I'm your man."

"There's no one left at *Bebe* who's going to appreciate how you keep that magazine moving, Cameron," Magnolia said. "You're its central nervous system." She started to cry, had no idea where her tissues were, and wiped away the tears with her hand.

"I'm going to try not to feel too sorry for myself," Cameron said in a serious voice Magnolia rarely heard. "Buck up. Keep your perspective. It's just a job."

She wondered if he'd give her a hug—or at least a tissue. He did not. Cam was halfway out the door when he turned. "I almost forgot—what's up with your friend Abbey? I read her personal online."

"You read the personals?" she asked, surprised. "I thought you had a girlfriend."

"Katya moved back to Prague."

"Which one was Katya?"

"Filmmaker. Leggy. Blond. Not important. Not anymore."

For no reason she could explain to herself, Magnolia felt intrigued to know this detail about Cameron. They were close, but only professional-close. They'd often spent fourteen-hour days together. She knew how he took his coffee and that he'd rather drink beer than wine. Magnolia could predict what he'd wear to work the following day and which movie he wouldn't see even if you tried to bribe him. But Cameron cruising the personals? What kind of woman would he be looking for? That she couldn't say.

"Who's your dream girl, Cam?" Magnolia asked.

"Maureen Dowd."

Shows you how little I know went through Magnolia's mind. "So what do you think about Abbey? You've met her—she *is* adorable."

"I don't know. I don't think I'm either the Paris flea market or Bergdorf's."

Magnolia could hear him chuckling as he walked down the hall. She logged on to her personal e-mail. Anything from Preacherman8? Just spam ads for drugs to make her penis bigger and a new diet pill that promised to pop cellulite like a bubble and burn an extra 937 calories per day.

Where was her radio? This office was a tomb. Pluck sucks.

Chapter 27

Angel Girl

"He asked for you again, Miss Gold," Manuel, the doorman said. "The gentleman from yesterday."

"Any message?" Magnolia asked.

"No, said he'd be back. Tried to get me to say when you'd be around but my lips are zipped." The doorman pulled his fingers across his lips in an exaggerated gesture.

"By any chance," she asked, "did this man have an accent?"

Manuel considered Magnolia's question as if the grand prize depended on it. "*Si. Si.* He did talk kinda funny."

"Thanks, Manuel," she said.

"One more thing."

"Yes, Manuel."

"I think I seen this guy hangin' around during my shift a few days ago."

She wondered whether she was getting an extra helping of attention because it was Christmastime, and her doorman pictured his hundred-dollar tip enjoying some jolly inflation. "Thanks again, Manuel," she said. "Don't work too hard."

Magnolia let herself into her apartment, kicked off her shoes, and returned her dogs' affection. Could the gentleman caller once again be Tommy? He'd phoned last week, eager to meet for a drink "now that Abbey and I are finished." Magnolia thought she'd spurned him with exquisite clarity, but Tommy was a no-means-yes guy—maybe he saw her exclamation-point rejection as a flirtatious semicolon begging for a repeat invitation.

Or was the visitor Harry, intoxicated with holiday spirit? Less than two months had elapsed since their split—he might consider their relationship under warranty, available for free repair. Harry swooping into her life was not beyond her imagination; the nonstop Christmas music everyone had to suffer through could wig out even the most stable person, subliminally programming him to find a mate, wait for Santa, and have compulsory intercourse.

She blinked away the thought. Magnolia was feeling doubtful of her resolve to turn away Harry—especially if he returned, bearing the Magnolia bracelet, although she knew she'd pay for it eventually when old St. Nick replaced it with a lump of disappointment.

Dogs fed, she settled at her computer to dash off the last of her holiday e-mails. But first she reread yesterday's message from Preacherman8: *Angel Girl, I hope u gt yr heart's desire. U 2,* she'd responded, in the language of the teenager she regressed to with Tyler. She hadn't heard from him today. But it must be a pastor's busy season.

She glanced outside. Like tiny doilies, snowflakes were beginning to fall, reflected in the high-intensity haze of yellow-white street lights. The holiday messages could wait. Best to take the dogs for their long walk.

It was the day before Christmas Eve, and the stock of the trees on Broadway had dwindled to the last lopsided orphans, although the scent of pine and balsam lingered, as did a gemütlichkeit that permeated the entire city. Magnolia walked south, down to Lincoln Center awash in twinkling light, then back again, enjoying the mood-elevating sociability that comes with being escorted by a matched set of canine extroverts. She could never walk a whole block without someone's stopping to converse, nose to nose, as if her animals were short, intelligent children. "Hello, sweetheart! How are you today?" And occasionally people talked to her, too.

Starbucks was as packed as on a Saturday morning, especially the tables favored by laptop users who turned them into private offices. Magnolia thought she saw a woman wave, and peered inside. It was Sasha, gathered with friends. Magnolia waved back—if she didn't have Biggie and Lola, she might have joined them—and as she turned, her eye caught the back of a man with a blue ski hat, sprinting uptown. Another Tyler doppelgänger—same long legs, same loping gait. What would Preacherman8 be doing now? Sledding with his kids under the endless black velvet of a starry prairie sky? Writing an antiadultery sermon? Arguing with little Jody Sunshine about whether to serve goose or turkey for Christmas dinner?

"Tyler—A Retrospective" had become Magnolia's favorite playlist on the iPod in her brain. When she left him in Fargo, she'd been relieved to escape into her real life, even if it was ruled by Jock and his harem of amped-up harpies. She knew there could never be anything real between her and Tyler Peterson; he'd hate the MTV-metabolism world she lived in, and she'd never find her place in a state with more cinnamon buns than bialys. In the absence of a flesh-and-blood boyfriend, however, she loved Tyler's attention. If this was twisted and pathetic, well, a therapist could make of that what she might. She told herself their harmless cyberflirtation would—out of mutual boredom or his fear of getting caught—soon fade.

Once home, she rubbed the salt off Biggie's and Lola's paws and took out her present for Abbey. The box was wrapped in shiny scarlet paper and a white silk bow, the tissue paper inside blanketing a bracelet-sleeved gold brocade jacket—circa 1962, but pristine—that Magnolia had found months ago in a downtown shop. She and Abbey planned to indulge tonight in many movies, spaghetti alla carbonara, a garlicky Caesar salad, Chianti, and—depending on the strength of their willpower—chocolate mousse cake.

"Let's make it a yearly ritual," Abbey had suggested. "Food and presents."

"You expect us to always be single forever?" Magnolia asked.

"I expect us to toast our friendship no matter what male baggage we trip over," she said.

As she turned into Abbey's building, she thought she saw the back of Blue Hat again. It probably wasn't the same guy—hard to tell in the dark. This man's hat might be navy or black or purple. As Magnolia rode up Abbey's elevator, she played the stranger game and began to weave stories about him.

Blue Hat was hurrying home to his wife for their twins' first birthday, an engraved silver spoon for each tot in his deep pockets. Blue Hat worked the Aspen ski patrol but flew in to see his widowed mother, who was on life support after a horse had bucked her in Central Park. Blue Hat owned a restaurant in Vermont and came to Manhattan to buy truffles for New Year's Eve. Blue Hat had got a glimpse of her on the subway and was traversing the streets, searching for his goddess. He would run, run, run until he found her.

The evening melted away with comfort food and Katharine Hepburn. Abbey danced around in her jacket, and Magnolia opened Abbey's gift to her, pale lilac crystals strung with tiny pearls in a lariat that would dangle enticingly between her breasts had she not been, at the moment, wearing a bulky cable knit. "I can see you in this with a low white dress," Abbey said.

"Something to look forward to," Magnolia said.

"Something to look forward to," she repeated to herself as she walked the ten blocks back home at one A.M. Manuel opened the door for her.

"You missed him," he said, excited. "The guy. Fifteen minutes ago."

"Did he leave a note?" Magnolia asked.

"Nothing."

"I'll live in suspense, Manuel," Magnolia said. "Thanks for the update."

Earlier in the evening, she'd shared the news of the visitor with Abbey. "It's getting a little unnerving," she said.

Abbey convinced her the guy was Harry. "He needs closure, Mags," she said. "The last word."

Upstairs, she decided to buttress the good mood the evening had brought by slipping into her white Jean Harlow nightgown and trying on her beads. Abbey was clairvoyant about trends. By next summer, when Magnolia would probably live in the pale lavender treasure, compliments would rain. She returned the necklace to its silk pouch and started to shut down her computer as an IM popped on the screen.

"Angel Girl," Preacherman8 said. *"Did u hav a gd evning?"*

Magnolia smiled. *"Lovely. U?"* she wrote back. It did feel lovely to end the day with someone who asked nothing of her and who made her ☺ and LOL.

"Brrrr. What did u do?"

"Party."

"Who with?"

"Aren't u being nosy?"

"Jealous type. Miss u. Visit?"

E-mail was Archie and Veronica, chaste and juvenile. An actual visit? Nightmare. Magnolia stared at the screen.

"Cat gt yr tung?" he wrote.

"I hve dogs."

"Duh. I repeat. Visit?"

"When?" she wrote, regretting the word as soon as she hit SEND.

"Now."

How slow could a woman be? He must be talking about cybersex. Was a semirepressed Midwestern preacher really capable of pounding out wet pussies, throbbing dicks, hot rods, tell me, higher, lower, there! Sucking trembling fondling licking slippery climaxes, oh oh oh yes yes

yes!!!!!!! *Ahh. . . . was it good for u, 2?* Or would it be the equivalent of an electronic dry hump?

Cybersex is definitely on my list of things to do before I die, Magnolia thought, but not tonight, not with Tyler. She wasn't going to peck away, pretending her keyboard was his pecker when it belonged to another woman, not to mention the Lutheran church.

"Gotta headache."

"Aw, let me make it better."

"Aren't u worried about J catching u?"

"Impossible."

"Anything's possible."

"Like your attitude. Visit?"

There was an easy way to get out of this rabbit hole.

"Merry XMAS & good night!" she wrote, switched off her computer, slammed it closed, and crawled into bed. Yet as she tried to read the bestseller on her nightstand, the unnerving image of Tyler as perv replaced every sentence. Ten minutes later, she turned off her light, pulled the covers to her chin, and begged for sleep.

In her dream, a phone rang. And rang. Magnolia awoke and recognized that the relentless trill was coming from her intercom. She stumbled to the hall and pressed the TALK button.

"The funny-accent guy, he's back," Manuel said. "Won't say his name."

"Well, don't send him up, Manuel," Magnolia said as she shivered.

"I ain't going to do that, Miss Gold. Wanted you to know, though. Now don't worry."

But she did. What if this Tommy-Harry-creep was a stalker? Over the last two years she'd received repeated, illiterate scrawls from a Florida prison inmate who, inspired by her *Lady* editor photo, professed to have fallen in love with her. While Scary's attorneys reassured her that the matter had been addressed, no one accused them of being a crack legal team. Could Fred the Felon have found out where she lived? Her phone number and address were unlisted, but a dedicated psycho had his ways.

Or what if Bebe had got completely unglued—enraged by the sum she was going to have to fork over to Prince Fine—and ordered another special delivery for her, this time in the form of someone a lot more like Tony Soprano? Knowing she'd been butted off *Bebe* might simply be a down payment toward the penance that woman felt she deserved. Bebe had to blame her for her public humiliation, and she couldn't inform her otherwise without exposing Sasha.

Magnolia was ready to call Abbey, who'd tell her whether she was having an attack of the paranoids, when she thought she heard someone shout her name. The snow was falling heavily now, and her view was blurred. She opened the window, letting a gust of cold rush into her bedroom. Yes, someone was shouting, "Maggie."

It wasn't Tommy, and it wasn't Harry. Blue Hat was standing below her window. Tyler in his blue ski hat.

"What are you doing?" was all she could think to yell back.

"Freezing my buns off," he said. "Can I come up?"

"You must be crazy," she shouted. She pressed her eyes shut. Was he transported here by burning lust, romantic ecstasy, or random lunacy?

"Please," he shouted back. "Maggie, I've come all this long way."

"No!" she shouted, but friends don't let friends wake the cranky couple in 2A, from which place an angry voice was already rumbling, "Hey, Romeo and Juliet, shut yer traps. People wanna sleep."

"Okay, I'm coming down," she gestured. "Go inside." She grabbed her parka and threw it over Jean Harlow, stepped into her dog-walking boots, and rode the elevator to the main floor. At the end of the hall that led to the entrance, a twelve-foot Christmas tree, switched off for the night, stood guard like a sinister totem. Magnolia's footfalls echoed as she rounded the corner, her nightgown dragging on the marble floor.

"You know this guy?" Manuel asked.

"I do," Magnolia said. "Old friend." She moved out of the doorman's earshot and fixed on Tyler. "Whatever are you thinking?" she whispered.

"Obviously, about you," he said, smiling slightly but looking like a child on the back of a milk carton.

"But to get on a plane and arrive unannounced?" Magnolia shook her head.

"*I'm aware it's a bold move.*'" She realized he was trying to mimic Jack Nicholson in a movie she'd seen on HBO.

"When did you arrive?"

"Two days ago. Staying at the Y. Walking the city. There are a lot of beautiful women here."

"Part of our regional charm."

"But you're the one I want." He paused. "I've been thinking . . ." And, apparently, following her.

Magnolia cut him off. "Why didn't you just call me?"

"I wanted it to be a surprise," he said, stepping closer.

"Believe me, it is."

This was the moment when a woman in love would reach out to the man, draw him close, kiss him tenderly, and know her life had forever changed. Magnolia searched her heart. It was . . . crowded. There was, she had to admit, warmth and not just of the chocolate chip cookie variety. Compared to most men she'd met, Tyler was forthright and kind and frighteningly handsome, especially out of his clothes. And while she was shocked by his kamikaze courting, she was less angry than overwhelmed that he'd flown thousands of miles to take a chance on her. Yet bigger than the intense pleasure of chemistry and flattery was an impenetrable layer of guilt from knowing her e-mails had apparently been misinterpreted.

Magnolia fumbled in her mental toolbox once more and pulled out . . . management skills. She took his hand. "Come upstairs," she said quietly, thinking out loud. "You'll call your wife—who must be a wreck." Magnolia turned to look at him. "Where does she think you are, by the way?"

"Visiting my brother in Butte," he said. He tapped his pocket. "Cell phone."

"We'll get you home by Christmas Eve," she murmured as they rode up in the elevator. "Your wife won't have to know." She couldn't say if the promise was directed to Mrs. Tyler Peterson or to him, or was for her own benefit.

Magnolia kindled a fire and settled Tyler across from her on the deep green velvet couch, a pot of herb tea and a plate of biscotti on the suede ottoman between them. Instead of lighting her chunky white candles, her usual custom with evening guests, she turned on a lamp. In the burnished glow, she saw him look around the room as if he were visiting the private quarters of the White House, and she felt embarrassed by her home's casual luxury. She'd never been so happy she had two sloppy dogs, who ran to him, placing their paws on his legs, looking for a scratch. He knew exactly how to please them.

"Talk to me," she said.

"I feel so trapped," he said. "Got it coming and going—listening to Jody complain about money and trying to comfort the people in my flock—plus the church is falling down on my head. Everywhere I look, complaints, complaints. I feel so alone. I'm thirty-eight and all used up. . . ." He looked into her eyes. "I was hoping you could be there for me."

"Tyler, I can't even imagine how hard your life must be," Magnolia said, and meant it. "What I do, compared to you, is . . . trivial. And I'm paid well to do it. Right now I'm feeling ashamed."

"Hey, you deserve it," he said. "Those magazines make folks happy. Either they look at celebrities' lives and thank God they're not one of them, or get a kick in the butt to change their ways. Jody is always clipping and quoting stuff she reads in magazines, yours included."

Magnolia felt too guilty to think about faraway, faceless Jody, and how she took to heart stories like "A Little to the Left—How to Say What You Want in Bed Without Bruising His Ego" or "Have You Let Yourself Go? Downsize Your Thighs in 4 Weeks."

"What I don't deserve is you, Tyler," she said.

He got up from his chair, sat next to her, and gently touched her face. His hands were still cold. She placed one of his hands between both of hers.

"I haven't felt this way in a long time," he said. "That weekend—there was something between us. Don't you love me, Angel Girl?"

Magnolia knew she wanted to be loved. But this was, she realized, irrelevant, because she didn't want to make her life with Tyler, and she couldn't return his love the way he hoped. "I'm someone who adores you, but I can't be your Angel Girl," she said. "I'm sorry if I misled you."

"Then are you my temptation?" he asked without a speck of detectable irony.

"When you use words like that, I can't answer," she admitted. "I'm still trying to believe that you went to all this trouble to surprise me here."

He looked to the other side of the room, but she knew she was reaching him.

"Tyler, listen to me. It's not our fate to be together." The Yiddish word *beshert*—destiny—popped into her mind—and not only wasn't he it, she didn't want to have to translate from Yiddish. "Tyler, I'm sorry, but I think it's best for everyone if you leave in the morning."

He nodded.

"Turning you away is very hard for me," she added, nervously twisting her hair. "I would love to play house with you, to show you Manhattan. To prove I'm not the ball-busting bitch people take me for."

"Maggie, if anyone knows that, it's me," he said, and let his lips graze hers. The graze turned into a long, deep kiss. "But I hear what you're saying. I don't like it, but I hear it." He stared into the fire. "And if this is your decision, I don't want to talk about it anymore." He pulled away. "All of a sudden I feel very tired."

She squeezed his hand.

"I do have one request," he said.

Magnolia brushed away a tear from her cheek.

"Let me borrow a dog for the night," he said, stretching out on the coach and pulling an ivory cashmere throw over his lanky frame. "If I can't have your warm body, at least let me hear a dog snoring." He shut his eyes and she tiptoed out of the room.

In the morning, Magnolia slept past ten. When she straggled out to the living room, Tyler was gone. "Dogs walked & fed," he'd written on a note. "Making 11:30 plane. Didn't want to wake you."

That night, Christmas Eve, she heard from him. *"Angel Girl, thank u for the wake-up call,"* he e-mailed. *"You will be forever in my heart. But I'm writing to say good-bye. P. S. I'm closing down this account."*

Chapter 28

One-Way Ticket to Siberia

"See you at the retreat," a new publisher at Scary boomed to Magnolia as he swung his duffel into the elevator on a late January morning. "You're speaking, right?" He'd started Monday and didn't know any better.

"Uh, no," Magnolia said. That would be the executive retreat at an upstate inn where anyone who wanted to present an idea had thirty minutes for her personal tap dance; the retreat capped by Pilates and outlet shopping, followed by an evening of fine food, good wine, and serious posturing—*that* retreat, the one a corporate editor whose job meant something would definitely be attending. She had the feeling—egocentric as it was—that the off-site gathering, which normally was held over the summer, had been moved up on the calendar simply so Jock could exclude her, enrage her, and get her to quit.

Magnolia opened the door to her office-in-exile and read her e-mail, which took only minutes now that she was no longer logging on to AOL six times a day to see what Preacherman8 had to say. To her relief, last week she'd got a handwritten letter from Tyler, who'd gone on a

Christian marriage weekend with Jody and was praying—which Mag-nolia took literally—that their marriage could be saved.

She followed her e-mail with her regular four newspapers plus the *Los Angeles Times*, then glanced at her yawning in-box. Even her magazine pile was low—she'd been reading issues cover to cover the minute they arrived. She opened this week's *New Yorker* and was idly flipping through the magazine, cartoon by cartoon, when Bebe clomped through the door.

"So what the hell are you doing in this job?" she asked by way of greeting, making a chair creak as she sat down. Either she'd gone on anabolic steroids or put on at least twenty pounds since the Polo episode. "Hanging out where you can call tips into tabloids more easily? Bankrupt a few more people?"

"Nice to see you, too, Bebe, and once more for the record, I wasn't the snitch," Magnolia said. "Not that I approved of what you were doing."

"And I am a natural redhead," Bebe said as she rolled her eyes. "You expect me to buy that?"

"I don't care what you buy," Magnolia said, wondering whether she came off as petulant as she sounded to herself. "If you're looking for an apology, you're not going to get one."

"Okay, keep your Girl Scout badge. That's not why I'm here."

"To what do I owe the honor?" Magnolia asked, genuinely curious.

Bebe looked around the office. "You know, this is really a dump. Remind me why you quit *Bebe*?"

"Quit?" The words flew out of her mouth.

Bebe raised her eyebrows. "Escaped, whatever?"

Magnolia weighed the advantage of revealing that her reassign-ment had been involuntary. She couldn't see the percentage. "If I told you what really went on," Magnolia said, "I'd have to kill you."

"Well," Bebe said. "You've made your point." Bebe studied her fin-gernails, long tips enameled in a blackened red. "Get your butt back."

Magnolia took a quick breath, turned and gazed out the window so Bebe couldn't see her shock. Suddenly, the sky looked bluer and was stenciled with wedding veil clouds. A pigeon landing on her ledge, she noticed, had feathers that shimmered silver-gray with a hint of pink. She used to think of them as flying rats, never appreciating how attractive pigeons—doves, yes?—actually were. She tried not to smile, but the sensation of Bebe asking her to return was sweet and as she savored the taste, time stood still.

"Well, don't just sit there," Bebe said, looking uncomfortable. She cleared her throat. "I'm not going to beg. What's your answer? Coming or not?"

As if Jock would let her kiss and make up with Bebe. Still, the pleasure of having Bebe ask was multiorgasmic. "I can't. Raven's here. The job's filled."

Bebe brushed away the thought and chortled. "Let Jock send her back."

"Not so simple," Magnolia said. "Scary jumped through hoops to get Raven a green card, rent her apartment, the whole bit." And, of course, that was only the public half of why Jock wouldn't make a change.

Bebe scowled.

"How *are* things with Raven, anyway?" Magnolia asked.

Bebe sat back, and the frown hardened. "I hate her," she said in a spasm of candor. "Eat Street this, Eat Street that. Who cares and where the hell is it, anyway?"

"It's 'Fleet Street.' Means she's a British journalist, that's all."

"And what's 'fine fettle'? The woman won't speak English." Bebe picked up an antique paperweight from Magnolia's desk and idly moved it from hand to hand. "I'd like to break her skinny little neck." Bebe stood, glanced back, and filled Magnolia's doorway. "So I gather your answer is 'no'?"

"Not for me to say," Magnolia said. "It's a Jock decision."

"If I can get him to throw her across 'the pond,' will you come back?"

"It could happen," Magnolia said, as Bebe walked off.

Since Jock had relocated her to Siberia, she'd only seen him twice, both times on his way to the men's room. But two could play the game. A few days after she'd been planted on the executive floor, he'd asked her, by e-mail, to analyze the covers of all the Scary magazines. Within a week she'd fulfilled the request, presented in a gleaming report which had been marking time on his desk for a week—if he hadn't filed it in the trash. Though she had virtually nothing to do, she was keeping regular hours, even if a considerable number of them each day were spent on obscure Web sites. Magnolia had been careful not to leave a computer trail that might suggest she was job hunting—she didn't want to give Jock grounds for firing with cause; there was too much money at stake. She had a contract, after all. Best to wait things out and hope that a mouthwatering job would come on the market, and she'd be on the short list.

She'd kill to see the look on Jock's face, though, when—and Bebe begged to get her back on *Bebe*. But Bebe had opted out of the retreat, so nothing would happen for days—if at all.

It was only eleven. Too early for lunch. Maybe she'd check in with the new couple. Or maybe not. Cameron and Abbey had gone out twice, and while neither claimed to be struck by lightning, they'd purchased tickets for an Off-Broadway play two weeks from that day, which, Magnolia decided, practically implied a betrothal. "She's good company" was the only reaction Magnolia could pry out of Cam, but on the subject of Cameron, Abbey was starting to sound like a 24/7 news network: how witty he was, how well-read, and how talented in the kitchen—on their second date he'd roasted a chicken for their dinner. Frankly, Abbey's oral reports were beginning to grate.

"Why didn't you ever hit on him, Magnolia?" Abbey had asked just the previous day.

"We've gone over this before," she said. "Did you forget that until five minutes ago I was his boss?" Not that the thought wouldn't have occurred to her—at least a hundred times.

As Magnolia was scrolling through her BlackBerry to see which neglected friend she could persuade to go to a movie with her this weekend, Natalie walked through her door. Today she was a gypsy queen in a flamenco skirt and a hip-slung leather belt heavy enough for a carpenter. Magnolia was surprised to see her—she and Natalie hadn't been talking since the Bebe-Polo dustup: She resented that Natalie's coolness suggested that she believed Magnolia was the one who tattled to the tabloid.

Yet she asked, "How you doing, Cookie?" as if they'd just chatted yesterday.

"How does it look like I'm doing, Natalie?" Magnolia said.

"I've seen worse," she said, sizing up Magnolia's office. "Anyway, I knew I wouldn't be seeing you this weekend—bonehead move on Jock's part to exclude you, if you ask me—and I wanted you to hear something." Natalie put on her glasses. The minute she saw it, Magnolia recognized the Smythsons of Bond Street envelope, from which Natalie withdrew a piece of paper of the sort used in the copying machine.

"Dear Mrs. Simon," Natalie read. "Magnolia Gold does not know I am writing you, but since she left *Bebe,* I can no longer live with my guilt. In case you are wondering, it was not Magnolia who informed the newspaper about Bebe Blake and Nathaniel Fine. I watched the whole thing, and I and I alone am responsible for disclosing this information to the press. I cannot reveal my identity, only that I am a member of the *Bebe* editorial staff and that I am sorry indeed for getting Magnolia in trouble." Natalie put the letter down. "It's signed, 'A friend.'"

Silence hung between them like a blast of drugstore air freshener. Magnolia hoped Natalie wasn't looking for a name to prosecute. "If you're wondering who Deep Throat is," she said, "I don't know, but it was big of her."

"Magnolia . . ." Natalie spoke in a voice usually reserved for guilty three-year-olds.

"You don't actually think I composed that letter and mailed it on my own behalf?" Magnolia asked incredulously.

Natalie stared at her while she ceremoniously removed her glasses.

"Think about it," Magnolia said. "What point would there be? I'm already so off the radar, no one would hear me if I sang grand opera."

"True," Natalie said, taking a moment to consider Magnolia's logic.

"So, I guess"—she walked around the desk to give Magnolia a hug—
"you deserve an apology. I owe you."

"Well, actually, now that you mention it," Magnolia said, "there's
something I want to run by you."

"Oh?" Natalie said.

"You're my second surprise today," Magnolia said. "Bebe was here
a few minutes ago. Odd as it may seem, she wants me back."

"Extraordinary," Natalie said. She took a moment to let it sink in.
"But what does this have to do with me?"

Magnolia put it out there: "I wouldn't mind returning to *Bebe*. Anything you could do to make that happen? Plant a seed with Jock at
your think weekend, let's say?"

"And where would Raven fly off to?" Natalie asked.

"I haven't thought it through, but you're so much better at those
moves than I am," Magnolia said.

Natalie put her chin in her hand and leaned forward on Magnolia's
desk, which she tapped nervously with her three middle fingers while
she appeared to weigh the request. The light on her biggest ring reflected
the afternoon sunlight. "Okay," Natalie said, after a moment. "If an
opening presents itself, I'll run it by him. But I can't make any promises."

"Fair enough," Magnolia said.

She could hear Natalie's flamenco skirt rustling as she walked down
the hall. The weather forecast for the weekend was suddenly looking
partly sunny.

Shipwrecked on Fantasy Island, Magnolia imagined a rever-
sal of fortune. If Bebe wanted her, seconded by Natalie, Jock would let
her return. One week drifted into the next, though, and she never
heard from him. The closest she got was a collision with Darlene.

"We missed you at the retreat," her former publisher boomed,
swooping down on her in Scary's lobby and kissing her on the right
cheek and then the left, a habit she kept going for a month or two after

her annual Alpine ski holiday. "No one understood why you weren't there, especially since we discussed new magazine ideas. They're your thing now, right?"

Good of you to point that out, Magnolia thought. "And how are Bebe and Raven hitting it off?" she said. "Bosom buddies?"

"Advertisers drooling over them," Darlene said, grinning.

"Must be quite a performance," Magnolia said. "Who gets the Oscar?"

"Oh, you do," Darlene said, turning away from Magnolia and talking loudly into the Bluetooth as she disappeared into a town car, her long black Prada coat flapping behind her.

The next day, Elvira called. Jock wanted to see her. The following day—Thursday—at ten A.M.

Now that she had the appointment, she invited Abbey and Cameron—who were going to be together that evening—for dinner. She wanted to poll them on how they thought her meeting would play out.

"He'll send you back to *Bebe*," Cam said, over grilled flank steak, a cut of beef Magnolia had learned that she couldn't destroy. As soon as he said it, Magnolia discounted his opinion, which she realized was more inspired by contempt toward Raven than his usual reliable logic. Cam had just spent the last ten minutes mimicking his new boss in a tweedy accent. "Hell of a bother to make the changes from those fact-checking cows," he'd quoted Raven as saying. "They seem to think readers give a damn whether the magazine is *true*. You've got scads too many people here anyway—in London we get a magazine out with half."

Abbey weighed in with "Jock? Admit he's wrong? No chance."

Magnolia reminded herself that Abbey was an outsider, unaware that far more curious developments took place regularly in the magazine industry; just last year a publisher bit a subordinate's nose; after an out-of-court settlement, the guy received a promotion and a raise.

"Maybe Jock has actual work for you," Abbey suggested. "Make you sweat for your paycheck." She decided Abbey was right. Jock probably wanted to hand her an endless, truly mind-numbing project—analyzing why Scary's postage costs were through the roof, let's say, which would require her to create enough Excel spread sheets to wallpaper her whole apartment before she blew her brains out.

At five minutes before ten on Thursday, Elvira phoned to say Jock had been delayed and moved the meeting to eleven, then two, then four-thirty, and ultimately to the next morning at ten. With each postponement, Magnolia felt increasingly like a force was at work to wring away every last drop of her composure, but when she walked into Jock's office, she faked a cheery smile—which he didn't return, motioning her to close the door. Magnolia sat in one of the armless chairs, facing him. He cleared his throat.

"Magnolia, I've reconsidered," he said.

"Really?" Relief surged through her like a current.

"Yes," he said, his face bleached of expression. "I've decided that with regard to the corporate editor position, we will go in another direction."

"What direction is that, Jock?" she asked. This time her smile wasn't entirely faked, though she did pray that the direction not lead to Excel spreadsheets.

He hesitated. "We will eliminate the position," he said.

"I see," Magnolia said, restraining herself from shooting Jock a high five. She wanted to get to the next bounce, when Jock would tell her—perhaps garnished with a compliment—either that she was headed back to *Bebe* because Bebe herself had demanded it, or that she would take on some sort of complex assignment that would make use of her unique talents.

"This hasn't been an easy decision," he added.

Yeah, yeah, yeah, Magnolia thought. Of course, it's hard—because he has to admit he's made a mistake—taking me off *Bebe*, even in starting the magazine in the first place, and not letting me renovate *Lady*. But does he think it's been a stroll on the beach to play the role of company loser? Let's get moving here, on to dessert.

"I respect that, Jock," Magnolia said, the only thing she could think of to say.

"Thank you, Magnolia," Jock said. "You're taking this well."

What an odd remark, Magnolia thought. What other way was there to take it? Does he actually think I'm going to miss being a corporate editor who does nothing?

She heard someone tapping softly at the door. Through the glass wall, Magnolia could see a man who worked at the other end of the executive floor. She remembered him as the dancing fool at the last Christmas party. Jock motioned for him to enter.

"Howard from Human Resources will explain everything you need to know," Jock said, as the man stood and stretched out his hand to shake Magnolia's. He wore a suit fit for an undertaker and an expression to match. Magnolia took it in and looked back to Jock.

Her stomach lurched. "What's going on?" she asked.

"Please don't make this difficult," Jock said.

"But, but," she sputtered, "what about my return to *Bebe*?"

"Excuse me?" Jock answered, and it was fair to say he snarled.

"Bebe . . ." Magnolia said. "She wants me to—"

Jock interrupted her. "That decision is mine and mine alone," he said, his voice rising. "Not Bebe Blake's. It's in the agreement she apparently never took the time to read. If that woman wanted to veto having Raven replace you, she had her chance months ago."

Whenever someone referred to *that woman,* Magnolia knew it wasn't good. A minute passed, or it could have been five. "Are you telling me I'm f-f-fired?" she asked, never remembering having stuttered in her whole life.

"No one is being 'fired,'" said the human resources representative, who had never sat down. "Your position is being e-lim-i-na-ted." He enunciated the word as if he were a speech therapist.

Magnolia's brain didn't seem connected to her mouth, if it had been connected at all for the last five minutes. "What are you saying?"

Jock and the HR heavy exchanged a glance. Magnolia now realized the reason she'd never had much contact with this man was because his primary job must be to show employees the door. When a company appoints fire marshals, is this what they mean?

"I think we're finished here," Jock said, evenly enough, though the look on his face read *Please, remove the dead rat from my rug*. "Let's not make this any more painful than it has to be."

Painful for whom, Magnolia wondered. Why did people who gave subordinates a pink slip suggest that the hurt was mutual? If her eyes had bullets, the men in the room would be on their way to the morgue.

When they were fired, some employees, Magnolia suspected, burst into tears or ran to the bathroom to vomit. Those must be people who could identify their emotions; she, however, didn't have a nerve ending in her body. All Magnolia could do was stand and meekly follow Howard-from-hell into the hall.

"Magnolia, don't worry," Howard said in a there-there-now-dear voice. "Someone will pack up your office. We'll send everything to your apartment. You can come to my office now—I'll explain your severance and you can sign off on the paperwork." He placed his hand on Magnolia's arm.

Magnolia shook it off. She stared at the man's moving mouth with its thin, colorless lips, and she began to come alive. Does he actually believe he's making this easier by telling me to get the hell out, she wondered? That packing my office is my highest concern? That I want my apartment littered with the residue of the last sixteen years of my work life? Does he think I plan to steal toilet paper, dozens of little green Post-it pads, a file cabinet of circulation records, perhaps. Was this Howard going to whistle for a police escort?

Magnolia straightened her shoulders and activated her voice to TAKE CHARGE mode. She'd be damned if, from this second on, anyone else at Scary would see her sweat or flinch or shed a tear.

"Howard, I think not," Magnolia said. "Those papers? I'll let you know my plans about them next week." She walked away before Howard could answer.

Magnolia returned to her office. She locked the door, blasted a rock station on her radio, and howled. It was a primal scream of rage, of frustration, of pain. Damn that spoiled pig Bebe for ever having convinced

Jock that her magazine deserved to exist. Damn that loudmouth Darlene for leading Bebe's charge and, most likely, working behind the scenes to assassinate her. Damn every boneheaded cretin at Scary for killing off *Lady* instead of letting her transform it into something special.

Magnolia moved to the next level of damnation—cursing herself for ever having got into such a vulnerable position, and for being deluded enough even as recently as ten minutes before in Jock's office to imagine her situation would improve. Instead of standing like a turkey in a shit storm, she should have had the guts to walk away from the money and quit months ago, to have already reinvented herself as a movie producer or the writer of a beach book.

But, mostly, damn Jock, for taking away the work she excelled at and adored. For coming on to her as if she were a happy little ho. Damn Jock for having the power to yank out her heart. Damn damn damn damn that asshole Jock.

Magnolia gasped, then laughed. She'd screamed for minutes and no one had even noticed. That's how important she wasn't.

She quickly changed her voice mail to give callers her cell phone number, sent out a mass e-mail to a select group of friends, and threw her BlackBerry into her bag. Magnolia took a look around her office, which she was still waiting for Scary to repaint even though she had moved in two months ago. I'm not going to miss this pit, she thought. Let the evil elves from Human Resources pack her.

She phoned Cameron.

"You're taking the afternoon off," she said. "I'm calling Abbey, and both of you are going to get me more drunk than I have ever been. Just name the place and don't ask why. I have only one requirement. Pick something obscenely expensive. Scary is paying—with your expense account. "

Cameron didn't skip a beat.

"The lounge at the Four Seasons?" Magnolia repeated, slipping into her coat. "Total rip-off. I love it. Meet you downstairs in five minutes."

Chapter 29

A Persistent Vegetative State

Magnolia awoke on Monday, and, with no compelling reason to get up in the cold, dim dawn, listened to the debate in her head. A kindly social worker's voice tried to soothe her back to sleep. "The dogs can wait," the voice said.

"Rise and shine, Missy," barked Drill Sergeant Haul Ass. "Run four miles. Blow your hair. Put on makeup. Dress up. Everyone hates a sloth."

"Ignore her," whispered the social worker, who had the voice of a yoga teacher. "Be good to yourself."

"Up, up," said Haul Ass. "Read your newspapers. Do a crossword. Rewrite your résumé. Sign up for Habitat for Humanity. Network. Visit a shut-in. Learn a language. . . ."

As the commands echoed, Magnolia buried her face in a pillow. Inertia sealed her eyelids and muffled any urge she might have had to mumble so much as a word. Suspended where disinterest meets disbelief, she surrendered to a lethargy one degree too tense to be called slumber.

As a four-year-old, Magnolia was the itty-bitty grandstander who relentlessly waved her hand in front of the nursery school teacher so she could explain "hibernation." At this moment her heartfelt wish was for just that, to sleep off the winter, emerging to a brighter spring. If the HR sherpa had wanted to be truly helpful, he might have tossed her a manual on how to get through the day, the following week, and who-knows-how-many months stretching before her. Magnolia felt better equipped to complete a long-form tax return than to figure out what to do next. And she suspected the tax return might be more interesting.

Minutes before ten o'clock, Lola began licking her face. She's probably afraid I'm dead, Magnolia realized. She placed both feet on the plush carpeting—and felt them sink into a warm spot of pee.

"Yech," she said, "Sorry, guys—won't happen again." She threw on a coat, stuffed her dirty hair under a hat, and found the leashes, which she'd dropped by the front door when she'd staggered in at midnight from Abbey's. On Broadway, she paused at the newsstand. Biggie pulled to keep moving, and she obliged. Perhaps the dogs intuitively knew she should avoid buying today's newspapers on the chance that media reporters had used their column inches as assault weapons aimed in her direction.

She had read one item about herself, on Saturday. One was enough. "Magnolia Gold has left her post at Scarborough Magazines for personal reasons." She wondered why any company thought they did you a favor by sending out a press release announcing you'd left for "personal reasons"? Short of their believing someone had contracted a life-threatening disease, did people suspect the *personal reason* was anything other than the minor detail of no longer having a job? Did readers imagine a more nuanced tale? She really, really wanted to get to know her cousins. She decided to go ahead with the sex change.

The sidewalks were dense with strangers—senior citizens, nannies pushing strollers, the occasional person in sleek business clothes rushing, perhaps late for a therapy appointment. She had no idea that during the workweek the Upper West Side was such a beehive of activity.

"Playing hooky?" Manuel, the doorman, asked with a wink as

Biggie and Lola stopped for their treats at his concierge desk. Ever since the evening with Tyler, Manuel seemed to think she and he were amigos. Would she need to come up with a story to explain her current life? "Got canned?" "Between jobs?" She worked up to "have a new schedule" and kept walking toward the elevator. Magnolia did not want to become one of those women whose best friend was the doorman.

Upstairs, she brewed a pot of coffee and logged on to her laptop. The day before and the day before that, she hadn't been willing to face her e-mail. She didn't know what she feared more, a tragically small number of messages from it's-not-enough-that-I-succeed-you've-got-to-fail acquaintances—or an avalanche. She didn't care what other people thought. Except when she did. Like, she had to admit, now.

"You've got mail," the friendliest voice she'd heard that day announced. Yes, she did—from scarborough.com, condenast.com, hearst.com, timeinc.com, meredith.com, and every other magazine company where she'd had lunch buddies and former colleagues. Clearly, the departing missive she'd hastily drafted had bounced all over town. There were fifty-two messages, divided almost evenly between sermon-spewers and the sympathetically bitchy, who realized that there but for the grace of God went they.

Group One apparently believed losing your job is a blessing in disguise; these things are always for the best; if life gives you lemons, make lemonade; one day Magnolia was going to thank herself for this happening; and—her favorite—when one window closes, another opens. What was she supposed to do, jump through it?

She noticed such wisdom tended to come from editors and publishers who'd rolled through life on a tide of professional good luck they'd grown to mistake for a birthright—though a few of the bromides were from less fortunate souls who simply appeared to have bought into their own magazines' spiritual porn and psychobabble.

Maybe the people who sent these words meant well, she reminded herself; they didn't have to write at all. But their lectures left a bitter aftertaste—the suggestion that nothing professionally rotten had happened and she should put her setback in perspective. Magnolia knew that's exactly what she would do—when she was good and ready, dammit—and she didn't need to get a push from editors still ruling tiny sovereign states.

Magnolia saved these glad tidings for a later response, along with those from the busier-than-thou's who suggested getting together for lunch—several months later, assuming their insane calendars ever allowed an opening.

She far preferred dear, sweet Group Two. Every one of their touching communiqués was poetry.

What the fuck happened?

Begin SSRI Rx ASAP.

This totally sucks.

Raw deal.

Which bitch is responsible? Bebe or Darlene?

Tell me the backstory.

Call! Any hour.

You've been robbed.

This happened to me, several times, and you couldn't get me out of bed for weeks.

Don't get mad—get even and, her favorite, a medley on the theme of Jock: Did a bigger jerk ever roam the earth?

These sentiments made Magnolia feel understood, and after she'd printed them out to savor, she responded to each. By the time she was finished, it was 2:30, and she'd set up fourteen breakfast, lunch, and cocktail dates for later in the month and into the next. Her lack of work was going to run up quite a tab on the corporate credit cards of industry pals who still had them. When life gives you lemons, order a gin and tonic.

At the moment, however, she was hypercaffeinated and famished, and realized she'd eaten through anything in her kitchen she could pretend was a meal. Order in lunch at home? Pathetic. Eat alone in a restaurant? Worse. Go hungry? Unthinkable. Go shopping? That's what a grown-up would do. Magnolia started making a grocery list just as the phone rang.

"Your boxes should arrive between four and eight," an unidentified wonk from Human Resources announced. "And Howard needs you to come in and sign your papers tomorrow at nine or ten. Which time works for you?"

Five minutes till never works for me, Magnolia thought. "I've had a dental appointment scheduled for months," she lied. "Can't make it until Thursday." That was the earliest she could picture herself walking through Scary's door.

"Howard's at a conference on Thursday—it'll have to be Friday. Ten."

Magnolia entered it in her calendar. She looked at this week and the next. Emptiness loomed like a persistent vegetative state.

As she went downstairs and out the door, the sergeant's voice started up again, and trailed her to the grocery store. Carpe diem, little unemployed princess. Now that you've received this unexpected gift of time, don't blow it.

Throwing groceries into her cart, Magnolia considered the arc of her life. Every summer during high school and college she'd merrily slaved away at some sort of internship, and since then had known nothing but a buzz of work. Many of her friends prayed for something they called me-time, dreaming of pedicures and trips to Patagonia—anything for a break from kids and pleasure-sucking jobs. Why couldn't one of them have been kicked out instead of her? For Magnolia, work was first-class fun attached to a paycheck.

She returned to her apartment, unloaded her bags of the six food groups—low-fat cottage cheese, Greek yogurt, strawberries, coffee ice cream, dark chocolate, and cashews. As she passed by the big, gilt mirror in her foyer, she caught a glimpse of herself and stopped for a closer look. She had a thought. This would be the perfect moment in which to disappear, let's say to Brazil, for breast implants. But she would never dare; it would be her karma to wind up profiled on *Date-line* with silicone dripping out of her nose.

She needed another idea. Take a course? The community center around the corner—a new building which had won architectural awards but could nonetheless be easily mistaken for a minimum security prison—had recently sent a catalog. She found it stuffed between overdue bills and unopened annual reports from companies in which she hadn't realized she'd invested.

Magnolia spent forty minutes studying the community center's offerings. Who knew, just blocks away, you could enroll in "Cheesecake," "Israeli Dancing with Shmulik," and "Mah-jongg for Beginners"? But what got Magnolia juiced was "Texas Hold 'Em." Poker chips! Free snacks! Then Magnolia read the fine print. The class was for forties and fifties singles.

She tossed the catalog in the garbage and curled up on her couch. What she wanted to do was . . . nothing. All the enticements that had drawn her to Manhattan, which she'd shoehorned into her frenetic schedule, suddenly seemed as appetizing as a black banana. Sample sales? For clothes to wear where? Galleries, the theater, ballet, opera, literary readings, scones with clotted cream at Lady Mendl's Tea Salon—the thought of indulging in any of them made her feel downgraded from bummed out to dejected, because there it was: she didn't want to be alone. Every friend who lived in the city was busy working, and her other buddies were young matrons exiled in the burbs, busy with lactation consultants and landscape gardeners.

A man in her life might be pleased to know she could steal away on an afternoon for a long lunch, with him for dessert. But there was no man, and she shouldn't be taking the time to look for one. She should be looking for a job.

Money wasn't her instant concern—she was still under contract with Scary as editor in chief of *Lady* and could handle the bills for a while. But soon enough she'd need a salary, and editor-in-chief positions didn't pop up often. She'd need to engineer meetings, light up the room like Forty-second Street, and be meticulous about what job she took next. Wrong choice? Hello, Has-Been.

Thinking about it all made Magnolia drowsy. If she closed her eyes, she could rouse herself in twenty minutes, shower, put on something other than her baggiest jeans and run to Zabar's. Sasha had just called to see if a group from *Bebe* could stop over after work with a bottle of wine. Magnolia would need at least some chips and salsa, and she definitely required a quickie blow-dry and Think Pink manicure.

A few minutes later—it felt like minutes, yet it was dark outside—Manuel buzzed to ask if he could send up some people who said they were from her office. Forget the blow-dry and manicure. She rushed to brush her teeth, but there was no time to change her clothes or even put on lipstick.

She opened the door. "Sign here," said a beefy messenger. "This is the first load. Where do you want 'em?" At least ten cartons as big as Bernese mountain dogs stood in the vestibule outside her door.

"Here will be fine." The delivery—which she'd forgotten about—was joined by a second load, then another. But it wouldn't be fine, seeing her work life reduced to thirty-two cartons she'd have no place to unpack. She supervised the messengers stacking the boxes in what now looked like a war memorial blocking her foyer mirror. At least she wouldn't have to look at the face of a whiny malcontent every time she walked to the kitchen.

"We're done," Mr. Muscle said. He gave her what she took as a meaningful once-over.

Is this guy coming on to me, she wondered, dressed the way I am, in a ratty Michigan sweatshirt? Then it occurred to Magnolia that he and his sidekick expected a tip. To have her apartment become a storage bin was going to cost her thirty bucks.

The intercom buzzed again. The *Bebe* gang was on its way up. Ruthie, Fredericka, Sasha, and Cameron trooped through the door, throwing their coats and bags on the boxes. She let herself be consumed by their embraces, not noticing that the door had opened again.

There was Felicity, lugging a case of beer. Bringing up the rear was Bebe, carrying numerous large pizza boxes.

"Magnolia, you look like shit," Bebe said.

If someone had used the Heimlich maneuver, they couldn't have got Magnolia to respond.

"C'mon, don't be a hard-ass," Bebe said, laughing. "I said it with love. Got a church key? Let's party like we actually like each other."

"Don't worry about a thing," Felicity said. In five minutes Felicity emerged from Magnolia's kitchen with dishes and silverware and placed them next to the pizza boxes on Magnolia's seldom used formal mahogany table. This was testimony to the historical footnote that ten years ago, as Mrs. Wally Fleigelman, she'd impersonated a grown-up and thrown dinner parties on wedding china. The group attacked the pizza and beer.

"To the enemy of my enemy!" Bebe said by way of a toast, clicking her beer bottle with Magnolia's. "May that twat Raven slit her throat with her own tongue."

Magnolia checked to see if the others—who had to take orders from Raven every day—were joining Bebe in the salutation. They were silent, except for Felicity's "Here, here."

Bebe went on. "Hell sized her up and took a dump in her office." Bebe's laughter ricocheted off Magnolia's living room walls.

Bebe took another beer. "That Jock, sense of humor like a chair," she said. No argument there, Magnolia agreed. "On his birthday, I had the art department mock up our gun cover, with me pointing the pistol at him. Damn, Fredericka, why didn't you bring a copy to show Magnolia? Dickhead couldn't crack a smile. Started going off on me about how that issue sucked, stores sending it back, Darlene needing to do a little dance about it to advertisers. In my face until I walked out on him."

A phone rang to the sound of the Patridge Family singing, "I Think I Love You." Felicity fished out her cell phone and took the call.

"Gotta tottle," Felicity said. "Pressing engagement."

"You with the 'pressing engagements,'" Bebe said to Felicity.

"Always disappearing." Bebe then shouted "Beer here!" to Cam as if he were hawking drinks at Yankee Stadium.

Bebe at center stage was, Magnolia realized, strangely relaxing. She felt like a throw pillow in her own living room and didn't even have to open her mouth. The others chimed in from time to time, but it was Bebe's show.

Magnolia wondered why she had come. It was too late for the two of them to become allies, if that's what the star wanted, and she doubted that Bebe genuinely liked or cared about her. Someone must have told her that it was good form to bond with your staff, and perhaps that's what the woman thought she was doing.

By eleven, one by one, Sasha, Cameron, Ruthie, and Fredericka peeled off, with the refuse from dinner bagged and ready to dump in the garbage. Only Bebe was left, downing the last beer.

"Nice place you've got here," she said to Magnolia, as if just noticing the surroundings. "Not what I would have pictured."

"Really?" Magnolia asked. "How did you see me living?"

"Truthfully?" Bebe asked. "Never thought about it." Her big laugh boomed again. "Hey, where's your john?" she asked. Magnolia pointed her toward the white marble powder room off the foyer. When Bebe emerged, Magnolia was glad to see her put on her coat.

"So, Magnolia, about the magazine?" Bebe asked on her way out.

"Yes, Bebe?" Why doesn't she just go home and Google herself for entertainment, Magnolia wondered.

"Give me your esteemed opinion," Bebe said in a surprisingly serious voice. "Should I cut my losses and pull out?"

"Of the magazine?"

"No, Iraq," Bebe said. "Of course, the magazine."

Was it the beer talking? From what Magnolia knew of the partnership with Scary, both parties were obligated for a lot longer than six months.

"If you do that, aren't there consequences?" Magnolia asked.

"Consequences?" Bebe said. "Honey, that's what lawyers are for."

"You know what I admire about you, Bebe—you're a risk taker," Magnolia said, thinking out loud. When she was involved in the magazine herself, Bebe's risks seemed inane, but, now, who was going to be hurt by them—Jock? Darlene? Magnolia had a glimmer of guilt when she considered that the *Bebe* staff would suffer from Bebe's missteps, but they were talented and versatile; she knew that if they floated their résumés, they'd be snapped up by other editors. "Honestly, I think you should take on more of the hot-button issues, Bebe," Magnolia said, her conviction growing. "The more controversial, the better. Let's think. How about gay marriage?" She had no idea where Bebe stood on the subject. It didn't matter. No matter her position, it would alienate half the country—and give Jock a coronary.

"Interesting," Bebe said. "Very interesting. It's my magazine. Why not get political? I could start endorsing candidates in my editor's letter."

"Now you're talking," Magnolia said.

"Or run for office myself."

"Yes!"

"Hey, I've got it," Bebe said. "Abortion. We'll do a special abortion issue." She high-fived Magnolia.

"Love it," Magnolia said. "It's genius, Bebe, genius." Could she think of one advertiser who would want to be in any magazine's special abortion issue? She could not. If Magnolia was lucky, there would be picketers outside Scary. Maybe a televised riot and a Michael Moore documentary.

"This was a hoot," Bebe said as the elevator door closed behind her. "Why weren't you this much fun when we worked together?"

Chapter 30

An Offending Prepositional Phrase

Magnolia had never visited the Human Resources department. In the past, HR always came to her. She wandered through Scary's basement and finally found Howard's pocket-sized office, where his assistant asked her to wait. Magnolia stared at a closed folder labeled with her name, hire date, and fire date. She was about to peek inside, when Howard entered and shook her hand with his clammy palm.

"Before we sign off on papers," he said without preamble, taking his chair, which was upholstered in purple squiggles, "it's customary to conduct an exit interview." Squarely in front of her, Howard placed a clipboard with a long, printed checklist. He cleared his throat. "Overall, Magnolia, how would you rate your experience here at Scarborough?" he read aloud.

"Would that be before or after?" Magnolia asked.

"Before or after?" Howard asked.

"Before or after *Lady*?" Magnolia asked. "Before or after Bebe Blake and *Bebe*? Before or after my corporate editor job?" She could hear her voice rising. "Before or after I got axed?"

Howard scribbled on the page. Probably identifying me as ready to go postal, Magnolia thought. "Start wherever you wish," Howard said.

"Being recruited as editor in chief of *Lady* was . . . terrific," she said, remembering the gigawatt glamour of being courted and cosseted for months—the counteroffer from her existing job that Scary topped, the breathless press release announcing her hire, and the veddy-veddy proper reception in her honor at Le Cirque. "I was thrilled to join this company. Everything after *Lady* . . ."

"Yes?" Howard prompted.

Should she say "sucked"? ". . . was less satisfying," Magnolia answered.

"Do you care to elaborate?" Howard asked.

"No," she said.

He raised one eyebrow. "Then on to the next question," he said, wearing the look of an ambulance technician trained to deal with trauma victims. "How would you describe Jock Flanagan, your supervisor here at Scarborough Magazines?"

"Aggressive," Magnolia said, after a split second's thought.

"Do you care to elaborate?" he asked.

Should she kick it up a notch? Magnolia settled on "inappropriate behavior," letting her fingers wink as quotations marks.

Howard raised both eyebrows and peered at Magnolia as if he were trying to imagine her naked—although maybe he was simply determining if she was an employee with a legitimate claim or a feminist who interpreted every innocent cheek peck as foreplay, and trying to recall a seminar he'd taken on how to know the difference.

"Care to elaborate?" Howard said.

"No," Magnolia said. "I don't."

"Nothing more you want to share?" This was like the moment in your appointment where the kindly gynecologist gives you the chance to reveal that your boyfriend is a drooling beast. But Magnolia couldn't see the point of screaming harassment now, when Jock would surely deny it, and she was already fired.

"Can we cut to the chase, please, and get to that?" Magnolia pointed to the bulging Magnolia Gold obituary folder.

"As you wish," Howard said, jotting a few notes on her form and putting it aside. "You have been a well-respected member of the Scarborough team," he recited. Magnolia wouldn't disagree. "In recognition of the contribution you've made here for the last few years, as well as your standing within the magazine community, Scarborough's board, under Jock's direction, has decided to give you more severance than you would, according to the employee guidelines, normally be accorded." Howard smiled beneficently.

Magnolia felt her heart beat a little faster. Jock must be feeling terrified, guilty, or both.

"We will double your severance," he said.

Her contract was good until the end of the year, and it was only January. She expected the silver lining of those eleven months' wages. But double! Almost two years. Holy crap, this was delicious. Her mind raced. She could postpone job hunting for at least six months and travel—take her parents to Israel maybe, and then see the Pyramids, and Turkey. She could finally visit Australia, then rent a flat in Paris. Magnolia pictured herself sitting at an outdoor café, wearing something by that dreamy Nicolas guy of Balenciaga. She'd pass the morning in the Musée d'Orsay and the afternoons lost in a novel—a French novel, because she'd have gone to Berlitz. Two years!

"So, if you'll sign off here," Howard said, opening the folder and offering Magnolia a pen.

Several pages of boilerplate stretched in front of her. Whereas, *yada, yada, yada,* herewith, *blah, blah, blah,* hereafter, in consideration of the payments and entitlements . . . therein her employment relationship with Scarborough Magazines, thereinunder . . . the termination of that relationship . . .

Whatever. Magnolia flipped to the final page. Gold shall receive monies equal to one month's employment.

Her brain flashed *does not compute.* Magnolia slowed down, and reread the last clause. A *month?* The words stood out like a tattoo.

"Excuse me, there's a typo," Magnolia said. She pointed to the offending prepositional phrase. "You said a minute ago that my payment would be doubled. I have a contract until the end of the year. So it comes to about two years, not a month."

Howard looked at the agreement. "No, it's correct. Perhaps there's been a misunderstanding," he added. "The contract you speak of was for when you were the editor in chief of *Lady.* That position ceased months ago. You've been corporate editor for a short time, with no contract. There was some discussion as to whether you were even entitled to two weeks of severance, but as I said, Jock has chosen to grant you a month. Now," he said, "if you'll sign."

The purple squiggles on the upholstery of Howard's chair swam like snakes in front of Magnolia's eyes. She wanted a glass of water, oxygen, Scotch. She wanted . . . a lawyer!

"You're right," she said. "I agree. There *has* been a 'misunderstanding.'" Magnolia repeated the winking finger gesture. She stood. "I'm not going to sign these. Now, if I may have those papers, please?"

"Magnolia, you've already taken almost a week to meet with me," Howard said, his patience having sprung a leak.

"Howard, I believe we're going to go in another direction here." She put out her hand. "Those papers?"

Howard handed them to Magnolia, who wandered into the hall, up the elevator, and out of Scary. She started walking blindly in the bracing cold until she found herself at the Starbucks she'd avoided since her blowup here with Harry. As she sat down, tears detonated.

Who could she call? Her professional support team consisted of a manicurist, a dog walker, a cleaning woman, Cam, and Abbey. The attorney who'd negotiated her *Lady* contract almost three years before was inconveniently incarcerated. The city was crawling with lawyers—that balding fellow at the next table, so engrossed in his phone conversation he didn't notice she'd come unhinged, was probably one. She definitely couldn't phone the environmental lawyer she'd dated two years ago. If you wanted to know about dog doo putrefying our water, he was your man, though. No, she'd need someone who could save her ass.

She finished her coffee and walked uptown, drifting in and out of stores to keep warm. At 1:30, she took herself to the café at Saks. Around her, pairs of glossy women chatted about mother-of-the-bride dresses and whether a five-carat ring was too-too.

Her phone rang. "Yes, I had the meeting," she told Abbey between sniffles. "Trying to stiff me out of my contract."

"Yikes, Jock's revenge," Abbey said. "You're not going to let him get away with it, are you?"

"I was just about to call one of those lawyers who advertise in the subway," Magnolia said. "1-800-SCREWED."

"Not funny," Abbey said. "What's plan B?"

"Tell me if I'm crazy," Magnolia said. "The person who keeps coming to mind to ask for help is Natalie."

"What makes you think you can trust her?" Abbey asked.

"With the bouquet she sent me—which was the most fabulous one I got, by the way—there was a note that read, 'Call me if you need help—with anything. I'm always here for you,'" Magnolia said. "I think that was code."

"Mags, I know this woman likes to find people furniture refinishers and gastroenterologists, but she's a card-carrying Scary person. You've lost your mind."

"You may be right," Magnolia admitted. She left Saks, walked all the way home, and reread her contract three times.

The next morning she flipped a coin, called Natalie's office, and left a message, which Natalie returned early that evening.

"Was hoping you'd call," Natalie asked. "How are you doing, Cookie?"

Natalie hated a whiner. "Pretty well," Magnolia said. "But I need some advice, and no one would know better than you."

"Love to talk, sweetie, but I've got a car downstairs and I've already kept it waiting for ten minutes," Natalie said. "Black-tie thing."

Was she saying I-can't-help-you now or I-can't-help-you-ever? "Shall I call you tomorrow in the office?" Magnolia ventured.

"Don't think we should be talking from office phones," Natalie said.

Strike two, Magnolia thought.

"But if you swing by the apartment tomorrow at five-thirty, we'll chat," Natalie suggested. "I know what you're going through."

I doubt that, Magnolia thought, thinking of Natalie's unblemished bio—Stanford, Columbia School of Journalism, perched at the top of a masthead for decades. She hated needing Natalie. But just now, she did.

"You're on," Magnolia said.

Chapter 31

What About the Obvious?

Upon close inspection a visitor could see that the volumes filling the mahogany shelves of the faux library lobby leaned heavily toward obsolete medical texts and encyclopedias. Still, the Fifth Avenue co-op building spoke of wealth, decorum, and an admissions board that subliminally whispered, "Are you kidding?" to 80 percent of its applicants.

"Penthouse it is, Miss," the elevator man said. Magnolia entered the private landing, wallpapered in a tangle of roses never seen in nature, and gently tapped a brass knocker.

"Welcome, Miss Gold," said the uniformed maid Natalie had employed at least since the era when mobile phones were as big as pound cakes. "Take your coat?"

"Thanks, Imogene," Magnolia said. "How are you?"

"Can't complain," Imogene said in a Jamaican lilt as she led Magnolia past the orchid-filled solarium. She moved so briskly, Magnolia barely got a glimpse of Natalie's newest collection, which covered the walls of a thirty-foot gallery tiled with antique limestone. When most people go to Australia, they return with kangaroo key chains. Not

Natalie, who now owned at least a dozen aboriginal paintings taller than most aborigines.

"What happened to the American folk art?" Magnolia asked. Not that she missed it. She could swear the eyes used to follow her from the portraits' bony faces.

"Mrs. Simon sold 'em at Sotheby's," Imogene said. Natalie must again be in a state of decorating flux, but Magnolia was glad to see that the red den, where they'd arrived, was intact. Like a quartet of plump dowagers, paisley club chairs faced the fireplace. Magnolia chose a seat nearest the hearth.

"Tea?" Imogene offered. "Cappuccino? A sherry?" The maid prodded the logs with an iron poker, and they responded in a blazing salute. Everything and everyone at Natalie's worked efficiently.

"Tea, please," Magnolia said, warming her hands by the crackling heat.

"The missus called to say she'll be here soon—make yourself at home."

Magnolia did. When Imogene left the room, she got up to scrutinize the vacation photos, framed identically in sterling silver. In each, Natalie was dead center—her husband, Stan, and three children flanking her. Magnolia knew many women who loved clothes, but no one liked them half as much as Natalie. On the Simons' recent Christmas trip to New Delhi, the family wore khaki—except for Natalie, a dead ringer for Princess of India Barbie in a billowing raspberry sari, matching tikka headdress, and a coordinating bindi glued to her forehead.

Magnolia sat again and began leafing through an *Architectural Digest*. As she took in the carefully crafted whimsy of Diane Keaton's kitchen, she heard Natalie's throaty alto echoing in the gallery.

"Magnolia," she shouted, her charm fully loaded. "Let me hang my cape and I'll be with you." By the time Magnolia had moved on to photos of a Bavarian castle, Natalie glided into the room, lit a Rigaud candle, and air kissed both of Magnolia's cheeks.

"So?" Natalie said, replacing her gray suede boots with red velvet slippers waiting by the fireplace.

"Hi, Nat," Magnolia said. "Thanks for having me over." She paused. Could this be more uncomfortable? "Anyway, without going into specifics, I need a lawyer," she said. "For my contract."

"No details, huh?" Natalie said, pouting in amusement. "Let me guess. Age discrimination generally begins at forty. Are you pregnant?"

"Definitely not, but can we not get into particulars, Natalie?" Magnolia begged. "And if this is awkward . . ."

"Stop right there," Natalie said, raising her hand like a traffic cop. "You know better than to take me for an obedient Scary stooge."

"Yes, but I was hoping you wouldn't put me in a corner," Magnolia said. "I just need the name of a smart lawyer . . . please."

"Because your contract, obviously, was written in invisible ink," Natalie said, laughing. "I'm playing with you. Jock tries this every time, in one way or another. It's a game. But I'm surprised you of all people are asking whom to call. What about the obvious?"

"And that would be . . . ?" she said. "I'm coming up empty here."

"I say 'married couple'; you say . . ."

"My parents, Franny and Eliot Goldfarb."

"Try again," Natalie said. "You and me doing the Macarena together at a wedding . . ."

A smile blossomed on Natalie's face as Magnolia began to remember. Centerpieces as dense as a tropical rain forest. A twenty-minute rendition of "Hot Hot Hot," which the bride had specifically placed at the top of the no-play list. A lumpish best man declaring that the couple's union would last forever. The groom telling three hundred reception guests he looked forward to the bride's being "a breeder."

"No!" Magnolia moaned. "Not him!"

"Why not?" Natalie asked. "Wally Fleigelman is one of the best labor lawyers in town, and I'm not saying that because he's my cousin."

"I am not using Wally," Magnolia said. "No! This is a guy who took the bar four times."

"Magnolia, you haven't kept up," Natalie said. "For the kind of mess you must be in, your ex is the gold standard."

"But we haven't spoken in years," Magnolia said, which was the least of it.

"Start," Natalie said. "Besides, if you handle yourself right, knowing Wally, he'll waive the fee."

"What do you take me for?" Magnolia looked at Natalie in mock shock.

"Get your mind out of the gutter—I didn't mean that at all," Natalie said. "According to my aunt Joyce, he's gaga for his wife."

"The lovely Whitney Fink Fleigelman?"

"You know her?"

"I hear things." And see things, like Whitney in a lineup of blondes photographed at the Central Park Conservancy annual spring lunch, though it was hard to see her face, given the enormous, flowered Queen Elizabeth hat.

Natalie reached for her brown lizard address book and copied Wally's number, which she pressed into Magnolia's hand as they walked to the front door.

"Thanks, Natalie," Magnolia said as Imogene magically appeared with her jacket and helped her into it.

"Anything more you want to tell me?" Natalie said mischievously as Magnolia buttoned up. "The reason why Jock would want to be an even bigger putz than usual, let's say?" An armful of Natalie's bangles jingled as she placed her hand on Magnolia's arm, "Listen," Natalie added, "I'm not Jock's type, but . . . I hear things."

Magnolia weighed Natalie's request for the fine points. "No, I'm good," she said, kissing her on both cheeks.

"Call him."

Magnolia stuffed the number in her pocket.

How do you start a conversation with a man who was your husband for a twelve-month eternity? It was nine thirty in the morning. If Wally was the Mr. Big that Natalie claimed, he'd surely be at his desk by now. She dialed his number: 212-644-0000. "Fleigelman's," a polite voice said.

No more Fleigelman Kelly Sinatra Rodriguez and Roth? Wally must be a lone ranger now.

"Mr. Fleigelman, please."

"Who may I say is calling?"

His ex-wife? An old friend? "Magnolia Gold."

"Hold, please."

A minute went by, then several, until a breathy voice came on the line.

"Mrs. Fleigelman speaking. May I help you?"

Damn that Natalie. Why did she give her Wally's home number? Magnolia wanted to hang up, but all Wally's wife had to do was *69 her and she'd be busted. "I was looking for Wally, please. This is . . . his first wife."

"Scarlett? Oh, excuse me. It's Melanie, isn't it?"

Magnolia did not care to guess how often she'd been the punch line of Wally and Whitney's jokes. "And you must be Tiffany," she said.

"Wally's at his office," Whitney Fleigelman said curtly. "May I know what this is in reference to?"

"Something personal. I mean, personal business. Well, really just business," she stammered. "I'll catch him another time. Sorry to bother you." She rushed off and called Abbey.

"I feel like such a twit," Magnolia said. "Natalie suggested I ask Wally for legal help—"

"Wally who?" Abbey asked.

"My starter husband," Magnolia said, pacing the room.

"Oh, Wally Finklestein," Abbey said.

"Close enough," Magnolia said. "Fleigelman."

"You were Magnolia Goldfarb Fleigelman?"

"Just barely," Magnolia said.

"That anchorwoman the network wanted to replace with the *American Idol* runner-up—a Walter Fleigelman I read about got her two million bucks. I kept meaning to ask if he's your ex."

"If he is, he's my guy," Magnolia said. "Oops, call waiting. Talk soon."

"Would this be the best damn ass in Manhattan?" the genial caller said. "The wildly successful magazine lady?"

The voice sounded even fuller of bravado than she remembered. "Not anymore, Wally," Magnolia said.

"You mean you didn't phone my home because you hoped to start things up again?" he said. "You're breaking my heart."

"How are you, Wally?"

"Can't complain," Wally said. "When you've got your health, you've got everything." He'd apparently morphed into his pinochle-playing grandfather. "Plus, in my case, seven-year-old twins; the wife, who's a looker, by the way . . ."

"That so?" Magnolia said.

". . . the apartment, Aspen, Southampton, solid practice—knock wood—and still shoot in the seventies. Over Christmas, my third hole in one. Boca's always been my lucky charm."

"So I recall," Magnolia said, remembering one of their more three-dimensional fights, which took place on a visit to his parents' condo there, and featured a redheaded tennis pro.

"Yes, Mrs. Fleigelman. Like I said, can't complain."

"Well, I can," Magnolia said. "My company's trying to pretend I don't have a contract. They eliminated my job and want to cut me loose with virtually no severance. I'm completely nuts. Don't know what I'll do for money. Sell my eggs?"

"Does this mean there's no Mr. Gold to pay your bills?"

"You know Daddy has never given me a dime."

"I'm thinking husband, Magnolia," Wally said, chuckling.

"Oh, one of those," she said. "Tried that. Didn't take."

"I can't believe you're still single, gorgeous girl like you. You're what now, thirty-six?"

"Give or take."

"Should have stayed with me, kid," Wally said and laughed again.

At this rate she and Wally would be kibitzing all morning. "Wally, I hate to hit you with this, but I was wondering if you'd take my case?" Magnolia said. "Please."

"So Maggie needs Wally, after all," he said. "Let's see. I have a load of depositions in Washington tomorrow, then off to Seattle Monday. May be there for a few weeks."

"If you don't have the time, I understand," she said.

"For you, I'll make time," he said. "Can you be in my office at three?"

Except for the cigar and a slightly higher forehead, Wally hadn't changed much. He was still broad-shouldered, bespeckled, and loud.

"How do I look?" he said, patting his head. "I'm one of those schmucks where Propecia did zip. The minute I turned forty, my dad's face started staring back at me in the mirror."

"You look like you," she said, kissing him on the cheek "Not a day older and oozing charm." She noticed that he still wasn't stingy with the aftershave, although along with a better wardrobe he'd upgraded to a more subtle scent than Old Spice. His suit was light gray wool; the shirt, red-striped with a white collar, French cuffs, and discreet gold cuff links; the shoes, soft, well-polished black leather oxfords; and the tie, subtle silk twill.

"You look like someone I was married to once, only prettier," Wally said, hanging up Magnolia's coat and motioning for her to sit at the couch in the corner of his office, where the wraparound windows looked north over the park and west toward the Hudson. On the

glass table in front of the couch were a stack of legal pads and a fountain pen.

"Nice outfit, by the way," he said. "My wife would approve."

For their meeting Magnolia pulled out her Chanel bag, a black
Dolce & Gabbana skirt—Wally had always complimented her legs,
whose calves, she thought, were a little too muscular, but were just
like his mother's—and a pale pink V-neck sweater that revealed a
peek of cleavage. She hoped her choices balanced needy female with
worth-every-damn-dime executive.

"Thanks, Wally," she said. "Love to see pictures of your kids."

He walked to his desk and returned, carrying a photograph of two
toothless tykes with long bangs and chin-length, dark brown hair.
"Harper and Morgan." Magnolia didn't want to ask if they were boys,
girls, or one of each.

"Adorable," she said.

"Take after their mommy," he said.

"You were always eager to be a dad," Magnolia said.

"Didn't that have something to do with our splitting up?"

That, the tennis pro, and an almost complete lack of shared interests, but who's keeping score? "We were just too young to be married,"
Magnolia said. "At least I was."

"So, tell Wally everything," he said. "You have a contract they
don't want to honor?"

"The company's claiming it's for a job that no longer exists," Magnolia said, and retold her story of *Lady* turning overnight into *Bebe*, of
being demoted to deputy editor of *Bebe*, then being switched to corporate editor of nothing.

"With all these different jobs, were you paid the same?"

"Yes, I was," she said, placing her contract on the table.

"And how much was that?"

She handed him pay stubs from each job.

Wally whistled. "Not bad," he said. "That's what you get for putting in commas? Wish my wife pulled in dough like this—I wouldn't

be busting my balls." As Magnolia scrolled through her brain for a response, he continued. "Just kidding—I love that Whitney's home with the kids. She's always bitching about how all those committees she's on are as much trouble as a job, though. You tell me."

"I wouldn't know," answered Magnolia, truthfully.

"So, anything more?" Wally asked.

Magnolia debated whether or not to tell Wally about Jock's come-on. As a lawyer, he'd surely heard far more lurid tales, but as an ex-husband who always accused her of being a flirt—despite the fact that he was the actual cheat—she hated the idea of Wally's judging her. She decided to edit that part of the story.

"Seems pretty clear to me," Magnolia said.

"Then I'll read this contract on the plane, sweetheart," he said. "Call you as soon as I can, and you call me if any other details come to mind."

"Thanks, Wally," she said, as he helped her into her sheared mink. "Your fees?"

"You can afford me," he said, laughing, and paused. "Hey, I'm thinking, why don't you come to our place Sunday? Whitney's having a bunch of friends in. Superbowl."

"Oh, I don't know, Wally," she said. "Don't you have to ask her first?" To get him to take her case, did she really have to sit through hours of Fleigelmans and football?

"What's to ask about?" he said. "We're at 740 Park. Any time after four."

"Sunday, then," Magnolia said. If she didn't come down with a twenty-four-hour virus and have to beg off.

"Just one more question," he said.

She knew it: he'd read her mind, and was going to nail her on the Jock proposition.

"Shoot," she said.

"What'd you do with the ring?"

"The ring?" Magnolia said.

"You forgot about a flawless three-carat emerald-cut stone set in platinum with two serious baguettes?" he asked. "Did you hock it? Turn it into a necklace? That's what Whitney did with her first ring. You need a loupe just to find the little fucker."

"The ring's in a safety-deposit box, Wally," she said. "I like knowing it's there."

"You always were such a Midwesterner," he said. "And I was some schmuck to let you keep both that ring and the apartment." He gave her a hug and patted her butt.

As Magnolia walked down the hall, she could still hear him laughing.

Chapter 32

A Defining Address

"Abbey, what do people wear to watch football?" Magnolia called to ask.

"Cameron, what do people wear to watch football?" Abbey shouted. At three o'clock on Sunday afternoon, it appeared that Saturday night hadn't ended for the newest couple on the Upper West Side. Magnolia didn't like to think of herself as a jealous person—not when it came to close friends—but the thought of Abbey and Cam having sex made her squirmy; not picturing-your-parents-in-bed squirmy, but close. Was it because she felt left out? One down? Proprietary about Cameron? Abbey kept insisting they hadn't slept together, but Magnolia found that hard to believe.

Cameron grabbed the phone. "Jeans, sweatshirts, and cheeseheads," he said.

"Cheeseheads are for Wisconsin," Magnolia said. "Even I know that. They're not playing, and I doubt this is a sweatshirt crowd. Put Abbey back on."

"Go with a sweater and good jeans," Abbey said, taking back the phone.

"You're sure? Friends don't let friends make fashion faux pas."

"Trust me."

"Boots: high or low?"

"Low," Abbey declared. "It's Sunday afternoon."

Of the better buildings on Park, 740 was even more persnickety about its owners' pedigrees than Jock's residence up the street or Natalie's co-op on Fifth. Rumor had it a co-op applicant needed a liquid net worth of more than $100 million to pass the board, which was rumored to have ixnayed showbiz types, including Barbra Streisand and Liz Taylor. It wasn't lost on Magnolia that Wally had probably extended his invitation to give her a taste of what she'd missed.

She checked the time that the game would start, and calibrated her five o'clock arrival to be late enough to avoid pregame chitchat, but not so late that Wally would consider her a brat unworthy of his help. Magnolia checked her coat in the lobby as the doorman directed, and rode the elevator to eleven.

Maybe this was a sweatshirt crowd: a pack of small boys in Manhattan private school sweatshirts opened the door and confidently yelled out, "Hello" like the type-A investment bankers and hedge-fund managers they would no doubt later become. Magnolia took a guess and addressed the tall child who resembled Wally's pre-braces, Raquette Lake Boys Camp photographs. "Are you Morgan?" she asked.

"Do I look like a girl?" he said. "I'm Harper. Who are you?"

"A friend of your daddy's," she said. "Magnolia Gold."

"Hi, Mrs. Gold," he said, and tore off up the staircase with his friends. She left the chocolates she'd brought next to a vase of white calla lilies on a large, exquisitely polished table. As Magnolia was trying to figure out her next move, one of the French doors at the end of the foyer opened. From a distant room in the generously proportioned apartment, she heard a buzz of conversation. A waitress walked toward her with a silver tray of empty champagne flutes.

"Hello, Mag—Miss Gold," she said.

"Hello," Magnolia said.

"I temped for you when Sasha was on vacation," she said. "Remember?"

"Of course," Magnolia said, drawing a blank. Magnolia prayed she'd done nothing to offend this girl, and that she wasn't marketing a novel based on an egomaniacal editor in chief.

"I'll be back with refills," the waitress said and pointed toward the doors. "Everyone's in the media room."

Magnolia entered a gathering of no less than a hundred people. The room smelled like a cigar bar crossed with the fragrance floor of Bloomingdale's. Every woman was perfectly blow-dried and the men——Magnolia couldn't see any men, although at the other end of the room, which had to be at least thirty-five feet long, she could pick out an enormous plasma television screen. Magnolia was always astonished that you could live in Manhattan for years, yet in a crowd notice no one familiar. An anthropologist could get loopy mapping the town's circles of influence——so many people considered themselves supremely important, yet relatively few circles overlapped.

As she searched the room for Wally, a trio of blondes seemed to be looking at her. Magnolia approached them. "Magnolia Gold," she said, extending her hand.

"Lizzie," the tall one said, "and this is Julia and Rachel." Each was dressed as if for the most important job interview of her life, except with more jewelry. Magnolia saw them eyeing her jeans. If they asked about them, she'd have to say she'd just come from mucking out her barn, that the horses couldn't wait.

"Are you a friend of Whitney's from nursery school?" asked the medium blonde.

"Did Whitney and I go to nursery school together?" Magnolia asked. What a peculiar question.

The women exchanged a glance. "Did your *child* go with the twins to the Ninety-second Street Y?" the short one asked. "We've never seen you up at Horace Mann."

"I don't have any kids," Magnolia said.

"Oh, forgive me," she said, casting her face in dramatic sympathy. "I am so sorry." Magnolia was afraid the three of them were going to hug her.

"It's fine, really," Magnolia said. This would have been a good time to add, "I work." Except she didn't.

"So how do you know Whitney—from a committee?" Lizzie asked.

"I don't," Magnolia said, "know Whitney, that is. Can you point her out?"

As the women turned to search for their hostess, Lizzie's long blond mane swatted Magnolia in the face. "That's Whitney over by the chairs," Julia-or-Rachel said. "Isn't it sweet the way she's made this look like a screening room?"

"Right," Magnolia said. All she could see of Whitney was that she was taller than Lizzie—and Wally, for that matter—and blindingly blond.

The four women stood together awkwardly. As Magnolia drilled deeper for schmooze material, she was grateful when Julia-or-Rachel spoke up. "Say, maybe you can help me," the short one said. "My housekeeper's gone AWOL. I'm losing my mind. My son, the apartment . . . It's been since Monday. Know of anyone? I'm ready to slit my wrists."

Magnolia's weekly cleaning woman had just lost one of her other day jobs. "Which day do you need?"

"Well, every day," the woman said, as if Magnolia were brain-damaged. "But for the right person I suppose I could give up Saturday."

"What are the responsibilities?" Magnolia asked.

"The usual. Laundry, ironing, cleaning, errands, cooking, dog walking. I like someone to help me get Joshy ready for school, so that means starting at seven, but she can go home after the dinner dishes are washed and put away. That's usually around nine thirty, some-times ten," the blonde said and smiled charmingly. "I'm flexible."

This woman worked Scary hours. She might be a brain surgeon, a district attorney, an Internet entrepreneur with an international travel schedule. Magnolia was intrigued. She asked the question asked of her at every New York social event for the last ten years, the one she was hoping no one would ask today. "What do you do?"

"*Do?*" the blonde replied in the mystified tone Parisians reserve for those who butcher their language.

"Your job?" Magnolia said. "It must be fascinating."

"I don't work," the blonde sniffed. "I'm *busy*."

Magnolia's comment hung in the air like a fart. She scoped out the room, caught Wally's eye, and waved enthusiastically. He walked over to Magnolia and embraced her from behind as she noticed Whitney noticing her.

"I see you've met Whitney's friends," he said. "Ladies, how do you like my ex-wife? See, I always get myself a looker. Mind if I steal her away from you beauties?"

Magnolia imagined they didn't.

"You might have told me your friends dress up to watch football," Magnolia said.

"Whitney's friends," he said. "Look at me—I'm the same old slob."

"Wally, I know that sweater," she said. "It's Tse cashmere."

"Doll, you look gorgeous," he said. "All the guys are looking at how you fill out those shrink-wrapped jeans."

While she knew she wasn't dressed like a Hassidic matron, neither did she want to be seen as a tart. Even worse, had she gained weight and not realized it? "Some apartment, Wally," Magnolia said, eager to change the subject. "This place is enormous."

"Five thousand square feet," he said. "With the kids, we need the space."

Need or want? Another Manhattanite who couldn't tell the difference, Magnolia thought.

"C'mon, let me show off my favorite room," he said. "We can talk business there. I've read your contract." He led her to his upstairs plaid-as-a-kilt study and closed the door. "Whitney had these shelves made for my trophies," he said, pointing to a wall of shiny, engraved silver cups from two decades of golf tournaments.

She really is a trophy wife. "Very impressive," Magnolia said.

"Who are you trying to kid—you hate golf," he said, grinning. He sat in one of two club chairs and patted the other. Magnolia sat down. "Listen, I've read over your particulars. It's an interesting case."

Magnolia didn't want her case to be interesting. She wanted it to be over, with her savings, pride, and future intact. "How so, Wally?"

"Well, your company—Scarborough, is it?—could argue that they acted in good faith. After they stopped publishing your magazine, they did, in fact, give you another job for quite a few months—until the end of the year—so they might say they fulfilled their end of the deal."

"I'm with you," she said.

"Then again, this new job, the 'corporate editor' thing, one might argue that it was bullshit . . ."

"One might."

". . . and that Scarborough did not, in fact, act in good faith—sticking you in a crappy job they planned to eliminate, and, if you'll pardon the expression, leaving you up shit's creek."

"That's my address, all right."

"Then again, had I been your legal counsel when you accepted this job, I'd have made damn sure we paid attention before you started, and addressed the contract issue then and there," he said. "You and your attorney were asleep at the wheel, toots."

"I didn't have an attorney," Magnolia admitted. She was suddenly afraid she might cry. Why hadn't she gone over the details with a lawyer? Because the thought had never occurred to her.

"That's my girl, Miss Naive and Frugal," Wally said in his own sweet way. He began to doodle on a legal pad. "I keep wishing there was more to this," he muttered. "Some point where I could really stick it to them. Got any help for me in that department?"

"You know I really didn't 'accept' this job," she said, after thinking it over. "There was never a choice."

"Why is that?" he asked.

Magnolia cleared her throat. "My boss," she said. "I mean my ex-boss, Jock Flanagan . . ." The tears started.

"What is it?" Wally said, without the bluster now.

"He propositioned me, that asshole," she said. "I rebuffed him. The corporate editor job was payback. I had to take it—or quit—which I thought meant I'd be breaking my contract, so I stuck it out, feeling like a horse's ass."

"Okay," Wally said, drawing out the word as if he were enjoying it as much as a long toke on a good joint. "Now we're getting somewhere. To the best of your recollection, what did you tell that sonofabitch?"

"Well, I can't remember, exactly," Magnolia said. "That I didn't think this was the time for him to make advances—the company was already in the middle of a scandal. Bebe had just been caught making sexual overtures to this boy, Nathaniel Fine, who worked as our intern. The press blasted her. The company was trying to clean up an enormous mess."

"I heard about that," Wally said. "The parents are members of our club and everyone was talking. Fourteen-karat gold gossip. I felt sorry for the kid, but it all went away. The Blake woman paid up big. Your company, too, up the wazoo."

"Scary paid?" Magnolia said. "Really? I never knew that. How do you know?"

"I was in a foursome with the kid's dad."

"How much did Scary pay?"

"Settled out of court, close to a half million from the publishing company, and more from the talk show gal. But stick to your story, darling," Wally said. "We might be on to something."

"I told Jock, 'I like the way things are now.'"

"Not sure I understand," Wally said. "What did you mean, 'I like the way things are now'?"

"I didn't want us to be a couple."

"I like the way things are." Wally let the phrase roll off his tongue. "'I like the way things are.' Now we're hot."

"I'm not the first woman Jock's tried to harass at work," Magnolia added quietly. "He's the matinee king. If you could get to Elvira, his secretary . . . She keeps his calendar, makes his reservations, pays the hotel bills. . . ."

Magnolia heard a knock at the door. "Just a minute," Wally said as he took notes. The knocking became a pound.

"Coming," Wally shouted. "Coming."

Wally got up to open the door as Whitney Fleigelman flew through it, blond hair flying.

"You fucking creep, Wally," she said, slapping him in the face. "Not again! 'I like the way things are,'" she mimicked. "How many times are you going to use that old line? And you!" She jabbed Magnolia with her finger, which had a long nail tip manicured the pink of a baby's tush. "You! 'I like us as a couple,'" she whined. "You had your nerve to call my home. You piece of dreck. And you come to my home in fuck-me jeans. Get out!" she ordered. "This minute!"

"Whew, Whitney, honey," Wally said, grabbing his wife by her narrow shoulders. "Calm down. You heard things wrong. And there's no need to insult Magnolia."

"Magnolia!" she said. "Like I care. And what kind of a bullshit name is that?"

"It's her name, Esther Rose!" Wally said. "Oh, excuse me, *Whitney*, the mother of Morgan and Harper. And what were you doing eavesdropping anyway?" His voice was as loud as Magnolia remembered it could be.

"Wally, I'll fuckin' listen to anything I want to in my own house, thank you very much," Whitney screamed, her face as red as her slinky sweater dress. Magnolia wondered if Whitney got a discount at Tse Cashmere or had just scored at the pre-Christmas sample sale.

"Magnolia! You've never gotten over that tramp, have you, Wally?"

"Get a grip, you crazy bitch," Wally said. "We have guests. You know, I shoulda stayed with Magnolia. At least she doesn't sit on her fat ass all day."

"You're saying my ass is fat?" Magnolia and Whitney asked the question in unison. But neither of the Fleigelmans heard Magnolia. They were too busy dismembering each other.

Magnolia left the study. "I'll call you," Wally yelled as she shut the door. "I've got an idea or two about your case."

Magnolia went downstairs. Guests were cheering in the media room, and the box of chocolates she'd brought was still sitting on the table where she'd left them.

"I forgot something," she said to the intern-turned-waitress, who just then walked through the foyer en route to the kitchen. Magnolia opened the box, offered a truffle to the waitress, and took one for herself. She closed the box, put it under her arm, and left.

Chapter 33

Yesterday's History, Tomorrow's a Mystery

"**You're getting a what?**" Magnolia asked Abbey as they trolled the Sunday flea market two weeks later.

"Getting a *get*," Abbey said. "A Jewish divorce."

"You're only half Jewish."

"My mother's Jewish—that's what counts." She rummaged through a box of old coins, examined one, and deemed it unfit for her new collection of chokers and charm bracelets.

"Tommy's conversion was pretty lightweight—you weren't even married by a rabbi." Magnolia had been the maid of honor at the wedding, which featured an officiating judge who couldn't have passed a breathalyzer test.

"Immaterial," Abbey said. "If a Jewish woman remarries without a proper religious divorce, any kids she might have in a second marriage are considered illegitimate," she recited, as if she were being tested on the answer. "Didn't you get one with Wally?"

"I refused. If his kids are bastards, I take no responsibility, and he's not going to hear it from me—not when he's been providing such excellent pro bono work on my behalf."

"How's that going?" Abbey asked.

"Scary caved some, but Wally's holding out for more," Magnolia said, putting down an art deco bracelet as soon as she saw the price tag. "Back to you—where's Tommy with all this?"

"In Australia with his new honey but willing to get it done," Abbey said. "He's flying in tonight, and I don't want to lose track of him again."

"But you certainly aren't getting any pressure from Cameron, that crusty old WASP," Magnolia said. "Are you?" She wasn't sure if she even wanted the answer.

Abbey grimaced, which with her delicate features managed to look enchanting. She struck some people as fragile, but Magnolia knew she was a waif built of titanium. "You're spending too much time with a lawyer—what's with the third degree?"

"Something's off," Magnolia said.

"What may be off is Cameron and me," Abbey said. "I like him— he's smart and makes me laugh and is a god under those flannel shirts and baggy jeans—"

Magnolia closed her eyes. "Too much information."

"—but I met someone on my trip to Paris. Someone *Juif.*"

"*Juif?*"

"French and Jewish. Gorgeous in that dark, brooding, existentialist way. He's been e-mailing, but he's very traditional and won't go out with me until I get a get."

"Does Frog Man have a name?"

"Daniel Cohen."

"A name that crosses borders," Magnolia said, "like the euro."

"He has piles of those. *Grandmère* is a Rothschild. They own vineyards." Abbey was practically bouncing. "So, will you come with me tomorrow afternoon when I get a get? Rabbi Nucki recommended that I bring a friend."

"As in nooky?"

"As in Nachum. Means 'wise.'"

"Sweetie, I'm so sorry, but I may be busy," Magnolia said. Everywhere, Magnolia heard doors slamming. She didn't want to be part of another ending, even if it was the conclusion of a marriage that never should have been.

"Busy how—cleaning your closets?"

"Don't mock your unemployed friend," Magnolia said. "Believe it or not, I have a job interview Wednesday, and I am devoting myself to maintenance—highlights, haircut, eyebrow and leg wax, manicure, and shoe shopping." Magnolia failed to mention that most of these events could wait for Tuesday. "But if this means a lot to you, I'll reschedule."

"Let's flip," Abbey said.

"Fair enough," Magnolia said. "Heads, I go." The brave on the buffalo nickel seemed to wink at her as he hit the table, face up. "Go-*get*ter reporting for duty," she said. "Tell me where to be."

Monday afternoon, address in hand, Magnolia searched a street for a stately cross between the neo-classic courthouse downtown— the one where Martha Stewart flirted with the press—and Temple Emanuel. Unless Abbey gave her the wrong information, however, the high rabbinical court of the land dwelt in a dingy, postwar building easily at home in any Communist-built section of Moscow. Magnolia checked the wall directory: twelfth floor, the Beth Din of America.

"Welcome," said a ruddy-faced receptionist, whose desk was crowded with a computer, an oversized box of tissues, and paper zinnias arranged in an empty seltzer bottle. She looked no older than twenty and wore a long, gathered denim skirt; a frilly, high-necked blouse, and a blond wig. "I'm Malka," she said as she extended her childlike hand, which featured a dainty diamond solitaire and a gold band. Around her wrist was a red string.

"*I'm* Malka!" Magnolia said, "I'm named for my father's great-aunt."

The only time she'd been called by that name was at her Bat Mitzvah on a windy November morning twenty-five years ago. Was she Malka bat Elliot? She couldn't recall her proper Hebrew name.

"So, we're like sisters," the receptionist said. "Are you here for your get?"

"I'm the support team," Magnolia said. "My friend will be here any minute now."

"So, Malka. Sit. Some tea maybe? Soda? Rugelah?"

"No, thanks," Magnolia said. "I'll settle in with my book."

She pushed aside the faded orange pillows on the brown foam sofa and opened Anna Wintour's unauthorized biography, which she hadn't been able to put down since she had started it the previous evening. Magnolia felt for Anna—no fewer than two hundred writers, photographers, and former colleagues of the *Vogue* editor in chief had gleefully tattled about how she was as cruel, cunning, and controlling as she was pin thin. On the other hand, the same crowd admitted she was brilliantly talented and industrious and could charm any snake slithering along her red-carpeted path. Magnolia thought she might learn a thing or two. How, for example, did Anna beguile every man she wanted for whatever purpose she had in mind?

She was at the part when Anna has chewed her way through a number of magazines no longer included on her résumé and lands an interview at *Vogue*. Its editor in chief at the time asks her what job she aspires to. "Actually, the job I'd like is yours," Anna answers before the woman ejects her from her office.

Do not—repeat, not—do that tomorrow, Magnolia warned herself. As she began to wonder where Anna got her mutant strain of monstrous confidence—clearly, they didn't grow it in North Dakota next to the amber waves of grain—Abbey walked through the door, Tommy at her side. For a couple planning to dissolve their marriage in the eyes of the tribe, they looked decidedly amicable.

"Hey, Magnolia," Tommy said, hugging her. "Sorry to hear about the end of your career."

This might, Magnolia realized, be his version of sensitivity. "Thanks, Tommy, but I'm hoping all that's ended is one bad job, not my whole brilliant career," she said, still simmering from his midnight visit months earlier.

"Mr.——" Malka was checking her paperwork. "O'Toole?" She pronounced the name as if she were sounding out a word in Urdu. "Rabbi Plotkin can take you in to see Rabbi Lipschitz now. Sign here, please." Tommy walked to the desk as a tall young man entered the reception room from another chamber.

"Rabbi Nachum Plotkin," he said, shaking Tommy's hand. "Or Nucki, your choice. Mrs. O'Toole, you stay—we'll call you soon. You brought a friend, yes?"

Abbey pointed to Magnolia.

"Malka," the receptionist said.

Rabbi Nucki approached Magnolia. "You are a good person to be here," he said. Magnolia put Anna in her bag, and extended her hand. The rabbi stepped back slightly, kept his hands by his sides, but smiled. Magnolia pulled back her hand. "Thank you, Malka," he said. "We'll talk later." He escorted Tommy into the next room and closed the heavy double doors behind them.

"Are you sure about this?" Magnolia whispered to Abbey. "You guys aren't even legally separated yet—and this step is terminal."

"I'm sure," Abbey whispered back. "It's over with Tommy, no matter what."

Magnolia noticed Malka looking at them and felt rude for whispering. "Malka, have you worked here long?" she asked.

"Since I graduated from Barnard last year," she said, "but I'm quitting soon." She smiled happily and patted her stomach.

"Congratulations," Magnolia said.

"Mazel tov," Abbey added.

"I'm blessed," she said. "My husband, Avi—he's a cardiology resident at Mount Sinai."

"Malkele," an older man's voice called from the other room. "Please send in Mrs. O'Toole."

Magnolia squeezed Abbey's hand as she got up to join Tommy and the rabbis.

"Malka, are you married?" the full-time Malka asked when they were alone.

"No. Well once, a long time ago," Magnolia said and decided to answer the inevitable question. "No kids."

"I know we've just met, but I'm wondering. Would you like to meet someone, Malka, a beautiful woman like you? Avi has an older brother, Chaim. He's thirty-nine. His wife—of blessed memory— died. Breast cancer. Tragic." Malka wiped away a tear. "Seven wonderful children who need a mother. It's been a year. You walking in today . . . You know *beshert*?"

"I know *beshert* and thank you for thinking of me, I'm very flattered, but . . ."

"But what?"

"But no," Magnolia said. "Though I thank you."

"You're not interested. I understand," Malka said and returned to her computer. In a moment she looked up. "Actually, I don't understand. If you don't mind me asking, if you're single, why wouldn't you want to meet such a good man?"

Magnolia put down her book. She began to feel like a tax return under audit. "I'm concentrating on work right now, that's all."

"What is it you do?"

"I work in magazines—although I don't have a job just now." She looked around, expecting to see at least a dog-eared *Reader's Digest*. Nothing. "Malka, do you read any magazines?"

"Yes, at the doctor's office," she said conspiratorially. "Especially fashion magazine—I like *Good Housekeeping, Woman's World, Vogue*."

Anna Wintour, meet your reader, Magnolia thought, as Rabbi Nucki walked out of the other room and sat across from her. It took a moment for Magnolia to calculate that minus the Old Testament beard and side curls, dressed in a suit that didn't hang on him as if he'd just lost thirty pounds, and with a spritz of bronzer to mitigate his indoor pallor, Rabbi Nucki could pass for a handsome Wall Streeter.

"It's sad when a marriage ends, yes, Malka?" he asked.

"Yes, Rabbi. But Abbey and Tommy—they'll meet other people. I'm sure of it."

"God willing. And you, Malka?"

Magnolia looked into his earnest face. A better shirt and tie wouldn't hurt, either. "My first priority is to find a new job, Rabbi," she said. "The man can come later," she added, surprised to be revealing anything to this ambassador from a galaxy far, far away.

"If you believe, they both will happen, Malka," he said. "Put your faith in the Almighty. As a great Talmudic scholar once said, and I paraphrase, yesterday's history, tomorrow's a mystery, and that's why they call today 'the present'—every day is a gift. *Forshtes*, Malka?"

"Yes, I understand," she said.

"If you work hard, Malka, and believe, God above will reward you," he said. "You want your dreams to come true? Then don't sleep, and when fortune calls, offer her a chair."

Rabbi Nucki rose to leave. "Thank you for coming today," he said. "It means a lot to your friend." He smiled kindly and returned to the inner sanctum, leaving Magnolia to decode his message. As soon as the door closed, however, Malka hurried over and sat down next to her.

"Malka," the young woman said, "put out your left wrist and close your eyes." When Magnolia opened them, she saw a delicate red thread tied next to her Cartier watch. "This will bring you blessings," Malka said, "and protect you against the evil eye of jealousy." A pity Scary didn't direct-deposit these bracelets with paychecks. "Thank you," Magnolia said.

"Don't thank me," Malka said. "This bracelet was meant for you. It will remind the One Above you want His protection. When you see it, you will remember to perform acts of kindness—like you have today—and that humility is an attribute of God."

I'm not sure I do humility, Magnolia thought.

"Don't take off the bracelet," Malka warned. "When the job is done, the bracelet will be gone, *Barusch Hashem*." She gave Magnolia a quick hug and returned to her computer as Abbey and Tommy opened the door, accompanied by Rabbi Nucki. Tommy's eyes were as red as Magnolia's newest accessory. Before he hurried out of the office, he shook the rabbi's hand, kissed Abbey on the cheek, and waved to Magnolia.

Magnolia and Abbey gathered their coats. "Go in peace, ladies," Rabbi Nucki said as Malka offered her good wishes. In the elevator, neither Abbey nor Magnolia spoke.

"You want to grab some coffee?" Magnolia asked when they reached the street. "Or just cab it uptown?"

"Caffeine," Abbey said. "I don't feel too steady." They walked a few blocks in silence, until they found a Starbucks.

"What was it like in there?" Magnolia asked, as they faced each other over cappuccino.

"I sat apart from Tommy," Abbey said quietly, "about twenty-five feet back from the rabbis and a scribe who wrote on parchment with a quill. Tommy had to read from a binder with plastic sleeves. Hebrew words written in English. He signed something. I don't have a clue what it said."

"So he might have traded you for three briskets and a she-goat?" Magnolia said. Abbey didn't laugh. "Did they ask why the marriage went bad?"

"They only wanted to know two things—if I kept kosher and Shabbat," Abbey said. "I assume they were disappointed on both counts."

"No chance to vent about what a rascal our Tommy was?" Magnolia asked. "Or for him to confess his sins?"

"No," she said. "At a certain point I had to pretend I was leaving with our marriage contract. They put a tiny cut in it and kept it. The people were gentle, but the whole thing was . . . formulaic." Abbey wiped away a tear. "A marriage, *poof,* gone. I don't know what I expected—more pomp and ceremony, certainly. I feel a lot more upset now than before."

Magnolia put her arm around Abbey's shoulder, and the two of them sat until Abbey stopped crying.

"I know you're going to be all right," Magnolia said softly. "A woman has to be open to possibilities, and you are."

Abbey looked unconvinced.

"When fortune calls, offer her a chair," Magnolia said.

"Today's horoscope?" Abbey sniffed, wiping her tears and finding a small smile.

"Something a wise man said," Magnolia said, pushing her red string under her sweater.

"Are you going to tell me to go on JDate, too?"

"Listen to Malka the wise," Magnolia said. "We've got to work hard at this happiness business."

"Thanks for coming," Abbey said. "I'm just rattled. Tommy broke down in the rabbi's office—it's only hitting him now that he blew it. I don't want to be with him anymore, but we loved each other once and I need to mourn. I'm going to go home, get in bed, and hope I'll sleep for twenty hours."

"If you want your dreams to come true," Magnolia said, "don't sleep."

Abbey looked at Magnolia as if she knew what she was talking about.

Chapter 34

What Would Anna Do?

"He'll be with you in a few minutes," the executive-floor receptionist said.

Should the interviewer want to see it, Magnolia had printed her résumé on paper with such a high fiber count a historian would be able to read it centuries from then. The best pages from *Lady* and a few from *Bebe* were tucked away in a black matte leather portfolio. Her new Jimmy Choos could pass muster here. The question was, could she?

If you visited the company's cafeteria, you'd know that three-fourths of the employees looked as bedraggled as much of the industry. A few six-foot swans contemplated whether to indulge in a leaf of radicchio, but you could count more jeans in the room than four-thousand-dollar suits, and most of the women actually had hips. Still, for a top job, Magnolia realized she'd be held to the highest standard.

If Magnolia knew what job she was being considered for—if, in fact, she was being considered for a real job, not simply being appraised like a piece of meat—she might be less nervous. But when the editorial director e-mailed her, he'd been cryptic, and you don't ask questions at Fancy—which is how Magnolia thought of this company. They weren't the biggest publisher, and despite their glossiness, you could subscribe to many of their magazines for five dollars a year on Mags4Cheap.com, but in the Triple Crown of hauteur, Fancy was a high horse indeed.

The editorial director met her himself in the outer lobby on his high floor. He walked her to his office, which, she was surprised to see, was smaller than her former suite at *Lady*.

"Magnolia Gold," he said. "At liberty, I understand."

"Free at last," she said.

"Bebe Blake, now there's a train wreck."

Knock Bebe and she'd come off as a whiner; say nothing and she'd bore this guy. Magnolia settled on: "Bebe looks out for herself—you've got to admire her grit."

"But why back her in a magazine?" he said. "What was Jock Flanagan thinking?"

Another land mine. For all Magnolia knew, Jock and her interviewer played squash together twice a week. Magnolia decided to respond with a laugh—not a guffaw or a giggle, more of an airy chuckle—although when she heard herself she was afraid she had whinnied like a sick pony. Damn, what would Anna Wintour do? By now he would have mortgaged his co-op to buy her a sable.

"How's *Bebe* selling?" the editorial director asked.

To say it was selling poorly wouldn't do her a bit of good. "Rather well, actually," Magnolia replied.

"Well, these numbers Darlene Knudson's spewing—are they for real?" he said. "Our publishers here aren't buying them."

"You'd really have to ask Jock or Darlene," Magnolia said, wishing he'd move to another topic.

He read her mind. "So what do you think of our magazines?" he said.

If she critiqued ferociously, he might kick her into the hall, a theme park of archival photographs and voices as muted as the color palette of the decor. Overpraise the magazines, and he'd think she was a suck-up with nothing to bring to his table. Magnolia decided to say only good things, sticking to magazines where she didn't stand a chance of ever becoming editor in chief, and emphasize how much she particularly loved the men's, home design, and food magazines.

"I dig almost all of what you do," she concluded. Did she just said *dig* in an interview?

"Any you don't dig?" the editorial director asked wryly.

This is where an interview could turn ugly. Why didn't this man stop torturing her and let her know why she was here? Should she happen to pounce on a magazine that he had decided was flawed and flay it in a manner he found cunning, at this notably mercurial company she might land herself a top job with a clothing allowance, a car and driver, and an interest-free loan for a country house. *But which magazine?* She could feel the seconds ticking away—or was that her pounding heart? She may as well have been on a TV game show.

"Your teen title," she finally said. "You could shake that one up, not be such a clone of the mother ship."

"Oh, really?" he said. "Do you think you're the right generation to lead that magazine?"

Ouch. Why didn't he come out and say it: you, Magnolia Gold, have aged out of the teen books, which were—inexplicably—how the industry referred to magazines. Perhaps this company hadn't heard that sixty was the new forty, and thirty-eight was a mere tot. She'd pretend he hadn't made the remark. "Oh, no, teen books—not my thing at all," Magnolia said, hating herself for being a weenie.

"Magnolia, I like you," he said. "You've done some lively work in a tired category. You have a good eye, an amusing voice, and you don't seem to take yourself too seriously." He made a sound that took Magnolia a second to realize was a laugh. "We're up to our eyeballs in divas here. . . ."

Magnolia felt her ego inflate like a beach ball. She was going to thank him, when he continued.

". . . and you have the common touch."

She'd been drop-kicked back to Fargo. Though their readers weren't any more gentrified than anyone else's, at Fancy it was all class all the time.

"I'm going to take that as a compliment," Magnolia decided. "I'd like to believe I can see into the soul of a fair number of women."

His half-smile returned. "You know, there's a new project we might talk about," he said. "It's flying a bit under the radar and goes by the code name *Voyeur*. You've heard about it, I assume."

Magnolia hadn't. "Of course," she said, and smiled in a way she hoped he took as knowing.

"Excellent," he said. He removed a short document from a folder on his big, uncluttered desk. "So if you'll sign this mutual confidentiality agreement, please."

Magnolia stared at the legal letter. Nobody said no to this company, but Wally would beat her with a nine iron if she made another forensic boo-boo. "I'm going to have to show this to my attorney," she said.

"Really?" he said, raising his eyebrows. "None of the other candidates have."

"Isn't it refreshing that I'm not like any of your other candidates?" Her remark failed to make him remove the agreement. Magnolia put down her silver fountain pen and closed her tiny blue leather notebook.

He took her measure. "We could handle this differently, if you wish," he said. "I won't show you our prototype, and you could simply hum a few bars and get back to me on paper."

"I could," Magnolia thought. Only she couldn't, since she hadn't a clue what *Voyeur* was. For all she knew, he had made up the name and project two minutes before. "But I really need to know a bit more. What I've heard, it's . . . sketchy."

He walked to his window, which had a commanding view of Times

Square. With his back turned to her, he spoke. "Think of the magazines that celebrate Hollywood. Now imagine something entirely original. That's *Voyeur.* Sex, glamour, dirty secrets."

"Aren't you describing *Vanity Fair*?" Magnolia said, not to mention *Dazzle* and all the others. Celebrity magazines had been popping out like free boob jobs in a San Fernando Valley shopping mall.

"Not literary," he said, as if that were obvious. "It would be for next-generation readers—and I use that term lightly—who prefer the celebrity blogs and webzines. I would think your experience with Bebe would allow you some insights." He gave her a sphinxlike glance. "We'll only run with this if we find the right vision," he said. "It's always about the editor."

"Deadline?" Magnolia asked.

"I'm leaving soon for the Oscars. A few weeks from now is fine."

"I'm on it," Magnolia said.

"By the way," he said, "the red bracelet? Nice touch. Very Madonna."

Chapter 35

Knickers in
a Twist

Magnolia didn't know whether her firing was an exclamation point at the end of a flickering work life or an ellipsis during a long, rambling passage, but one thing she did know was if she was going to breakfast with Natalie, she'd need the holy trinity—good hair, good shoes, and a good bag. One, two, three, blastoff.

As Magnolia pushed open the door to Michael's crowded entry and deposited her coat, someone jostled her from behind. She turned in time to see Jock roaring out the door, his head a black comet careening across Fifty-fifth Street. Darlene was the comet's tail, her long Prada coat flying. But before her former publisher could cut and run into the cold morning, she turned to Magnolia and yowled two words: "Whip smart."

Escorted by the maître d', Magnolia walked to Natalie's usual table, nervously waiting for faces to turn and inspect her. Every diner, however, was buried in a paper. Magnolia thought she heard someone say the identical words Darlene had shrieked, but she couldn't hear— the room was rocking as if it were the White House Correspondents dinner and the First Lady had got off a zinger piercing the president's ego.

"Fresh orange juice?" the waiter said, barely concealing a giggle.

"Just coffee, please," Magnolia answered.

"Mrs. Simon phoned to say she was running late," he continued, his snicker exploding. He paused until he controlled himself. "May I bring you a newspaper, Miss Gold? *Wall Street Journal*, the *Times*—"

"The *Post*, please," Magnolia said. With today's thorough primping, she hadn't read it. The waiter placed the tabloid in front of her, folded. All she could see was the business end of a whip dangling by a pair of sturdy, fishnet-clad legs and thigh-high, nosebleed stiletto boots. She unfolded the paper. Before her was a middle-aged matron wearing a diabolical expression, a black leather thong, and a laced bustier that any lingerie saleswoman worth her microfiber would instantly dismiss as several sizes too small. The determined face looked familiar; the cleavage, terrifying; the headline—WHIPSMART.

Holy latex G-string! Felicity Dingle, you snake in the grass, Magnolia thought. No wonder your cell phone is always going off. "I Think I Love You," my big foot.

"We're a family newspaper, friends, so turn the page if you'll blush over your morning java and spank us if you think we're naughty," the page-two article began, "but perhaps Bebe Blake isn't keeping Felicity Dingle sufficiently busy whipping things into shape at *Bebe*, her eponymous magazine. Or maybe her day-job's salary is so stingy, the poor dear needs to moon . . . light. Our exclusive sources inform us that in the evening hours, the high-ranking *Bebe* editor, aka Mistress Whipsmart, finds career satisfaction by, uh, dominating some of the city's finest, as she had for years among the House of Lords, where she was known professionally as Nasty Nanny and, in later years, Madame Mumsy. In London, she is reputed to have carried the tools of her trade in a large handbag purchased at Her Majesty's favorite leather shop. . . ."

Magnolia read quickly until she got to a quote from Felicity. "Don't get your knickers in a twist," Mistress Whipsmart told *Post* insiders. "It's not as if I opened a dungeon next to a day-care center. I provide a needed public service, like the National Health. Oh, forgive me. You don't have that here in the States. More's the pity.

"On the subject of humiliation, neither Jock Flanagan, president of Scarborough Magazines—which has a multimillion-dollar stake in *Bebe*, launched last year to replace the venerable *Lady*—nor Bebe Blake, the magazine's editor, nor its publisher, Darlene Knudson, could be reached for comment."

As Magnolia read the item for the third time, Natalie tapped her on the shoulder and sat down next to her.

"If you looked any happier, I'd say you had a new boyfriend or a new job," Natalie said. "Which is it?"

"I wish," Magnolia said. "Natalie, I know a lot of people at Scary have a shoe fetish, but this is taking it too far, don't you think?" she added, laughing so hard, coffee almost shot out her nose.

"What are you jabbering about?" Natalie said.

"You didn't see the *Post*?"

"*The Washington Post?*" Natalie said. "Of course. Why?" Natalie always waited to read the juiciest morsels in the *New York Post* after she arrived in the office and her assistant presented clips to her.

"Have a look," she said, waving the tabloid. Natalie's eyes got as big as the mantilla comb supporting her updo.

"Oh. My. God," Natalie said. "Elizabeth is going to flip her wig on this one."

"Elizabeth Lester Duvall's joining the Witness Protection Program," Magnolia said. "Who do you think spilled this story?"

"Who cares?" Natalie said. "What's important now is for us to look like it's inconsequential."

"Why does that matter to me, Natalie?" Magnolia said. "Scary gave me the boot."

"Of course," Natalie said. "What am I thinking? But be a pal and stop gloating." The waiter came to take their order. "Excuse me for a minute, Magnolia," Natalie said as she left, presumably to make a call or two to ensure that none of Scary's newest scandal stuck to her. In the ten minutes she was gone, several editors stopped by Magnolia's table to offer breathless variations on the theme of "You look fabulous! I've been meaning to call—I'll have my assistant set up coffee or lunch. Okay?"

"So?" Magnolia said, when Natalie returned. "How do you think this one's going to play out? Scary paid for the Polo incident and it went away."

"This one's not coming at a particularly propitious time," Natalie said, in a low voice. She shot Magnolia one of her cryptic looks.

"What is it?" she asked.

Natalie turned to her right, then left. One pleasure of eating at Michael's was that the tables were far enough apart so that people could shake on deals and share names of matrimonial attorneys without being overheard. Still, Natalie hadn't stayed in the industry for decades by taking chances. "You didn't hear it from me, Cookie, but the circulation numbers for *Bebe*—well, let's just say Darlene is a very creative accountant," she said even more quietly.

When it served their purposes, the editors in chief at Scary were loyal to the company, but as was true of any dysfunctional family, sibling rivalry could pop out at any time. If someone else's magazine took a tumble, you could smell the schaudenfreude like blood at a slaughter.

"She's cooking the books?" Magnolia asked.

"Of course I'm not a hundred percent sure, but my friends in circulation are dropping hints along those lines." Natalie made it her business to stay on excellent terms with that particular back-office department, which, on any given day, had the pulse of how each magazine was selling.

"*Bebe*'s not a rip-roaring success?" Magnolia said, clutching her chest. "I'm shocked. Shocked."

"Like I say, these are speculations, but subscribers are apparently canceling like crazy," Natalie said, looking smug. "The business with

Nathaniel Fine and that gun cover . . . Advertisers are cutting loose, too. Darlene's putting out numbers that are pure fiction."

"With Jock's blessing?" Magnolia asked.

"Naturally," Natalie said.

"Does Bebe know?" Magnolia asked.

Now it was Natalie's turn to laugh. "Not if Jock can help it. You know how these contracts work. If *Bebe* fails to clear certain hurdles, Bebe's allowed to pull out—and if she does that, then Scary will never make back its investment. But—of course—I don't know any of this for a fact. It may be innuendo from some bean counter with an ax to grind because Darlene wouldn't dance with him at the Christmas party."

Magnolia took it all in while Natalie finished the last bite of her egg-white omelet.

"How are you, by the way?" Natalie said. "Cousin Wally coming through?"

"Wally's a prince," Magnolia said absentmindedly while she absorbed the enormity of Natalie's news.

"Glad to hear it," Natalie said. "Now, how's the job hunt?"

Magnolia decided not to report on her *Voyeur* conversation. Natalie was, after all, the editor in chief of *Dazzle*—theoretically, a competitor. "It's nowhere," she complained. "When you're a publisher, people assume if you can sell ads in one magazine, you can sell anything. But as an editor"—Magnolia knew she sounded kvetchy—"there's this idea that you have to be a walking mission statement for your magazine. Anyway, there are zero jobs now. Somebody would have to be assassinated to make room for me."

"You have to get out, be seen," Natalie said. "Make a job find you."

"From your mouth to God's ears," Magnolia said, touching the red bracelet hidden under her sleeve. "What's new with you—besides Mistress Burberry's bombshell?"

"Well, *Dazzle* couldn't be hotter," Natalie said, as she always did.

"Up ten percent on the newsstand and surpassing last quarter with ads. But it sounds as if Scary's going to be depending on us more than ever to be a cash cow. The pressure . . ." She looked at her watch. "Gotta run. Can I give you a lift? My car's waiting."

"No, I'm headed uptown," Magnolia said. "I have a meeting, too," she said—with Biggie and Lola.

As she walked to the subway, her BlackBerry beeped. Bebe. She hadn't heard from her in months. Magnolia called back on the cell number she had given her only after Bebe decided Raven was a she-devil.

"Magnolia, that you?" Bebe said, answering on the first ring. "Can you believe this?"

"Did you have any inkling?" Magnolia asked.

"Well, a pair of handcuffs once fell out of her bag, but who doesn't own a pair?" Bebe said. "Now Jock's ordered me to dump poor Felicity. Just because he took a boondoggle to China, he thinks he's the little emperor. It's my magazine. Mine. I'd like to take one of his suspenders and strangle that preppy asshole. . . ."

Magnolia held the phone away from her ear while Bebe ranted.

"Magnolia, you there?" Bebe shouted. "I asked you a question."

"Excuse me," Magnolia said. "There's a lot of traffic—I couldn't hear you."

"I asked you if you'd come back," Bebe said. "Poor Felicity deserves a long vacation."

"Aren't you forgetting Jock dumped me?" Magnolia said.

"But these are extraordinary circumstances," Bebe said. "Damn. Hang on. Another call."

The pause gave Magnolia a chance to savor the moment. Even if she hadn't been fired by Scary and wasn't disputing her severance, this wouldn't be the burning building she'd pick to run back into.

"It's my agent," Bebe said. "*Good Morning America* and *Today* are fighting over me for tomorrow morning, and tonight I'm doing *Larry King* and *Letterman.* No time to fly to L.A. for *Leno.* Rats." She clicked off.

Magnolia dialed another number.

"Cameron," she said, leaving a message. "Want to come over tonight for *Larry King* and *Letterman?* Bring Abbey. Bring the world. I'm celebrating."

"Where's Abbey?" Magnolia asked Cameron as he walked through her door. He kissed her on the cheek, hung his overcoat in the closet, and in a few giant steps made himself at home in front of her television.

"Wouldn't know," he said, flipping channels till he found *Larry King Live.* "Abbey and I had the let's-be-friends talk."

"Sorry to hear that," Magnolia said. And surprised, since Abbey hadn't returned her last two calls.

"Don't be. Some Frenchman she met's in town. Frankly, I'm relieved. I'd been rehearsing the same speech for weeks. She's sweet, Abbey. I didn't know how to put it to her."

Magnolia fixed Cam with a long, quizzical stare, searching for a sign that Abbey's rejection had wounded his heart or at least stung his pride. She had an impulse to push up the glasses that had slipped down his nose, but the Continental Divide of boss-employee relations wouldn't close, despite the fact that they hadn't worked together for months.

"What?" he said. "Really, it's over. *Finito.* Abbey's great, but there was zero chemistry. Not enough meat on her bones. And not only do I not know a radiant cut from a rat's ass, I don't want to know."

In truth, everything about the way Cam's lanky, blue-jean-clad legs stretched in front of him looked relaxed as a breeze. Magnolia shrugged and walked into her kitchen.

"There she is," he shouted as she pulled two beers out of her refrigerator to accompany the chips she'd put on a tray. "White beluga sighting! Gold, get in here."

So now she was Gold. Magnolia bolted to the TV. For her appearance,

Bebe had chosen a bustier, form-fitting jeans, and go-go boots, all in Clorox white.

"I guess this is her idea of a virginal look," Magnolia said. "Drive home the old 'If you think I'm a dominatrix, think again' message."

Bebe leaned toward Larry King, her breasts pouring over her bodice, and beamed a smile that stopped short of her eyes.

"Bebe, when you started your magazine, did you ever think it would be this hard?" Larry asked her.

In the second that Bebe hesitated, Magnolia could sense this wasn't the question she had expected. "Hard, Larry?" she said. "We're starting this out by talking about who's hard?" She let loose her boisterous cackle.

Larry smiled slightly. "Seriously, every year almost a thousand magazines launch," he said. "*Naked Dachshunds* and yours were just two last year. Anyone who can start a fire, it seems, can start a magazine, and usually all that happens is they burn a lot of money. Most new magazines fail."

Larry did like to hear himself talk.

"How much money has *Bebe* burned?" he finally asked.

"He's a meanie tonight," Magnolia said.

"Just jerking her chain," Cameron said.

"Larry, honey, nobody said putting out a good magazine is gonna be cheap," Bebe countered, her smile vanished. "I'm not about cheap. *Bebe* will cost what it costs. It's my magazine."

"Sort of," Magnolia said, imagining Jock's blood pressure soaring as he watched the interchange. He was probably pulling up his copy of their partnership agreement this very instant and exercising every four-letter word he knew. Magnolia turned to Cameron. "You're the managing editor—how over-the-top are her costs?"

Cameron rolled his eyes and waved his hand above his head but shushed Magnolia so he could fixate on Bebe, who'd moved to a vigorous defense of Felicity's right to whip anyone she felt like in the privacy of a boudoir.

"You and I can agree on that, Bebe," Larry said, "but will your readers? They're a conservative crowd. Won't they feel Miss Dingle is an abomination?"

As the censors bleeped out Bebe's response, Larry turned straight to the camera. "On that subject, I wonder what tonight's other guest has to say? Dr. Laura Schlessinger, are you standing by in Los Angeles?" The camera panned back to Bebe in time to catch the fury contorting her face. Had she been unaware that a virtue-hawk was the other guest? Bebe dipped into her décolleté, fished out her mike, and—making a clatter—stood.

"Bebe," Larry said. "Where you headed, girl?"

"Outta here, my friend," Bebe snapped. "It's been a pleasure, but I know a setup when I see it."

"C'mon, Bebe," Larry said. "Let's calm down."

"Let's not," she said.

"Bebe, you're a talk show host yourself—you know this is just . . . television," Larry said, shaking his head. But Bebe had already stomped off.

Cameron and Magnolia stared at the screen. "Did we just see what we just saw?" she asked.

"Career annihilation in the making?" Cameron said. "Thought our Bebe was a cooler cucumber."

"Jock must actually be getting to her," Magnolia said. "Can't wait to see how she's going to handle *Letterman*."

Cameron looked at his watch. "Wish I could stay but," he said, "gotta write."

"How's that book coming?" Magnolia asked. As far as she knew, Cameron had been writing the same book for the full four years she had known him. Although maybe he already had a best seller or two under a pseudonym. Maybe even a series. That's how little he mentioned this side of his literary life.

"On the home stretch. My agent e-mails me every day to make sure I don't have a minute's fun."

"What's the book about?" Magnolia asked coyly, as she had many times before. Cameron just laughed and gave her an amused look.

"Can you at least tell me what kind of novel it is? Mystery? Thriller?"

"None of the above," he said.

"You're writing chick lit! God knows you could, working at a women's magazine. No, I've got it. You're doing male chick lit. Yes! Dick lit!"

"Pardon me, Ms. Gold," Cameron said in an imperious tone, "but even if all gentlemen do is reflect on their tiny penises and ample love handles, what we write are called *books*. Got that? *Literature*. Even if the title is *The Unibrow Diaries*."

"*The Devil Wears Tighty Whiteys?*"

"He always does," he said. With that, he gave her an unexpectedly huge hug, grabbed his jacket, and left.

Magnolia walked back to her TV. Since her one and only current job prospect was *Voyeur* over at Fancy, she'd decided she needed to steep herself in pop culture and had been TiVo-ing every celebrity program, cable and network. The chuga-chuga-chuga of celebrity's gossip train was roaring through her brain. She might know diddly-squat about what river flows from the Allegheny and the Mononga-hela, or take a day to recall the name of the newest Supreme Court justice, but she'd developed an encyclopedic knowledge of whose cel-lulite was the most cottage cheesy, which bride in a Vera Wang gown was a lipstick lesbian, and the name of which star was caught in flagrante delicto with his personal chef. Ask her anything, and Mag-nolia could lob back the answer faster than you could spit the word "spin." She wasn't proud of this ability, but she knew it might eventu-ally pay her way.

Besides, celebrity shows passed the time, and when she became utterly brain-dead, there was always *Jewels of Vegas*. Magnolia had just bought her mother a pink sapphire and amethyst ring for only

$139 (there were only ten available—she had to act fast) when she decided to catch a tiny catnap so she could stay awake for *Letterman.*

She opened her eyes at what seemed like ten minutes later, but Dave was already finishing his "top ten" list.

"And the number one reason why no one should ever start her own magazine," Dave said, "is that the swimsuit issue of *Naked Dachshunds* may outsell you." To applause, he held up a cover featuring a pregnant dachshund posing with her belly proudly displayed like Demi Moore on *Vanity Fair.* "And now, welcome our next guest, my very good friend Bebe Blake."

Bebe had changed out of her dress whites. In solidarity with serious editors, she'd switched to black. Feathers, however, engulfed her. She looked like Big Bird in mourning.

"Dave, you're not going to ambush me, are you?" Bebe said, twinkling a laugh.

"Bebe, wouldn't dream of it," he said.

"Would you mind if a friend joined me?" she said, smoothing her feathers as she sat with a thunk on the couch.

"Not a dachshund, is it?" he said. "No stupid pet tricks tonight."

"It's my dear colleague, Felicity Dingle," Bebe said. Felicity walked out, carrying her infamous leather satchel. "In case you need to be whipped into shape." Dave and the audience joined her in a roar of laughter. The three of them chattered, every remark as sweet as cherry pie, even a long yak that contrasted sexual habits of Americans to those in the UK.

Magnolia was getting ready to turn off the show, when Dave turned to Felicity, "Bebe seems content, doesn't she? True, Bebe?" he added.

"I am—now," she answered, a grin splitting her face.

"How's that?" he said.

"Now that I'm quitting the magazine," she said, looking entirely pleased with herself. She opened Felicity's satchel and pulled out at least a dozen copies of *Bebe,* which she dropped on the floor, then punted off the set. "I made my decision earlier today. I don't know what happened to freedom of the press, among other freedoms, but no one's going to tell me what to put on the cover of my own magazine, or who to hire to run it. I can't put up with any more abuse and interference. You heard it here. My magazine is history."

Dave's eyebrows went up. "Now, Bebe—say it ain't so. *Bebe*'s a mere babe, and you're no quitter."

"If something's not working, don't drag it out. I've been married twice and when the relationships stopped working, I moved on. Men, magazines—all the same. Ciao. Adios. Life's too short for aggravation."

"Haven't you been having fun, Bebe?" Dave said. "And that gun cover—well, you were making quite a statement." He held up the gun cover issue, which had been conveniently placed on his desk.

"Do I have to spell it out, Dave?" Bebe said. "I quit. Q-U-I-T. Scarborough Magazines can take their magazine and put it where the sun don't shine."

"Oooh, harsh, Bebe. Harsh." Dave said, then looked into the camera. "Ladies and gentlemen, you heard it here first. How about it? Bebe Blake calling it quits to her beloved magazine. It will be dearly missed. Especially among gun lovers. It's bye-bye, *Bebe,* bye-bye. Or shall we say bang-bang, *Bebe,* bang-bang?"

The next thing Magnolia knew, a car commercial replaced David Letterman's face. Magnolia immediately called Cameron, but his line was busy—because he was dialing her cell.

"Didn't I say that Bebe was going to quit tonight?" Magnolia asked. "I knew it!"

"No," Cameron said. "You didn't say it, and you didn't know it."

"But I was thinking it," Magnolia said. "I swear."

"I don't even want to imagine what goes on in that brain of yours, Magnolia," Cameron said. "Anyway, it's probably Bebe's idea of a publicity stunt. Make Jock sweat and beg to take her back on her terms."

It occurred to Magnolia that what he said made sense—and that she'd just displayed the sensitivity of a tank. If Bebe quit, Cam would be out of a job. She better back down. "Thanks for stopping by this evening," she said. "You're definitely right, as always."

"Pleasure's all mine," he said. "And, you know, I was wondering . . ."

The phone indicated another call. "Could you hold on, Cam? Just a second . . ."

"Surprised?" Bebe said.

"Nothing surprises me anymore," Magnolia answered. "But why now?"

"Jock, Raven, Darlene, bunch of losers," Bebe said. "Who needs this shit? Nobody tells Bebe Blake what to do. I hope they'll have fun putting out *The Magazine Formerly Known as Bebe.*"

"Bebe, if you weren't serious about the magazine, why did you start it?" Magnolia said. *And bomb my life?*

But Bebe didn't answer. She had already hung up. Magnolia went out to walk her dogs and, when she returned, promptly fell asleep. Only the next morning did she remember she'd never got back to Cameron.

Chapter 36

It's a Hard-Knock Life

"My name is Magnolia," she began, stepping into the inferno of a crowded subway car in July. "I know you hate people interrupting your morning, but I just need a moment." Most of the commuters resolutely read religious tracts, swayed to their music, or looked through her, their goal to avoid eye contact—and, if possible, skin contact—with fellow passengers. "A short time ago, I had a good job and benefits. Now I'm homeless.

"I don't rob. I don't steal. I don't do drugs." Technically true, if you discounted the occasional joint at parties. "If you could find it in your heart to help me—money, food, whatever—anything will be appreciated." She walked the length of the car, her Tod's tote open. "Just thinkin' about tomorrow clears away the cobwebs and the sorrow," she sang in her wobbly voice with its five-note range. One man yelled, "Put a lid on it," but as Magnolia hit "I love ya tomorrow—you're always a day away," a woman opened her own Tod's bag and tossed a half-eaten box of Good & Plenty into Magnolia's bag.

"Good luck," the woman said with deep sincerity as she squeezed

Magnolia's hand, her manicure impeccable in contrast to Magnolia's own ragged nail stubs.

Magnolia kicked off her heavy comforter and woke in a puddle of sweat, her heart throbbing like percussion at the MTV Music Video Awards. Damn—she shouldn't have visited that storefront psychic yesterday, but its handout beckoned: "Are you depressed, anxious, losing peace of mind?" All of the above, she decided. "Stop feeling sorry for yourself. This gifted European spiritual adviser will remove negative energy and help you achieve inner serenity." The next thing Magnolia knew, Svetlana of West Seventy-eighth Street was predicting "a dazzling future" but warning her, as she chewed what Magnolia hoped was gum and not tobacco, to "not keep repeating mistakes and put what happened yesterday behind you."

Which psychic phenomenon from yesterday? Svetlana didn't specify. Bebe abandoning *Bebe*? How could this touch her now that she was unemployed and possibly unemployable? Two months had passed, and while she'd been feted at breakfasts, lunches, and cocktail hours, all that happened was that she'd listened to no fewer than twenty-seven editors bitch about their own work. Despite a five-pound weight gain, after each date Magnolia felt a little emptier, exactly the emotion she experienced handing the gifted Svetlana twenty bucks.

Svetlana may have exorcized energy all right. Magnolia collapsed that night at eight-thirty. Now she stumbled into her shower and washed away the dream. As she was getting ready to scrub off yesterday's mascara as well, her phone rang.

"Magnolia, she who snoozes loses," Wally crooned. "Pick up, my princess."

She rushed, dripping, to the phone she'd left on the sink.

"Wally, I've been hoping to hear from you," she said. For the last six weeks, her case had progressed in slow motion, keeping pace with the rest of her life. Wally split a hair. Scary split another. Every few days he sent her an e-mail reporting that little had developed. Twice

Magnolia had been ready to ditch the whole exercise, but "This is how lawyers show how big their dicks are," Wally insisted. "When the schmucks at your old company make a dumb-ass move, I just laugh, let it sit for a few days, then go back for more. Not to worry."

If her dream was a barometer, however, she was worrying. "Any developments on my case?" she asked.

"Tell you in person, kiddo. Can you be in my office in, say, an hour?" he asked. "I'm leaving this afternoon for Aspen with Whitney and the kids, but you and I gotta talk."

"Good news?"

"Is my name not Wally Fleigelman?" he responded. Unfortunately, it was.

"See you soon," she said.

For their ten o'clock meeting, Wally had ordered breakfast. He carefully prepared a bagel for her, smearing it with chive cream cheese, adding two glistening slices of Nova Scotia salmon, and topping it with a thick slab of Bermuda onion.

"Oops, forgot you hate onion on Nova," he said. "Little hick. I'll take yours." He plucked off the onion and placed the extra slice on his own bagel tower. "It's not like you're going to kiss me—though you should."

Magnolia glanced pointedly at the photo of Whitney and the twins.

"I deserve a kiss—I've been a champ," he added. He poured them each a large cup of coffee from a silver Georg Jensen pot.

"How's that, Wally?" Magnolia asked.

"Let me first tell you that your old company's legal department should stick to copyrights and libel. What is it you call your company?" Wally asked. "Scary?"

"Very," she said.

"Okay. Scary failed to consider, when they switched you to deputy editor and then corporate editor, that the term of your contract for editor in chief was still in effect," he began. "They screwed up royally with that one."

"Goody," she said. "So, we have a case?"

"Patience, darling. It gets better," he said. "Turns out your other lawyer wasn't such a putz after all. There was a clause in your contract stipulating that in order for Scary to change your title, they needed your written consent."

"Really?" Magnolia asked.

"Which, obviously, they didn't get. Don't you love it? God is in the details."

"So, is that our case?"

"Magnolia, you'd think you were paying me by the hour. That's just the beginning of our case. No check to cash just yet."

Her smile vanished.

"Scary isn't talking big enough numbers." He quoted her a figure.

"That's almost my salary for the rest of the year, Wally," she said, shifting to panic. "Can't you just say yes, and stop the games?"

"They said take it or leave it, so I said shove it," he said. "Chump change."

Why did I ever get involved with Wally? Magnolia asked herself. Why? Was this what the psychic meant about not repeating mistakes? She rubbed her temples.

"Stop stressing, Mags. Believe in Wally, who is pulling another card out of his pretty little deck."

"And that would be?" Magnolia said.

"A little gem called quid pro quo sexual harassment." Wally's face lit up as if someone had offered him a blow job. "So, if you don't mind, I'm going to turn on my tape recorder and ask you a few questions."

Magnolia suddenly felt dirty. She'd rather analyze her sex life with her own father than do a play-by-play with Wally. But there he was, wired and ready.

"Did Jock Flanagan make sexual advances or requests to you, or otherwise engage in conduct of a sexual nature?" he began. At least his tone was quiet and professional.

Magnolia nodded yes.

"Speak up, please, Magnolia."

"Yes, he did," she said. "Jock Flanagan did make sexual advances to me."

He nodded yes and smiled. "Was the sexual conduct welcomed by you?" he asked.

"What do you think?" she said, looking at him as if he had the IQ of a matzo ball.

"Magnolia, a simple yes or no?"

"No," she said, recalling Jock's paw on her leg, his fingers running up and down her thigh.

"Did you reject his advances?"

"Yes!" Magnolia was surprised by the steel in her voice. "Of course."

"And after that incident were the terms or conditions of your employment adversely affected?"

"After that I was moved from being deputy editor to corporate editor, and soon after that I was fired." It wasn't cancer. It wasn't even a broken arm or a classic broken heart. She hesitated but said, "I call that 'adverse,' yes."

Wally turned off his tape recorder. "Was that so bad?" he said. "We've had worse conversations over what color white to paint the living room."

Magnolia remembered and laughed. "You and Whitney agree on all that?"

"I pick my battles, doll," he said. "Marriage—who ever thought that one up?" He began to tidy his desk. Magnolia considered that perhaps she should leave, but then Wally started talking. "By the way, were you surprised by the lawsuit?"

Magnolia had rushed out without reading the paper or listening to any morning television. What new national or international scandal didn't she know about? Her face registered empty. Lately, she'd been focusing so much on celebrity journalism—if that wasn't an oxymoron—that *The New York Times* kept piling up unread.

"Oh, you didn't hear?" Wally said matter-of-factly. He broke into a grin. "That's right. I forgot. You couldn't have heard. Nobody knows yet." He paused for dramatic effect. "Scary's suing Bebe Blake. For breach of contract. You heard it here first. The story's going to break in an hour or two."

"Who told you this?"

"A friend handling the case," he said. "Yes, ma'am. Scary's suing for damages, punitive and actual. Three hundred big ones."

"Three hundred thousand dollars?"

"Oh, you are an innocent. Million, honey. Million. Claims your Bebe Blake breached her contract. Behaved erratically. That true?"

It was Magnolia's turn to laugh. "Honestly, Wally, Bebe defines 'erratic.' One day she sends you the best birthday gift you ever received, and the next day you're afraid she might steal your dog."

"So, did you see it coming?"

"Wally, if you're asking me if I'm surprised that Scary would sue, no. It's Jock, down to his boxers. Ego the size of Alaska."

"Guess that means you're rooting for Bebe?"

Magnolia spoke very, very slowly. "Wally, honey. If Scary has money to throw around on vanity lawsuits, I'm rooting for *me*. Pull out every card in that pretty little deck of yours. Go get Magnolia a nice, six-figure check."

He smiled. "Now you're talking."

"This is for you, Wally," she said, ignoring his onion breath and kissing him on the lips. "Get lucky. Get very lucky."

Chapter 37

See You in Court

"Miss Gold, delivery coming up." The doorman purred over Magnolia's creaky intercom. "Flowers for the lady."

Magnolia hadn't received a bouquet in months. The only blossoms that weren't on her wallpaper were from the deli. Just this morning she'd trashed two dozen roses which after only twenty-four hours had arrived at death's door, bending over as if they were praying.

Someone pressed her bell with short, urgent blasts. "Hold on," she sang out, as she squinted through the peephole. All she could see were Smurf-blue carnations. Her fleeting thought was that this was Cameron's idea of humor. Magnolia opened the door, hoping he was attached to the flowers.

A squat, middle-aged man held tightly to the carnations. His greasy hair was combed over a shiny bald spot, and he wore an overcoat that appeared to have been plucked from the annual New York Cares coat drive. Magnolia reached for the neon bouquet, but the man pulled it back while he shoved an envelope in her face.

"Consider yourself served," he said before he slunk back into the elevator, carnations in hand, like a villain in a 1942 comic book.

Magnolia ripped open the envelope. "You are hereby commanded to appear in the offices of . . ." She read the name of a patrician law firm and noted a place, date, and time the following week. Strange that Wally hadn't mentioned anything about a command legal performance, Magnolia thought, as she walked to her desk to check her calendar. "No can do," she said aloud, noting a conflict with an appointment she'd scheduled weeks ago to put a blast of bling in her highlights—the winter was long enough without hair the color of burnt toast. She looked up Wally's cell phone number to call and ask what this summons had to do with her contract dispute, then remembered it was far too early to reach him in Colorado. Magnolia tossed the letter onto a pile of unpaid bills and returned to her television. She could crash in several episodes of third-tier celebrity shows before meeting Abbey.

She'd been missing Abbey. The velocity of their IM-ing, text messaging, and phone calls had petered out to half the norm. At least that's how it felt to Magnolia, who for the first time in her adult life didn't have to multitask while she and her only true confidante gave each other full accountings of daily minutia, the dull as well as the droll. Now, Abbey seemed to be abbreviating every conversation. Her business had taken off. Bergdorf's had requested three dozen pairs of sea-foam sapphire earrings, Fred Segal was offering an exclusive for all of la-la land if she could whittle down the price and do them up in lemon jade, and Anthropologie would be willing to place an order that was seven times the size of the others combined.

Yet Magnolia knew this flurry of entrepreneurial hyperbole didn't explain Abbey's attention deficit, and she didn't think for a second that Abbey was cheating on her with another friend, someone who might be—at the moment—a whole lot perkier. Abbey had a low tolerance for perky, which was one of the qualities she and Magnolia shared. No, there was only one explanation. A man. To be specific, a *French*man.

Magnolia walked the long white runway that led to MoMA, where they planned to meet at one o'clock. Advancing out of the tunnel, she felt as if she should wind up in heaven, not a swanky café. Planted under an enormous leafy photo was Abbey, who in her scarlet coat looked like Little Red Riding Hood lost in the forest.

Abbey waved gaily. "You look gorgeous!" she said, stretching to hug Magnolia.

"You do and I don't, but let's not discuss it," Magnolia said, returning the hug, reassured by the all's-well-in-the-world comfort she got when she looked into her friend's dark almond eyes. "What I want to know is—everything. And—now that I don't have to worry about falling asleep at my desk—let's hear it over a drink." One of a platoon of waiters in charcoal Nehru jackets showed them to a choice table with a view of the ghostly crystalline garden and its ice-frosted Calders. "To you," she said, toasting Abbey with her glass. "My own jewel of Las Vegas."

"To Magnolia, who I can count on never to set foot in Las Vegas," Abbey said.

"So? Is this Daniel Cohen the One?" Magnolia took a sip, put her glass on the table, and smiled warmly at Abbey. "He is! You're blushing!" Abbey's cheeks were rapidly turning the pink of a sweet sixteen party.

"I can't get enough of this guy," Abbey said. She started counting his virtues while tapping her delicate, white index finger on the digits of her left hand. "He's charming, he's handsome, he's brilliant, he's sexy." She switched to the right hand. "He's got an accent I could listen to even if he were reading a grocery list, he's totally into me—"

"That should be number one," Magnolia said, cutting her off. "I get it. He's the anti-Tommy."

"Right, except Tommy did have bedroom appeal. Let's give him that. On the other hand, Daniel's a grown-up," Abbey said. "He's older—thirty-nine—but mostly it's his Frenchness. Even a Parisian sixteen-year-old seems older than Tommy."

"Where do you go from here?"

"Literally?"

"Cosmically," Magnolia said.

"I only know literally," she answered. "To Paris again this weekend. He keeps sending me tickets. And in a few weeks he's coming here and I'm planning to introduce him to my nearest and dearest. Cocktails at my place. You're not going to be away, I hope?"

"For the near future I expect to be epoxied to my armchair with a view of the TV."

"It would never be a party without you. Oh, and Cameron," she said, as she took a bite of smoked eel. Love seemed to have sparked Abbey's appetite.

"Cameron's made your A-list?" Magnolia asked, truly surprised. "How do you do it? All my exes despise me." Except Tyler, who every once in a while sent her a friendly, funny e-mail from his regular Pastorpeterson account. Harry? Had he thought to send her as much as an e-mail expressing sympathy about her job loss—which he had to know about, given its tabloid coverage? She'd concluded that Harry was a user, and at the moment she wasn't even useful enough to be his friend.

"To begin with, Cam and I never got near lust," Abbey said. "He's just not the one to own my heart—"

"Whoa. You're forgetting our rule," Magnolia said. "No Country Western lyrics until after two or more beers."

"Plus, I know I don't do it for him," Abbey continued, ignoring her. "I can never tell if he's laughing with me or at me. You get him a lot better than I do, but I do see where he's hot, if that's what you're wondering."

Magnolia let the last bubble of conversation float in the air until it disappeared, then attacked her gâteau, a rich pastry featuring crispy potato and escargot. If you can't eat carbs when you're unemployed, she'd decided, you just don't love yourself enough.

"Back to Daniel Cohen," she said. "You deserve this, Abbey. I am so happy for you that—look at me—I'm going to cry."

This was true. Magnolia blinked away tears. She was almost sure she was ready to shed them entirely on Abbey's behalf and not because her friend's attachment to the perfect Daniel might mean one more shutter closed in her shrinking, darkening world. You are pathetic, Magnolia told herself, brushing away both the thought and the tear. Also selfish. Jealous. Small-minded. You adore Abbey. You will find your own man. You will not be alone. Or a bag lady. Shoulders back, girl.

"Dessert?" Magnolia asked as a cart sailed past, laden with chocolate napoleons and pale, lemony petits fours lined up like ballerinas.

"Not today," Abbey said. "Got to get back to my studio. Call you tonight?"

"Date," Magnolia said. They finished their espressos, split the bill, and left the restaurant. Magnolia wandered through a few cavernous, sparely hung galleries, then out on Fifty-third Street. She began to walk uptown toward Columbus Circle where she could catch a train.

As she crossed Fifty-seventh Street, someone bellowed her name. "Over here," said the voice. "In the limo."

Magnolia swiveled to avoid oncoming traffic. A Stretch Hummer had stopped across the street. "Where you headed, Bebe?" she shouted back.

"My lawyer's," Bebe said.

"What's the occasion?" Magnolia asked when she got close to the car's window. "Let me guess. You need another prenup. Are congratulations in order?"

"I need another husband like I need a third boob," Bebe said. "Or like I needed a magazine. But Jock's going to pay. He's in for a little surprise." She rubbed her hands together like an eager cannibal. "Don't stand there shivering—I'll fill you in. C'mon—Gold. Chop, chop."

"But I'm going uptown," Magnolia said.

"So we'll take a ride." Bebe gathered her plentiful fox coat with its hanging tails and tassels and patted the seat next to her. Magnolia climbed into the car. "Like I was saying, our countersuit is almost ready to rock and roll. Scary and Jock won't know what hit 'em. I'm talking major artillery shelling." Bebe grabbed Magnolia's arm—

hard—and wasn't letting go. "You didn't honestly think I'd sit still for those mental midgets to steal my money, not when Jock and Darlene and all the others have treated me like pond scum, did you? Well, did you?"

"Bebe, I've been trying not to think about any of this," Magnolia pleaded. "I'm sorry you're being sued," she fibbed, "but you did publish a cover that was blatant gun-lobby propaganda. You weren't always the easiest person to work with and, damn it, you fired me." She wrested away her arm.

"*Jock* fired you!" Bebe said. "I wanted you."

"Revisionist history. Jock may have pulled the trigger," Magnolia said, figuring it was a metaphor Bebe would understand, "but I don't recall an enormous show of support at the time."

"You don't know what you don't know. I was behind the scenes, saying I wanted you. All along. You know I hate that eye-rolling bitch Raven. Tried to shoot down my ideas like they were enemy Black Hawks. And Jock! Did you know he had a security guard lock me in my office? I was stuck there for ninety minutes. Thought I'd have a stroke."

"I heard something about that," Magnolia said. "But you'd threatened to kick Raven in the teeth."

"I believe I identified a different body part," Bebe said. "Lower down." She stopped talking for a minute. "This is an absurd conversation. It's all very simple. I need to pull out before I lose more dough," she said after a minute of meditation. "Like my ma always said, she didn't raise no stupid kids."

Bebe may have calmed down, but Magnolia hadn't. "Shall we talk money now?" She asked. "How about the hundred people who got fired when *Bebe* closed—what about them? All they got was a month's severance."

"That's what Scary decided to give them, cheap bastards," she said. "Though half that money came from me, which Jock neglected to mention. I also wrote checks out of my own pocket for at least a thousand dollars each to every single person on the masthead."

"Really? That was incredible," Magnolia admitted. Cameron had e-mailed her about Bebe's gesture, and in fact, he had received two thousand dollars, as had Fredericka, Phoebe, Ruthie, and Sasha. As the star of her own tragedy, Magnolia had forgotten all about that.

"After Jock ordered all those wimps not to talk to me or Felicity!" Spittle landed on Magnolia's cheek as Bebe yelled.

"Speaking of Felicity," Magnolia said. "What do you think Ms. Whipsmart cost the magazine and the company?" Magnolia realized that now she was hollering as well. And probably spitting. "And what about coming on to Nathaniel? How perverted was that?"

"Who?" Bebe looked puzzled.

"Our intern, Polo? How soon we forget."

"That kid wanted it!" Bebe leaned back in the seat, turned her head to the window, and began to pout. The car stopped at a light on Central Park West about ten blocks from Magnolia's building.

"Driver, I'll get out here, please," Magnolia decided and motioned to him through the class partition. "Thanks for the lift." She put her hand on the door and began to open it.

"Magnolia, I was hoping for some support from you," Bebe said. "It wasn't that bad, our working together." She sighed. "But it doesn't really matter one way or another—you'll be hearing from my attorney. He's going to depose you. We've already discussed it." This seemed to cheer up Bebe, who put a smile back on her face. "You know what? I'll see you in court." She laughed. "I've always wanted to say that. 'I'll see you in court.'"

As the car sped away, Bebe blew Magnolia kiss after kiss.

Magnolia walked to her apartment. It was just past lunchtime in Aspen and perhaps she could catch Wally; he'd be the kind of guy who'd ski with a cell phone.

He answered on the first ring.

"Fleigelman," he said.

"Gold," she said. "How's the snow?"

"Sixteen inches of powder last night," he said. "Drifts up to my tuches. Which is where I spend my time here. It's Whitney who can ski like a movie star. She did a double black diamond with Goldie Hawn." He nattered on about nine-hundred-dollar-a-night rooms and steaks the size of thighs. "What can I do for you?" he finally asked. "If you're wondering when we'll work through your contract, hold your water, doll face."

"Wally, I'm sure it's nothing, but this morning I got a peculiar letter." She speed-read it to him. "I just wanted to know what this has to do with my case?"

"Absolutely nothing," he replied. "Was that letter delivered by a greasy little troll in a bad suit?"

"More or less," she said.

"Your company is deposing you in their claim against Bebe Blake." Wally explained. "Standard procedure. No big whoop."

"I have to do it, even though they're trying to stiff me out of my money?" Magnolia asked. "This seems so unfair. Jeez."

"I love when you talk all Fargo," Wally said. "God bless America, darling. This is what they call justice."

"And Bebe's lawyers can ask me, too?"

"Now you're getting ahead of yourself. It's Scary suing Bebe. She's the defendant."

"Oh, you didn't know? That's right. I forgot. You couldn't have heard. Because nobody knows yet. She's going tit for tat. Suing back."

Wally laughed. "That Bebe is my kind of broad! So now she's a plaintiff, too?" he said. "Must be a *Law & Order* junkie. I'm only sorry she didn't hire me to represent her."

"Wally, my question?" Magnolia asked.

"Oh, sure, speaking of asses, I'd expect that both sides will want a piece of that pretty little butt of yours."

Chapter 38

Blue-Blooded Butt-Head vs. the White-Trash Nympho

"Good morning," croaked the wrenlike receptionist in a surprisingly low voice. "May I help you?"

"I'm Magnolia Gold—for a meeting at ten," Magnolia said. "My attorney, Walter Fleigelman, will be joining me."

The woman looked down at her desk. "According to our schedule, your appointment is for eleven," she said before she returned to her Mary Higgins Clark mystery.

Magnolia had been sure about ten. "Could you double-check please?"

The receptionist looked up briefly and shook her head. "No, no mistake. If you'd like to make yourself comfortable . . ."

To even their score with Bebe Blake, Scarborough Magazines and John Crawford Flanagan Jr., its CEO, had engaged Cromwell, Adams, and Case, one of the whitest, white-shoe law firms in all Manhattan. Magnolia entered their burnished mahogany offices on the fifty-fifth floor of Rockefeller Center. Magnolia breathed in. Her nose picked up a delicate bouquet of Shalimar wafting from the receptionist, an under-note of Murphy's Oil Soap, and the slight rankness of upholstery dating from 1972. Ah, WASP incense, she thought; the scent of old money.

After selecting the least worn sofa in the cavernous reception area, Magnolia pulled out her newspapers and a fresh batch of celebrity tabloids. In early press reports of their mutual sniping, Jock and Bebe displayed a certain dignity. "We couldn't permit *Bebe* to migrate into a manifesto for its namesake's personal views," Jock stated in a haughty tone Magnolia knew well. "I wouldn't abide Jock Flanagan's interference," Bebe replied with surprising restraint. But as each side began leaking succulent morsels about the other, Jock's suit and Bebe's countersuit began pulsating beyond the business section. Every news-paper and all of the blogs were covering the story. Yesterday Bebe referred to Jock as "that blue-blooded butt-head with the overbite and pruney moneybags wife," and he called her "a white-trash nympho with the talent of a Dorito."

As Magnolia read today's smears—the *Daily News* reported Jock's wife's affair with his twin brother—she didn't realize she was laugh-ing aloud until she heard Darlene. "You think this is funny?" her for-mer publisher asked, crossing her arms atop the mountain of her pregnant belly.

"Darlene," Magnolia said. "You're looking well. Finally having a boy?" The two of them hadn't spoken since Darlene's sympathy call after Scary ditched her, when Magnolia matched Darlene's mock sin-cerity with her own feigned serenity.

"A boy? That'll happen when pigs fly," Darlene said, sitting heavily in a chair across from Magnolia. She patted her Lycra-bound tummy. "No, Georgina here is a little clone of her three big sisters. And based on her kicking, she's an animal just like her mama." Darlene con-sidered it high praise when Jock described her as being the sort of pub-lisher who would happily wrestle clients to the ground on Madison Avenue to land the last Cool Whip ad. Darlene tapped out a few mes-sages on her BlackBerry, but soon enough Magnolia felt her stare.

"I hope you're on our side," she said.

"How's that possible?" Magnolia answered, looking up from *Us*. "I'm sworn to tell the truth."

"Bebe sabotaged the magazine," Darlene said.

"She got as good as she gave," Magnolia said.

"Try selling ads with the pervert twins hogging the headlines and covers that frighten small children," Darlene harrumphed. "I've been a miracle worker." Magnolia noticed Darlene's eyes downshift to her wrist. "Why are you wearing that red string?" she asked suspiciously.

Magnolia was about to explain the bracelet when she heard a racket at the other end of the room. Wally. He checked in with the receptionist and hobbled over to Magnolia on crutches, his right leg in a blazing orange cast.

"Good God—what happened?" Magnolia said, rising to kiss his sunburned cheek.

"Schmuck here tried to show off on his last day in Aspen," Wally said, and shrugged as well as a man on crutches could. "From now on, golf, period." He sat on the other end of the love seat. "You ready, kid? Anything you want to go over?"

Magnolia cleared her throat and tilted her head slightly toward her former publisher. "Darlene," she said, "I'd like you to meet my . . . attorney," she said. "Walter Fleigelman."

As Darlene looked up, Wally assumed an expression of hangdog sadness. "And former husband," he added, extending his hand to shake Darlene's

"Magnolia, you sneak," Darlene said. "How long were you married?"

"We were madly in love for eleven minutes," Magnolia said.

Both of them turned to Wally. With his raccoon tan, he looked like a masked sidekick—Slalom the Blind Skier perhaps. "Happy to meet you, Walter." Darlene gave him one of her billboard-big publisher's smiles.

"Darlene, I'm sure when we worked together, you remember that I talked about Wally," Magnolia said. "Maybe you don't recall."

But Magnolia was saved from further discussion. The reception-ist announced that Darlene's appointment would be starting, and she walked swiftly—considering the bulk she was balancing on stilettos—into the bowels of Cromwell, Adams, and Case.

Magnolia and Wally sat side by side. "'*I don't recall*,'" she repeated. "I've been practicing that line."

"Good girl," Wally said. When he'd rehearsed Magnolia for today's deposition, he'd browbeaten her with a careful instruction. "When-ever you cannot exactly remember an event or incident that the lawyer deposing you describes, you are allowed to say, 'I don't recall.' For example, let's say every workday at precisely three o'clock you had the habit of going down to the lobby for a Diet Coke. The lawyer asks 'On June 1, did you get yourself a Diet Coke at three o'clock? Unless you can actually remember the details of buying that can of soda on that specific June 1, you are allowed to say 'I don't recall.'"

"Sweet," Magnolia had replied. "Got it."

"The deposition was supposed to be on for ten, right?" Wally asked.

"So I thought," Magnolia answered.

"Keep us waiting—oldest trick in the book," Wally said. "Don't let it rattle you. Here—look at my pictures." He pulled a digital camera from his briefcase and showed her a good hundred images of Fleigel-mans squinting into the sun. Nearly an hour later, she and Wally entered the Cromwell, Adams, and Case conference room.

"Walter, good morning," boomed a tall, broad-shouldered man in gray pinstripes that appeared to be cut from the same cloth as Wally's. Wally's suit, however, was a 38 short; the other attorney's, 44 long.

"Sky," Wally boomed back. "Let me introduce my client, Miss Magnolia Gold. Magnolia? James Skyler, Esquire."

James Skyler looked like an aristobrat born to scull at Choate and Harvard. He locked eyes with Magnolia. When he smiled, his per-fectly straight teeth sported a God-given gleam that bleaching can never mimic. "Mind if I take off my jacket?" he asked, rhetori-cally. In shirtsleeves, his shoulders looked as broad as a superhero's, and Magnolia could see that his waist, encased in fine lizard, was no wider than thirty-two inches. He slowly rolled up each cuff. The golden hair on his arms matched the thatch on his head.

Magnolia took in the performance, which, she guessed, was for her benefit. If the lawyer had been a woman, by now she'd be playing with her hair and licking her lips. "The attorney is going to try to seduce you," Wally had warned. "Remember, he is not your next boyfriend. Don't fall for his schmaltz."

"Miss Gold, could you give me your full name, please?" James Skyler asked.

"Magnolia Gold." Had she just perjured herself? She'd never formally changed her name from Goldfarb. And what about Fleigelman? Did she have to say that for less than a year she was Magnolia Goldfarb Fleigelman?

"Magnolia, charming name. Has it been passed down in your family?"

As if—and what did this have to do with Scary's case? Magnolia wondered.

"No," she said. Stay cool, Magnolia, she reminded herself.

Skyler had her résumé in front of him. "Could you briefly describe your work history?" he asked.

Magnolia compressed thirteen years into three minutes.

"So, you were effectively demoted when you were switched from *Lady*'s editor in chief to deputy editor of *Bebe*?"

Magnolia felt Wally's leg. Don't let yourself get pissy, the cast seemed to say. "Yes," she answered, evenly.

"Did Bebe Blake make all of the key decisions at the magazine?" the attorney asked.

Magnolia looked at Wally. "Am I allowed to ask what a 'key decision' is?" she said.

"Could you please rephrase the question for my client?" Wally asked.

"Certainly," he said. "Let me be more specific. Who selected the image for this cover?" He held up the premiere issue in all its leopard splendor.

"Bebe did," Magnolia said.

"This one?"

"Bebe." He must be trying to rankle her by showing covers she didn't get to choose herself. It wasn't going to work. Magnolia stayed steady while the lawyer ran through every one of the issues and moved on to stacks of proofs and headlines.

"Do you recognize this signature?" he asked.

"Yes."

"Whose is it?"

"Mine."

"Do you remember signing this?"

Every month she okayed hundreds of proofs. "I don't recall," she said.

Next he pulled out a school photograph. "Can you, please, identify this person?"

"Yes," she said. "That's Nathaniel Fine, our former intern."

"Did you see Bebe Blake, uh, make sexual advances to Mr. Fine?"

Magnolia stretched her mind back to December. She remembered going into the fashion closet. She recalled hearing a rustle and a conversation between Bebe and Polo. But did she actually see Bebe do anything to him? The fashion closet had been filled with racks of clothing that stood between her and the couple like size-four artillery. Had she simply, based on the conversation she'd overheard, imagined the worst?

"Miss Gold?" the attorney asked.

"I don't recall," she said—and said again, and again, and again.

"As a decision maker, how would you describe Bebe Blake?"

Wally broke in. "I object."

"I'll rephrase. Do you think it's fair to describe Ms. Blake as unpredictable?"

Magnolia thought it over. "Yes."

"Did Ms. Blake have a clear vision for her magazine?"

Magnolia ruminated and shook her head. "No."

"Did the staff like Ms. Blake?"

Did some of the staff like Bebe? Probably, considering how Americans devoured celebrity gossip as if it were hot-buttered popcorn. "I honestly don't know," she finally answered. The questions bombarded her until she wanted to crawl under the nineteenth-century conference room table. The next time she had insomnia, she would reconstruct this legal snooze.

"Thank you, Ms. Gold," the attorney said. "That will be all. I appreciate your help." James Skyler, Esq., smiled coolly at Magnolia as he put down his pen and legal pad. She and Wally walked to the street and his waiting car.

"You did good," he said.

"Really?" She sighed. "Scary won't call me as a witness, will they?"

Wally threw his arms up in the air, then caught his crutches before they fell. "Don't think about it," he said. "Compartmentalize."

"I can't," Magnolia said as the two of them started driving uptown. "My mind is a big, open loft, which is currently a mess." She turned to look at Wally. "Will you come to the trial—for moral support?"

"C'mon, you'll be fine," he said. "Bebe's lawyer will try to get you to admit Jock attempted to cramp her style, usurp her good name, force a different editor on her, and make her life unadulterated hell. You decide if it's true or not. I don't need to be your little pit bull."

"You do!" Magnolia said.

"Okay, Mags. Then you and I are breaking up before the Mrs. changes the locks."

Chapter 39

Guts and Roses

"You must be Magnolia," said a tall, thin man with black hair curling over his collar. He kissed her on both cheeks. "Abbey was right. You are beautiful."

"Thank you," Magnolia said, standing in Abbey's foyer. "Abbey forgot to mention your eyes. Not many of us have green eyes." His were like olives, lightly flecked with caramel. If you took his face apart, feature by feature, you wouldn't expect it to be reassembled in such a handsome fashion. His nose was long. Under his eyes were slight shadows, faintly lavender, like matching bruises. But it all worked, especially the smile, which fanned a delicate web of early lines toward each silver-laced temple.

"When the Moors invaded France, they left behind green eyes," he said. "In Brazil, with all their mixed bloodlines, green eyes exist in the most exotic medleys of skin and hair. Green eyes come when opposites attract." His accent was heavy, and his voice low. "Daniel Cohen," he said. "I am so happy we finally meet."

"I see you've found each other," Abbey said, linking her arm through both his and Magnolia's. Next to Daniel, she looked even more fragile than usual. She wore a white lace minidress, its high neck pinned with a garnet and diamond bumblebee Magnolia had never seen.

"From Daniel," Abbey said, touching the brooch. "His great-grandmother's."

"Because Abbey reminds me of a bee—small, busy, making sweetness and beauty wherever she lands."

If an American man had said this, Magnolia would have wanted to stick a finger down her throat. From Daniel, the sentiment sounded poetic.

"The dress suits you, Magnolia," Daniel said.

"I knew it would," Abbey added. "I found it in the Paris flea market and wanted you to have it for tonight."

That morning a messenger had delivered a large, white box tied with a silky bow and filled with layers of chartreuse tissue paper. Magnolia pulled out a chocolate brown velvet dress, cut deep at the décolleté, which was frosted with lace and beads. The skirt, layered with rows of small, horizontal ruffles, was longer than Magnolia's usual length. "For tonight—with your spiky, brown boots," the note from Abbey commanded. It was a dress that Magnolia would have never tried on in a store. She was fairly sure it made her resemble a poodle, especially because Abbey had requested she wear her hair, which hadn't been cut in three months, loose and curly.

"You don't think I'm old for ruffles? I'm feeling like I escaped from the Moulin Rouge."

"You can bring it off," Abbey said.

When she had tried on the dress, Magnolia wondered if perhaps tonight would be some kind of covert costume ball and everyone would be similarly coiffed and clothed. That, however, was not the case. The rest of the crowd—which, when she arrived, already overflowed Abbey's foyer, dining room, and living room and stood deep in the hall leading to her bedroom and library—wore the usual black and charcoal wools of a Manhattan Sunday night in March.

Servers in tuxedos circulated with trays bearing white roses—her favorite flower—and tuna tartare; flaky, Brie-filled biscuits; and roasted red peppers and chèvre on tiny baguettes. In the corner of the living room, a pianist played jazz, and the piano sounded—for the first time ever—perfectly in tune. Abbey had put in all three leaves of her dining room table and set it with an old-world damask cloth, tall white tapers in mismatched sterling silver holders, and her usual garden of flowered Limoge. For a centerpiece, hundreds of ranunculus and lilies of the valley were packed tight with miniature white roses in an ornate silver ice bucket.

"How did you pull off this party so quickly?" Magnolia asked when Daniel rushed over to greet a handsome older couple and a woman about Magnolia's age, all regal and slim.

"It's amazing how freedom can kick-start your engine," Abbey said. "Turns out, our divorce was about the only thing Tommy and I agreed on. He met someone else, and wanted to move fast. Let me keep everything. The minute the paperwork was signed, I felt I could fly."

"When will the divorce come through?" Wally and Magnolia's split had been reasonably amicable and yet it had taken almost a year.

"Yesterday," she whispered in Magnolia's ear. "I'm single!"

"Abbey!" Magnolia said. "I don't even know what to say. Congratulations?"

"I accept," she said. "Now go mingle. This is my night, and you have to promise to enjoy yourself."

"You're getting pretty damn pushy," Magnolia said. She kissed her on the cheek and walked off to the bar for a glass of champagne—except for water, the only beverage available. She scanned the room and noticed a bearded man in his thirties who looked vaguely familiar.

"Do I see you around the track?" she asked.

"Four times a week," he said, introducing himself. "Matthew Hirsch, die-hard runner. Not that many of us crazies keep going through the winter."

"How do you know Abbey?" she asked. It seemed odd that he was here—when they ran together, Abbey had never greeted him at the Reservoir.

"We just met—the other day," he said. "On some business."

Abbey's next-door neighbor joined their conversation. "Good evening, Rabbi Hirsch—may I steal you away?"

"Rabbi?" Magnolia asked. Now it clicked. "Are you the rabbi the Ben Stiller character was based on in *Keep the Faith*?" She'd rented that DVD twice.

"Guilty as charged," Rabbi Hirsch said with a dimpled smile. He hurried away with Abbey's neighbor, leaving Magnolia to penetrate the crush of guests in the hallway.

"She knows how to throw a party, huh?" Cameron said, coming up to her from behind. "Now I see why she didn't get jazzed when my idea of a great date was Niko's on Broadway."

"You can feed me their moussaka any day, but Abbey's allergic to plastic grapes dangling from ceilings," Magnolia said, smoothing her ruffles. "By the way, I'm only in this ridiculous dress because Abbey forced me to wear it."

"I was just thinking I like you all girly," Cameron said, clicking her glass with his.

"That's high praise coming as it does from a man whose idea of sartorial elegance is L.L. Bean."

"You just wish you owned a cap that repels ticks," he said. "And I'm pretty sure I've seen you in a Bean Mad Bomber hat."

"I'm pretty sure you gave me that hat," Magnolia said. "And, for the record, I love it."

The two of them wandered back to the bar for refills. "By the way, you actually look very handsome tonight." He did. Magnolia couldn't remember the last time she'd seen Cameron in a sport coat. They leaned against the dining room wall, which was painted a deep persimmon, a perfect backdrop for Magnolia's brown gown. "How did your Bebe deposition go?" Magnolia wasn't the only one who'd been living in lawyers' offices.

"Interminable," Cam said. "Was it true that during Ms. Blake's vacation in Baja you sent her two hundred e-mails in one day? Did you hear Jock Flanagan say Ms. Blake would be thrown off the magazine if she had any more 'bullshit hissy fits'? Did you call Felicity Dingle a 'harpy'? Like that. And by the way I didn't call Felicity a harpy. I called her something much worse."

"So how are you spending your time when you're not in a lawyer's office?" Magnolia asked. Phoebe was staying home with her baby, Sasha was studying for the LSAT, Ruthie got nabbed by *Lucky*, and Fredericka was skiing in Switzerland with a German school friend who now owned half of Hamburg.

"Write, write, write."

"You're not job hunting?"

"I think my illustrious career as a managing editor may have ground to a halt," Cam said, as his cell phone rang. He looked at the name. "Find you later. Got to take this."

Magnolia began to search for someone else to talk to when Abbey walked over. "Can I steal you away?" she said. She pointed toward the hall. "In my bedroom."

Abbey closed the door behind them. She kicked off her silver sandals, pushed aside a profusion of embroidered silk pillows, and crawled onto her bed. From the bedside table, she handed Magnolia a small box. "For you," she said.

"Another gift?" Magnolia said. "It's not my birthday, Abbey. You're spoiling me." She shook the box. Maybe it was the spiral earrings Bergdorf's ordered. Inside, however, was a small gold locket that dangled from an almost invisible chain. Magnolia opened it to find a picture of the two of them, victorious after their first six-mile race. They looked very young, very sweaty, and very happy.

"Put it on," Abbey insisted. The locket sat below Magnolia's collarbone at exactly the right spot. "It's my way of thanking you."

"For what?" Magnolia said. "Being a best friend doesn't require thanks." She gave Abbey a lingering hug.

"Being a maid of honor does," Abbey whispered, still embraced in Magnolia's arms.

Magnolia pushed her away so she could see her face and said very quietly. "Excuse me? You're getting *married*?" Magnolia decided not to add "again."

"Yes!" Abbey said and started to cry. "I know it's abrupt, but he's the one. Daniel and I together are magic."

Magnolia fell back on the bed and stared at the ceiling. "When's the wedding?" she asked.

"Soon," Abbey said.

"How soon?"

She heard Abbey draw a breath. "In ten minutes."

Magnolia bolted upright. Abbey grabbed a tissue next to her bed so the tears streaming down her face wouldn't drop on her dress. Her wedding dress. "Hold on." She darted into her bathroom.

Hold on, that's for damn sure. Get a grip, Magnolia thought, as she fell back on the bed and began to take short, hyperventilated breaths. Abbey walked out of her bathroom, holding two nosegays: one with white roses and lilies of the valley tied with garnet-red silk ribbon and another of chocolate brown rununculus and lilac roses, which she handed to Magnolia.

"Your bouquet," Abbey said, placing her own bouquet on the bed. "Now, please help me with this veil. It's your *job*." From her closet she pulled out a wisp of tulle attached to a comb jeweled with garnets that matched her bee pin. "I stayed up all night, trying to get this right."

She sat down at her silvery mirrored antique desk and faced its matching mirror. Magnolia put the veil on Abbey's head but it wound up crooked. Abbey looked deranged. Magnolia tried again, but her hands were shaking too hard to get the comb in place. Abbey gently pulled Magnolia's hand off the headpiece and futzed with it until she looked like the bride on the top of a cake. She grabbed Magnolia's hand. "I know you think I'm making a mistake—another mistake, even bigger than Tommy."

"That's not what I'm thinking," Magnolia said, "because I don't know what to think."

"It's crazy, but it's good crazy," Abbey said. "We'll live here and Daniel will commute, and in the summers we'll live in France near his vineyards, and of course I'll go to Paris whenever I can." Abbey's words were flying faster than Magnolia could catch. "I love his family, and they love me."

Magnolia stared at Abbey in continued shock. There was a tap at the door.

"Who is it?" Abbey said.

"Véronique," a French-accented voice said.

"Entrez, s'il vous plaît," Abbey said. The lissome blonde whom Magnolia had seen Daniel greet entered the room. "Magnolia, I'd like you to meet Daniel's sister, Véronique. Véronique, *mon amie,* Magnolia." The blonde kissed Abbey, and then Magnolia, three times each—on their right cheek, left cheek, and then right again.

"Tu est prête, ma chérie?" Véronique said.

"Ready," Abbey replied, as Véronique returned to the living room.

From faraway, Magnolia heard the music switch from jazz to "Chapel of Love." "That's your cue," Abbey said. "Just walk out the door and down the hall through the living room. My brother will have already asked people to be still. You'll figure out the rest."

Magnolia stood up and smoothed her ruffled dress as best she could. She grasped the bouquet, holding it tightly in front of her galloping heart, and walked out of Abbey's bedroom. The rooms at the end of the hall were silent. A blur of faces turned to look at her as she walked toward the candlelight. The guests had parted, leaving a wide swath. The chapel of love, Abbey's dining room, seemed fifty miles away.

As Magnolia walked closer, she saw that Véronique, Abbey's brother and sister-in-law, and Abbey's college roommate were each holding a pole that supported an embroidered Spanish shawl that usually hung on the grand piano. Under the canopy, Daniel stood next to the older man she'd seen with him before—now, his best man.

Matthew Hirsch, in a black velvet yarmulke and a tallis over his Armani suit, winked at Magnolia as she walked toward the chuppah. Daniel bowed to her slightly and offered a half-smile. A white rosebud was now in his lapel.

The pianist changed to "Here Comes the Bride." Magnolia hadn't taken her friend for the sort of woman who would want that song played at her wedding, but it certainly got everyone's attention. Every eye turned to Abbey as she proceeded through her living room, twinkling like a small star.

Later, when friends asked Magnolia to describe the ceremony, all she could remember was that Abbey circled Daniel seven times, there were vows in three languages—English, French, and Hebrew—and the bride and groom each sipped from a tall silver goblet of wine, presumably poured from an excellent Rothschild vintage and a very good year. The rabbi spoke of fate, of people coming together, and used the word *beshert*. Magnolia glanced down to see if her red bracelet was still there. It had disappeared. "*When the job is done, the bracelet will be gone*," she remembered Malka as saying. But she couldn't contemplate what the missing bracelet might mean, because just then Daniel stepped on the glass and kissed Abbey like the actor in the favorite movie of Magnolia's mother, *A Man and a Woman*. Shouts of mazel tov and *bonne chance* echoed through the apartment.

As the piano played Cole Porter, waiters circulated with champagne and more champagne. There was dancing, singing, and shrieks of joy. The pianist struck up "Hava Nagila," and Rabbi Hirsch grabbed Magnolia by the waist for several loops of the hora. Abbey broke away from Daniel, took both of Magnolia's hands, and began twirling with her in the center of a circle of clapping friends and relatives.

"If you expect me to do the cancan, forget it," Magnolia said.

"Thanks for being so *sportive* about wearing the dress," Abbey said. "It didn't come from the flea market, by the way."

"Oh, really?" Magnolia said, half out of breath as the two of them whirled.

"It was Daniel's mother's. *Couture.* From her trousseau."

"Do I have to give it back?" Magnolia said. "I like it better now."

"It's yours," Abbey said. "The least I can do."

At midnight waiters brought out a four-layer wedding cake of chocolate iced in white fondant. Chocolate piping replicated the embroidery from the shawl that had doubled as the wedding canopy. The couple cut the cake and fed each other pieces, and then everyone gorged on cake, profiteroles, and lemon squares. Well past one-thirty, the bride and groom bid the crowd adieu and guests started to drift away. Magnolia found her boots—which she'd pulled off hours before and left in a corner—and went to Abbey's bedroom to put them on. Ringlets stuck to her face. She looked as if she'd been to a hockey game, not a wedding.

"Magnolia Gold, I don't believe I've ever seen you this ripped," Cameron said as she walked out of the bedroom.

She'd danced with him hours before. Then he'd switched to Véronique as a partner, and Magnolia had got into a long, inebriated conversation with Daniel's father, who promised Magnolia an invitation to the Cohen villa in St. Tropez, providing she didn't keep her bikini top on like a typical American. Magnolia had agreed.

"Hmmm," Magnolia said to Cameron, swaying in the boots, which felt staggeringly high. "I might have had a little too much to drink." Feeling at risk of falling, she put her arms around his neck.

In Abbey's hallway, as a clock chimed, she suddenly gave him a sloppy, lingering kiss. He kissed her back. His tongue tasted like chilled champagne.

"C'mon, Mags," he said, grabbing her around the waist. "I'm walking you home."

A fine rain fell as they strolled, wordlessly, down Central Park West, then past brownstones on the side streets where more sensible people had gone to bed hours before.

"I can't believe she did it," Magnolia said, several times. "It took such guts."

"Sometimes guts is all you need," Cam said.

"Guts and roses."

They arrived at her building. Magnolia was still happily intoxicated, but not so skunk-drunk that she didn't remember that fifteen minutes before she'd kissed her longtime former employee and current friend. And he hadn't pulled away. Quite the opposite.

As if she were a documentary filmmaker shooting from across the street, she saw—in black and white—a man and a woman holding each other. The couple looked as if they belonged together. Magnolia wondered what would happen next. But mist blurred the image, and she was suddenly exhausted.

It was hard to tell whether what she was seeing was real or a champagne dream.

Magnolia awoke at noon and forced herself out of a catatonic sleep. She was wearing her underwear and she was alone, which she decided were both good things. She remembered enough about last night to wonder if Cameron would be there and if they'd both be naked. She winced.

Once she'd published an article in *Lady* that said if you have a hangover you should make yourself a fruit smoothie from a banana, soy milk, and a handful of vitamins. Magnolia opened her refrigerator. It contained batteries, leftover pad thai, and some rather nasty carrots. She filled a glass with water, drank it down with two aspirin, and filled it again.

How big a fool had she made of herself? Enough so that her first instinct was to go back to bed. This is why people have dogs, she reminded herself as she cleaned up Biggie and Lola's mess, to make sure that they don't simply pull the covers over their heads and never get up after they have thoroughly embarrassed themselves. She fell into some jeans and a sweatshirt, grabbed a raincoat and hat, and attached the dogs' leashes.

"Some mail was dropped off for you, Miss Gold," her doorman said as she walked out.

More subpoenas? They could wait. "I'll get it on the way back," she said. Magnolia took the dogs to Central Park; the day was surprisingly warm, with the promise of spring in the air, and the rain stopped the minute she started walking. You weren't supposed to let dogs loose at this time of the day, but what the hell—in the ranking of mistakes she might have made in the last twelve hours, the offense was small. She unhooked Biggie's and Lola's leashes and for a full hour watched them revel in the wet grass. Her headache faded, she walked back home, and brought up the mail. Sure enough, the thin letter was a subpoena. Bebe and Jock's trial would be starting next week, and she was cordially invited to appear in court.

The second piece of mail was large and heavy, taped shut in a big manila envelope with no stamps or return address. Inside was another sealed envelope, and a handwritten note.

"Magnolia," it read. "I've been wanting to show you my book for a long time. My agent called last night to say it sold. If you'd do me the favor of reading it, I would be very grateful. Also, I need some help with the dedication and acknowledgments."

Magnolia ripped open the second envelope to find a manuscript of more than five hundred typed pages. The first page had only a few words: *A Friend Indeed* by Cameron Dane.

She walked to her living room couch, and began to read. Magnolia read through the afternoon, well into the night, and long past sunrise, stopping only for coffee.

At nine, she dialed Cameron's number. His voice mail picked up.

"If you wanted to ask me out," she said, "you could have just called."

Chapter 40

A Goose Is Cooked

Magnolia slipped into a seat in the remarkably unsupreme courtroom. Elizabeth Lester Duvall, her short hair shorter than usual, had parked herself next to the *Post*'s Mike McCourt, most likely willing him to cover the trial through her own eyes. Darlene Knudson sat behind a row of attorneys—although the lawyer who'd administered Magnolia's deposition was conspicuously absent. Had he been hired by Central Casting, she wondered, to try to unhinge her? On the far right, Felicity Dingle—whose knitting needles were clicking furiously on a long, drab garment—was stationed next to Arthur Montgomery, Bebe's lead lawyer.

"All rise," said a court officer. As everyone in the courtroom stood, a short, stout woman in half-glasses waddled to the judge's chair. Magnolia deflated. She'd been expecting the smash of a gavel and, in the role of judge, was thinking along the lines of Meryl Streep. The crowd had barely taken their seats when "the defense calls John Crawford Flanagan Jr., CEO of Scarborough Magazines" rang out in the room. Jock—on this, the second day of the trial—strolled to the witness stand for his swearing-in.

"Why did you enter into an agreement to publish a magazine with Ms. Bebe Blake?" a lawyer from Team Bebe said. Jock pondered the question as if he'd been asked to name and spell the capital of Uzbekistan. After a moment, he furrowed his brow and said, "We thought it was a potentially profitable idea."

"Could you please define 'we'?"

"Our team of top executives," he said with a thinly disguised tone of contempt, reeling off a list that included Darlene's name but, Magnolia noted, not her own.

Yesterday, Magnolia had stayed home and tried to focus on her proposal for *Voyeur*. She'd been advised that she might be called to testify later in the week and had dutifully turned in an overflowing box of notes and files. But knowing the trial was taking place just miles from her home had made her too twitchy to work. That, and the fact that she couldn't stop thinking about Cameron, who she thought might be there. Today she boarded the subway and found the State Supreme Court of New York.

As soon as she sat down, she scanned the courtroom for Cameron. She couldn't, however, find his face in the crowd.

Several days had passed before Cameron returned the phone message Magnolia had left after she read his manuscript. This gave Magnolia ample time to impale herself with regret. Could she have misread his book? With Abbey, her reality meter, away on her honeymoon, she went into a spin, obsessing day and insomnia-filled night.

Ultimately, she decided she'd got the subtext of the book just fine; there was, in fact, nothing sub about it. The heroine was one Daisy Silver, a magazine editor, albeit taller, slimmer-hipped, and blonder than she. The hero—a shy, wry colleague—yearned for her. The sex was hot, the love scenes graphic but romantic, and the dialogue, steamy and real. There were a few testosterone explosions along the way—a murder, a terrorist act, the requisite car chase—but the ending was pure Hollywood, and the writing, clear, clever, and poignant.

Maybe it was her assessment of the writing—or rather her lack of assessment—that had tripped her up. Maybe she'd been so focused on the plot she hadn't made it evident to Cam that his talent took her breath away. Maybe he was horribly and legitimately disappointed, not to mention furious, on that count. Maybe he now regretted revealing his feelings.

As the days passed, Magnolia's worry crescendoed to the most painful possibility of all—maybe their one high-as-a-kite kiss had succeeded in terminating his fantasy. When Cameron did finally call, he talked about everything except what had happened between them. Then he flew to California on a mission he didn't explain.

Magnolia was left with her maybes, including maybe on Cameron's return she should beg him to retreat to friendship, with its comforts of weightless silence, scrubbed-face honesty, and chaste but unconditional love—if such a state were now possible.

She looked up. Jock was still on the stand.

"How long does it take for most new magazines to turn a profit?" the lawyer asked him. "Ballpark figures."

"A year or two," Jock said. Above his eye, a blue vein throbbed like a tiny blinker flashing "stress." The lawyer reminded him he'd sworn to tell the truth, the whole truth, and nothing but the truth. "But more often it takes five years, or even longer," he added.

"So it was unreasonable to expect *Bebe* to be profitable anytime soon?" he asked. Jock answered with a flurry of figures, but all eyes—even the judge's—had turned to the back of the room. In a tweed suit and a boa, Bebe sashayed to the front of the room. She was treating the courtroom's center aisle as if it were a red carpet, looking from side to side and smiling for invisible paparazzi. Like the wave, a buzz moved forward as she progressed to her seat.

"Don't mind me," she said loudly to no one in particular. "The president is in town. Traffic sucks." Everyone stared. She shrugged. "Don't blame me—I didn't vote for him."

Judge Tannenbaum looked over her glasses and gave Bebe a stern stare. "Glad you could join us, Miss Blake," she said. "Mr. Montgomery, please, continue."

"I have concluded," he said. One of Cromwell, Adams, and Case's lead attorneys stepped forward to cross-examine.

"Mr. Flanagan," he said, "how much money does Scarborough Magazines stand to lose by Bebe Blake abandoning your co-venture?"

"One hundred million dollars," he said.

Magnolia was familiar with Scary's case. Who wasn't, the way it was being tried in the papers? But where Jock was getting this number, she didn't know.

When the court officer declared an adjournment until two, Magnolia made her way through the crowds to the steps outside court. As she reached the bottom, someone shouted her name, startling her. She stumbled into a large puddle of mud and soaked her best black suede boots. Magnolia looked up in time for a television camera to catch her saying, "Fuck."

"How do you think Scary's doing?" a second voice shouted. It was Mike McCourt, approaching with a notebook.

"No comment," she said. Wally had warned her not to talk to the press while her settlement was dragging on, as it was, like a Wagnerian opera.

"Is it true you're on the short list to start a new magazine for another company?" Mike asked. Who fed this guy his intelligence? Abbey and Cam were the only people she'd told about *Voyeur*, and neither one would squeak a word. The leak had to be from Fancy.

"No comment," she said.

"So, I guess that means 'yes'?" Mike asked. Magnolia was considering if she should say, "No comment" once more when Mike craned his neck to her left.

"Mr. Dane?" Mike yelled. "Mr. Dane, that you?"

Magnolia turned as well, and saw Cameron walking toward her.

"Some book deal I'm hearing rumors about," Mike said to Cam.

"Hardcover rights, paperback, audio, foreign in fourteen countries, and a possible TV series and film option. What's up?"

"You must have me confused with someone else, buddy," Cameron said amiably, as he walked toward Magnolia, grabbed her elbow, and steered her out of the throng.

"Cam, is what Mike says true?" Magnolia asked.

He laughed off the question. "Hungry?"

"When have I ever not been hungry?"

"I'm in the mood for dim sum," he said. "Want to join me?"

They began walking to Mott Street. "Did you catch my grand legal performance yesterday?" he asked.

"Really?" Magnolia asked. "You testified?" There had been no report of it on television, online, or in the press.

"Chapter and verse about how much money *Bebe* spent on this and that," Cam said. "I assure you, *Court TV* is not flashing a contract in my face."

"I'm praying I won't be called," she said. "It would kill me to help any of these barbarians win a dime."

They reached the restaurant and continued to dissect the trial. But what Magnolia wanted to talk about was them. As Cameron's hand reached for a sparerib, she imagined it under her skirt, above her soggy boot, inching upward.

"Chicken feet?" he said.

In her mind, the hand warmed her as its sensuous journey continued.

"Magnolia?"

"Excuse me," she said. "What's this about cold feet?"

He looked at her strangely. "Chicken feet. You don't like these suckers, do you?" The dim sum lady was standing by their table, trying to tempt them with some sad little body parts that looked like the last remains after a nuclear holocaust.

"I'll pass," she said. "Thanks."

"The desserts, please," Cam said. A few Chinese words flew across the room like insects. Sesame rice dumplings, mango pudding, and sticky buns in lotus leaves appeared on a cart beside their small table, which was nestled underneath a window. As Cam leaned forward to check them out, his thigh brushed hers. He poured the last drops of green tea into their cups and raised one. It looked fragile and small in his hand.

"You've been on my mind," he said.

Finally, Magnolia thought. She took a deep breath. "You've been on my mind, too," she admitted.

"I originally called my book *The Shy Guy*, but the editor changed it," he said. "Deal point." He laughed a musical bass that Magnolia realized had been an essential background noise in her life for several years. "Shoot me. I'm talking like some L.A. studio exec." He shifted to an imperious voice. "*'Hello, my name is Trevor, and I demand that my pathetically underpaid assistant roll my calls the minute people who've tried to reach me walk out of their offices.'*"

"Please, don't start walking around, wearing a headset," she said.

"Promise," he said. As Magnolia waited for Cameron to pick up his original train of thought, they heard a bang on the window.

"Get your butts out here," Bebe mouthed through the glass.

Cam and Magnolia looked at each other. "The queen beckons," he said. Cam paid the bill, and they gathered their coats and umbrellas and met her outside.

"I haven't been to Chinatown in years," Bebe said gaily, her arms filled with large, flimsy plastic sacks. For a woman who, according to every paper and newsmagazine, was worried about a twenty-million-dollar investment going south, her spirits were remarkably intact. "Here, have a bag," she said, handing Magnolia a Gucci knockoff fashioned of industrial-strength vinyl. She cocked her head, sized up Cam, and fished out a pimp-worthy faux gold Rolex Oyster, which she attached to his wrist. "For the gentleman," she said.

"Thanks, Bebe," he said. They all began walking back to the courthouse. "How do you think the trial's going?"

"Are you kidding?" Bebe snorted. "Fabulous! That judge loathes Jock. Can't you see the venom in her eyes?"

"You think?" Cameron said.

"What's your esteemed opinion, Magnolia?" Bebe asked.

"Honest, Bebe, I can't even see the judge's eyes," she said, "with the glasses and all."

Bebe stopped and scowled at Magnolia. "Why am I asking you anyway? I'm not supposed to even talk to either one of you." She ducked into yet another handbag stall. "Later!" she yelled.

Magnolia and Cam reached the courthouse. She returned to her seat, and Cameron joined her. Darlene was now on the stand, explaining her role as *Bebe*'s publisher. "I was in charge of the magazine's business department," she said. "Ad sales and marketing."

Magnolia was tuning out Darlene, concentrating only on Cam's closeness—until a document flashed on an overhead screen.

"Is this your pay stub?" the lawyer asked.

"Yes, it is," Darlene said, swelled with both pregnancy and pride. Magnolia had always suspected Darlene made a lot more money than she did, but with the evidence bigger than life, she sat there, her shoulders hunched, and slumped.

"Could you cringe more quietly?" Cameron whispered. "I can hear your teeth grinding."

"What galls me is she still has a job," Magnolia whispered. Darlene had been moved to Scary's business development unit, and insiders expected her to soon replace the current publisher of *Dazzle*.

Darlene's paycheck made way for wearying charts of ad revenues, which Darlene interpreted for the lawyer in anesthetizing detail.

"Want to duck out?" Magnolia whispered to Cameron. "Catch a movie at the Angelika?"

"Let's wait a few minutes," he said. "It looks like Bebe's attorney's going to cross-examine." Arthur Montgomery stepped forward.

"Is this your signature?" he asked Darlene.

"Yes, it is," she said. On the screen was a statement from the auditing bureau which tracks magazines' circulations. "I see that *Bebe* sold 480,500 copies per issue during its year of publication. Is that true?"

Anyone in the courtroom who wasn't blind could see that.

"Yes," Darlene said.

"So, can you explain these figures for me, please?" On the screen, to the right of the statement, a second document appeared, but this one stated that *Bebe* had sold, on average, only 278,935 copies per issue.

Darlene's eyes darted to Jock, the screen, and then to her attorneys. One of them sprung up from his chair and waved his hand like the smartest kid in the class. "I object," he said. "Your honor, I object."

The judge peered down at him. "Would counsel approach the bench, please," she said. All Magnolia could make of the conversation—which lasted for a few minutes—were aggressive hand gestures on the attorney's part.

"Counsel may continue," Judge Tannenbaum said to Bebe's lawyer.

"May I remind you, Mrs. Knudson, that you are under oath," Arthur Montgomery said. "Which of these two statements is correct?"

Darlene mumbled softly.

"Could you speak up for everyone to hear, please?" the judge directed.

Darlene returned to her normal speaking voice. "The one on the right," she blared.

"Now let me understand," Arthur Montgomery said very slowly. "I am reading from the joint-venture agreement." He quoted a jumble of legalese. Magnolia leaned forward in her chair and listened carefully, which wasn't hard, because the courtroom had become silent as a cave.

She turned to Cameron. "Are we hearing what I think we're hearing?" she said, getting close enough to smell the clean sweetness of his skin. "It sounds like Bebe was allowed to walk away from the magazine if it sold fewer than 350,000 copies per issue."

"That's exactly what it says," Cameron whispered back. His breath in her ear made her tingle.

"And could you explain this?" the attorney asked. On the screen an e-mail appeared to Darlene from Jock, who directed her to "manage the financials."

Cameron and Magnolia looked at each other and just as she was saying, "Scary goosed the numbers," he noted, "They've been caught red-handed cooking the books." As everyone reached the same conclusion, the courtroom came alive like an Italian soccer game. Felicity dropped her knitting needles, stood up, and high-fived Bebe, who whooped, "Hot damn. I knew it. Hot, fuckin' damn!"

"Order in the court," the judge said. "Order in the court." Magnolia got to hear the crash of a gavel after all. "Court will convene tomorrow at ten," Judge Tannenbaum said, finally, in disgust.

As they left Supreme Court, Magnolia and Cam stopped and listened to Jock giving an ad hoc press conference. "It's common industry practice to estimate the sales of a magazine before final numbers are in, and occasionally the two figures differ," he said to a growing audience of reporters. "Scarborough Magazines didn't do anything that every other magazine company doesn't do all the time."

As the statement leaped out of Jock's mouth, Magnolia knew it was destined to become the caption for tomorrow's picture in the *Post*—perhaps even the epitaph on his professional tombstone. So much for damage control. Elizabeth would probably return to her office and fax her résumé to every other publisher in the country.

"Don't you just love magazines?" Cam said to Magnolia.

"I do," she said. "In any other industry, if the president of a company stood up and said, 'I cheat. We all cheat. We're an entire industry of liars and cheaters,' he'd be found with two broken legs, groaning and bleeding, in a New Jersey garbage dump."

Magnolia and Cam watched Bebe walk past Jock. She didn't say a word but gave him her most high-voltage smile as she swirled her boa, which almost tickled his face.

"Smile all you want, Bebe," Jock snarled at her. "It's never over till the fat lady sings."

Chapter 41

The Curse of the Perfect Memory

"I'd sooner miss the Oscars than this," Natalie said airily as she took the seat next to Magnolia. The trial had become a spectator sport for every key Scary employee. As always, Natalie looked camera-ready. Velvet peep-toe pumps showed off her elegant feet and dark red pedicure. Magnolia was fairly sure, however, that if Natalie were photographed in the plaid coat she was wearing today, she'd wind up captioned in one of the Fashion Police columns with "Woof! I liked this better on my basset hound's bed."

Judge Margaret Ruth Tannenbaum had turned out to be a no-nonsense jurist. She was moving along the trial at a whirlwind clip, whacking lawyers' statements in midsentence. Yesterday, to the amusement of another full house, Felicity got her turn as a witness, and today Magnolia expected that Big Mama herself would take the stand. She could imagine no other reason for Bebe to sport a Miss Marple fedora.

The court officer stepped forward. "The plaintiffs call Magnolia Gold," he said. Magnolia froze. "The plaintiffs call Magnolia Gold," he shouted out again.

Natalie nudged her. Magnolia knew her name was on the list of witnesses who would be required to testify. By now, however, well into the trial's second week, she'd convinced herself that neither side must feel she could fuel their arguments and maybe she'd be granted a pass. She got up out of her chair and sleepwalked to the front. From a remote brain cell the thought occurred to her that at least she was wearing a sober black suit, not a ruffled cancan dress. On her way to the bench, from the corner of her eye, Magnolia saw Bebe offer a thumbs-up.

Magnolia lifted her right hand and swore her oath.

"What is your relationship to Scarborough Magazines?" asked their lead attorney.

Magnolia doubted *adversarial* was the answer they wanted. "Could you clarify the question, please?" she asked.

"I believe Counsel wants to know your work history and current association with the company," the judge said.

"Currently, I am no longer employed at the company, but before it was turned into *Bebe* I was the editor in chief of *Lady* magazine," Magnolia began.

"Solid magazine," Judge Tannenbaum interrupted. "My mother always subscribed, and so did I."

"We had four million readers," Magnolia said.

"I liked those little paper dolls."

"That was *McCall's*," Magnolia pointed out but continued to beam.

"I get them all mixed up."

"Everyone does."

As this homey banter continued, the Scarborough attorney glowered. Judge Tannenbaum eventually gestured for him to continue.

"Can you, please, explain why *Lady* was turned into a magazine for Bebe Blake?" he asked.

"No," Magnolia answered.

"Shall I clarify? Can you explain why the failing financials of *Lady* paved the way for *Bebe*?"

"I can't," Magnolia said. She looked at the judge to see if she was allowed to continue. Judge Tannenbaum nodded. "You see, the magazine wasn't failing. Our newsstand sales were reasonably strong, and according to the business meetings I was invited to, we were profitable."

"Then can you explain this?" the attorney asked. A document appeared on the overhead screen showing that *Lady*, in the last year of her life, clearly belonged in a financial hospice.

"No," she said. "I can't."

"Shall we call an expert witness to interpret these figures?"

Magnolia was quite certain no one missed his tone of condescension. "I *understand* them," she said. "I can't *explain* them."

"Why not?" the attorney asked petulantly.

"Because they conflict with these," she said. From her Tod's tote, Magnolia pulled out her own white rabbit, Darlene's update from the final *Lady* business review. It was Wally who insisted she open and sort the tower of boxes sent from Scary that had been collecting dust in her foyer. With Sasha's help, she spent the better part of the previous weekend digging through them.

"According to this memo," Magnolia said, handing it to the attorney, "the magazine wasn't losing money."

Scary's lawyer put on his reading glasses and examined the memo. As he huddled with Jock, Darlene, and the other Scarborough lawyers, Magnolia strained, unsuccessfully, to hear their conversation. There were several minutes of animated discussion after which Magnolia's memo was labeled and entered as evidence. Then the lawyer looked at the judge and said, "We are finished with this witness."

Magnolia's hands were trembling so obviously, she grabbed both sides of the chair. Under her jacket, her starched white shirt felt damp.

"Mr. Montgomery, do you care to cross-examine?" the judge asked.

"Thank you," he said in his courtliest Southern accent. "I do." Arthur Montgomery stood in front of Magnolia and clasped his hands behind his back. His genial smile revealed his large teeth. "Miss Gold, did you support the concept of turning *Lady* into *Bebe*?"

Magnolia thought back to the previous June's original meeting, the lunacy of which she could recall as if it had happened the day before. "No," she replied, "I did not." As she spoke the words, she could feel the blitzkrieg of Bebe's menace roll toward her like World War III.

"When Scarborough Magazines presented the idea to you, what, exactly, did you say?"

Magnolia hesitated. She reminded herself she was obligated to tell the truth.

"I said that Bebe didn't stand for anything bigger than herself, that she was a collection of interests that didn't add up to a clear vision for a magazine." The courtroom had become quiet except for Felicity's saying, "That little ferret."

"Was there anything else you said about my client, Miss Blake?" the attorney asked.

There are times in life when a perfect memory is a curse. "That she could be a player," Magnolia said. She was certain she'd used that word instead of nympho, slut, or child molester. "And difficult to work with." Magnolia began to hear laughter, which started lightly and multiplied with such volume that Judge Tannenbaum got another chance to exercise her gavel. "Order," the judge demanded as she crashed it on the bench. "Order."

The room complied.

"Did you become an editor on the magazine?"

"Yes," Magnolia said.

"Mr. Montgomery, is there a point here?" the judge asked.

"Yes, your honor." A smile broadened on his sharp, lupine face. "Miss Gold, given your distaste for Miss Blake's idea," he articulated loudly, as if he were trying to communicate with a mute, "is it not fair to say that you may have undermined Miss Blake in her best efforts to publish her magazine?" Montgomery pronounced "undermined" as if it were in boldface.

"No!" Magnolia said, more emotionally than she intended. "I was always professional."

"Did you resent that you had to take direction from Bebe Blake?" he asked with forced casualness.

Do you resent that you are an ugly little man with hair sprouting from your ears, Magnolia wanted to ask back. Do you resent that ninety-nine women out of a hundred would rather clean a toilet than sleep with you?

"Miss Gold, answer Mr. Montgomery's question," the judge demanded.

"Yes," she said, a nasty bile rising in her throat.

"Thank you, Miss Gold," he said. "That will be all."

Magnolia wanted to let out a primal scream. She turned to the judge with a pleading look.

"Miss Gold, you may return to your seat."

She walked back, willing herself to stand straight and tall. How dare he? Without her sweat equity, *Bebe* never would have happened. Magnolia sat on the hard bench. Natalie took her hand and stroked it. She wished the stroking were coming from Cameron, but she hadn't seen him anywhere in the courtroom.

"Relax, Cookie," Natalie said. "That ambulance-chasing jackass isn't worth getting worked up about. Anyway, you look gorgeous when you're pissed. That's all anyone will remember." From a black patent Gucci bag large enough to carry a cocker spaniel, she pulled out a tissue which she handed to Magnolia, who flicked away a tear.

"The court calls Bebe Blake," Magnolia heard the words from a far-off place. Bebe marched to the witness stand for her swearing-in.

"Finally!" Bebe said, straightening her hat.

"May I remind you that you will speak only when called on," the judge said.

"Sorry, Your Honor," Bebe said. Scary's attorneys started in on her, and Bebe was thoroughly engaging—even when the gun cover was shown, bigger than life, like an advertisement for mental illness. Magnolia wondered if the attorneys would try to nail her as a sexual deviant, but it appeared that they were steering clear of that line of questioning.

"Before a business trip, did you have one of the *Bebe* assistants show you Polaroids of hotel suites so you would pick the best one?" the attorney asked.

"Yes, doesn't everyone?" she answered. The courtroom laughed.

"At the *Bebe* sales conference in Palm Beach, is it true that you had a silver Corvette driven all the way from Atlanta and that when you didn't like it, you had the same automobile brought in from Sarasota in red?"

"I don't recall," Bebe said with a big grin.

At one o'clock, after Bebe had much of the courtroom chuckling along with her, the court officer announced a lunch break.

"Want to grab a bite?" Natalie said.

"I'm fried," Magnolia said. "Going to head uptown and work." She hadn't written so much as a sentence of her *Voyeur* proposal in more than a week.

"Work?" Natalie said.

Natalie would be the last person she'd tell about her Fancy meeting.

"Oh, you know, letters, basic drudgery," Magnolia said. "Have to beat the bushes."

She walked to the checkroom to retrieve her phone and put on her Chanel sample sale raincoat, which she was wearing for the first time that day. Outside, she caught her reflection in the glass front of a restaurant she passed on the way to the subway. This coat makes me look like a heifer, she decided. Tomorrow, I'll ship it to Mom.

Magnolia played back her messages. There were two—the first from Wally; the second, Cameron. An empty cab passed, its yellow light a taunting reminder not to splurge on a $25 fare.

She dialed Cam's number. He was back in California, his message had said, but all he shared was that negotiations on his book had got complicated. He didn't answer his telephone.

"It's the person who's probably just handed Bebe a two-hundred-million-dollar victory," she said in her message. "Call if you want to make fun of me."

She pressed the buttons on her phone for Wally, who was now on speed dial. "Mr. Fleigelman, please?" she said to his assistant. "It's Magnolia Gold."

Wally got on the line right away. "Hi, gorgeous," he said. "In the mood for news?"

"Only if it's good," she said.

"Well, in that case . . ." Wally said solemnly.

"Oh-h-h," Magnolia groaned. "No!"

"Just kidding," he said and laughed loudly. "Listen to this." He paused for dramatic effect. "Scary is offering two years' salary."

"Wally!" Magnolia said. "That's amazing. Beyond amazing! Tell me everything!" She was screaming so loudly, people were turning to stare.

"They came around yesterday," he said. "Turns out, you weren't the first woman to charge sexual harassment. Your Mr. Flanagan had a history." Wally switched to his serious lawyer voice. "Employers are liable for sexual harassment of employees by their managers and Scarborough had done nothing to reprimand Jock, despite numerous complaints."

"Dickheads," she said.

"You're right on that one. And the Scary dickheads are not too pleased with their boy now that the world knows he cooks the books and, you'll pardon my French, he's basically accused the whole industry of being a lying sack of shit," he said. "But back to you. At first Scary was only going to come through with one year of salary. Then I let them know you were planning to sue."

"I was?"

"You were."

"I am one ballsy chick, aren't I, Wally?"

"I'm afraid I'm not done yet, Mags," Wally said. "There's a bit more to it."

It *had* sounded too good to be true, Magnolia thought.

"I let Jock's attorney know you were planning to sue Jock person-ally, which—by the way—is perfectly legal. And, an hour ago, the damnedest thing happened. The attorney found $200,000 for you. Funny how that happens. Guess Mr. Flanagan sold a painting."

Magnolia gasped.

"You there, Mags?" Wally shouted. "I've got to know if these terms sound acceptable, or you want to go back for more." There was only breathing from Magnolia's end of the phone. "Magnolia?"

"I'm here, Wally, talking to you from euphoria," she said. "Magno-lia Gold accepts—with pleasure."

Chapter 42

Fired, Finished, Decapitated

"I missed you."

"I missed you, too."

After two weeks in Italy and one in Paris, Abbey had returned. Daniel wouldn't be visiting for several more weeks, and Magnolia was just slightly ashamed of being elated to have the new Madame Cohen all to herself. "I can't figure out what's changed about you," she said as they began their early morning run. A moisturizer sold only in Europe? A subtly different hair color? "Your face looks softer," she decided. "Is this what happiness looks like?"

"This is what five pounds looks like," Abbey said, puffing her cheeks and patting her tummy, which—to Magnolia—looked as concave as ever. "And at my height, my five is your ten. Great food, great wine–that was my honeymoon. Well, not quite." She paused, apparently to recollect a moment she didn't care to share.

As they ran, Abbey reviewed every four-star restaurant they visited. "And by the way, forget the hype—the real reason Frenchwomen don't get fat is that they smoke." She stopped as they finished their second loop. "But enough about me. Your settlement! You must be crazy happy."

They walked briskly toward their coffee shop. "Oh, I am," Magnolia said. But she considered herself an ingrate not to be radiating ostentatious glee. "Wally's a prince, and my financial adviser—I have one now, can you believe it?—put almost all the money in something she insists I don't touch for years. Except for the pittance I plan to live off, I'm pretending my windfall doesn't exist. This is what good Fargo girls do—hoard."

"Come on," Abbey said. "Indulge yourself. At least a little bauble?" Their regular waiter appeared as they grabbed the prime corner booth. "Just tea for me this morning, nothing to eat," Abbey said as the waiter welcomed them back.

"The usual, please," Magnolia said, then turned back to Abbey. "I wrote checks to ten charities, and I'm sending my parents on a cruise of the Greek islands."

Abbey raised her eyebrows. "That's noble, but what about you?"

"I'm replacing my kitchen countertops." Magnolia brushed poppy seeds from her bagel into a tiny black pyramid. "What do you think of white marble? Not practical, huh?"

"Magnolia?" Abbey sounded dubious.

"Truth? I'm too agitated to spend a cent," she said, staring at the table. "My inner bag lady is shouting, 'Watch out—you'll never work again.' I'm beginning to feel this firing is The End."

"C'mon—it may take a while to find a dream job—you told me that yourself," Abbey said. "At least plan a trip while you're waiting. You can use Daniel's apartment in Paris." She stopped herself. "*Our* apartment."

"I don't feel like traveling alone," she snapped and immediately regretted it. Throwing guilt bombs at Abbey hadn't been her plan. "Forget I said that. I couldn't go anywhere even if I wanted to—still polishing my Fancy proposal."

"You were working on that before I left."

"Every time I think I'm finished I start over. Maybe I have a learning disability."

"Clinical ambivalence," Abbey said and gently poked Magnolia's arm. "Do you even want that job?"

"I'm not sure there even is a job," she said. "Fancy might just be picking my brains." Magnolia put her hand in the pocket of her windbreaker and pulled out a ten dollar bill, which she laid on the table. "This one's on me. Welcome back. Movie tonight?"

"Whatever you want to see," Abbey said. They stood up and layered on their scarves, gloves, and hats. The calendar read April, but it still felt like the winter of Magnolia's discontent.

She walked west, toward her apartment. While Abbey had been away they'd e-mailed every few days, so Abbey was up to speed about the trial and the sale of Cam's book, though not its plot, and definitely not the kiss. What else was there to tell, really? That she and Cam had each made a move but ultimately retreated to their passion-free comfort zones? True, they'd been talking, e-mailing, and IM-ing since he'd returned to Los Angeles for more meetings. Yet in every way there was a continent between them.

Now Cam wanted her to visit. She'd been telling him she couldn't leave town because of her *Voyeur* proposal. Magnolia knew she was a freeze-dried liar.

"You'd love running on the beach," he'd said last night. His publisher, or maybe it was his agent—Cam was vague on this point—was putting him up at the Shutters in Santa Monica, and his room had a view of the Pacific. He hadn't exactly said that he wanted her to *share* that room, however, and Magnolia felt uncomfortable asking.

Maybe Abbey was right, though. She should get out of town. What would be the worst that might happen? She and Cam would laugh at the absurdity of thinking they could hook up, then buy a movie star map, rent a red convertible, and prowl the city.

Every trip she'd ever made to L.A. had been in tandem with a publisher for the sole purpose of selling ads. Magnolia associated the city with predawn wake-up calls, six meetings per day, and ten P.M. exhaustion. As pure R&R, it might be different. She and Cam could gorge on overpriced sushi, go to comedy showcases, and visit the wineries in Santa Barbara. When Cam was busy, she'd dress in aggressively casual left coast clothes and get some practically iridescent highlights or do a Pilates class and rub shoulders with celebrities she'd been scrutinizing ad nauseam on television and in magazines. Maybe she'd even discreetly check out plastic surgeons; by L.A. standards, surely thirty-eight was past the legal limit to be walking around with a face and body that hadn't been reengineered. On the weekend, the two of them could stop by that enormous swap meet at the Rose Bowl or wind their way up the coast, stay in Big Sur, and end in Napa, where they'd drink even more wine.

It could be chummy—or better than chummy—and at the very least shake her out of the New York blahs. Anyone could get cranky living through a damp Manhattan winter. She always felt far more shivery here than in the arctic desert of North Dakota.

By the time Magnolia arrived at her apartment, she'd decided to call Cam and announce her plans to take the trip. She looked at her watch. Five o'clock in the morning in California. Better wait. She left her running clothes in a heap on her bathroom floor and hopped in the shower. In the steam, she let herself imagine a second kiss with Cam. And more. Much more. She heard the phone ring. As the fantasy flowed into every tributary of her unloved body, she let it ring and ring.

After drying herself with a towel she'd warmed on the radiator, Magnolia found her most extravagant lotion—no Vaseline Intensive Care today—and lovingly massaged it into her skin, inch by inch. She stood in front of the opened armoire and reached for a variation on her ongoing work uniform—flannel pajama bottoms and a baggy T-shirt. No thanks, she decided. From a drawer, Magnolia unearthed some excellent underwear and pale blue cashmere sweatpants with a matching hoodie. The unworn set was still wrapped in tissue paper from last Christmas and felt like kitten fur against her newly silken skin. Her fantasy intact, she logged on to her computer and, using miles to upgrade to first class, made an airline reservation for two days later. Within ten more minutes, she'd booked a car to take her to the airport and arranged for Biggie and Lola to be kenneled.

Magnolia felt better already.

Yet it was still too early to call Cam. She decided to e-mail. "In the mood for sushi after all. See you Thursday at LAX," she wrote. "I've missed you," she added and immediately substituted the sentiment with "Talk later. M."

Magnolia thought through what else she'd need to do before she left. A haircut and root job, definitely. Maybe someone would already be at Frédéric Fekkai and be able to book an appointment. She got to her phone and noticed she had a message that must have arrived when she was showering. "Turn on your TV pronto, Magnolia," Natalie's recorded voice said. "The verdict's in. Call me. ASAP."

Magnolia ran to her TV. She'd missed the last round of news, so she checked online. There were no postings she could locate. She returned to channel surf.

Throughout the trial, Judge Tannenbaum made no secret that she had bigger legal fish to fry and that the plaintiffs, defendants, and all their lawyers were wasting her precious time. "This trial never should have happened, and these two are just a pair of playground bullies," she'd carped about Jock and Bebe, "but there's no client like a rich, angry one." Nonetheless, everyone Magnolia knew was betting that Bebe would clean up—big. As she continued to flip channels, Magnolia started pacing as if she were waiting to see whether a pregnancy test would turn blue.

". . . and the victor in the infamous trial between talk show personality Bebe Blake and Scarborough Magazines, the publisher of her eponymous magazine, *Bebe*, is . . ."

Why did she care? Strictly speaking, was she even *in* the magazine industry anymore?

". . . absolutely no one," the newscaster said. "That's right, folks. Judge Margaret Ruth Tannenbaum of the Supreme Court of the State of New York has essentially said a pox on both your houses." The screen flashed to footage of the judge. "There is no proof that *Bebe* magazine would ever have made a dime," the judge lectured, "so neither side deserves monetary damages."

"In further comments," the reporter continued, "Judge Tannenbaum stressed that she thought it was 'a crime that *Lady* magazine was sacrificed to a narcissistic celebrity so she could be the hood ornament for a pointless magazine.' Both the judge and her mother had been longtime *Lady* subscribers. 'I miss their recipes,' said the judge, who is widely known for her home-baked biscotti, 'and the article on pet psoriasis saved my Max from considerable heartbreak.'"

Magnolia switched to other channels, searching for more coverage. Bebe popped up.

"Viewers," she heard Matt Lauer say, "Bebe Blake is standing by. How do you feel about the verdict on your lawsuit, Bebe?"

Bebe's face looked terrifyingly large as it filled Magnolia's TV screen. "This is a huge victory," Bebe said. "Huge."

"But, Bebe, you didn't get a dime," Matt countered.

"That's not the point," Bebe said. "Justice has prevailed. I don't care what it cost—I care about the principle, and the important thing is that Scarborough Magazines didn't win a dime. And," Bebe continued, pausing for a split second to catch her breath, "we're going after those suckers to recover legal fees, which are substantial." She raised her arm in a victory salute. "They started this war!"

"You did quit your own magazine," Matt pointed out. "And weren't there some improprieties on the part one of your editors, Felicity Dingle—and a few other, uh, bumps along the way?"

Bebe failed to respond, which caused Matt to catapult another question into the dead air. "Your future plans, Bebe? What can your fans look forward to now that *Bebe* magazine is over? Are the rumors true that you are also quitting your television show?"

"You nailed that one!" said Bebe, who made a gagging sound and motion. "I'm sure you can relate."

Matt ignored the comment and sound effect. "So tell our audience—what's up?"

"I'm starting a business," Bebe said. "The Slut Hut."

"Excuse me?" he asked.

"Got ya, Matt," Bebe said. "Ha. For real? My friend Barbra wants me for the lead in *Yentl,* which she's bringing to Broadway. Plus my new blog."

"Boy, everyone's a blogger. What's yours called?"

"Bebe's Bull—" Bebe's face disappeared as the censors bit off the end of the name.

Magnolia had seen enough. She returned the call to Natalie, who was in a meeting, so she dived into her newspapers. The trial story was too new for the morning editions, but in the *Post* there was Jock's face, his mouth agape. The article reported that Jock's wife was leaving him. Pippi wanted $57,000 a month for alimony and child support, which included $14,000 for Little Jock's rented horse, even if it meant that Big Jock had to abandon his $10,000-a-month pied-à-terre.

The phone rang. "So, Cookie," Natalie trilled. "What do you think?"

"I'm loving it!" Magnolia admitted. "Both sides got what they deserve. Oops, rewind," Magnolia said. "How insensitive of me." She realized Scary's ignominious loss would be bad business for a company where Natalie continued to work.

"Good God, Magnolia," Natalie said. "Don't apologize. Everybody here thinks Jock's the most arrogant scum-bucket who ever lived. There's a special circle in corporate hell for a CEO who squanders millions on an embarrassing trial, tops it off with sexual harassment problems and his puss splashed over the papers for his divorce, and tries to drag his peers down with him."

"So you think the Scary boys will have him eat dirt for a while?" The very thought made her want to stand up and sing, "I'm Gonna Wash That Man Right Outta My Hair."

"Are you kidding?" Natalie said. "'Eat dirt?' He's over."

"Define 'over.'"

"Fired, finished, decapitated. If the Scary boys could waste him, they would."

"Really?" Sweet, she thought. "What's going to happen now?"

"Well . . ." Natalie abandoned all dignity. It was fair to say she squealed. "You can congratulate me, Natalie Simon, the newly appointed CEO of Scarborough Magazines!"

Magnolia screamed.

"Thanks—I'll take that as mazel tov. And if you can clear your busy schedule, Miss Gold, Chairman Simon would like to take you to lunch. See you Friday at Michael's."

Chapter 43

Passion in Flip-flops

An enormous bouquet of orange gerbera daisies arrived as Magnolia left to meet Abbey at a downtown theater. "To my Daisy Silver," Cameron's note said. "You finally made the right decision. Looking forward, C."

Throughout the movie, Magnolia deliberated on those daisies, which now filled her three tallest vases and every corner of her brain.

"Keanu Reeves's kiss—did you have the feeling it was the beginning of the end or the end of the beginning?" Abbey had to repeat the question twice before Magnolia answered.

"Hmmm . . ." Magnolia answered, as they walked into Lil' Frankie's. "Not sure."

"Did that plot work for you?"

Magnolia could barely remember it. "Uh, yeah," she said.

"Fascinating," Abbey said, picking up a menu. "Okay, what kind of pizza should we order?"

"Whatever," Magnolia said. "You know what I like."

Abbey thwacked her with a stare. "Magnolia, you're phoning in this whole evening. Hardly said a word in the cab. Forgot to pick up our Raisinettes. What's up?"

"I'm . . . preoccupied."

"Your 'preoccupied' is not an orgy of fun, my friend," Abbey said. "Is it that you think the verdict wasn't fair?"

Magnolia leaned her head on her arm. "Judge Tannenbaum's verdict was eminently fair," she said, "but it's put me in a corner, that's all."

"You're going to have to connect the dots for me," Abbey said. "I know I've been out of the country for a few weeks, but . . ."

"Okay," Magnolia said, and launched into a short, sweet synopsis of where she and Cam stood or didn't stand, that she was looking forward to visiting him and he apparently felt the same way, but how Natalie had thrown a monkey wrench into her plan by scheduling a command performance for Friday.

"Now that's a story line," Abbey said, looking appropriately flabbergasted. "You and Cam!" She squeezed Magnolia's hand. "I was wondering when you'd notice you're perfect for each other. It seemed quite apparent to me when he couldn't stop talking about you." She was grinning. "So, what's the big deal?" The pizza arrived and Abbey bit into a hot, cheesy slice. "You just reschedule Natalie."

"People don't 'reschedule' Natalie," Magnolia said. "Certainly not now that she's CEO. You're not getting how important this might be. She's invited me to Michael's. In practically her first public act. It's living theater."

"I don't know," Abbey said. "She might just want to gloat before an adoring audience. Put her off. By the way, what have you told Cameron?"

Magnolia sucked in a big gulp of air. "Nothing," she admitted. "There, I said it. I'm dodging. He called at ten, and twice later, and I didn't pick up."

"Magnolia, what's gotten into you? You're being a child—and cruel," Abbey said none of this kindly or quietly.

"Thank you," Magnolia hissed. "I really needed to hear that and so did the people at the next table." The heavily pierced, tattooed recent college graduates were looking at Magnolia as if she were wearing Mom jeans and sensible shoes. She glanced at her Pumas. She *was* wearing sensible shoes.

"If you don't need my advice, then just pull the petals off your daisies to decide."

"I also don't need your sarcasm."

"But the answer is obvious." Abbey sat forward until her face was less than a foot away from Magnolia's. "Follow your heart." She did that thing where she zipped her lips in a tight line and crossed her arms, offering Magnolia an excellent view of the chunky diamonds blinking from her wedding band.

"Abbey, you met Daniel, bells chimed, and now you're married with so many residences you need a new address book. You own vineyards! Your heart knew what it wanted. Mine needs a fucking GPS! I can't trust it. It led me to Harry, to Tyler." She wiped away tears with her sleeve. "It led me to Wally!"

Abbey laughed. "Who may have been a keeper and you never noticed."

"Precisely. Why should I let myself believe a flirtation with Cameron is passion in a flannel shirt? Actually, now he probably wears Hawaiian shirts and flip-flops. My instincts suck. I can't run away. What I need is a job—a plan—and then maybe I'll start thinking straight."

"Didn't Mark Twain say, 'Life is what happens to you when you're busy making other plans,'" Abbey asked.

"No, but John Lennon did."

"Whatever. 'Love is the flower you've got to let grow,'" Abbey sang.

"'The more I see the less I know,'" Magnolia sang back.

"All I am saying is give Cam a chance," Abbey said. "You owe him. At least explain." They finished their dinner, split the bill, and began a painfully quiet ride uptown. Halfway there, Magnolia's phone rang.

"Hello, dear," Felicity said. "Bebe would love you to join us for an impromptu fete. Her friend Mario is pulling out all the stops here at Babbo. We have food for fifty. Quite a do." In the background, Magnolia could hear Bebe's laugh maxxed out to top volume.

Magnolia put her hand over her phone and whispered to Abbey, "Apparently, Bebe's gotten over my testimony. Want to go to her celebration party? You've got to admit that woman does know how to move on."

"Pass," Abbey said without a moment's hesitation.

"Felicity, I just stuffed myself. But have a great time. And thanks for asking."

"You sure? You'd especially like the piñata," she said. "It's Jock's likeness."

"Tell Bebe to give it a good whack on my behalf," Magnolia said. Bebe carrying on as if she'd won Wimbledon? It made no sense, but not much did today.

The taxi dropped off Abbey. Magnolia got out a few blocks later and gave Biggie and Lola an extra long walk before she had the nerve to see if Cam had called again. He had. She walked to her computer, started to write, but decided only a candy-assed coward would e-mail.

He answered on the first ring.

"Cameron?"

"Mags." He said her name with a glint of joy and intimacy she could hear and feel three thousand miles away. "I was beginning to worry."

"I'm sorry I haven't been able to call back," she said. "I got totally in the zone with my proposal—you know how that happens—then suddenly it was six-thirty and I'd promised to meet Abbey and then I forgot my phone." She was a terrible liar, spilling out her explanation in a breathless gasp.

"Un-huh," he said.

"I love the flowers," she said. "Thank you." Why hadn't she gushed her gratitude immediately?

"They're thinking of calling the movie *Daisy Chain*. I hate it."

"Movie? What movie?"

"The movie being made from my book. My agent did the deal. The book's optioned, and the studio wants me to collaborate here on the screenplay."

"Cameron," she shrieked. "That's incredible. This is huge. Huge! Congratulations. I am so impressed. You, a Hollywood screenwriter. You're going to win an Oscar."

"Enough," he said. He sounded neither happy nor excited. In fact, at the other end of the phone she thought she heard him sigh, but the sound might have come from her. "You've decided not to visit, haven't you?"

"Everything's taken a turn for the complicated," she said softly. "Jock was fired."

"Are there spontaneous outbursts of jubilation throughout the city?"

"There's one here in this apartment."

"The people who despise that guy could fill Roseland."

"Natalie's getting his job."

"Hmmm . . . Interesting. I can see that," he said. "The woman turned *Dazzle* into an ATM."

"She wants to have lunch Friday."

"You have to take the meeting."

Magnolia laughed. "Talking like an L.A. boy. You like it there?"

"I didn't think I would," he said. "But writers run around in T-shirts and cutoffs and work at the Coffee Bean. It has its charms." As if he'd selected a different font, his tone had downshifted to friendship. Magnolia wanted to get back what had already slipped away.

"I'm disappointed, you know," she said. "About this weekend."

"Me, too," he said. The dead air hung between them.

"Tell me what I'll miss."

"Dinner on Friday at this tapas place. Saturday I thought you might go house-hunting with me. Sunday morning, the Rose Bowl swap meet, and then a drive to Malibu or those Santa Barbara wineries."

"From *Sideways?*"

"From *Sideways.*"

"Roll back to house-hunting. Does this mean you're going to be there permanently?"

"No, but at least six months . . . It would be a rental—near the beach or in one of those coyote-filled canyons."

Cameron of California was beginning to come into focus and he felt unknown and far, far away. There wasn't much to say after that. Except good night.

She called her dogs. "You guys—bedtime. It's an order." Biggie and Lola leaped up and settled in for a cozy snooze. The same could not be said for Magnolia. She pictured Cam going from project to project as Hollywood's hot, new script doctor. Two years from now, he'd be picking up an Oscar for best screenplay—looking cute in a tuxedo. He'd accept with a wry comment, which would make most people scratch their heads, but she would get it. She'd call to congratulate him. His assistant would take a message. "We'll return," the assistant would lie.

When the phone rang at two A.M., Magnolia welcomed the interruption.

"The thing I want to know is," he said, "after the screwing you've gotten in magazines and the rodeo down at the courthouse, why would you ever want to try to stay in that business and hang around just to get beat up again? What's that thing you always said to me—it's okay to make a mistake but just don't keep making the same mistake?"

Magnolia waited to see if there was more to the tirade. She wondered if he'd been drinking.

"I'm asking as a friend," he added. He sounded sober, too sober.

"Cam, you clearly have all sorts of talents," she said. Even some she only suspected, and would like to experience—in every way—firsthand. "But working in magazines is what I do. I'm a monkey with one trick."

"You don't know that," he said. "You're just terrified. I'll only say this once. Forget about being an editor. Move in with me. We'll discover L.A. together. Fresh start. You got to Manhattan from Fargo. How hard could this town be?"

"You think the movie business is any better than magazines?" Her voice wasn't sleepy anymore. "Film companies give themselves names like Pariah and nobody blinks. L.A. is where people eat their young. And speaking of young, by Hollywood standards, I'm not."

"Magnolia, none of that matters. Goddammit, you are one stubborn woman." He paused. "Is this why I love you or do I love you in spite of this?"

Chapter 44

The Devil's Work?

"**Congratulations.**" Air kisses. "Perfect choice." Hugs. "Can't wait to see what you'll do." Big smooch. "Success becomes you."

With Michael's patrons genuflecting to Natalie as they arrived and departed in their spiffy best, Magnolia's lunch dragged into its second hour. Finally, cappuccinos and cookies arrived on a small silver tray, and Natalie beamed her attention toward Magnolia. "You must feel vindicated," she said. In her new role as Scary's president and CEO, Natalie had arrived on a crimson tide of a red suit and Christian Louboutin T-strap heels.

"How's that?" Magnolia wondered.

"Pundits are spinning the trial as a retroactive win for *Lady*."

"One pundit in one ultraconservative newspaper with a circulation of ten thousand."

"Cookie, you're not hearing what I'm hearing. Your stock is way up on the magazine NASDAQ."

"Well, thanks Natalie," she said. "But the last time I looked I was still unemployed."

"I hear you may be starting a new celebrity magazine," Natalie said.

"Don't believe everything you hear," she said, smiling coyly. A more accurate answer would be "fat chance," since she hadn't massaged her *Voyeur* proposal to anywhere near perfection or even given herself a deadline to set up an appointment at Fancy. The editorial director there had probably forgotten they'd ever met.

"We can't have you working for a competitor now, can we?" Natalie said, nibbling one of Michael's decadent butter cookies. "You know, I'm going to be replacing myself at *Dazzle*."

Two months before, Magnolia wouldn't have felt the least bit qualified to lead a magazine that depended not only on being able to distinguish Jessica Simpson from Jessica Alba but knowing what, exactly, each was famous for; and, more important, the names of their butt doubles. Yet after dedicating herself to nonstop celebrity watching, she'd got it. She'd got it fine.

Magnolia was just about to say she'd be thrilled to discuss *Dazzle* when Darlene stopped by the table, grunted a hello to her, and swooped down on Natalie. "I hope you got my flowers, Natalie," she said in a voice the whole restaurant could hear. "I am so thrilled for you. I can't think of a better choice for Scarborough, and I know the two of us are going to work together famously and make a ton. A ton!" Were those tears in her eyes or was Darlene just allergic to sincerity?

"Thank you, sweetie," Natalie said, patting Darlene's sturdy hand. "The flowers are gorgeous." She took a sip of cappuccino. "So, we'll be seeing each other today at four?"

Confusion blew over Darlene's face. Magnolia thought she saw a sign on her forehead say, "What the fuck?" but Darlene recovered. "Of course," she said. "Later!"

As soon as she had left, Natalie leaned her head close to Magnolia's. "She's history," she whispered without moving her lips. "I just decided this very minute that we'll have 'the talk' at four, and if I'm lucky I will never see that loudmouth bitch again. She's a walking speaker phone." Natalie picked up her BlackBerry and sent a message to her assistant instructing her to set up an appointment with Darlene.

"Those manufactured circ numbers . . . and does she think I don't know she's had her nose up everyone's butt for a new job?" Natalie ate another cookie. "I think I am going to like being CEO."

"You'll be brilliant," Magnolia said and meant it. But why can't we return to the topic on the table before Darlene appeared? Natalie looked at her watch.

"You were mentioning *Dazzle*," Magnolia said. She hoped the desperation in her voice didn't come across like ticker tape.

"Oh, right," Natalie said. She pulled out her corporate AmEx card, which was identical to the one Magnolia had to shred when her little pink slip arrived. "Do you think you might be interested?"

"I think I would," she said.

"Being a weekly, you pretty much have to be on call three hundred fifty-two days of the year," Natalie said. You've never *done* a weekly—that's what she was really saying. Or even worked on a celebrity magazine or been an entertainment editor. Neither had Natalie when she'd talked her way into becoming *Dazzle*'s editor in chief. But Magnolia understood. Natalie wanted her to scrawl, "I will die if you don't hire me" on the white tablecloth in her own blood, then jump on the chair, beat her chest, and declare undying love for *Dazzle*.

Dazzle led the media parade that revered fame. Op-Ed page critics could make a strong case for why it was the kind of scandal sheet that made teenagers want to grow up to become stars of their own reality TV shows instead of schoolteachers and pediatricians, but hadn't Anne Frank had photographs of celebrities in her hiding place? Working at *Dazzle* wasn't the devil's work, Magnolia told herself. It was just entertainment—and the most lucrative editor-in-chief job at Scary.

She swallowed hard. "Natalie, I am shocked and flattered. I would be completely honored to lead *Dazzle*," she said. "Of course, I would have very big shoes to fill . . ."—rats. Unfortunate choice of phrase, Natalie being vain about her size-five, triple-A feet—"but especially during my, uh, hiatus, I've become utterly enamored of the current celebrity culture in the United States. Ask me anything! Brangelina's baby's middle name. Jennifer Lopez's preferred underarm deodorant. Salma Hayek's electrolysis technician . . ."

Natalie was smiling beautifully, thoroughly enjoying the groveling. "I think I could be a highly effective, energetic editor in chief of *Dazzle*," Magnolia continued. "As far as its being a weekly goes, you know how fast I am, Natalie. You know I never stop working for a damn second. I am always ahead of schedule. 'Anal retentive' is my middle name . . ."

"Okay, okay," Natalie said. "You're in."

"I'm in? Great!" Magnolia said. She felt light-headed and thought she needed water. Then the wires in her brain connected. What, exactly, did "in" mean?

"I'd love you to be a candidate," Natalie continued. "Several editors on my staff have spoken to me about the job, and Raven, of course. Plus, I've gotten calls from several other strong contenders from the company, as well as from *Vanity Fair*, *People*, *Us*, the *Star*, *InTouch*." Natalie stood to leave. "Interest in the job is off the charts."

"Understandable," Magnolia mumbled.

"Anyone who wants to be considered needs to give me their vision for the magazine, in less than thirty pages—including visuals—by Monday at ten."

Chapter 45

Best Picture

"Amélie is here," the voice said, sounding exhausted but happy. "She wants to meet you."

"Oh, my God," Magnolia said groggily. "I'll get there as fast as I can." No one expected Amélie for several weeks. "How is she?"

"Beautiful."

Magnolia scrambled into yesterday's clothes, which she'd tossed on the chair when she'd got home past midnight, and grabbed the present hiding in her closet. She stopped on Columbus Avenue at the posh new florist—they were overpriced, but she didn't care—and asked for four dozen tiny white tea roses packed tightly in a square glass vase.

It was snowing and taxis were scarce. Snowflakes blew sharply in her face as she stood, burdened with her gifts, looking for an empty cab. After fifteen minutes, one found her.

"Mount Sinai Hospital," she said to the driver. The taxi skidded along the icy streets and through the park and, ten minutes later, stopped on Fifth Avenue and 100th Street. A nurse directed Magnolia to the room. She stood in the doorway and watched Daniel sitting on the edge of the bed, stroking Abbey's hair. He bent over and gave his wife a tender caress.

"Knock, knock," Magnolia said softly.

"Magnolia," Abbey said sleepily. "Have you seen her yet?"

"You first," Magnolia answered, as she placed the roses on the windowsill and the bag next to the bed. She hugged Abbey and then Daniel. "How do you both feel?"

"Surprised," Abbey said, "elated, exhausted."

"*Très content,*" he said.

"A long labor?"

"C-section at three-ten this morning," she said. "We got here at eleven. I thought it was a false alarm until my water broke—it happened fast after that." In slow motion, Abbey shifted her position. "I want you to see her."

"She is in the front left corner," Daniel said, "with the long, dark coiffure."

At five pounds, thirteen ounces, Amélie Charlotte Rothschild Cohen looked about as big as a Perdue oven-stuffer. She was sleeping peacefully in a tightly swaddled blanket, a curl escaping from a small pink cap. Already, she had a certain je ne sais quoi.

"Welcome, little angel," Magnolia cooed through the glass. "I'm your auntie Magnolia and wait till you see the layette I bought you at Barney's. It's at home." Amélie yawned. "Okay, if you don't like it, we can exchange. I'm telling you now—this is a promise—I will be your fairy godmother. We are going to explore New York together, and I plan to teach you everything I know." Magnolia was fairly sure Amélie opened her eyes and held her gaze. Maybe one day I'll produce a friend for you, she thought.

She returned to the room. With Daniel's help, Abbey sat up. "I'm duct-taped together," she said and winced. "I can't believe Nurse Ratched out there expects me to take a walk."

"This is for you," Magnolia said, handing her the large box in the bag. Abbey opened it carefully. Inside was a peach chiffon bed jacket

Magnolia had found two months ago on Portobello Road. "There," Magnolia said, as she helped Abbey slip it on. "You look like some- body's very well-kept mistress, circa 1955."

"Thanks, Mags," Abbey said. "For everything."

"Sorry those lessons of ours turned out to be irrelevant," Magnolia said, puffing out a few shallow Lamaze breaths. "We were world-class."

"Thank you for being there," Daniel said in his deep voice. "Now I stay in Manhattan for three months. And next week, Marie-France will arrive."

"She takes care of *les enfants* Rothschild," Abbey said. "Don't you love it?"

"Abbey, I want your life," Magnolia said, though both of them knew it wasn't true.

"I'm so sorry I have to leave this afternoon."

"As I recall, you have a plane to catch."

"Not for five hours, and I'm already packed."

"Which dress are you wearing?"

"The Armani sequins. Definitely not the Dolce & Gabbana. I'm aiming for elegant, not 'I work at Hooters.'"

"I loved you in the Dolce."

"Because you're obsessing about nursing," Magnolia said. "I just hope you aren't one of those mommies who whips out her huge titties every chance she gets."

"Stop—it hurts when I laugh," Abbey said, holding her stomach. Wind howled against the windows. "I really think you should get to the airport early," she urged.

"Unfortunately, I believe you're right," Magnolia said, as she stood to leave. "As usual."

It had been almost a year since Magnolia had become editor in chief of *Dazzle*. Her weeks of drafting and redrafting the *Voyeur* proposal allowed her to submit—almost overnight—a fully hatched vision of how she could attract new, younger readers to *Dazzle* and give it an edge.

"Cookie, you nailed it," Natalie had called to say the very day she turned in her pitch, complete with eight sample covers on which Magnolia had worked with Fredericka, with the understanding that if she got the job, Fredericka would have one, too. "When can you start?"

"Thanks, Natalie," she said. "I'll start as soon as Wally looks over my contract."

"Fair enough," Natalie answered.

A week later, she moved into Natalie's old office, which Natalie agreed to let her redecorate—smart of Wally to ask for that, Magnolia thought, along with weekly flowers in lieu of the standard health club. Magnolia wasn't ready to give up running with Abbey.

The walls were now a whispery violet repeated on the soft, low mohair sofas that flanked the fireplace, which Magnolia had kept ablaze since Halloween. She was back to working at the same long, antique pine table—unearthed from Scary's netherworld—that she'd used at *Lady*. There were big windows and huge bulletin boards layered with photographs and in-progress pages from the magazine. It was a spare, calming work space, which was good, since her days began before eight and ended after ten.

True to Natalie's prediction, Magnolia had been working seven days a week, including traveling at least once a month with the magazine's publisher, Malachy Jones. They'd made sales calls in San Francisco, Atlanta, Chicago, Minneapolis, Detroit (twice), Boston, Houston, and London. This trip would be their first to Los Angeles.

There were two aspects of travel with Malachy Jones that Magnolia particularly appreciated. The first was that in every city he seemed to have a boyfriend, which meant her evenings always ended by nine. The second: he wasn't Darlene Knudson; he was quiet and thoughtful. What had become of Darlene since the firing, nobody was certain. Some said she and Jock were selling condos in Queens, which they were marketing as "the new downtown." Others declared that Darlene had launched a tween girls' clothing line with prices starting at a thousand dollars.

Almost every day at *Dazzle* brought the rush of New Year's Eve, minus the champagne. Magnolia had more than kept up her end of the bargain. The magazine wasn't just Scary's queen breadwinner—newsstand, subscriptions, and ads were all soaring. There were two good reasons why. First, a long overdue redesign by Fredericka. The second, Magnolia's secret weapon, Sasha.

"Do you want to work for me again?" she'd asked Sasha. "You'll be my first hire."

"As your assistant?" Sasha asked. Magnolia could hear her disappointment. "You know I'm applying to law school."

"You'd be a staff writer," Magnolia said. Sasha accepted the position on the spot, and every week generated headline-grabbing articles, like her exclusive on those nasty rumors about one of President Bush's daughters.

The rest of the staff, which she'd inherited from Natalie, wasn't just efficient—she liked them. And the person she liked the best was Stella, her number-two geisha, whom Natalie had left behind. With her MBA from the Natalie Simon School of Office Protocol, Stella arranged every detail with what was once quaintly known as military precision. Before a trip, for instance, she anticipated Magnolia's needs down to the location of each airport's ladies' rooms.

Today, the moment Magnolia arrived home after visiting Abbey, Stella was on the line, assuring her that the car she reserved to take her to the airport was—amazingly, considering the blizzard—on time. Magnolia thanked her profusely and opened the shiny black folder Stella had messengered over with its hour-by-hour itinerary amended with tickets, directions, and vouchers.

What she looked at first, of course, was the large, square engraved invitation, not unlike the one she'd received last week for her cousin's daughter's Bat Mitzvah in Boca Raton. "The Academy of Motion Picture Arts and Sciences invites Ms. Magnolia Gold to the Academy Awards . . ." This year she would be watching the Oscars not from her living room but from the Kodak Theater, in one of the two seats traditionally accorded to *Dazzle*. Magnolia wondered if Malachy, her date, would actually wear socks with his evening shoes.

Magnolia reached the airport with more than an hour to spare, but soon enough she settled into her seat—first class—and eyed her heavy bag of manuscripts. Usually, she couldn't wait to read and comment. Today she had other plans. Magnolia took out the bound, uncorrected galley of the book Stella had worked her contacts to chase down just the previous day. The cover showed the back of a couple embracing. *A Friend Indeed*. She was glad Cameron had won the war with his publisher over the name.

She looked first for the dedication and acknowledgments, her heart racing, but they were TK—publisher's jargon for "coming later." She flipped to the end for the author's bio: "Cameron James Dane was raised in Burlington, Vermont," it said. "He received his bachelor's degree from Williams College and a master's in fine arts from Yale University. *A Friend Indeed*, his first novel, is being published in fourteen countries and made into a major motion picture. He lives in Malibu with his rescue dog, Mags." The photograph showed Cam with a pup whose fur was the same dirty-blond as that of her owner, who was walking barefoot on the beach, his face hidden by sunglasses.

Magnolia opened to the first page, telling herself she was just curious to see whether Cam's editor had macerated his deceptively simple prose. *"Jake Hawkins had loved Daisy Silver for four years. Five, if you counted the year when he only admired her from his desk in the office three doors down. He loved the way her laugh sounded like the charm bracelet that never left her slim wrist, and he wondered whether she kept it on, even when ..."*

As she devoured the pages, she could see that the decorum committee at Cam's publishing house had convened and blessed the sex scenes, which were now more fruitful and had multiplied. But, otherwise, the book was as she remembered. Cam's voice was still strong. In fact, she felt as if he were dictating into her ear and she luxuriated in every word. When the captain announced they were landing at LAX, she was only half finished, having—at strategic points—allowed her mind to swerve into territory no one would call virginal.

Magnolia deplaned and found her waiting town car. The Four Seasons in Beverly Hills couldn't be less like its forbidding Manhattan cousin. She was admiring its warm, old-world ambience, waiting for her room key, when she heard her name.

"Mag-knowl-ya."

"Bebe!" she said, spinning around to face her. "Hello." Bebe had lost a good fifty pounds and had dyed her hair black.

"I hear you're in town for the Oscars."

"And you're making a movie."

"Don't you think I'm perfect for the Elizabeth Taylor role?" Bebe said. "As soon as I started Hellcat—that's my production company—I knew *The Taming of the Shrew* had to be our first release."

"Sorry *Yentl* closed so soon," Magnolia said.

Bebe dismissed the four performances with a wave of her hand. "Those Broadway audiences don't get subtlety," she said. Magnolia saw a fleet of Louis Vuitton luggage roll by. "Great, my bags are finally here. So, can I take you to dinner?"

"Sorry, Bebe, but my publisher has us seeing a client," Magnolia said. "But thanks."

"Breakfast tomorrow?"

"Same."

"Drink then?" Bebe said. "The bar here, say about ten?"

"I'd love to, but we'll be meeting with other clients later," Magnolia lied. "You know how it is—sell, sell, sell."

"Well, catch you later," Bebe said, unfazed. "And think cover. I want a fabulous cover just like this!" she said as she put on white movie-star sunglasses.

"Yes, I know," Magnolia said. Bebe had been agitating for a cover on *Dazzle* since Magnolia had got her job.

"Promise?" Bebe said, winking.

She winked back.

A bellman ushered Magnolia into her suite. She tipped him generously. On one table stood a bottle of Cristal chilling in a silver bucket. "Cookie, enjoy the Oscars," the card from Natalie said, "and thanks for *your* wonderful performance." Magnolia hadn't known what to expect of Natalie as a boss, but she quickly learned that as long as she kept *Dazzle* solidly in the black and favorably in the news, they'd get along famously.

Two large bouquets crowded the coffee table. One was a tall stand of mango calla lilies, their bright orange a lightning bolt in the tastefully beige room. She ripped open the card. "Orange you glad we're going to the Oscars?" Malachy's jokes sometimes fell a bit short on the wit meter, but unlike Darlene, at least he tried. The second bouquet was an extravagance of peonies, hydrangeas, and full-blown red roses accompanied by a gardenia-scented candle and two pounds of dark Belgium chocolates. "Welcome to the town where more is more, Big smooch, BEBE," the card read.

Magnolia unpacked, carefully hanging her gown on a heavily padded silk hanger. She lined up her Cinderella-worthy sandals on the closet floor and stowed this year's birthday present from Abbey—jade and moonstone drop earrings—in the safe. The Balenciaga evening bag, filmy wrap, and silky lingerie, still with their tags on, she slipped into the drawers.

In fifteen minutes, she was due downstairs to meet Malachy. She considered—as she had, constantly, for the last few weeks—whether she should call Cameron. She hadn't seen Cam at all since she aborted her trip to visit him the past spring and once her job started, their e-mails had dwindled to nothing. "Hi, there. Want to get together? In town for the Oscars!" Magnolia practiced saying the lines out loud, trying to imbue them with a blithe insouciance.

She couldn't do it. She'd make the call later.

Later, however—after dinner with four obstreperous, twenty-eight-year-old cosmetic clients who seemed to especially enjoy that the mojitos were on Scary—she fell dead into bed. Amélie's arrival,

the time difference, her months and months of fatigue . . . in two minutes, she was out cold. On Sunday, she nearly overslept, and before the
nine o'clock appointment Malachy had lined up for them, barely had
time for a swipe of lip gloss before meeting him downstairs. Magnolia
had scant conversation to share as they drove in their rented convertible to Doughboys on Third and La Jolla.

As the group gorged on flaxseed pancakes, Magnolia discreetly
checked her itinerary. After breakfast she'd be back at the Four Seasons, at the spa. Eleven o'clock: manicure and pedicure; twelve o'clock:
massage; and one o'clock: the house specialty, margarita body polishes:
she'd be rubbed with juices from limes, oranges, and tangerines mixed
with sunflower oil, salt, and tequila. Magnolia hoped she wouldn't
walk away, smelling like a Tijuana bar. After the spa, she'd return to
her room to meet a hair and makeup stylist. Assuming no snafus, she
and Malachy would connect at three-thirty.

Which was how it worked out. Having been pummeled, exfoliated,
and transformed by a team of dedicated Southern California professionals, slipping into her sequins and shoes was the quickest thing she
did all day. As she fastened her earrings and admired the way they
caught the light, there was a knock.

"Flowers," the bellman said. "Again." She peeked through the
chained door and saw a bouquet in each of his hands.

"Kisses from the Cohens—Abbey, Daniel, and Amélie," said the
card attached to the lavender roses in a silver cache. The other blossoms were creamy white and starlike, on branches that appeared to
have been recently cut from a backyard garden. She breathed in their
unmistakable fragrance, as sweet as a June twilight on the delta.
Magnolias.

There was no card. Did she dare think they might be from Cam?
They were probably from a publicist who would follow up later, per-
haps with skywriting promoting a miracle depilatory she wanted
Dazzle to feature. Although they might be from Rabbi Hirsch. They'd

gone out six times, and although Magnolia felt he was a good deal more appropriate for her than Tyler Peterson, she couldn't see herself with a man who might expect her to bake a kugel every Friday night.

Magnolia locked her cell phone in the safe—her evening bag was barely bigger than a six-year-old's hand—and checked her reflection. No one was going to mistake her for a best-actress wannabe, but a documentary short subject nominee perhaps. She went downstairs to meet Malachy.

"You look lovely, Ms. Gold," he said, offering his arm. Magnolia hoped she looked half as pretty as he did. Malachy-the-metrosexual had eyelashes she would kill for, not a pore in sight, and highlights so deceptively natural she wished she had the nerve to ask for the name of his colorist.

"You, Mr. Jones, will be mistaken for a star," she said. "In fact, I do believe you will get lucky tonight."

"I believe I have gotten lucky already," he said. "Did you see the tall Spanish guy at the bar around eleven? Great abs?"

"I am sorry to say at that hour I was asleep."

"Well, here's the deal," Malachy said, as he helped her into the limo. "He's a seat filler tonight, and we're going to meet at the end of the evening. But don't worry. The car will still pick you up to take you to the party."

"Got it," Magnolia said, as a surge of Fargo shyness kicked in at the thought of having to navigate an Oscar bash solo. But, she told herself, like everything else this year, it would be character-building.

Given the crush of limos, it took almost thirty minutes to drive twenty blocks on Sunset Boulevard, and the car came to a complete halt on Hollywood, two blocks from Highland.

"Let's walk," Malachy suggested. They joined the swarm of other guests already perspiring under the blinding afternoon sun. It took twenty-five minutes to get near the red carpet.

But there it was. Hair extensions! Cleavage! A lyric poem to excess, the epicenter of hyperbole. Vince Vaughn, Nicole Kidman, and Bill Murray looked taller than she had imagined; Jude Law, Reese Witherspoon, and Ralph Fiennes, shorter. Two feet from her, Catherine Zeta-Jones dissed Renee Zellweger, who turned to chat up a man in a cowboy hat. Her ex? No, Tim McGraw, with Faith Hill.

A man bumped into her as she and Malachy got pushed to one side.

"That you, Magnolia?"

"Hugh!" Magnolia said, but when she blinked, he was gone.

"You know Hugh Grant?" Malachy asked.

"Long story," she said.

In one corner, a phalanx of reporters and photographers charged Angelina Jolie, dressed tonight as an impossibly beautiful angel of death. A rogue state of hip-hop artists, led by Jay-Z and Sean Diddy Combs, all but danced its way across the carpet, nearly colliding with a frizzy-haired, fashion-resistant gentleman Magnolia recognized as the director of the creature feature nominated for best picture. From far across the red carpet, she spotted Joan Rivers accosting Bebe, though it might be the other way around. Oprah and her best friend Gayle— in Magnolia's exact gown—arrived, bejeweled and bemused, and ex-changed compliments with Cate Blanchett. Everyone greeted Jack Nicholson as if he were Jesus, Buddha, and Muhammad combined.

Prada, Yves Saint Laurent, Gucci, Ralph Lauren, Jean Paul Gaultier, J. Mendel, Vera Wang, Dior, Chanel, and Armani—the gang was all here. The tuxedos were exceptional, especially Ellen DeGeneres's. Magnolia wished Abbey could be here just to do a head count of the eight-carat-and-larger diamonds, although it would be more fun to critique the fashion boo-boos. In eighty-degree heat, why was Hilary Swank in chinchilla? Did Penélope Cruz think a bubble skirt flattered anyone over the age of ten? Magnolia hoped she wasn't watching it all with her mouth agape. She circled wide-eyed through the crowd, knowing it wasn't just fodder for *Dazzle* but the world's best cocktail party.

Eventually, Malachy grabbed her hand as they were ushered into the theater. Passing through a glass curtain, she wanted to study the photos from the previous years' Best Pictures, but like a herd of royal cattle, she, Malachy, and the other three-thousand-plus chosen ones were verbally prodded toward their seats. The two of them headed for the uppermost balcony. It didn't matter, at least not to Magnolia. Tonight was the best one she'd had in—well, ever. If celebrity worship were religion, this was Jerusalem. The thought of Cameron bounced in and out of her brain—how great it would be to chew over this vaudeville of narcissism with him—but then the overture began. She leaned back.

Malachy seemed far less taken with it all than Magnolia. He fiddled with the digital buttons next to his seat, ordered them cocktails, and any number of times checked his BlackBerry. But for Magnolia, it didn't matter if it was for Best Actress or Best Sound Mixing—when a winner was announced she cheered as if her mother had won.

"Excuse me for just a minute," Malachy said as the third hour of the ceremony began. "I'm going to the little boy's room." Magnolia barely heard him, since the next award was for Best Actor. The bright lights beamed on every face, each trying harder than the next to look as if he didn't give a flying fuck.

And the winner is . . . "Johnny Depp!"

The auditorium erupted in applause. Magnolia stood up and started clapping. "Johnny—I love you," she shouted in a rebel yell. She may have actually whistled. Until he spoke, however, she barely noticed that a body had slid in next to her, filling Malachy's empty seat.

"That guy your type?" said the seat filler.

She whipped her head around so fast an earring flew off.

"Cameron?" Magnolia blinked in disbelief.

"Hey, aren't you that magazine chick?" he asked.

"And aren't you the writer whose novel's getting all that buzz?"

"Good dress," he said.

She wanted to answer with something appropriate, but had no idea what appropriate might be. He looked as good in a tuxedo as she had imagined, from his piqué shirt, to studs the exact blue of his eyes, right down to his feet, shod in dignified black, and not—thank God—in velvet slippers embroidered with martini glasses, like the stranger to her left. She continued to stare. "What a coincidence," she finally sputtered.

"Do you think maybe we should sit down?" he said. After one of the more abbreviated speeches, Johnny Depp had already left the stage. Magnolia and Cam were the only people in their corner of the third balcony left standing. Hands all around were motioning for them to stop blocking the view. But first, Cameron bent over and retrieved her earring, which had landed—like an offering—directly at his feet.

He took her hand and laughed as he placed the earring in it. "Magnolia, it's good to see you," he said as he slid his cool fingers down her bare back, let them rest above her hip, and pulled her as close as he could. "What a guy has to do to get your attention."

She leaned into Cam both to steady her balance and to see if he was real. "How'd you come up with this idea?"

"Abbey."

"Really?" was all she could say.

"And your publisher, Malachy—great guy—engineered it. The magnolias, though," he said, nodding his head up and down, "my idea. All mine."

The clapping started again, but Magnolia was no longer paying attention. "I love those flowers." She started to cry and opened her tiny bag in search of a tissue. Fortunately, anticipating her reaction to the film clip of the year's dead Academy members, she'd packed as thick a wad as her tiny bag would allow. "I absolutely love them." Her hands were shaking.

"I've missed you," he said, and sounded not one bit flip.

Say something, Magnolia. Say something that shows this man he's been in your dreams for the last year, that every day you've asked yourself whether you made the right decision. Do. Not. Blow. It.

"I've been kind of an ass," she said. It wasn't poetry, but it was utterly from the heart.

"That you have," he said. "But I have always kind of liked your ass—and I've been kind of an ass, too."

"Congratulations on your second book deal," she said. "I've read about it everywhere." Now that Leo DiCaprio was signed to play the lead in *A Friend Indeed*, Cameron's advance for his next novel commanded a jaw-dropping sum.

"Thanks, but now I have to write it in one year, which is already ticking away. Those advances you hear about—you only get a sliver at the beginning. You've actually got to write the sucker to see any real money. Imagine that?" As he smiled, he pushed up his glasses in that little boy way Magnolia never got tired of seeing. "Congratulations on your job, which, I guess, isn't that new anymore."

"With the shelf life of editors, ten months is a lifetime."

"Do you love it?" he asked. What he was really saying was *you better love it, fool, because look what you gave up.*

Magnolia certainly didn't like analyzing the rising and falling futures of celebrities as if they were pork bellies, and she hated to think that at the end of her life, her finest accomplishment would have been to have persuaded the movie-star-of-the-month to do a *Dazzle* cover. But all the standard editor hash—that she loved as much as always. She'd be lying if she denied it.

"I like it fine," she said, "for however long it lasts—but I have no illusions about growing old in this or any job. Being editor in chief of *Dazzle* could last for twenty years—or twenty more minutes."

"So it's right up there in security with writing books and screenplays."

"Like trying to weather a hurricane in an inflatable kayak."

It felt good just to be talking to Cam, but the people around her didn't see it that way. She realized she'd best cut to the chase.

"Are you coming back to New York?" she asked, and didn't care if she came off borderline psycho for being direct. Cameron was here next to her. Now.

He shrugged. "I'm house-sitting till May. After that, who can say?"

Don't expect too much, she chanted to herself. *Enjoy this little moment, even if that's all it is.* Yet the editor in her was already writing the headline: MAGS AND CAM—THEY'RE BA-A-A-CK.

"Could you see yourself ever moving out here?" he asked.

"I'm the kind of bike rider who never likes to shift gears," she admitted. She knew there was no way she'd give up her job.

"What do you say we just think about tonight then," he said. "That is, if you don't have some fabled party to attend."

"I do," she whispered and ran her fingers up his arm. "But I heard about this far more exclusive party. At the Four Seasons. Suite 492. The champagne is ready, the room is full of flowers, and I can guarantee an enthusiastic showing of your fan base."

"Ah, the director proposes a Hollywood ending?" he asked.

"Too big a cliché for you?"

"Let's stay on point here. As the writer, I will consider the suggestion, but I have one immediate thought—a proper Hollywood ending needs to include a kiss."

"Interesting," Magnolia said, softly. "Show me how you'd write that."

He did.

From the front of the auditorium the nominees for Best Picture were being announced. The room thundered. An entourage of winners ascended the stage and began thanking everyone from their baby's nanny to their brother's chiropodist. Every eye in the theater focused on the stage. All except four.

"Who *are* these people?" Magnolia asked, taking one last look at the stage before she put Cameron's hand in hers and nodded toward the exit. "I have never been more bored with anything in my life. C'mon."

Magnolia and Cameron looked at each other. "What the hell?" he said, and standing up and wrapping his arm around Magnolia's waist, he started leading her toward the door. "We've got work to do."

This was a job at which Magnolia had a feeling she would excel.

Readers Guide

1. The author has pulled back the curtain on the magazine industry, and the portrayal reveals backstabbing, superficiality, and greed. Which industries in America do you think have similar corporate cultures? Do you think that the magazine industry is worse than, say, academia? Financial institutions? American government? A place where you've worked?

2. *Little Pink Slips* reflects on the extent to which celebrity mania infiltrates American society. We often know more intimate details about stars than we do our best friends. Why do you think this trend has taken root in the United States? Do you feel it's innocent or damaging? Do you feel this trend should be reversed and if so, how could we make that happen?

3. Magnolia Gold, the heroine of *Little Pink Slips*, is a small-town girl who dreams of bright lights and the big city. Do you think that Magnolia would behave any differently if she were born in an urban area? Do you feel that values are different in large urban areas from what they are in smaller cities, the country, or the suburbs? What are your personal biases about different regions of the United States?

4. If you were Magnolia, would you have quit rather than try to work with Bebe?

5. Magnolia's love life is rocky, and even at the end of the book, her romantic future remains unclear. Do you think that women in powerful positions have a harder time than other women in building relationships? Do you think men shy away from such women? If so, is this changing?

6. If you could start a magazine, what would you name it and what would it contain?

7. Magnolia has a fling with an old high school boyfriend. What is there about teenage boyfriends that mature women can sometimes never get over?

8. Magnolia helps her friend Abbey write a personal ad. What kind of personal ad would you write for yourself?

9. Did you feel that the friendship between Abbey and Magnolia realistically captures a friendship between two American women today? What qualities do you think are important for close female friendships?

10. Did you get a kick out of Bebe? Despise her? When celebrities do outrageous things, do you suspect that much of their behavior is calculated simply to grab headlines?

11. If you were Magnolia, would you have quit your job at the end of the book and moved to Los Angeles to be with Cameron? Would you have written the ending differently?

12. The author says that she wrote this book to try to show personal resilience and get over a disappointment—in her case, losing a job. What have you done in your life to bounce back from a stressful situation?

13. Have you ever been fired? If so, did you think that your "little pink slip" was fair? How did it feel to be fired? How did you get over that hardship?